PII D1628131

When William Golding was awarded the Nobel Prize in Literature, the Nobel Foundation said of his novels that they 'illuminate the human condition in the world of today'. Born in Cornwall in 1911, Golding was educated at Marlborough Grammar School and Brasenose College, Oxford. Before becoming a writer, he was an actor, a lecturer, a small-boat sailor, a musician and a schoolteacher. In 1940 he joined the Royal Navy and saw action against battleships, submarines and aircraft, and also took part in the pursuit of the *Bismarck*.

Lord of the Flies, his first novel, was rejected by several publishers and one literary agent. It was rescued from the 'slush pile' by a young editor at Faber and Faber and published in 1954. The book would go on to sell several million copies; it was translated into 35 languages and made into a film by Peter Brook in 1963. He wrote eleven other novels, *The Inheritors* and *The Spire* among them, a play and two essay collections. He won the Booker Prize for his novel *Rites of Passage* in 1980, and the Nobel Prize in Literature in 1983. He was knighted in 1988. He died at his home in the summer of 1993.

www.william-golding.co.uk

C334036532

Books by
Sir William Golding
1911–1993
Nobel Prize in Literature

Fiction
LORD OF THE FLIES
THE INHERITORS
PINCHER MARTIN
FREE FALL
THE SPIRE
THE PYRAMID
THE SCORPION GOD
DARKNESS VISIBLE
THE PAPER MEN
RITES OF PASSAGE
CLOSE QUARTERS
FIRE DOWN BELOW
TO THE ENDS OF THE EARTH
(comprising *Rites of Passage, Close Quarters* and *Fire Down Below* in a
revised text; foreword by the author)
THE DOUBLE TONGUE

Essays
THE HOT GATES
A MOVING TARGET

Travel
AN EGYPTIAN JOURNAL

Plays
THE BRASS BUTTERFLY
LORD OF THE FLIES
adapted for the stage by Nigel Williams

WILLIAM GOLDING: A CRITICAL STUDY OF THE NOVELS
by Mark Kinkead-Weekes and Ian Gregor

WILLIAM GOLDING

Pincher Martin

With an afterword by Philippa Gregory

FABER & FABER

First published in 1956
by Faber & Faber Limited
Bloomsbury House, 74–77 Great Russell Street, London WC1B 3DA
This paperback edition first published in 2015

Printed and bound by CPI Group (UK) Ltd, Croydon, CR0 4YY

A CIP record for this book is available from the British Library

ISBN 978–0–571–32274–9

2 4 6 8 10 9 7 5 3

1

He was struggling in every direction, he was the centre of the writhing and kicking knot of his own body. There was no up or down, no light and no air. He felt his mouth open of itself and the shrieked word burst out.

"Help!"

When the air had gone with the shriek, water came in to fill its place—burning water, hard in the throat and mouth as stones that hurt. He hutched his body towards the place where air had been but now it was gone and there was nothing but black, choking welter. His body let loose its panic and his mouth strained open till the hinges of his jaw hurt. Water thrust in, down, without mercy. Air came with it for a moment so that he fought in what might have been the right direction. But water reclaimed him and spun so that knowledge of where the air might be was erased completely. Turbines were screaming in his ears and green sparks flew out from the centre like tracer. There was a piston engine too, racing out of gear and making the whole universe shake. Then for a moment there was air like a cold mask against his face and he bit into it. Air and water mixed, dragged down

1

into his body like gravel. Muscles, nerves and blood, struggling lungs, a machine in the head, they worked for one moment in an ancient pattern. The lumps of hard water jerked in the gullet, the lips came together and parted, the tongue arched, the brain lit a neon track.

"Moth——"

But the man lay suspended behind the whole commotion, detached from his jerking body. The luminous pictures that were shuffled before him were drenched in light but he paid no attention to them. Could he have controlled the nerves of his face, or could a face have been fashioned to fit the attitude of his consciousness where it lay suspended between life and death that face would have worn a snarl. But the real jaw was contorted down and distant, the mouth was slopped full. The green tracer that flew from the centre began to spin into a disc. The throat at such a distance from the snarling man vomited water and drew it in again. The hard lumps of water no longer hurt. There was a kind of truce, observation of the body. There was no face but there was a snarl.

A picture steadied and the man regarded it. He had not seen such a thing for so many years that the snarl became curious and lost a little intensity. It examined the picture.

The jam jar was standing on a table, brightly lit from O.P. It might have been a huge jar in the centre of a stage or a small one almost touching the face, but it was interesting because one could see into a little world there which was quite separate but which one could control.

2

The jar was nearly full of clear water and a tiny glass figure floated upright in it. The top of the jar was covered with a thin membrane—white rubber. He watched the jar without moving or thinking while his distant body stilled itself and relaxed. The pleasure of the jar lay in the fact that the little glass figure was so delicately balanced between opposing forces. Lay a finger on the membrane and you would compress the air below it which in turn would press more strongly on the water. Then the water would force itself farther up the little tube in the figure, and it would begin to sink. By varying the pressure on the membrane you could do anything you liked with the glass figure which was wholly in your power. You could mutter,—sink now! And down it would go, down, down; you could steady it and relent. You could let it struggle towards the surface, give it almost a bit of air then send it steadily, slowly, remorselessly down and down.

The delicate balance of the glass figure related itself to his body. In a moment of wordless realization he saw himself touching the surface of the sea with just such a dangerous stability, poised between floating and going down. The snarl thought words to itself. They were not articulate, but they were there in a luminous way as a realization.

Of course. My lifebelt.

It was bound by the tapes under that arm and that. The tapes went over the shoulders—and now he could even feel them—went round the chest and were fastened in front under the oilskin and duffle. It was almost deflated

3

as recommended by the authorities because a tightly blown-up belt might burst when you hit the water. Swim away from the ship then blow up your belt.

With the realization of the lifebelt a flood of connected images came back—the varnished board on which the instructions were displayed, pictures of the lifebelt itself with the tube and metal tit threaded through the tapes. Suddenly he knew who he was and where he was. He was lying suspended in the water like the glass figure; he was not struggling but limp. A swell was washing regularly over his head.

His mouth slopped full and he choked. Flashes of tracer cut the darkness. He felt a weight pulling him down. The snarl came back with a picture of heavy seaboots and he began to move his legs. He got one toe over the other and shoved but the boot would not come off. He gathered himself and there were his hands far off but serviceable. He shut his mouth and performed a grim acrobatic in the water while the tracer flashed. He felt his heart thumping and for a while it was the only point of reference in the formless darkness. He got his right leg across his left thigh and heaved with sodden hands. The seaboot slipped down his calf and he kicked it free. Once the rubber top had left his toes he felt it touch him once and then it was gone utterly. He forced his left leg up, wrestled with the second boot and got it free. Both boots had left him. He let his body uncoil and lie limply.

His mouth was clever. It opened and shut for the air

4

and against the water. His body understood too. Every now and then it would clench its stomach into a hard knot and sea water would burst out over his tongue. He began to be frightened again—not with animal panic but with deep fear of death in isolation and long drawn out. The snarl came back but now it had a face to use and air for the throat. There was something meaningful behind the snarl which would not waste the air on noises. There was a purpose which had not yet had time and experience to discover how relentless it was. It could not use the mechanism for regular breathing but it took air in gulps between the moments of burial.

He began to think in gulps as he swallowed the air. He remembered his hands again and there they were in the darkness, far away. He brought them in and began to fumble at the hard stuff of his oilskin. The button hurt and would hardly be persuaded to go through the hole. He slipped the loop off the toggle of his duffle. Lying with little movement of his body he found that the sea ignored him, treated him as a glass figure of a sailor or as a log that was almost ready to sink but would last a few moments yet. The air was regularly in attendance between the passage of the swells.

He got the rubber tube and drew it through the tapes. He could feel the slack and uninflated rubber that was so nearly not holding him up. He got the tit of the tube between his teeth and unscrewed with two fingers while the others sealed the tube. He won a little air from between swells and fuffed it through the rubber tube. For uncounted numbers of swell and hollow he taxed the air that might have gone into his lungs until his heart was staggering in his body like a wounded man and the green tracer was flicking and spinning. The lifebelt began to firm up against his chest but so slowly that he could not tell when the change came. Then abruptly the swells were washing over his shoulders and the repeated burial beneath them had become a wet and splashing slap in the face. He found he had no need to play catch-as-catch-can for air. He blew deeply and regularly into the tube until the lifebelt rose and strained at his clothing. Yet he did not stop blowing at once. He played with the air, letting a little out and then blowing again as if frightened of stopping the one positive action he could take to help himself. His head and neck and shoulders were out of the water now for long intervals. They were colder than the rest of his body. The air stiffened them. They began to shake.

He took his mouth from the tube.

"Help! Help!"

The air escaped from the tube and he struggled with it. He twisted the tit until the air was safe. He stopped shouting and strained his eyes to see through the darkness but it lay right against his eyeballs. He put his hand before his eyes and saw nothing. Immediately the terror of blindness added itself to the terror of isolation and drowning. He began to make vague climbing motions in the water.

"Help! Is there anybody there? Help! Survivor!"

He lay shaking for a while and listened for an answer but the only sound was the hissing and puddling of the water as it washed round him. His head fell forward.

He licked salt water off his lips.

"Exercise."

He began to tread water gently. His mouth mumbled.

"Why did I take my sea boots off? I'm no better off than I was." His head nodded forward again.

"Cold. Mustn't get too cold. If I had those boots I could put them on and then take them off and then put them on——"

He thought suddenly of the boat sinking through water towards a bottom that was still perhaps a mile remote from them. With that, the whole wet immensity seemed to squeeze his body as though he were sunk to a great depth. His chattering teeth came together and the flesh of his face twisted. He arched in the water, drawing his feet up away from the depth, the slopping, glutinous welter.

"Help! Help——"

He began to thresh with his hands and force his body round. He stared at the darkness as he turned but there was nothing to tell him when he had completed the circle and everywhere the darkness was grainless and alike. There was no wreckage, no sinking hull, no struggling survivors but himself, there was only darkness lying close against the balls of the eyes. There was the movement of water.

He began to cry out for the others, for anyone.

7

"Nat! Nathaniel! For Christ's sake! Nathaniel! Help!"

His voice died and his face untwisted. He lay slackly in his lifebelt, allowing the swell to do what it would. His teeth were chattering again and sometimes this vibration would spread till it included his whole body. His legs below him were not cold so much as pressed, squeezed mercilessly by the sea so that the feeling in them was not a response to temperature but to weight that would crush and burst them. He searched for a place to put his hands but there was nowhere that kept the ache out of them. The back of his neck began to hurt and that not gradually but with a sudden stab of pain so that holding his chin away from his chest was impossible. But this put his face into the sea so that he sucked it into his nose with a snoring noise and a choke. He spat and endured the pain in his neck for a while. He wedged his hands between his lifebelt and his chin and for a swell or two this was some relief but then the pain returned. He let his hands fall away and his face dipped in the water. He lay back, forcing his head against the pain so that his eyes if they had been open would have been looking at the sky. The pressure on his legs was bearable now. They were no longer flesh, but had been transformed to some other substance, petrified and comfortable. The part of his body that had not been invaded and wholly subdued by the sea was jerking intermittently. Eternity, inseparable from pain was there to be examined and experienced. The snarl endured. He thought. The thoughts were laborious, disconnected but vital.

8

Presently it will be daylight.

I must move from one point to another.

Enough to see one move ahead.

Presently it will be daylight.

I shall see wreckage.

I won't die.

I can't die.

Not me——

Precious.

He roused himself with a sudden surge of feeling that had nothing to do with the touch of the sea. Salt water was coming fast out of his eyes. He snivelled and gulped.

"Help, somebody—help!"

His body lifted and fell gently.

If I'd been below I might have got to a boat even. Or a raft. But it had to be my bloody watch. Blown off the bloody bridge. She must have gone on perhaps to starboard if he got the order in time, sinking or turning over. They'll be there in the darkness somewhere where she sank asking each other if they're down-hearted, knots and stipples of heads in the water and oil and drifting stuff. When it's light I must find them, Christ I must find them. Or they'll be picked up and I'll be left to swell like a hammock. Christ!

"Help! Nathaniel! Help——!"

And I gave the right orders too. If I'd done it ten seconds earlier I'd be a bloody hero—Hard a-starboard for Christ's sake!

9

Must have hit us bang under the bridge. And I gave the right order. And I get blown to buggery.

The snarl fixed itself, worked on the wooden face till the upper lip was lifted and the chattering teeth bared. The little warmth of anger flushed blood back into the tops of the cheeks and behind the eyes. They opened.

Then he was jerking and splashing and looking up. There was a difference in the texture of the darkness; there were smears and patches that were not in the eye itself. For a moment and before he remembered how to use his sight the patches lay on the eyeballs as close as the darkness had been. Then he firmed the use of his eyes and he was inside his head, looking out through the arches of his skull at random formations of dim light and mist. However he blinked and squinted they remained there outside him. He bent his head forward and saw, fainter than an afterimage, the scalloped and changing shape of a swell as his body was lifted in it. For a moment he caught the inconstant outline against the sky, then he was floating up and seeing dimly the black top of the next swell as it swept towards him. He began to make swimming motions. His hands were glimmering patches in the water and his movements broke up the stony weight of his legs. The thoughts continued to flicker.

We were travelling north-east. I gave the order. If he began the turn she might be anywhere over there to the east. The wind was westerly. That's the east over there where the swells are running away down hill.

10

His movements and his breathing became fierce. He swam a sort of clumsy breast-stroke, buoyed up on the inflated belt. He stopped and lay wallowing. He set his teeth, took the tit of the lifebelt and let out air till he was lying lower in the water. He began to swim again. His breathing laboured. He stared out of his arches intently and painfully at the back of each swell as it slunk away from him. His legs slowed and stopped; his arms fell. His mind inside the dark skull made swimming movements long after the body lay motionless in the water.

The grain of the sky was more distinct. There were vaporous changes of tone from dark to gloom, to grey. Near at hand the individual hillocks of the surface were visible. His mind made swimming movements.

Pictures invaded his mind and tried to get between him and the urgency of his motion towards the east. The jam jar came back but robbed of significance. There was a man, a brief interview, a desk-top so polished that the smile of teeth was being reflected in it. There was a row of huge masks hung up to dry and a voice from behind the teeth that had been reflected in the desk spoke softly.

"Which one do you think would suit Christopher?"

There was a binnacle-top with the compass light just visible, there was an order shouted, hung up there for all heaven and earth to see in neon lighting.

"Hard a-starboard, for Christ's sake!"

Water washed into his mouth and he jerked into consciousness with a sound that was half a snore and half a

11

choke. The day was inexorably present in green and grey. The seas were intimate and enormous. They smoked. When he swung up a broad, hilly crest he could see two other smoking crests then nothing but a vague circle that might be mist or fine spray or rain. He peered into the circle, turning himself, judging direction by the run of the water until he had inspected every part. The slow fire of his belly, banked up to endure, was invaded. It lay defenceless in the middle of the clothing and sodden body.

"I won't die! I won't!"

The circle of mist was everywhere alike. Crests swung into view on that side, loomed, seized him, elevated him for a moment, let him down and slunk off, but there was another crest to take him, lift him so that he could see the last one just dimming out of the circle. Then he would go down again and another crest would loom weltering towards him.

He began to curse and beat the water with the flat of his white hands. He struggled up the swells. But even the sounds of his working mouth and body were merged unnoticed in the innumerable sounds of travelling water. He hung still in his belt, feeling the cold search his belly with its fingers. His head fell on his chest and the stuff slopped weakly, peristently over his face. Think. My last chance. Think what can be done.

She sank out in the Atlantic. Hundreds of miles from land. She was alone, sent north-east from the convoy to break WT silence. The U-boat may be hanging round to

12

pick up a survivor or two for questioning. Or to pick off any ship that comes to rescue survivors. She may surface at any moment, breaking the swell with her heavy body like a half-tide rock. Her periscope may sear the water close by, eye of a land-creature that has defeated the rhythm and necessity of the sea. She may be passing under me now, shadowy and shark-like, she may be lying down there below my wooden feet on a bed of salty water as on a cushion while her crew sleeps. Survivors, a raft, the whaler, the dinghy, wreckage may be milling about only a swell or two away hidden in the mist and waiting for rescue with at least bully and perhaps a tot.

He began to rotate in the water again, peering blearily at the midst, he squinted at the sky that was not much higher than a roof; he searched the circle for wreckage or a head. But there was nothing. She had gone as if a hand had reached up that vertical mile and snatched her down in one motion. When he thought of the mile he arched in the water, face twisted, and began to cry out.

"Help, curse you, sod you, bugger you—Help!"

Then he was blubbering and shuddering and the cold was squeezing him like the hand that had snatched down the ship. He hiccupped slowly into silence and started to rotate once more in the smoke and green welter.

One side of the circle was lighter than the other. The swell was shouldering itself on towards the left of this vague brightness; and where the brightness spread the mist was even more impenetrable than behind him. He

13

remained facing the brightness not because it was of any use to him but because it was a difference that broke the uniformity of the circle and because it looked a little warmer than anywhere else. He made swimming movements again without thought and as if to follow in the wake of that brightness was an inevitable thing to do. The light made the sea-smoke seem solid. It penetrated the water so that between him and the very tops of the restless hillocks it was bottle green. For a moment or two after a wave had passed he could see right into it but the waves were nothing but water—there was no weed in them, no speck of solid, nothing drifting, nothing moving but green water, cold persistent idiot water. There were hands to be sure and two forearms of black oil-skin and there was the noise of breathing, gasping. There was also the noise of the idiot stuff, whispering, folding on itself, tripped ripples running tinkling by the ear like miniatures of surf on a flat beach; there were sudden hisses and spats, roars and incompleted syllables and the soft friction of wind. The hands were important under the bright side of the circle but they had nothing to seize on. There was an infinite drop of the soft, cold stuff below them and under the labouring, dying, body.

The sense of depth caught him and he drew his dead feet up to his belly as if to detach them from the whole ocean. He arched and gaped, he rose over the chasm of deep sea on a swell and his mouth opened to scream against the brightness.

14

It stayed open. Then it shut with a snap of teeth and his arms began to heave water out of the way. He fought his way forward.

"Ahoy—for Christ's sake! Survivor! Survivor! Fine on your starboard bow!"

He threshed with his arms and legs into a clumsy crawl. A crest overtook him and he jerked himself to the chest out of water.

"Help! Help! Survivor! For God's sake!"

The force of his return sent him under but he struggled up and shook the wave from his head. The fire of his belly had spread and his heart was thrusting the sluggish blood painfully round his body. There was a ship in the mist to port of the bright patch. He was on her starboard bow—or—and the thought drove him to foam in the water—he was on her port quarter and she was moving away. But even in his fury of movement he saw how impossible this was since then she would have passed by him only a few minutes ago. So she was coming towards, to cut across the circle of visibility only a few yards from him.

Or stopped.

At that, he stopped too, and lay in the water. She was so dull a shape, little more than a looming darkness that he could not tell both her distance and her size. She was more nearly bows on than when he had first seen her and now she was visible even when he was in a trough. He began to swim again but every time he rose on a crest he screamed.

"Help! Survivor!"

15

But what ship was ever so lop-sided? A carrier? A derelict carrier, deserted and waiting to sink? But she would have been knocked down by a salvo of torpedoes. A derelict liner? Then she must be one of the Queens by her bulk—and why lop-sided? The sun and the mist were balanced against each other. The sun could illumine the mist but not pierce it. And darkly in the sun-mist loomed the shape of a not-ship where nothing but a ship could be.

He began to swim again, feeling suddenly the desperate exhaustion of his body. The first, fierce excitement of sighting had burned up the fuel and the fire was low again. He swam grimly, forcing his arms through the water, reaching forward under his arches with sight as though he could pull himself into safety with it. The shape moved. It grew larger and not clearer. Every now and then there was something like a bow-wave at the forefoot. He ceased to look at her but swam and screamed alternately with the last strength of his body. There was green force round him, growing in strength to rob, there was mist and glitter over him; there was a redness pulsing in front of his eyes—his body gave up and he lay slack in the waves and the shape rose over him. He heard through the rasp and thump of his works the sound of waves breaking. He lifted his head and there was rock stuck up in the sky with a sea-gull poised before it. He heaved over in the sea and saw how each swell dipped for a moment, flung up a white hand of foam then disappeared as if the rock had swallowed it. He began to think swimming motions but knew

16

now that his body was no longer obedient. The top of the next swell between him and the rock was blunted, smoothed curiously, then jerked up spray. He sank down, saw without comprehension that the green water was no longer empty. There was yellow and brown. He heard not the formless mad talking of uncontrolled water but a sudden roar. Then he went under into a singing world and there were hairy shapes that flitted and twisted past his face, there were sudden notable details close to of intricate rock and weed. Brown tendrils slashed across his face, then with a destroying shock he hit solidity. It was utter difference, it was under his body, against his knees and face, he could close fingers on it, for an instance he could even hold on. His mouth was needlessly open and his eyes so that he had a moment of close and intent communion with three limpets, two small and one large that were only an inch or two from his face. Yet this solidity was terrible and apocalyptic after the world of inconstant wetness. It was not vibrant as a ship's hull might be but merciless and mother of panic. It had no business to interrupt the thousands of miles of water going about their purposeless affairs and therefore the world sprang here into sudden war. He felt himself picked up and away from the limpets, reversed, tugged, thrust down into weed and darkness. Ropes held him, slipped and let him go. He saw light, got a mouthful of air and foam. He glimpsed a riven rock face with trees of spray growing up it and the sight of this rock floating in mid-Atlantic was so dreadful that he wasted his

17

air by screaming as if it had been a wild beast. He went under into a green calm, then up and was thrust sideways. The sea no longer played with him. It stayed its wild movement and held him gently, carried him with delicate and careful motion like a retriever with a bird. Hard things touched him about the feet and knees. The sea laid him down gently and retreated. There were hard things touching his face and chest, the side of his forehead. The sea came back and fawned round his face, licked him. He thought movements that did not happen. The sea came back and he thought the movements again and this time they happened because the sea took most of his weight. They moved him forward over the hard things. Each wave and each movement moved him forward. He felt the sea run down to smell at his feet then come back and nuzzle under his arm. It no longer licked his face. There was a pattern in front of him that occupied all the space under the arches. It meant nothing. The sea nuzzled under his arm again.

He lay still.

2

The pattern was white and black but mostly white. It existed in two layers, one behind the other, one for each eye. He thought nothing, did nothing while the pattern changed a trifle and made little noises. The hardnesses under his cheek began to insist. They passed through pressure to a burning without heat, to a localized pain. They became vicious in their insistence like the nag of an aching tooth. They began to pull him back into himself and organize him again as a single being.

Yet it was not the pain nor the white and black pattern that first brought him back to life, but the noises. Though the sea had treated him so carefully, elsewhere it continued to roar and thump and collapse on itself. The wind too, given something to fight with other than obsequious water was hissing round the rock and breathing gustily in crevices. All these noises made a language which forced itself into the dark, passionless head and assured it that the head was somewhere, somewhere—and then finally with the flourish of a gull's cry over the sound of wind and water, declared to the groping consciousness: wherever you are, you are here!

Then he was there, suddenly, enduring pain but in deep communion with the solidity that held up his body. He remembered how eyes should be used and brought the two lines of sight together so that the patterns fused and made a distance. The pebbles were close to his face, pressing against his cheek and jaw. They were white quartz, dulled and rounded, a miscellany of potato-shapes. Their whiteness was qualified by yellow stains and flecks of darker material. There was a whiter thing beyond them. He examined it without curiosity, noting the bleached wrinkles, the blue roots of nails, the corrugations at the finger-tips. He did not move his head but followed the line of the hand back to an oilskin sleeve, the beginnings of a shoulder. His eyes returned to the pebbles and watched them idly as if they were about to perform some operation for which he was waiting without much interest. The hand did not move.

Water welled up among the pebbles. It stirred them slightly, paused, then sank away while the pebbles clicked and chirruped. It swilled down past his body and pulled gently at his stockinged feet. He watched the pebbles while the water came back and this time the last touch of the sea lopped into his open mouth. Without change of expression he began to shake, a deep shake that included the whole of his body. Inside his head it seemed that the pebbles were shaking because the movement of his white hand forward and back was matched by the movement of his body. Under the side of his face the pebbles nagged.

The pictures that came and went inside his head did

not disturb him because they were so small and remote. There was a woman's body, white and detailed, there was a boy's body; there was a box office, the bridge of a ship, an order picked out across a far sky in neon lighting, a tall, thin man who stood aside humbly in the darkness at the top of a companion ladder; there was a man hanging in the sea like a glass sailor in a jam jar. There was nothing to choose between the pebbles and pictures. Sometimes one was uppermost, sometimes the other. The individual pebbles were no bigger than the pictures. Sometimes a pebble would be occupied entirely by a picture as though it were a window, a spy-hole into a different world or other dimension. Words and sounds were sometimes visible as shapes like the shouted order. They did not vibrate and disappear. When they were created they remained as hard enduring things like the pebbles. Some of these were inside the skull, behind the arch of the brow and the shadowy nose. They were right in the indeterminate darkness above the fire of hardnesses. If you looked out idly, you saw round them.

There was a new kind of coldness over his body. It was creeping down his back between the stuffed layers of clothing. It was air that felt like slow fire. He had hardly noticed this when a wave came back and filled his mouth so that a choke interrupted the rhythm of shaking.

He began to experiment. He found that he could haul the weight of one leg up and then the other. His hand crawled round above his head. He reasoned deeply that

21

there was another hand on the other side somewhere and sent a message out to it. He found the hand and worked the wrist. There were still fingers on it, not because he could move them but because when he pushed he could feel the wooden tips shifting the invisible pebbles. He moved his four limbs in close and began to make swimming movements. The vibrations from the cold helped him. Now his breath went in and out quickly and his heart began to race again. The inconsequential pictures vanished and there was nothing but pebbles and pebble noises and heart-thumps. He had a valuable thought, not because it was of immediate physical value but because it gave him back a bit of his personality. He made words to express this thought, though they did not pass the barrier of his teeth.

"I should be about as heavy as this on Jupiter."

At once he was master. He knew that his body weighed no more than it had always done, that it was exhausted, that he was trying to crawl up a little pebble slope. He lifted the dents in his face away from the pebbles that had made them and pushed with his knees. His teeth came together and ground. He timed the expansion of his chest against the pebbles, the slow shaking of his body till they did not hold up the leaden journey. He felt how each wave finished farther and farther down towards his feet. When the journey became too desperate he would wait, gasping, until the world came back. The water no longer touched his feet.

His left hand—the hidden one—touched something that did not click and give. He rolled his head and looked up under the arch. There was greyish yellow stuff in front of his face. It was pock-marked and hollowed, dotted with red lumps of jelly. The yellow tents of limpets were pitched in every hole. Brown fronds and green webs of weed hung over them. The white pebbles led up into a dark angle. There was a film of water glistening over everything, drops falling, tiny pools caught at random, lying and shuddering or leaking down among the weed. He began to turn on the pebbles, working his back against the rock and drawing up his feet. He saw them now for the first time, distant projections, made thick and bear-like by the white, seaboot stockings. They gave him back a little more of himself. He got his left hand down beneath his ear and began to heave. His shoulder lifted a little. He pushed with feet, pulled with hands. His back was edging into the angle where the pools leaked down. His head was high. He took a thigh in both hands and pulled it towards his chest and then the other. He packed himself into the angle and looked down at the pebbles over his knees. His mouth had fallen open again.

And after all, as pebbles go there were not very many of them. The length of a man or less would measure out the sides of the triangle that they made under the shadow of the rock. They filled the cleft and they were solid.

He took his eyes away from the pebbles and made them examine the water. This was almost calm in comparison

23

with the open sea; and the reason was the rock round which the waves had whirled him. He could see the rock out there now. It was the same stuff as this, grey and creamy with barnacles and foam. Each wave tripped on it so that although the water ran and thumped on either side of the cleft, there was a few yards of green, clear water between him and the creamy rock. Beyond the rock was nothing but a smoking advance of sea with watery sunlight caught in it.

He let his eyes close and ignored the pictures that came and went behind them. The slow movement of his mind settled on a thought. There was a small fire in his body that was almost extinguished but incredibly was still smouldering despite the Atlantic. He folded his body consciously round that fire and nursed it. There was not more than a spark. The formal words and the pictures evolved themselves.

A seabird cried over him with a long sound descending down wind. He removed his attention from the spark of fire and opened his eyes again. This time he had got back so much of his personality that he could look out and grasp the whole of what he saw at once. There were the dark walls of rock on either side that framed the brighter light. There was sunlight on a rock with spray round it and the steady march of swells that brought their own fine mist along with them under the sun. He turned his head sideways and peered up.

The rock was smoother above the weeds and limpets

24

and drew together. There was an opening at the top with daylight and the suggestion of cloud caught in it. As he watched, a gull flicked across the opening and cried in the wind. He found the effort of looking up hurt him and he turned to his body, examined the humps that were his knees under the oilskin and duffle. He looked closely at a button.

His mouth shut then opened. Sounds came out. He readjusted them and they were uncertain words.

"I know you. Nathaniel sewed you on. I asked him to. Said it was an excuse to get him away from the mess-deck for a bit of peace."

His eyes closed again and he fingered the button clumsily.

"Had this oilskin when I was a rating. Lofty sewed on the buttons before Nathaniel."

His head nodded on his knees.

"All the blue watch. Blue watch to muster."

The pictures were interrupted by the solid shape of a snore. The shiverings were less dramatic but they took power from his arms so that presently they fell away from his knees and his hands lay on the pebbles. His head shook. Between the snores the pebbles were hard to the feet, harder to the backside when the heels had slid slowly from under. The pictures were so confused that there was as much danger that they would destroy the personality as that the spark of fire would go out. He forced his way among them, lifted his eyelids and looked out.

25

The pebbles were wavering down there where the water welled over them. Higher up, the rock that had saved him was lathered and fringed with leaping strings of foam. There was afternoon brightness outside but the cleft was dripping, dank and smelly as a dockside latrine. He made quacking sounds with his mouth. The words that had formed in his mind were: Where is this bloody rock? But that seemed to risk something by insult of the dark cleft so that he changed them in his throat.

"Where the hell am I?"

A single point of rock, peak of a mountain range, one tooth set in the ancient jaw of a sunken world, projecting through the inconceivable vastness of the whole ocean—and how many miles from dry land? An evil pervasion, not the convulsive panic of his first struggles in the water, but a deep and generalized terror set him clawing at the rock with his blunt fingers. He even got half-up and leaned or crouched against the weed and the lumps of jelly.

"Think, you bloody fool, think."

The horizon of misty water stayed close, the water leapt from the rock and the pebbles wavered.

"Think."

He crouched, watching the rock, not moving but trembling continually. He noted how the waves broke on the outer rock and were tamed, so that the water before the cleft was sloppily harmless. Slowly, he settled back into the angle of the cleft. The spark was alight and the heart

26

was supplying it with what it wanted. He watched the outer rock but hardly saw it. There was a name missing. That name was written on the chart, well out in the Atlantic, eccentrically isolated so that seamen who could to a certain extent laugh at wind and weather had made a joke of the rock. Frowning, he saw the chart now in his mind's eye but not clearly. He saw the navigating commander of the cruiser bending over it with the captain, saw himself as navigator's yeoman standing ready while they grinned at each other. The captain spoke with his clipped Dartmouth accent—spoke and laughed.

"I call that name a near miss."

Near miss whatever the name was. And now to be huddled on a near miss how many miles from the Hebrides? What was the use of the spark if it winked away in a crack of that ludicrous isolation? He spat his words at the picture of the captain.

"I am no better off than I was."

He began to slide down the rocks as his bones bent their hinges. He slumped into the angle and his head fell. He snored.

But inside, where the snores were external, the consciousness was moving and poking about among the pictures and revelations, among the shape-sounds and the disregarded feelings like an animal ceaselessly examining its cage. It rejected the detailed bodies of women, slowly sorted the odd words, ignored the pains and the insistence of the shaking body. It was looking for a thought. It found

27

the thought, separated it from the junk, lifted it and used the apparatus of the body to give it force and importance.

"I am intelligent."

There was a period of black suspension behind the snores; then the right hand, so far away, obeyed a command and began to fumble and pluck at the oilskin. It raised a flap and crawled inside. The fingers found cord and a shut clasp-knife. They stayed there.

The eyes blinked open so that the arch of brows was a frame to green sea. For a while the eyes looked, received impressions without seeing them. Then the whole body gave a jump. The spark became a flame, the body scrambled, crouched, the hand flicked out of the oilskin pocket and grabbed rock. The eyes stared and did not blink.

As the eyes watched, a wave went clear over the outer rock so that they could see the brown weed inside the water. The green dance beyond the pebbles was troubled. A line of foam broke and hissed up the pebbles to his feet. The foam sank away and the pebbles chattered like teeth. He watched, wave after wave as bursts of foam swallowed more and more of the pebbles and left fewer visible when they went back. The outer rock was no longer a barrier but only a gesture of defence. The cleft was being connected more and more directly with the irrestible progress of the green, smoking seas. He jerked away from the open water and turned towards the rock. The dark, lavatorial cleft, with its dripping weed, with its sessile, mindless life

28

of shell and jelly was land only twice a day by courtesy of the moon. It felt like solidity but it was a sea-trap, as alien to breathing life as the soft slop of the last night and the vertical mile.

A gull screamed with him so that he came back into himself, leaned his forehead against the rock and waited for his heart to steady. A shot of foam went over his feet. He looked down past them. There were fewer pebbles to stand on and those that had met his hands when he had been washed ashore were yellow and green beneath a foot of jumping water. He turned to the rock again and spoke out loud.

"Climb!"

He turned round and found handholds in the cleft. There were many to choose from. His hands were poor, sodden stuff against their wet projections. He leaned a moment against the rock and gathered the resources of his body together. He lifted his right leg and dropped the foot in an opening like an ash-tray. There was an edge to the ash-tray but not a sharp one and his foot could feel nothing. He took his forehead away from a weedy surface and heaved himself up until the right leg was straight. His left leg swung and thumped. He got the toes on a shelf and stayed so, only a few inches off the pebbles and spreadeagled. The cleft rose by his face and he looked at the secret drops of the stillicide in the dark angle as though he envied them their peace. Time went by drop by drop. The two pictures drifted apart.

29

The pebbles rattled below him and a last lick of water flipped into the crevice. He dropped his head and looked down over his lifebelt, through the open skirt of the oilskin to where the wetted pebbles lay in the angle of the cleft. He saw his seaboot stockings and thought his feet back into them.

"I wish I had my seaboots still."

He changed the position of his right foot cautiously and locked his left knee stiffly upright to bear his weight without effort. His feet were selective in a curious way. They could not feel rock unless there was sharpness. They only became a part of him when they were hurting him or when he could see them.

The tail end of a wave reached right into the angle and struck in the apex with a plop. A single string of spray leapt up between his legs, past the lifebelt and wetted his face. He made a sound and only then found how ruinous an extension of flesh he carried round him. The sound began in the throat, bubbled and stayed there. The mouth took no part but lay open, jaw lying slack on the hard oilskin collar. The bubbling increased and he made the teeth click. Words twisted out between them and the frozen stuff of his upper lip.

"Like a dead man!"

Another wave reached in and spray ran down his face. He began to labour at climbing. He moved up the intricate rock face until there were no more limpets nor mussels and nothing clung to the rock but his own body and tiny barnacles and green smears of weed. All the time the wind pushed him into the cleft and the sea made dispersed noises.

The cleft narrowed until his head projected through an opening, not much wider than his body. He got his elbows jammed on either side and looked up.

Before his face the rock widened above the narrowest part of the cleft into a funnel. The sides of the funnel were not very smooth; but they were smooth enough to refuse to hold a body by friction. They sloped away to the top of the rock like a roof angle. The track from his face to the cliff-like edge of the funnel at the top was nearly twice the length of a man. He began to turn his head, slowly, searching for handholds, but saw none. Only at about halfway there was a depression, but too shallow for a handhold. Blunted fingers would never be safe on the rounded edge.

There came a thud from the bottom of the angle. Solid water shot into the angle, burst and washed down again. He peered over his lifebelt, between his two feet. The pebbles were dimmed, appeared clearly for a moment, then vanished under a surge of green water. Spray shot up between his body and the rock.

He pulled himself up until his body from the waist was leaning forward along the slope. His feet found the holds where his elbows had been. His knees straightened slowly while he breathed in gasps and his right arm reached out in front of him. Fingers closed on the blunted edge of the depression. Pulled.

31

He took one foot away from a hold and edged the knee up. He moved the other.

He hung, only a few inches from the top of the angle, held by one hand and the friction of his body. The fingers of his right hand quivered and gave. They slipped over the rounded edge. His whole body slid down and he was back at the top of the crevice again. He lay still, not seeing the rock by his eyes and his right arm was stretched above him.

The sea was taking over the cleft. Every few seconds there came the thump and return of a wave below him. Heavy drops fell and trickled on the surface of the funnel before his face. Then a wave exploded and water cascaded over his legs. He lifted his face off the rock and the snarl wrestled with his stiff muscles.

"Like a limpet."

He lay for a while, bent at the top of the crevice. The pebbles no longer appeared in the angle. They were a wavering memory of themselves between bouts of spray. Then they vanished, the rock vanished with them and with another explosion the water hit him from head to foot. He shook it from his face. He was staring down at the crevice as though the water were irrelevant.

He cried out.

"Like a limpet!"

He put his feet down and felt for holds, lowered himself resolutely, clinging each time the water hit him and went back. He held his breath and spat when each wave left him. The water was no longer cold but powerful rather. The nearer he lowered his body to the pebbles the harder he was struck and the heavier the weight that urged him down at each return. He lost his hold and fell the last few inches and immediately a wave had him, thrust him brutally into the angle then tried to tear him away. Between waves when he staggered to his feet the water was knee-deep over the pebbles and they gave beneath him. He fell on all fours and was hidden in a green heap that hit the back of the angle and climbed up in a tree-trunk of spray. He staggered round the angle then gripped with both hands. The water tore at him but he held on. He got his knife free and opened the blade. He ducked down and immediately there were visions of rock and weed in front of his eyes. The uproar of the sea sank to a singing note in the ears. Then he was up again, the knife swinging free, two limpets in his hands and the sea knocked him down and stood him on his head. He found rock and clung against the backwash. When the waves left him for a moment he opened his mouth and gasped in the air as though he were winning territory. He found holds in the angle and the sea exploded, thrust him up so that now his effort was to stay down and under control. After each blow he flattened himself to escape the descent of the water. As he rose the seas lost their quality of leaden power but became more personal and vicious. They tore at his clothing, they beat him in the crutch, they tented up his oilskin till the skirt was crumpled above his waist. If he looked down the

33

water came straight at his face, or hit him in the guts and thrust him up.

He came to the narrowest part and was shoved through. He opened his eyes after the water gushed back and breathed wetly as the foam streamed down his face. A lock of hair was plastered just to the bridge of his nose and he saw the end of it, double. The chute struck him again, the waterfall rushed back and he was still there, wedged by his weight in the narrowest part of the crevice where the funnel began and his body was shaking. He lay forward on the slope and began to straighten his legs. His face moved up against the rock and a torrent swept back over him. He began to fumble in the crumples of his oilskin. He brought out a limpet and set it on the rock by his waist. Water came again and went. He reversed his knife and tapped the limpet on the top with the haft. The limpet gave a tiny sideways lurch and sucked itself down against the rock. A weight pressed on him and the man and the limpet firmed down against the rock together.

His legs were straight and stiff and his eyes were shut. He brought his right arm round in a circle and felt above him. He found the blunted dent that was too smooth for a handhold. His hand came back, was inundated, fumbled in oilskin. He pulled it out and when the hand crawled round and up there was a limpet in the palm. The man was looking at the rock an inch or two from his face but without interest. What life was left was concentrated in the crawling right hand. The hand found the blunted hollow, and

34

pitched the limpet beyond the edge. The body was lifted a few inches and lay motionless waiting for the return of the water. When the chute had passed the hand came back, took the knife, moved up and tapped blindly on rock. The fingers searched stiffly, found the limpet, hit with the haft of the knife.

He turned his face, endured another wave and considered the limpet above him gravely. His hand let the knife go, which slid and clattered and hung motionless by his waist. He took the tit of the lifebelt and unscrewed the end. The air breathed out and his body flattened a little in the funnel. He laid the side of his head down and did nothing. Before his mouth the wet surface of the rock was blurred a little and regularly the blur was erased by the return of the waterfall. Sometimes the pendant knife would clatter.

Again he turned his face and looked up. His fingers closed over the limpet. Now his right leg was moving. The toes searched tremulously for the first limpet as the fingers had searched for the second. They did not find the limpet but the knee did. The hand let go, came down to the knee and lifted that part of the leg. The snarl behind the stiff face felt the limpet as a pain in the crook of the knee. The teeth set. The whole body began to wriggle; the hand went back to the higher limpet and pulled. The man moved sideways up the slope of the roof. The left leg came in and the seaboot stocking pushed the first leg away. The side of the foot was against the limpet. The

35

leg straightened. Another torrent returned and washed down.

The man was lying with one foot on a limpet, held mostly by friction. But his foot was on one limpet and the second one was before his eyes. He reached up and there was a possible handhold that his fingers found, provided the other one still gripped the limpet by his face. He moved up, up, up and then there was an edge for his fingers. His right arm rose, seized. He pulled with both arms, thrust with both legs. He saw a trench of rock beyond the edge, glimpsed sea, saw whiteness on the rocks and jumble. He fell forward.

3

He was lying in a trench. He could see a weathered wall of rock and a long pool of water stretching away from his eye. His body was in some other place that had nothing to do with this landscape. It was splayed, scattered behind him, his legs in different worlds, neck twisted. His right arm was bent under his body and his wrist doubled. He sensed this hand and the hard pressure of the knuckles against his side but the pain was not intense enough to warrant the titanic effort of moving. His left arm stretched away along the trench and was half-covered in water. His right eye was so close to this water that he could feel a little pluck from the surface tension when he blinked and his eyelashes caught in the film. The water had flattened again by the time he saw the surface consciously but his right cheek and the corner of his mouth were under water and were causing a tremble. The other eye was above water and was looking down the trench. The inside of the trench was dirty white, strangely white with more than the glossy reflection from the sky. The corner of his mouth pricked. Sometimes the surface of the water was pitted for a moment or two and faint, inter-lacing circles spread over it from each pit. His left eye watched them, looking through a kind of arch of darkness where the skull swept round the socket. At the bottom and almost a straight line, was the skin colour of his nose. Filling the arch was the level of shining water.

He began to think slowly.

I have tumbled in a trench. My head is jammed against the farther side and my neck is twisted. My legs must be up in the air over the other wall. My thighs are hurting because the weight of my legs is pushing against the edge of the wall as a fulcrum. My right toes are hurt more than the rest of my leg. My hand is doubled under me and that is why I feel the localized pain in my ribs. My fin-gers might be made of wood. That whiter white under the water along there is my hand, hidden.

There was a descending scream in the air, a squawk and the beating of wings. A gull was braking widely over the wall at the end of the trench, legs and claws held out. It yelled angrily at the trench, the wide wings gained a purchase and it hung flapping only a foot or two above the rock. Wind chilled his cheek. The webbed feet came up, the wings steadied and the gull side-slipped away. The commotion of its passage made waves in the white water that beat against his cheek, the shut eye, the corner of his mouth. The stinging increased.

There was no pain sharp enough to compel action. Even the stinging was outside the head. His left eye watched the whiter white of his hand under water. Some of the memory pictures came back. They were new ones of a man climbing up rock and placing limpets.

The pictures stirred him more than the stinging. They made his left hand contract under the surface and the oilskin arm roll in the water. His breathing grew suddenly fierce so that waves rippled away along the trench, crossed and came back. A ripple splashed into his mouth.

Immediately he was convulsed and struggling. His legs kicked and swung sideways. His head ground against rock and turned. He scrabbled in the white water with both hands and heaved himself up. He felt the too-smooth wetness running on his face and the brilliant jab of pain at the corner of his right eye. He spat and snarled. He glimpsed the trenches with their thick layers of dirty white, their trapped inches of solution, a gull slipping away over a green sea. Then he was forcing himself forward. He fell into the next trench, hauled himself over the wall, saw a jumble of broken rock, slid and stumbled. He was going down hill and he fell part of the way. There was moving water round flattish rocks, a complication of weedy life. The wind went down with him and urged him forward. As long as he went forward the wind was satisfied but if he stopped for a moment's caution it thrust his unbalanced body down so that he scraped and hit. He saw little of the open sea and sky or the whole rock but only flashes of intimate being, a crack or point, a hand's breadth of

39

yellowish surface that was about to strike a blow, unavoidable fists of rock that beat him impersonally, struck bright flashes of light from his body. The pain in the corner of his eye went with him too. This was the most important of all the pains because it thrust a needle now into the dark skull where he lived. The pain could not be avoided. His body revolved round it. Then he was holding brown weed and the sea was washing over his head and shoulders. He pulled himself up and lay on a flat rock with a pool across the top. He rolled the side of his face and his eye backwards and forwards under water. He moved his hands gently so that the water swished. They left the water and reached round and gathered smears of green weed.

He knelt up and held the smears of green against his eye and the right side of his face. He slumped back against rock among the jellies and scalloped pitches and encampments of limpets and let the encrusted barnacles hurt him as they would. He set his left hand gently on his thigh and squinted sideways at it. The fingers were half-bent. The skin was white with blue showing through and wrinkles cut the surface in regular shapes. The needle reached after him in the skull behind the dark arch. If he moved the eyeball the needle moved too. He opened his eye and it filled immediately with water under the green weed.

He began to snort and make sounds deep in his chest. They were like hard lumps of sound and they jerked him as they came out. More salt water came out of each eye and joined the traces of the sea and the solution on his cheeks. His whole body began to shiver.

There was a deeper pool on a ledge farther down. He climbed slowly and heavily down, edged himself across and put his right cheek under again. He opened and closed his eye so that the water flushed the needle corner. The memory pictures had gone so far away that they could be disregarded. He felt round and buried his hands in the pool. Now and then a hard sound jerked his body.

The sea-gull came back with others and he heard them sounding their interlacing cries like a trace of their flight over his head. There were noises from the sea too, wet gurgles below his ear and the running thump of swells, blanketed by the main of the rock but still able to sidle round and send offshoots sideways among the rocks and into the crannies. The idea that he must ignore pain came and sat in the centre of his darkness where he could not avoid it. He opened his eyes for all the movement of the needle and looked down at his bleached hands. He began to mutter.

"Shelter. Must have shelter. Die if I don't."

He turned his head carefully and looked up the way he had come. The odd patches of rock that had hit him on the way down were visible now as part of each other. His eyes took in yards at a time, surfaces that swam as the needle pricked water out of him. He set himself to crawl back up the rock. The wind was lighter but dropping trails of rain still fell over him. He hauled himself up a cliff that was no higher than a man could span with his arms but it was

41

an obstacle that had to be negotiated with much arrangement and thought for separate limbs. He lay for a while on the top of the little cliff and looked in watery snatches up the height of the rock. The sun lay just above the high part where the white trenches had waited for him. The light was struggling with clouds and rain-mist and there were birds wheeling across the rock. The sun was dull but drew more water from his eyes so that he screwed them up and cried out suddenly against the needle. He crawled by touch, and then with one eye through trenches and gullies where there was no whiteness. He lifted his legs over the broken walls of trenches as though they belonged to another body. All at once, with the diminishing of the pain in his eye, the cold and exhaustion came back. He fell flat in a gully and let his body look after itself. The deep chill fitted close to him, so close it was inside the clothes, inside the skin.

The chill and the exhaustion spoke to him clearly. Give up, they said, lie still. Give up the thought of return, the thought of living. Break up, leave go. Those white bodies are without attraction or excitement, the faces, the words, happened to another man in another place. An hour on this rock is a lifetime. What have you to lose? There is nothing here but torture. Give up. Leave go.

His body began to crawl again. It was not that there was muscular or nervous strength there that refused to be beaten but rather that the voices of pain were like waves beating against the sides of a ship. There was at the centre of all the pictures and pains and voices a fact like a bar of steel, a thing—that which was so nakedly the centre of everything that it could not even examine itself. In the darkness of the skull, it existed, a darker dark, self-existent and indestructible.

"Shelter. Must have shelter."

The centre began to work. It endured the needle to look sideways, put thoughts together. It concluded that it must crawl this way rather than that. It noted a dozen places and rejected them, searched ahead of the crawling body. It lifted the luminous window under the arch, shifted the arch of skull from side to side like the slow shift of the head of a caterpillar trying to reach a new leaf. When the body drew near to a possible shelter the head still moved from side to side, moving more quickly than the slow thoughts inside.

There was a slab of rock that had slipped and fallen sideways from the wall of a trench. This made a triangular hole between the rock and the side and bottom of the trench. There was no more than a smear of rainwater in this trench and no white stuff. The hole ran away and down at an angle following the line of the trench and inside there was darkness. The hole even looked drier than the rest of the rock. At last his head stopped moving and he lay down before this hole as the sun dipped from view. He began to turn his body in the trench, among a complication of sodden clothing. He said nothing but breathed heavily with open mouth. Slowly he turned until his white

43

seaboot stockings were towards the crevice. He backed to the triangular opening and put his feet in. He lay flat on his stomach and began to wriggle weakly like a snake that cannot cast its skin. His eyes were open and unfocused. He reached back and forced the oilskin and duffle down on either side. The oilskin was hard and he backed with innumerable separate movements like a lobster backing into a deep crevice under water. He was in the crack up to his shoulders and rock held him tightly. He hutched the lifebelt up till the soft rubber was across the upper part of his chest. The slow thoughts waxed and waned, the eyes were empty except for the water that ran from the needle in the right one. His hand found the tit and he blew again slowly until the rubber was firmed up against his chest. He folded his arms, a white hand on either side. He let the left side of his face fall on an oilskinned sleeve and his eyes were shut—not screwed up but lightly closed. His mouth was still open, the jaw fallen sideways. Now and then a shudder came up out of the crack and set his head and arms shaking. Water ran slowly out of his sleeves, fell from his hair and his nose, dripped from the rucked-up clothing round his neck. His eyes fell open like the mouth because the needle was more controllable that way. Only when he had to blink them against water did the point jab into the place where he lived.

He could see gulls swinging over the rock, circling down. They settled and cried with erect heads and tongues, beaks wide open on the high point of the rock.

44

The sky greyed down and sea-smoke drifted over. The birds talked and shook their wings, folded them one over the other, settled like white pebbles against the rock and tucked in their heads. The greyness thickened into a darkness in which the few birds and the splashes of their dung were visible as the patches of foam were visible on the water. The trenches were full of darkness for down by the shelter for some reason there was no dirty white. The rocks were dim shapes among them. The wind blew softly and chill over the main rock and its unseen, gentle passage made a continual and almost inaudible hiss. Every now and then a swell thumped into the angle by the safety rock. After that there would be a long pause and then the rush and scramble of falling water down the funnel.

The man lay, huddled in his crevice, left cheek pillowed on black oilskin and his hands were glimmering patches on either side. Every now and then there came a faint scratching sound of oilskin as the body shivered.

4

The man was inside two crevices. There was first the rock, closed and not warm but at least not cold with the coldness of sea or air. The rock was negative. It confined his body so that here and there the shudders were beaten; not soothed but forced inward. He felt pain throughout most of his body but distant pain that was sometimes to be mistaken for fire. There was dull fire in his feet and a sharper sort in either knee. He could see this fire in his mind's eye because his body was a second and interior crevice which he inhabited. Under each knee, then, there was a little fire built with crossed sticks and busily flaring like the fire that is lighted under a dying camel. But the man was intelligent. He endured these fires although they gave not heat but pain. They had to be endured because to stand up or even move would mean nothing but an increase of pain—more sticks and more flame, extending under all the body. He himself was at the far end of this inner crevice of flesh. At this far end, away from the fires, there was a mass of him lying on a lifebelt that rolled backwards and forwards at every breath. Beyond the mass was the round, bone globe of the world and himself hanging inside. One half of this world burned and froze but with a steadier and bearable pain. Only towards the top half of this world there would sometimes come a jab that was like a vast needle prying after him. Then he would make seismic convulsions of whole continents on that side and the jabs would become frequent but less deep and the nature of that part of the globe would change. There would appear shapes of dark and grey in space and a patch of galactic whiteness that he knew vaguely was a hand connected to him. The other side of the globe was all dark and gave no offence. He floated in the middle of this globe like a waterlogged body. He knew as an axiom of existence that he must be content with the smallest of all small mercies as he floated there. All the extensions with which he was connected, their distant fires, their slow burning, their racks and pincers were at least far enough away. If he could hit some particular mode of inactive being, some subtlety of interior balance, he might be allowed by the nature of the second crevice to float, still and painless in the centre of the globe.

Sometimes he came near this. He became small, and the globe larger until the burning extensions were interplanetary. But this universe was subject to convulsions that began in deep space and came like a wave. Then he was larger again, filling every corner of the tunnels, sweeping with shrieking nerves over the fires, expanding in the globe until he filled it and the needle jabbed through the corner of his right eye straight into the darkness of his

47

head. Dimly he would see one white hand while the pain stabbed. Then slowly he would sink back into the centre of the globe, shrink and float in the middle of a dark world. This became a rhythm that had obtained from all ages and would endure so.

This rhythm was qualified but not altered in essentials by pictures that happened to him and sometimes to someone else. They were brightly lit in comparison with the fires. There were waves larger than the universe and a glass sailor hanging in them. There was an order in neon lighting. There was a woman, not like the white detailed bodies but with a face. There was the gloom and hardness of a night-time ship, the lift of the deck, the slow cant and bumble. He was walking forward across the bridge to the binnacle and its dim light. He could hear Nat leaving his post as port look-out, Nat going down the ladder. He could hear that Nat had walking shoes on, not seaboots or plimsols. Nat was lowering his un-handy spider-length down the ladder with womanish care, not able now after all these months to wear the right clothes or negotiate a ladder like a seaman. Dawn had found him shivering from inadequate rig, the mess-deck would find him hurt by the language, a butt, humble, obedient and useless.

He looked briefly at the starboard horizon then across to the convoy, bulks just coming into view in the dawn light. They interrupted the horizon like so many bleak iron walls where now the long, blurred tears of rust were nearly visible.

48

But Nat would be fumbling aft, to find five minutes' solitude by the rail and meet his aeons. He would be picking his diffident way toward the depth-charge thrower on the starboard side not because it was preferable to the port rail but because he always went there. He would be enduring the wind and engine stink, the peculiar dusty dirt and shabbiness of a wartime destroyer because life itself with all its touches, tastes, sights and sounds and smells had been at a distance from him. He would go on enduring until custom made him indifferent. He would never find his feet in the Navy because those great feet of his had always been away out there, attached by accident while the man inside prayed and waited to meet his aeons.

But the deck-watch was ticking on to the next leg of the zigzag. He looked carefully at the second hand.

"Starboard fifteen."

Out on the port bow *Wildebeeste* was turning too. The grey light showed the swirl under her stern where the rudder had kicked across. As the bridge canted under him *Wildebeeste* seemed to slide astern from her position until she was lying parallel and just forrard of the beam.

"Midships."

Wildebeeste was still turning. Connected by the soles of his feet through steel to the long waver and roll of glaucous water he could predict to himself the exact degree of her list to port as she came round. But the water was not so predictable after all. In the last few degrees of her turn he saw a mound of grey, a seventh wave slide by her bows and pass under her. The swing of her stern increased, her stern slid down the slope and for that time she had carried ten degrees beyond her course, in a sudden lurch.

"Steady."

And curse the bloody Navy and the bloody war. He yawned sleepily and saw the swirl under *Wildebeeste*'s stern as she came back on course. The fires out there at the end of the second crevice flared up, a needle stabbed and he was back in his body. The fire died down again in the usual rhythm.

The destroyers in a V screen turned back together. Between orders he listened to the shivering ping of the Asdic and the light increased. The herd of merchantmen chugged on at six knots with the destroyers like outriders scouring the way before them, sweeping the sea clear with their invisible brooms, changing course together, all on one string.

He heard a step behind him on the ladder and busied himself to take a bearing because the captain might be coming. He checked the bearing of *Wildebeeste* with elaborate care. But no voice came with the steps.

He turned casually at last and there was Petty Officer Roberts—and now saluting.

"Good morning, Chief."

"Good morning, sir."

"What is it? Wangled a tot for me?"

The close eyes under their peak withdrew a little but the mouth made itself smile.

50

"Might, sir——"

And then, the calculation made, the advantage to self admitted, the smile widened.

"I'm a bit off me rum these days, somehow. Any time you'd care to——"

"O.K. Thanks."

And what now? A draft chit? Recommend for commission? Something small and manageable?

But Petty Officer Roberts was playing a game too deep. Whatever it was and wherever the elaborate system of obligations might lead to, it required nothing today but a grateful opinion of his good sense and understanding.

"About Walterson, sir."

Astonished laugh.

"My old friend Nat? What's he been doing? Not got himself in the rattle, has he?"

"Oh no, sir, nothing like that. Only——"

"What?"

"Well, just look now, sir, aft on the starboard side."

Together they walked to the starboard wing of the bridge. Nathaniel was still engaged with his aeons, feet held by friction on the corticene, bony rump on the rail just aft of the thrower. His hands were up to his face, his improbable length swaying with the scend of the swells.

"Silly ass."

"He'll do that once too often, sir."

Petty Officer Roberts came close. Liar. There was rum in his breath.

"I could have put him in the rattle for it, sir, but I thought, seeing he's a friend of yours in civvy street——"

Pause.

"O.K., Chief. I'll drop him a word myself."

"Thank you, sir."

"Thank *you*, Chief."

"I won't forget the tot, sir."

"Thanks a lot."

Petty Officer Roberts saluted and withdrew from the presence. He descended the ladder.

"Port fifteen."

Solitude with fires under the knees and a jabbing needle. Solitude out over the deck where the muzzle of X gun was lifted over the corticene. He smiled grimly to himself and reconstructed the inside of Nathaniel's head. He must have laid aft, hopefully, seeking privacy between the crew of the gun and the depth-charge watch. But there was no solitude for a rating in a small ship unless he was knowing enough to find himself a quiet number. He must have drifted aft from the mob of the fo'castle, from utter, crowded squalor to a modified and windy form of it. He was too witless to understand that the huddled mess-deck was so dense as to ensure a form of privacy, like that a man can achieve in a London crowd. So he would endure the gloomy stare of the depth-charge watch at his prayers, not understanding that they would keep an eye on him because they had nothing else to do.

"Midships. Steady."

52

Zig.

And he is praying in his time below when he ought to be turned in, swinging in his hammock, because he has been told that on watch he must keep a look-out over a sector of the sea. So he kept a look-out, dutiful and uncomprehending.

The dark centre of the head turned, saw the port lookout hutched, the swinging RDF aerial, the funnel with its tremble of hot air and trace of fume, looked down over the break of the bridge to the starboard deck.

Nathaniel was still there. His improbable height, combined with the leanness that made it seem even more incredible, had reduced the rail to an insecure parapet. His legs were splayed out and his feet held him by friction against the deck. As the dark centre watched, it saw Nathaniel take his hands down from his face, lay hold of the rail and get himself upright. He began to work his way forrard over the deck, legs straddled, arms out for balance. He carried his absurd little naval cap exactly level on the top of his head, and his curly black hair—a trifle lank for the night's dampness—emerged from under it all round. He saw the bridge by chance and gravely brought his right hand toward the right side of his head—taking no liberties, thought the black centre, knowing his place, humble aboard as in civvy street, ludicrous, unstoppable.

But the balance of the thin figure was disturbed by this temporary exercise of the right hand; it tottered sideways, tried for the salute again, missed, considered the problem gravely with arms out and legs astraddle. A scend made it rock. It turned, went to the engine casing, tried out the surface to see if the metal was hot, steadied, turned forrard and slowly saluted the bridge.

The dark centre made itself wave cheerfully to the foreshortened figure. Nathaniel's face altered even at that distance. The delight of recognition appeared in it, not plastered on and adjusted as Petty Officer Roberts had smiled under his too-close eyes: but rising spontaneously from the conjectural centre behind the face, evidence of sheer niceness that made the breath come short with maddened liking and rage. There was a convulsion in the substrata of the globe at this end so that the needle came stabbing and prying towards the centre that had floated all this while without pain.

He seized the binnacle and the rock and cried out in an anguish of frustration.

"Can't anyone understand how I feel?"

Then he was extended again throughout the tunnels of the inner crevice and the fires were flaring and spitting in his flesh.

There came a new noise among the others. It was connected with the motionless blobs of white out there. They were more definite than they had been. Then he was aware that time had passed. What had seemed an eternal rhythm had been hours of darkness and now there was a faint light that consolidated his personality, gave it bounds and sanity. The noise was a throaty cluck from one of the roosting gulls.

He lay with the pains, considering the light and the fact of a new day. He could inspect his wooden left hand if he was careful about the management of the inflamed corner of his eye. He willed the fingers to close and they quivered, then contracted. Immediately he was back in them, he became a man who was thrust deep into a crevice in barren rock. Knowledge and memory flowed back in orderly succession, he remembered the funnel, the trench. He became a castaway in broad daylight and the necessity of his position fell on him. He began to heave at his body, dragging himself out of the space between the rocks. As he moved out, the gulls clamoured out of sleep and took off. They came back, sweeping in to examine him with sharp cries then sidling away in the air again. They were not like the man-wary gulls of inhabited beaches and cliffs. Nor had they about them the primal innocence of unvisited nature. They were wartime gulls who, finding a single man with water round him, resented the warmth of his flesh and his slow, unwarranted movements. They told him, with their close approach, and flapping hover that he was far better dead, floating in the sea like a burst hammock. He staggered and struck out among them with wooden arms.

"Yah! Get away! Bugger off!"

They rose clamorously wheeling, came back till their wings beat his face. He struck out again in panic so that one went drooping off with a wing that made no more

55

than a half-beat. They retired then, circled and watched. Their heads were narrow. They were flying reptiles. An ancient antipathy for things with claws set him shuddering at them and thinking into their smooth outlines all the strangeness of bats and vampires.

"Keep off! Who do you think I am?"

Their circles widened. They flew away to the open sea.

He turned his attention back to his body. His flesh seemed to be a compound of aches and stiffnesses. Even the control system had broken down for his legs had to be given deliberate and separate orders as though they were some unhandy kind of stilts that had been strapped to him. He broke the stilts in the middle, and got upright. He discovered new fires—little islands of severer pain in the general ache. The one at the corner of his right eye was so near to him that he did not need to discover it. He stood up, leaning his back against the side of a trench and looked round him.

The morning was dull but the wind had died down and the water was leaping rather than progressing. He became aware of a new thing; sound of the sea that the sailor never hears in his live ship. There was a gentle undertone compounded of countless sloppings of wavelets, there was a constant gurgling and sucking that ranged from a stony smack to a ruminative swallow. There were sounds that seemed every moment to be on the point of articulation but lapsed into a liquid slapping like appetite. Over all this was a definable note, a singing hiss, soft touch of the air

56

on stone, continuous, subtle, unending friction.

A gull-cry swirled over him and he raised an arm and looked under the elbow but the gull swung away from the rock. When the cry had gone everything was gentle again, non-committal and without offence.

He looked down at the horizon and passed his tongue over his upper lip. It came again, touched experimentally, vanished. He swallowed. His eyes opened wider and he paid no attention to the jab. He began to breathe quickly.

"Water!"

As in the sea at a moment of desperate crisis his body changed, became able and willing. He scrambled out of the trench on legs that were no longer wooden. He climbed across fallen buttresses that had never supported anything but their own weight; he slithered in the white pools of the trenches near the top of the rock. He came to the edge of the cliff where he had climbed and a solitary gull slipped away from under his feet. He worked himself round on his two feet but the horizon was like itself at every point. He could only tell when he had inspected every point by the lie of the rock beneath him. He went round again.

At last he turned back to the rock itself and climbed down but more slowly now from trench to trench. When he was below the level of the white bird-droppings he stopped and began to examine the rock foot by foot. He crouched in a trench, gripping the lower side and looking at every part of it with quick glances as if he were trying

57

to follow the flight of a hover-fly. He saw water on a flat rock, went to it, put his hands on either side of the puddle and stuck his tongue in. His lips contracted down round his tongue, sucked. The puddle became nothing but a patch of wetness on the rock. He crawled on. He came to a horizontal crack in the side of a trench. Beneath the crack a slab of rock was falling away and there was water caught. He put his forehead against the rock then turned sideways until his cheek rested above the crack—but still his tongue could not reach the water. He thrust and thrust, mouth ground against the stone but still the water was beyond him. He seized the cracked stone and jerked furiously until it broke away. The water spilled down and became a film in the bottom of the trench. He stood there, heart thumping and held the broken stone in his hands.

"Use you loaf, man. Use your loaf."

He looked down the jumbled slope before him. He began to work the rock methodically. He noticed the broken stone in his hands and dropped it. He worked across the rock and back from trench to trench. He came on the mouldering bones of fish and a dead gull, its up-turned breast-bone like the keel of a derelict boat. He found patches of grey and yellow lichen, traces even of earth, a button of moss. There were the empty shells of crabs, pieces of dead weed, and the claws of a lobster.

At the lower end of the rock there were pools of water but they were salt. He came back up the slope, his needle and the fires forgotten. He groped in the crevice where he had lain all night but the rock was nearly dry. He clambered over the fallen slab of stone that had sheltered him.

The slab was in two pieces. Once there must have been a huge upended layer of rock that had endured while the others weathered away. It had fallen and broken in two. The larger piece lay across the trench at the very edge of the rock. Part of it projected over the sea, and the trench led underneath like a gutter.

He lay down and inserted himself. He paused. Then he was jerking his tail like a seal and lifting himself forward with his flippers. He put his head down and made sucking noises. Then he lay still.

The place in which he had found water was like a little cave. The floor of the trench sloped down gently under water so that this end of the pool was shallow. There was room for him to lie with his elbows spread apart for the slab had smashed down the wall on the right-hand side. The roof stone lay across at an angle and the farther end of the cave was not entirely stopped up. There was a small hole high up by the roof, full of daylight and a patch of sky. The light from the sky was reflected in and from the water so that faint lines quivered over the stone roof. The water was drinkable but there was no pleasure in the taste. It tasted of things that were vaguely unpleasant though the tastes were not individually identifiable. The water did not satisfy thirst so much as allay it. There seemed to be plenty of the stuff, for the pool was yards long before him and the farther end looked deep. He lowered his head and

59

sucked again. Now that his one and a half eyes were adjusted to the light he could see there was a deposit under the water, reddish and slimy. The deposit was not hard but easily disturbed so that where he had drunk, the slime was coiling up, drifting about, hanging, settling. He watched dully.

Presently he began to mutter.

"Rescue. See about rescue."

He struggled back with a thump of his skull against rock. He crawled along the trench and clambered to the top of the rock and peered round and round the horizon again. He knelt and lowered himself on his hands. The thoughts began to flicker quickly in his head.

"I cannot stay up here all the time. I cannot shout to them if they pass. I must make a man to stand here for me. If they see anything like a man they will come closer."

There was a broken rock below his hands, leaning against the wall from which the clean fracture had fallen. He climbed down and wrestled with a great weight. He made the stone rise on an angle; he quivered and the stone fell over. He collapsed and lay for a while. He left the stone and scrambled heavily down to the little cliff and the scattered rocks where he had bathed his eye. He found an encrusted boulder lying in a rock pool and pulled it up. He got the stone against his stomach, staggered for a few steps, dropped the stone, lifted and carried again. He dumped the stone on the high point above the funnel and came back. There was a stone like a suitcase balanced on the wall of a trench and he pondered what he should do. He put his back against the suitcase and his feet against the other side of the trench. The suitcase grated, moved. He got a shoulder under one end and heaved. The suitcase tumbled in the next trench and broke. He grinned without humour and lugged the larger part up into his lap. He raised the broken suitcase to the wall, turned it end over end, engineered it up slopes of fallen but unmanageable rock, pulled and hauled.

Then there were two rocks on the high part, one with a trace of blood. He looked once round the horizon and climbed down the slope again. He stopped, put a hand to his forehead, then examined the palm. But there was no blood.

He spoke out loud in a voice that was at once flat and throaty.

"I am beginning to sweat."

He found a third stone but could not get it up the wall of the trench. He retreated with it, urged it along the bottom to a lower level until he could find an exit low enough for him to heave it up. By the time he had dragged it to the others his hands were broken. He knelt by the stones and considered the sea and sky. The sun was out wanly and there were fewer layers of cloud. He lay down across the three stones and let them hurt him. The sun shone on his left ear from the afternoon side of the rock.

He got up, put the second stone laboriously on the third and the first on the second. The three stones measured

61

nearly two feet from top to bottom. He sat down and leaned back against them. The horizon was empty, the sea gentle, the sun a token. A sea-gull was drifting over the water a stone's throw from the rock, and now the bird was rounded, white and harmless. He covered his aching eye with one hand to rest it but the effort of holding a hand up was too much and he let the palm fall back on his knee. He ignored his eye and tried to think.

"Food?"

He got to his feet and climbed down over the trenches. At the lower end were cliffs a few feet high and beyond them separate rocks broke the surface. He ignored these for the moment because they were inaccessible. The cliffs were very rough. They were covered with a crust of tiny barnacles that had welded their limy secretions into an extended colony that dipped down in the water as deep as his better eye could see. There were yellowish limpets and coloured sea-snails drying and drawn in against the rock. Each limpet sat in the hollow its foot had worn. There were clusters of blue mussels too, with green webs of weed caught over them. He looked back up the side of the rock—under the water-hole for he could see the roof slab projecting like a diving-board—and saw how the mussels had triumphed over the whole wall. Beneath a defined line the rock was blue with them. He lowered himself carefully and inspected the cliff. Under water the harvest of food was even thicker for the mussels were bigger down there and water-snails were crawling over

62

them. And among the limpets, the mussels, the snails and barnacles, dotted like sucked sweets, were the red blobs of jelly, the anemones. Under water they opened their mouths in a circle of petals but up by his face, waiting for the increase of the tide they were pursed up and slumped like breasts when the milk has been drawn from them.

Hunger contracted under his clothes like a pair of hands. But as he hung there, his mouth watering, a lump rose in his throat as if he were very sad. He hung on the creamy wall and listened to the washing of water, the minute ticks and whispers that came from this abundant, but not quite vegetable, life. He felt at his waist, produced the lanyard, swung it and caught the knife with his free hand. He put the blade against his mouth, gripped with his teeth and pulled the haft away from it. He put the point under a limpet and it contracted down so that he felt its muscular strength as he turned the blade. He dropped the knife to the length of the lanyard and caught the limpet as it fell. He turned the limpet over in his hand and peered into the broad end. He saw an oval brown foot drawn in, drawn back, shutting out the light.

"Bloody hell."

He jerked the limpet away from him and the tent made a little flip of water in the sea. As the ripples died away he watched it waver down whitely out of sight. He looked for a while at the place where the limpet had disappeared. He took his knife again and began to chisel lines among the barnacles. They wept and bled salty, uretic water. He

63

poked an anemone with the point of the knife and the jelly screwed up tight. He pressed the top with the flat of the blade and the opening pissed in his eye. He jammed the knife against the rock and shut it. He climbed back and sat on the high rock with his back against the three stones—two broken and an encrusted one on top.

Inside, the man was aware of a kind of fit that seized his body. He drew his feet up against him and rolled sideways so that his face was on the rock. His body was jumping and shuddering beneath the sodden clothing. He whispered against stone.

"You can't give up."

Immediately he began to crawl away down hill. The crawl became a scramble. Down by the water he found stones but they were of useless shape. He chose one from just under water and toiled back to the others. He changed the new one for the top stone, grated it into place, then put the encrusted one back. Two feet, six inches.

He muttered.

"Must. Must."

He climbed down to the rock-side opposite the cliff of mussels. There were ledges on this side and water sucking up and down. The water was very dark and there was long weed at the bottom, straps like the stuff travellers sometimes put round suitcases when the locks are broken. This brown weed was collapsed and coiled over itself near the surface but farther out it lay upright in the water or moved slowly like tentacles or tongues. Beyond that there

64

was nothing but the blackness of deep water going down to the bottom of the deep sea. He took his eyes away from this, climbed along one of the ledges, but everywhere the rock was firm and there were no separated pieces to be found, though in one place the solid ledge was cracked. He pushed at this part with his stockinged feet but could not move it. He turned clumsily on the ledge and came back. At the lower end of the great rock he found the stones with the wrong shape and took them one by one to a trench and piled them. He pried in crevices and pulled out blocks and rounded masses of yellowing quartz on which the weed was draggled like green hair. He took them to the man he was building and piled them round the bottom stone. Some were not much bigger than potatoes and he knocked these in where the big stones did not fit until the top one no longer rocked when he touched it. He put one last stone on the others, one big as his head.

Three feet.

He stood away from the pile and looked round him. The pile reached in his view from horizon level to higher than the sun. He was astonished when he saw this and looked carefully to establish where west was. He saw the outlying rock that had saved him and the sea-gulls were floating just beyond the backwash.

He climbed down the rock again to where he had prised off the limpet. He made a wry face and pushed his doubled fists into the damp cloth over his belly. He hung on the little cliff and began to tear away the blobs of red jelly with his fingers. He set them on the edge of the cliff and did not look at them for a while. Then he turned his one and a half eyes down to them and inspected them closely. They lay like a handful of sweets only they moved ever so slightly and there was a little clear water trickling from the pile. He sat by them on the edge of the cliff and no longer saw them. His face set in a look of agony.

"Bloody hell!"

His fingers closed over a sweet. He put it quickly in his mouth, ducked, swallowed, shuddered. He took another, swallowed, took another as fast as he could. He bolted the pile of sweets then sat rigid, his throat working. He subsided, grinning palely. He looked down at his left hand and there was one last sweet lying against his little finger in a drip of water. He clapped his hand to his mouth, stared over the fingers and fought with his stomach. He scrambled over the rocks to the water-hole and pulled himself in. Again the coils of red silt and slime rose from the bottom. There was a band of red round the nearer end of the pool that was about half an inch across.

When he had settled his stomach with the harsh water he came out of the hole backwards. The sea-gulls were circling the rock now and he looked at them with hate.

"You won't get me!"

He clambered back to the top of the rock where his three-foot dwarf stood. The horizon was in sight all round and empty. He licked a trace of drinkable water from his lips.

"I have enough to drink——"

He stood, looking down at the slab over his drinking water where it projected like a diving-board. He went slowly to the cliff, got down and peered under the slab. The seaward end of the pool was held back by a jumble of broken stones that were lodged against each other. Behind the impaired window of his sight he saw the red silt rising and coiling. The stuff must lie over the inner side of these stones, sealing them lightly against the water's escape. He had a quick vision of the hidden surfaces, holes that time had furred with red till they were stopped and the incongruous fresh water held back among all the salt; but held back so delicately that the merest touch would set his life irrevocably flowing——

He backed away with staring eyes and breath that came quick.

"Forget it!"

He began to thrust himself backwards into the sleeping crevice. He got almost to his ears out of sight and filled the hole with his body and heavy clothing. He pulled the sleeves of his duffle out of the oilskin tubes until they came over the backs of his hands. After a little struggling he could grip them with his fingers and double his fists so that they were hidden in the hairy duffle. The lifebelt supported his chest and throat once more and he pillowed his left cheek on his forearm. He lay so, shivering now that the sun had gone down, while the green sky turned blue, dark blue and the gulls floated down. His body yielded to

67

the shivers but between the bouts it lay quite still. His mouth was open and his eyes stared anxiously into the darkness. Once, he jerked and the mouth spoke.

"Forget it!"

A gull moved a little then settled down again.

5

But he could not fall into the pit because he was extended through his body. He was aware dimly of returning strength; and this not only allowed him to savour the cold and be physically miserable but to be irritated by it. Instead of the apocalyptic visions and voices of the other night he had now nothing but ill-used and complaining flesh. The point of the needle in his eye was blunted but instead of enduring anything rather than its stab he had continually to rub one foot over the other or press with his body against the slab of rock in an effort to shut off the chill on that side, only to find that the other side required attention more and more insistently. He would heave the globe of darkness in which he most lived off a hard, wooden surface, rotate it and lay the other hemisphere down. There was another difference between this night and the last. The fires had died down but they were still there now he had the time and the strength to attend to them. The stiffness had become a settled sense of strain as if his body were being stretched mercilessly. The rock too, now that he had a little strength to spare was forcing additional discomfort on him. What the globe had taken in its extreme exhaustion for a smooth surface was in fact undulating with the suggestion of prominences here and there. These suggestions became localized discomforts that changed in turn to a dull ache. Allowed to continue, aches became pains then fires that must be avoided. So he would heave his thigh away or wriggle weakly only to find that the prominence was gone and had left nothing but an undulation. His thigh would flatten down again and wait in the darkness for the discomfort, the ache, the pain, the fire.

Up at the top end now that the window was dark the man found the intermissions of discomfort were again full of voices and things that could not but be seen. He had a confused picture of the passage of the sun below him beyond the central fires of the earth. But both the sun and the fires were too far away to warm him. He saw the red silt holding back the fresh water, a double handful of red sweets, an empty horizon.

"I shall live!"

He saw the sun below him with its snail movement and was confused inside his head by the earth's revolution on its axis and its year-long journey round the sun. He saw how many months a man must endure before he was warmed by the brighter light of spring. He watched the sun for months without thought or identity. He saw it from many angles, through windows of trains or from fields. He confused its fires with other fires, on allotments,

70

in gardens, in grates. One of these fires was most insistent that here was reality and to be watched. The fire was behind the bars of a grate. He found that the grate was in a room and then everything became familiar out of the past and he knew where he was and that the time and the words were significant. There was a tall and spider-thin figure sitting in the chair opposite. It looked up under its black curls, as if it were consulting a reference book on the other side of the ceiling.

"Take us as we are now and heaven would be sheer negation. Without form and void. You see? A sort of black lightning destroying everything that we call life."

But he was laughing and happy in his reply.

"I don't see and I don't much care but I'll come to your lecture. My dear Nathaniel, you've no idea how glad I am to see you!"

Nathaniel looked his face over carefully.

"And I, too. About seeing you, I mean."

"We're showing emotion, Nat, We're being un-English."

Again the careful look.

"I think you need my lecture. You're not happy, are you?"

"I'm not really interested in heaven either. Let me get you a drink."

"No, thanks."

Nathaniel uncoiled from the chair and stood with his arms out on either side, hands bent up. He looked, first at nothing, then round the room. He went to the wall and

71

perched himself absurdly high up with his bony rump on the top of a shelf. He pushed his incredible legs out and splayed them apart till he was held insecurely by the friction of the soles of his feet. He looked up at the reference book again.

"You could call it a talk on the technique of dying."

"You'll die a long time before me. It's a cold night—and look how you're dressed!"

Nathaniel peered at the laughing window then down at himself.

"Is it? Yes. I suppose I am."

"And I'm going to have a damned long life and get what I'm after."

"And that is——?"

"Various things."

"But you're not happy."

"Why do you spill this over me, of all people?"

"There's a connection between us. Something will happen to us or perhaps we were meant to work together. You have an extraordinary capacity to endure."

"To what end?"

"To achieve heaven."

"Negation?"

"The technique of dying into heaven."

"No thanks. Be your age, Nat."

"You could, you know. And I——"

Nat's face was undergoing a change. It turned towards him again. The flush on the cheeks was painful. The eyes

72

loomed and impended.

"—And I, have a feeling. Don't laugh, please—but I feel—you could say that I know." Below the eyes the breath came out in a little gasp. Feet scraped.

"—You could say that I know it is important for you personally to understand about heaven—about dying—because in only a few years——"

For a while there was silence, a double shock—for the bells ceased to toll beyond the windows of the room as though they had stopped with the voice. A vicious sting from his cigarette whipped along the arm into the globe so that he flicked it away and cried out. Then he was flat on the floor, fumbling for the stub under the armchair and the undulations of the floor were a discomfort to the body. Lying there, the words pursued him, made his ears buzz, set up a tumult, pushed his heart to thump with sudden, appalled understanding as though it were gasping the words that Nathaniel had not spoken.

"—because in only a few years you will be dead."

He cried out against the unspoken words in fury and panic.

"You bloody fool, Nat! You awful bloody fool!"

The words echoed in the trench and he jerked his cheek up off the oilskin. There was much light outside, sunlight and the crying of gulls.

He shouted.

"I'm damned if I'll die!"

He hauled himself quickly out of the crevice and stood

73

in the trench. The sea and sky were dark blue and the sun was high enough not to make a dazzle from the water. He felt the sun on his face and rubbed with both hands at the bristles. He looked quickly round the horizon then climbed down to a trench. He began to fumble with his trousers, glancing furtively behind him. Then for the first time on the rock he broke up the bristly, external face with a shout of jeering laughter. He went back to the dwarf and made water in a hosing gesture at the horizon.

"Gentlemen are requested to adjust their dress before leaving."

He began to fumble with the buttons of his oilskin and lugged it off fiercely. He picked and pulled at the tapes that held his lifebelt inside the duffle. He slipped both off and dumped them in a heavy heap and stood there looking down. He glanced at the two wavy lines of gold braid on either arm, the gilt buttons, the black doeskin of his jacket and trousers. He peeled himself, jacket, woollen sweater, black sweater, shirt, vest; pulled off his long stockings, his socks, his pants. He stood still and examined what he could see of his body.

The feet had been so thoroughly sodden that they seemed to have lost their shape. One big toe was blue and black with bruise and drying blood. There were bruises on either knee that ended in lacerations, not cuts or jabs but places the size of a sixpence where the skin and flesh had been worn off. His right hip was blue as though someone had laid a hand dipped in paint on it.

74

He examined his arms. The right elbow was swollen and stiff and there were more bruises about. Here and there on his body were patches, not of raw flesh but of blood flecks under the skin. He felt the bristles on his face tenderly. His right eye was fogged and that cheek was hot and stiff.

He took his vest and tried to wring out the body but there was water held in the material that would not come free. He put his left foot on one end of the twisted cloth and screwed the other with both hands. Dampness appeared and moistened the rock. He did this in turn to each piece of clothing and spread the lot in the sun to dry. He sat down by the dwarf, fumbled in his jacket and brought out a sodden packet of papers and a small brown booklet. The colour had run from the booklet and stained the papers as if they were rusting. He spread the papers out round him and rummaged through his pockets in turn. He found two pennies and a florin. He laid them by the dwarf in a little heap. He took his knife on its lanyard from the pocket of his oilskin and hung it round his neck. When he had done that he put up his hand and tugged gently at the small brown disc that was tied round his neck by a white thread. He bent his face into a grin. He got up and scrambled over the rocks to the water-hole. He eased himself in and leaned forward. The red coils rose and reminded him of the other tamped end of the pool. He backed out carefully, holding his breath.

He climbed down over the trenches to the lower end of

75

the rock. The water was low and tons of living jelly was spread in armour over the cliffs. Where he stood with his toes projecting over the edge the food was dry, and talked with continual tiny crepitations. The weed was transparent over the shells and only faintly green. He clambered down from handhold to handhold, wincing as he caught the sharp shells with his feet. He pulled at mussels but they would not come away. He had to twist them out as if he were breaking bones away from their tendons, screwing them out of the joints. He jerked them over his head so that they arched up and fell clattering on the rock. He worked among the sharp shells over the wavering water until his legs were trembling with strain. He climbed the cliff, rested, came back and twisted out more. There was a scattered harvest of them on the rock, some of them four inches long. He sat down, breathless in the sun and worked at them. They were not vulnerable like the red sweets; they were gripped and glued tight and there was nowhere to get the blade of the knife in. He put one on the rock and beat it with the haft of his knife until the shell fractured. He took out the complicated body and looked away over the sea.

"The Belgians do."

He gulped the body down. He set his teeth, broke another shell. Soon he had a heap of raw flesh that lay, white and yellow on the dry rock. His jaws moved, he looked away at the horizon. The fogged side of his right eye was pulled slightly as he ate. He felt round with his hand and

76

the heap was gone. He climbed down the cliff and got more. He opened each of these with a sudden downward jab of his knife. When they were gone he forced the red sweets from the rock and popped them in his mouth. He made no distinction between green and red. He took a wisp of green seaweed and chewed it like a leaf of lettuce. He went back to the water-hole, inserted himself and lay for a moment, looking down at the gleaming surface. He moistened his lips, so that the coils of red slime only stirred a little then lay down again. He eased himself out, clambered to the top of the rock and looked round. The horizon was ruled straight and hard in every part. He sat down.

The papers and booklet were still damp but he took up the booklet and opened it. Inside the cover was a transparent guard over a photograph. He peered through the cover and made out a fogged portrait. He could see a carefully arranged head of hair, a strong and smiling face, the white silk scarf round the neck. But detail had gone for ever. The young man who smiled dimly at him through fog and brown stains was distant as the posed portraits of great-grandparents in a faint, brown world.

Even so, he continued to look, searching for the details he remembered rather than saw, touching his bristled cheek while he divined the smiling smoothness of the one before him, rearranging the unkempt hair, feeling tenderly the painful corner of an eye. Opposite the photograph was writing in a slot but this too was smeared and washed into

77

illegibility. He put the booklet down and felt for the brown disc hanging round his neck. He lifted the disc as far as the string would allow until it was close to his left eye. He strained back and got it far enough away from him.

CHRISTOPHER

HADLEY

MARTIN

TY. LIEUT., R.N.V.R.

C. OF E.

He read the inscription again and again, cut by cut. His lips began to move. He dropped the disc, looked down at his salted legs with their scars, at his belly and the bush of hair over his privates.

He spoke out loud, using his voice hoarsely and with a kind of astonishment.

"Christopher Hadley Martin. Martin. Chris. I am what I always was!"

All at once it seemed to him that he came out of his curious isolation inside the globe of his head and was extended normally through his limbs. He lived again on the surface of his eyes, he was out in the air. Daylight crowded down on him, sunlight, there was a sparkle on the sea. The solid rock was coherent as an object, with layered guano, with fresh water and shell-fish. It was a position in a finite sea at the intersection of two lines, there were real ships passing under the horizon. He got quickly to his feet and laboured round the rock, turning his clothes in the sun.

78

He sniffed the pants and laughed. He went back to the papers and turned them. He took up the coins, chinked them in his hand for a moment and made as if to toss them in the sea. He paused.

"That would be too cracker-motto. Too ham."

He looked at the quiet sea.

"I don't claim to be a hero. But I've got health and education and intelligence. I'll beat you."

The sea said nothing. He grinned a little foolishly at himself.

"What I meant was to affirm my determination to survive. And of course, I'm talking to myself."

He looked round the rock.

"The first thing to do is to survey the estate."

The rock had diminished from an island to a thing. In the sunlight and absence of cold the whole could be inspected not only with eyes but with understanding. He saw at once that the trenches were the worn ends of vertical strata and the walls between them, harder layers that had worn more slowly. They were the broken end of a deep bed of mud that had been compressed by weight until the mud had heated and partly fused. Some convulsion of the upper layers, an unguessable contortion, a gripe of the earth's belly had torn the deep bed and thrust this broken end up vertically through mud and clay until it erupted as the tooth bursts out of the fleshy jaw. Then the less compressed layers had worn away into trenches full of edges like the cut pages of a book. The walls too were broken in

79

places and modified everywhere by local hazard. Some of the walls had fallen and lay jumbled in the trenches. The whole top of the rock tended down, trench by trench, from the west to the east.

The cliff sides of the rock concealed the stratification for they were water-worn and fretted into lace by the plant-animals that clustered so thickly on them. This top was concreted with whiteness under stinking water but down there where the blue and shattered mussel-shells lay scattered, the rock was clean or covered with barnacles and weed. Beyond the rock was a gap of shallow water, then another smaller rock, another and another in a slightly curving line. Then there was a pock that interrupted the pattern of the water and after that, the steep climb of the sea up to the sky.

He looked solemnly at the line of rocks and found himself thinking of them as teeth. He caught himself imagining that they were emerging gradually from the jaw—but that was not the truth. They were sinking; or rather they were being worn away in infinite slow motion. They were the grinders of old age, worn away. A lifetime of the world had blunted them, was reducing them as they ground what food rocks eat.

He shook his head irritably then caught his breath at the sudden pain in his neck.

"The process is so slow it has no relevance to——"

He stopped. He looked up into the air, then round over his shoulder. He repeated the words carefully, with the same intonation and at the same strength.

"The process is so slow——"

There was something peculiar about the sound that came out of his mouth. He discounted the hoarseness as of a man recovering from a cold or a bout of violent shouting. That was explicable.

He sang loudly.

"Alouette, gentille Alouette——"

He held his nose with his right hand and tried to blow through it until the pressure rounded his cheeks. Nothing cracked in his ears. His eyes hurt and water ran round them. He bent down, put his hands on his scarred knees and turned his head sideways. He shook his head violently, ignoring the pain in his neck and hoping to feel the little wobbling weight that would tell of water caught in his ears.

He stood up, facing a whole amphitheatre of water and sang a scale.

"Lah-la, la, la, la, la la-lah!"

The sound ended at his mouth.

He struck an attitude and declaimed.

> *The weary moon with her lamp before*
> *Knocks even now upon dawn's grey door——*

His voice faltered and stopped. He brought his hand down, turned the wrist, held the palm about a foot in front of his mouth.

81

"Testing. Testing. I am receiving you, strength——"

He closed his lips, lowered his hand slowly. The blue, igloo-roof over the rock went away to a vast distance, the visible world expanded with a leap. The water lopped round a tiny rock in the middle of the Atlantic. The strain tautened his face. He took a step among the scattered papers.

"My God!"

He gripped the stone dwarf, clutched himself to the humped shoulders and stared across. His mouth was open again. His heart-beats were visible as a flutter among the ribs. The knuckles of his hands whitened.

There was a clatter from the dwarf. The head stone thumped and went knock, knock, knock down the cliff.

Flumf.

He began to curse. He scrambled down the rock, found a too heavy stone, moved it about a yard and then let go. He threw himself over the stone and went cursing to the water. But there was nothing visible within reach that he could handle. He went quickly to the top again and stood looking at the headless dwarf in terror. He scrambled back to the too heavy stone and fought with it. He moved it, end over end. He built steps to the top of a wall and worked the great stone up. He drew from his body more strength than he had got. He bled. He stood sweating among the papers at last. He dismantled the dwarf and re-built him on the stone that after all was not too heavy for education and intelligence and will.

Four feet.

He jammed in the dry, white potatoes.

"Out of this nettle danger——"

The air sucked up his voice like blotting-paper.

Take a grip.

Education and intelligence.

He stood by the dwarf and began to talk like a man who has an unwilling audience but who will have his say whether anyone listens to him or not.

6

"The end to be desired is rescue. For that, the bare minimum necessary is survival. I must keep this body going. I must give it drink and food and shelter. When I do that it does not matter if the job is well done or not so long as it is done at all. So long as the thread of life is unbroken it will connect a future with the past for all this ghastly interlude. Point one.

"Point two. I must expect to fall sick. I cannot expose the body to this hardship and expect the poor beast to behave as if it were in clover. I must watch for signs of sickness and doctor myself.

"Point three. I must watch my mind. I must not let madness steal up on me and take me by surprise. Already—I must expect hallucinations. That is the real battle. That is why I shall talk out loud for all the blotting-paper. In normal life to talk out loud is a sign of insanity. Here it is proof of identity.

"Point four. I must help myself to be rescued. I cannot do anything but be visible. I have not even a stick to hoist a shirt on. But one will come within sight of this rock without turning a pair of binoculars on it. If they see the rock they will see this dwarf I have made. They will know that someone built the dwarf and they will come and take me off. All I have to do is to live and wait. I must keep my grip on reality."

He looked firmly at the sea. All at once he found that he was seeing through a window again. He was inside himself at the top end. The window was bounded above by the mixed, superimposed skin and hair of both brows, and divided into three lights by two outlines or shadows of noses. But the noses were transparent. The right-hand light was fogged and all three drew together at the bottom. When he looked down at the rock he was seeing the surface over the scrubby hedge of his unshaven upper lip. The window was surrounded by inscrutable darkness which extended throughout his body. He leaned forward to peer round the window-frame but it went with him. He altered the frame for a moment with a frown. He turned the three lights right round the horizon. He spoke, frowning.

"That is the ordinary experience of living. There is nothing strange in that." He shook his head and busied himself. He turned the windows on his own body and examined the skin critically. Great patches were pink over the scars and he cried out.

"Sunburn!"

He grabbed his vest and pulled it on. The material was so nearly dry that he accepted it as such and shuffled into his pants. The luminous windows became the ordinary way

85

of seeing. He gathered his papers, put them in the identity book and stowed the whole packet in the pocket of his reefer. He padded round the top of the rock, handling his clothes and testing them for dryness. They did not feel damp so much as heavy. There was no moisture that would come off on the fingers or could be wrung out, but where he lifted them from the rock they left their shapes in darker stone that faded slowly in the sun.

He spoke flatly against the blotting-paper.

"I wish I'd kept my seaboots."

He came to his oilskin and knelt, looking at it. Then suddenly he was rummaging through the forgotten pockets. He drew out a sou'wester from which the water ran, and a sodden balaclava. He unfolded the sou'wester and wrung out the balaclava. He spread them and dived at the other pocket. An expression of anxious concentration settled on his face. He fumbled and drew out a greening ha'penny, some string and the crumpled wrapping from a bar of chocolate. He unfolded the paper with great care; but there was nothing left inside. He put his face close to the glittering paper and squinted at it. In one crease there was a single brown grain. He put out his tongue and took the grain. The chocolate stung with a piercing sweetness, momentary and agonizing, and was gone.

He leaned back against the stone dwarf, reached for his socks and pulled them on. He took his seaboot stockings, rolled down the tops and made do with them for boots.

He let his head lie against the dwarf and closed his eyes.

The sun shone over his shoulder and the water washed. Inside his head the busy scenes flickered and voices spoke. He experienced all the concomitants of drowsiness but still there did not come the fall and gap of sleep. The thing in the middle of the globe was active and tireless.

"I should like a bed with sheets. I should like a pint or two and a hot meal. I should like a hot bath."

He sat for a while, silent, while the thing jumped from thought to thought. He remembered that speech was proof of identity and his lips began to move again.

"So long as I can want these things without finding the absence of them unendurable; so long as I can tell myself that I am alone on a rock in the middle of the Atlantic and that I have to fight to survive—then I can manage. After all, I am safe compared with those silly sods in H.M. ships. They never know when they're going to be blown up. But I should like to see the brick that could shift this rock."

The thing that could not examine itself danced on in the world behind the eyes.

"And anyway I must not sleep in the daytime. Save that for the miserable nights."

He stood up suddenly and looked round the horizon.

"Dress and eat. Dress for dinner."

He kicked off the seaboot stockings and got into his clothes, all but the duffle and oilskin. He pulled the stockings up over his trousers to the knees. He stood and became voluble in the flat air.

"I call this place the Look-out. That is the Dwarf. The

87

rock out there under the sun where I came swimming is Safety Rock. The place where I get mussels and stuff is Food Cliff. Where I eat them is—The Red Lion. On the south side where the strap-weed is, I call Prospect Cliff. This cliff here to the west with the funnel in it is——"

He paused, searching for a name. A sea-gull came swinging in under the sun, saw the two figures standing on the Look-out, screamed, side-slipped crazily and wheeled away. It came straight back but at a lower level on his right hand and vanished into the cliff. He edged forward and looked down. There was a sheer, almost un-broken descent on the left and then the cleft in the middle of the cliff, and above that, the funnel. To the right the foot of the cliff was hidden for the highest corner of the Look-out leaned out. He went on hands and knees to the edge and looked down. The cliff was visible for a yard and then turned in and hid itself. The rock began again near the bottom and he could see a glint of feather.

"A lump has fallen out of the cliff."

He searched the water carefully and thought he could make out a square shape deep under the surface. He backed away and stood up.

"Gull Cliff."

The horizon was still empty.

He climbed down the rock to the Red Lion.

"I wish I could remember the name of the whole rock. The Captain said it was a near miss and he laughed. I have it on the tip of my tongue. And I must have a name for this habitual clamber of mine between the Look-out and the Red Lion. I shall call it the High Street."

He saw that the rock on which he sat was dark and glanced over his shoulder. The sun was just leaving him, going down behind the Dwarf, so that the piled stones had become a giant. He got up quickly and lowered himself down the plastered Food Cliff. He hung spreadeagled, traversed a couple of yards and twisted out mussels. The deep sea tide was up now and he had much less scope. He had to lean down and work the mussels loose under water. He climbed back to the Red Lion and began to eat. The great shape of the rock had lost detail and become a blotch against the evening sky. The shadow loomed, vast as a mountain peak. He looked the other way and there were the three rocks diminishing into a dark sea.

"I name you three rocks—Oxford Circus, Piccadilly and Leicester Square."

He went to the dark water-hole and pulled himself in. A little light still came from the hole in the jumbled stones at the other end and when he drank he could see ripples faintly but the red coils were invisible. He put his forefinger straight down into the water and felt the slimy bottom. He lay very still.

"It will rain again."

Then he was jumping and shuddering for there was someone else in the hole with him. Or there was a voice that spoke almost with his, from the water and the slab. As his heart eased he could think coherently of the sound

89

as a rare and forgotten thing, a resonance, an echo. Then immediately he could reason that his voice was full-sized in here so he quietened his body and spoke deliberately.

"Plenty of identity in here, Ladies and Gentlemen——"

He cut his voice off sharply and heard the rock say, "—men——"

"It will rain."

"—ain."

"How are you?"

"—u?"

"I am busy surviving. I am netting down this rock with names and taming it. Some people would be incapable of understanding the importance of that. What is given a name is given a seal, a chain. If this rock tries to adapt me to its ways I will refuse and adapt it to mine. I will impose my routine on it, my geography. I will tie it down with names. If it tries to annihilate me with blotting-paper, then I will speak in here where my words resound and significant sounds assure me of my own identity. I will trap rainwater and add it to this pool. I will use my brain as a delicate machine-tool to produce the results I want. Comfort. Safety. Rescue. Therefore to-morrow I declare to be a thinking day."

He backed out of the water-hole, climbed the High Street and stood on the Look-out by the Dwarf. He dressed in everything, pulled on the damp balaclava and drew the sou'wester round his head with the chinstay down. He looked quickly round the horizon, listened to the faint movement from the invisible aery half-way down

90

Gull Cliff. He went down the High Street, came to his crevice. He sat on the wall by the crevice, put his feet in the grey sweater and wrapped it round them. He got down and wormed his way into the crevice, pushing down his duffle and oilskin. He blew the lifebelt up tight and tied the two breast ends of the tube together with the tape. The lifebelt made a pillow big enough for his head and very soft. He lay on his back and rested his head in the sou'wester on the soft pillow. He inched his arms down on either side of him in the crevice. He spoke to the sky.

"I must dry seaweed and line this crevice. I could be as snug as a bug in a rug."

He shut his eyes.

"Relax each muscle in turn."

Sleep is a condition to be attained by thought like any other.

"The trouble with keeping house on a rock is that there's so much to do. But I shan't get bored, that's one thing."

Relax the muscles of the feet.

"And what a story! A week on a rock. Lectures——"

How to Survive. By Lieutenant—but why not Lieutenant-Commander? Or Commander? Brass Hat and all.

"You men must remember——"

His eyes fell open.

"And I never remembered! Never thought of it! Haven't had a crap for a week!" Or not since before I was blown off

91

the bloody bridge anyway.

The flaps of his sou'wester prevented him from hearing the flatness of his voice against the sky. He lay and meditated the sluggishness of his bowels. This created pictures of chrome and porcelain and attendant circumstances. He put the toothbrush back, and stood, looking at his face in the mirror. The whole business of eating was peculiarly significant. They made a ritual of it on every level, the Fascists as a punishment, the religious as a rite, the cannibal either as a ritual or as a medicine or as a superbly direct declaration to conquest. Killed and eaten. And of course eating with the mouth was only the gross expression of what was a universal process. You could eat with your cock or with your fists, or with your voice. You could eat with hobnailed boots or buying and selling or marrying and begetting or cuckolding——

Cuckolding reminded him. He turned from the mirror, bound his dressing-gown with the cord and opened the bathroom door. And there, coming towards him, as if the rather antiquated expression had conjured him up was Alfred. But it was a different Alfred, pale, sweating, trembling, coming at a run toward. He took the wrist as the fist came at his chest and twisted it till Alfred was gritting his teeth and hissing through them. Secure in his knowledge of the cosmic nature of eating he grinned down at him.

"Hullo, Alfred!"

"You bloody swine!"

"Nosey little man."

92

"Who've you got in there? Tell me!"

"Now, now. Come along quietly Alfred, we don't want any fuss."

"Don't pretend it's someone else! You bastard! Oh Christ——"

They were by the closed door. Alfred was crying into the lines round his mouth and struggling to get at the door handle.

"Tell me who she is, Chris. I *must* know—for God's sake!"

"Don't ham it, Alfred."

"And don't pretend it's not Sybil, you dirty, thieving bastard!"

"Like to look, Alfred?"

Hiccups. Weak struggles.

"You mean it's someone else? You're not fooling Chris, honestly?"

"Anything to cheer you up old man. Look."

The door opening; Sybil, giving a tiny shriek and pulling the sheet up to her mouth as if this were a bedroom-farce which, of course, in every sense, it was.

"Honestly, Alfred old man, anyone would think you'd married the girl."

But there was a connection between eating and the Chinese box. What was a Chinese box? A coffin? Or those carved ivory ornaments, one inside the other? Yet there was a Chinese box in it somewhere——

Astonished, he lay like a stone man, open-mouthed and

93

gazing into the sky. The furious struggle against his chest, the slobbering sobs of the weak mouth were still calling their reactions out of his stronger body when he was back in the crevice.

He cleared his throat and spoke aloud.

"Where the hell am I? Where was I?"

He heaved over and lay face downwards in the crevice, his cheeks on the lifebelt.

"Can't sleep."

But sleep is necessary. Lack of sleep was what sent people crazy. He spoke aloud and the lifebelt wobbled under his jaw.

"I was asleep then. I was dreaming about Alfred and Sybil. Go to sleep again."

He lay still and considered sleep. But it was a tantalizingly evasive subject.

Think about women then or eating. Think about eating women, eating men, crunching up Alfred, that other girl, that boy, that crude and unsatisfactory experiment, lie restful as a log and consider the gnawed tunnel of life right up to this uneasy intermission.

This rock.

"I shall call those three rocks out there the Teeth."

All at once he was gripping the lifebelt with both hands and tensing his muscles to defeat the deep shudders that were sweeping through him.

"No! Not the Teeth!"

The teeth were here, inside his mouth. He felt them

with his tongue, the double barrier of bone, each known and individual except the gaps—and there they persisted as a memory if one troubled to think. But to lie on a row of teeth in the middle of the sea——

He began to think desperately about sleep.

Sleep is a relaxation of the conscious guard, the sorter. Sleep is when all the unsorted stuff comes flying out as from a dustbin upset in a high wind. In sleep time was divorced from the straight line so that Alfred and Sybil were on the rock with him and that boy with his snivelling, blubbered face. Or sleep was a consenting to die, to go into complete unconsciousness, the personality defeated, acknowledging too frankly what is implicit in mortality that we are temporary structures patched up and unable to stand the pace without a daily respite from what we most think ours——

"Then why can't I sleep?"

Sleep is where we touch what is better left unexamined. There, the whole of life is bundled up, dwindled. There the carefully hoarded and enjoyed personality, our only treasure and at the same time our only defence must die into the ultimate truth of things, the black lightning that splits and destroys all, the positive, unquestionable nothingness.

And I lie here, a creature armoured in oilskin, thrust into a crack, a morsel of food on the teeth that a world's lifetime has blunted.

Oh God! Why can't I sleep?

Gripping the lifebelt in two hands, with face lifted,

95

eyes staring straight ahead down the gloomy tunnel, he whispered the answer to his own question in a mixture of astonishment and terror.

"I am afraid to."

7

The light changed before the staring eyes but so slowly that they did not notice any difference. They looked, rather, at the jumble of unsorted pictures that presented themselves at random. There was still the silent, indisputable creature that sat at the centre of things, but it seemed to have lost the knack of distinguishing between pictures and reality. Occasionally the gate in the lower part of the globe would open against the soft lifebelt and words come out, but each statement was so separated by the glossy and illuminated scenes the creature took part in that it did not know which was relevant to which.

"I said that I should be sick."

"Drink. Food. Sanity. Rescue."

"I shall call them the——"

But the glossy images persisted, changed, not as one cloud shape into another but with sudden and complete differences of time and place.

"Sit down, Martin."

"Sir."

"We're considering whether we should recommend you

97

for a commission. Cigarette?"

"Thank you, sir."

Sudden smile over the clicked lighter.

"Got your nickname on the lower deck yet?"

Smile in return, charming, diffident.

"'Fraid so, sir. Inevitably, I believe."

"Like Dusty Miller and Nobby Clark."

"Yes, sir."

"How's the life up forrard?"

"It's—endurable, sir."

"We want men of education and intelligence; but most of all, men of character. Why did you join the Navy?"

"One felt one ought to—well, help, sir, if you see what I mean?"

Pause.

"I see you're an actor in civvy street."

Careful.

"Yes, sir. Not a terribly good one, I'm afraid."

"Author?"

"Nothing much, yet, sir."

"What would you have liked to be then?"

"One felt it was—unreal. Not like this. You know, sir! Here in this ship. Here we *are* getting down to the basic business of life—something worth doing. I wish I'd been a sailor."

Pause.

"Why would you like a commission, Martin?"

"As an ordinary seaman, sir, one's the minutest cog in a

machine. As an officer one would have more chance of hitting the old Hun for six, sir, actually."

Pause.

"Did you volunteer, Martin?"

He's got it all on those papers there if he chooses to look it up.

Frank.

"Actually, no sir."

He's blushing, under that standard Dartmouth mask of his.

"That will be all, Martin, thank you."

"Aye, aye, sir, thank you, sir."

He's blushing like a virgin of sixteen.

"She's the producer's wife, old man, here where are you going?"

An exceptionally small French dictionary, looking like an exceptionally large red eraser.

A black lacquer cash-box on which the gilt was worn.

The Chinese box was evasive. Sometimes it was the fretted ivories, one inside the other, sometimes it was a single box like a cash-box. But however evasive, it was important and intrusive.

She's the producer's wife, old man. Fat. White. Like a maggot with tiny black eyes. I should like to eat you.

99

I should love to play Danny. I should love to eat you. I should love to put you in a play. How can I put you anywhere if I haven't eaten you? He's a queer. He'd love to eat you. And I should love to eat you too. You're not a person, my sweet, you're an instrument of pleasure.

A Chinese box.

A sword is a phallus. What a huge mountain-shaking joke! A phallus is a sword. Down, dog, down. Down on all fours where you belong.

Then he was looking at a half-face and crying out. The half-face belonged to one of the feathered reptiles. The creature was perched on the slab and looking down sideways at him. As he cried out the wide wings beat and flapped away and immediately a glossy picture swept the blue sky and the stone out of sight. This was a bright patch, sometimes like a figure eight lying on its side and sometimes a circle. The circle was filled with blue sea where gulls were wheeling and settling and loving to eat and fight. He felt the swing of the ship under him, sensed the bleak stillness and silence that settled on the bridge as the destroyer slid by the thing floating in the water—a thing, humble and abused and still, among the fighting beaks, an instrument of pleasure.

He struggled out into the sun, stood up and cried flatly in the great air.

"I am awake!"

Dense blue with white flecks and diamond flashes.

Foam, flowering abundantly round the three rocks.

He turned away from the night.

"Today is a thinking day."

He undressed quickly to his trousers and sweater, spread his clothing in the sun and went down to the Red Lion. The tide was so low that mussels were in sight by the ship load.

Mussels were food but one soon tired of them. He wondered for a moment whether he should collect some sweets but his stomach did not entertain the idea. He thought of chocolate instead and the silver paper came into his mind. He sat there, chewing mechanically while his mind's eye watched silver, flashing bright.

"After all, I may be rescued today."

He examined the thought and found that the whole idea was neutral as the mussels had become, harsh and negative as the fresh water. He climbed to the water-hole and crawled in. The red deposit lay in a band nearly two inches wide at the nearer edge.

He cried out in the echoing hole.

"It will rain again!"

Proof of identity.

"I must measure this pool. I must ration myself. I must force water to come to me if necessary. I must have water."

A well. Boring through rock. A dew pond. Line with clay and straw. Precipitation. Education. Intelligence.

He reached out his hand and prodded down with the finger. When his hand had submerged to the knuckles

101

his finger-tip met slime and slid. Then rock. He took a deep breath. There was darker water farther on under the window.

"A fool would waste water by crawling forward, washing this end about just to see how much there is left. But I won't. I'll wait and crawl forward as the water shrinks. And before that there will be rain."

He went quickly to his clothes, took out the silver paper and the string and climbed back to the Dwarf.

He frowned at the Dwarf and began to talk into the blotting-paper.

"East or west is useless. If convoys appear in either of those quarters they would be moving towards the rock anyway. But they may appear to the south, or less likely, to the north. But the sun does not shine from the north. South is the best bet, then."

He took the Dwarf's head off and laid the stone carefully on the Look-out. He knelt down and smoothed the silver paper until the sheet gleamed under his hand. He forced the foil to lie smoothly against the head and bound it in place with the string. He put the silver head back on the Dwarf, went to the southern end of the Look-out and stared at the blank face. The sun bounced at him from the paper. He bent his knees until he was looking into the paper at eye-level and still he saw a distorted sun. He shuffled round in such arc as the southern end of the Look-out would allow and still he saw the sun. He took the silver head off the Dwarf again, polished the silver on

102

his seaboot stockings and put it back. The sun winked at him. There stood on the Look-out a veritable man and one who carried a flashing signal on his shoulders.

"I shall be rescued today."

He fortified and deepened the meaningless statement with three steps of a dance but stopped with a grimace.

"My feet!"

He sat down and leaned against the Dwarf on the south side.

Today is a thinking day.

"I haven't done so badly."

He altered the arch over his window with a frown.

"Ideally of course, the stone should be a sphere. Then no matter where the ship appears in an arc of one hundred and eighty degrees the sun will bounce straight at her from the Dwarf. If a ship is under the horizon then the gleam might fetch her crow's-nest, following it along like a hand of arrest on the shoulder, persisting, nagging, till even the dullest of seamen would notice and the idea sink in."

The horizon remained empty.

"I must get a sphere. Perhaps I could beat the nearest to it with another stone until it rounds. Stone mason as well. Who was it cut stone cannon-balls? Michael Angelo? But I must look for a very round stone. Never a dull moment. Just like Itma."

He got up and went down to the sea. He peered over the edge of the little cliff by the mussels but saw nothing worth having. There was green weed and a mass of stone

103

between him and the three rocks but he turned away from it. He went instead to Prospect Cliff, climbed down the ledges to low water. But here there was nothing but masses of weed that stank. His climb tired him and he clung over the water for a moment, searching the surface of the rock with his eyes for anything of value. There was a coralline substance close to his face, thin and pink like icing and then not pink as though it were for ever changing its mind to purple. He stroked the smooth stuff with one finger. They called that paint Barmaid's Blush and splashed on gallons with the inexpert and casual hand of the wartime sailor. The colour was supposed to merge a ship into the sea and air at the perilous hour of dawn. There were interminable hard acres of the pink round scuttles and on gun shields, whole fields on sides and top hamper, hanging round the hard angles, the utilitarian curves, the grudgingly conceded living quarters of ships on the Northern Patrol, like pink icing or the coral growths on a washed rock. He took his face away from the casing and turned to climb the ladders to the bridge. There must be acres of the stuff spread on the childtime rocks at Tresellyn. That was where Nat had taken her—taken her in two senses, grateful for the tip.

The ship rolled heavily and here was Nat descending the upper ladder like a daddy-longlegs, carefully placing the remote ends of the limbs for security and now faced with a crisis at the sight of the face and the cap. Here is Nat saluting as ever off balance, but this time held in pos-

104

ition by one arm and two legs.

"Wotcher, Nat. Happy in your work?"

Dutiful Nat-smile though a little queasy. See the bright side.

"Yes, sir."

Amble aft you drawn-out bastard.

Climb, climb. The bridge, a little wind and afternoon.

"Hallo. Mean course o-nine-o. Now on zag at one-one-o. And I may say, dead in station, not wandering all over the ocean the way you leave her. She's all yours and the Old Man is in one of his moods, so watch out for sparks."

"Zig coming up in ten seconds? I've got her."

"See you again at the witching hour."

"Port fifteen. Midships. Steady."

He looked briefly round the convoy and then aft. Nat was there, tediously in his usual place, legs wide apart, face in hands. The corticened deck lurched under him, re-arranged itself and he swayed on the rail. The luminous window that looked down at him bent at the sides in a snarl that was disguised as a grin.

Christ, how I hate you. I could eat you. Because you fathomed her mystery, you have a right to handle her transmuted cheap tweed; because you both have made a place where I can't get; because in your fool innocence you've got what I had to get or go mad.

Then he found himself additionally furious with Nath-aniel, not because of Mary, not because he had happened on her as he might have tripped over a ring-bolt but

105

because he dared sit so, tilting with the sea, held by a thread, so near the end that would be at once so anguishing and restful like the bursting of a boil.

"Christ!"

Wildebeeste had turned seconds ago.

"Starboard thirty! Half-ahead together!"

Already, from the apex of the destroyer screen, a light was stabbing erratically.

"Midships! Steady. Slow ahead together."

There was a clatter from the ladder. The Captain burst at him.

"What the bloody hell are you playing at?"

Hurried and smooth.

"I thought there was wreckage on the starboard bow, sir, and couldn't be sure so I maintained course and speed till we were clear, sir."

The Captain stopped, one hand on the screen of the bridge and lowered at him.

"What sort of wreckage?"

"Baulks of timber, sir, floating just under the surface."

"Starboard look-out!"

"Sir?"

"Did you see any wreckage?"

"No, sir."

"—I may have been mistaken, sir, but I judged it better to make sure, sir."

The Captain bored in, face to face so that his grip on the rock tightened as he remembered. The Captain's face was

106

big, pale and lined, the eyes red-rimmed with sleeplessness and gin. It examined for a moment what the window had to exhibit. The two shadowy noses on either side of the window caught a faint, sweet scent. Then the face changed, not dramatically, not registering, not making obvious, but changing like a Nat-face, from within. Under the pallor and moist creases, in the corners of the mouth and eyes, came the slight muscular shift of complicated tensions till the face was rearranged and bore like an open insult, the pattern of contempt and disbelief.

The mouth opened.

"Carry on."

In a confusion too complete for answer or salute he watched the face turn away and take its understanding and contempt down the ladder.

There was heat and blood.

"Signal, sir, from Captain D. 'Where are you going to my pretty maid?'"

Signalman with a wooden face. Heat and blood.

"Take it to the Captain."

"Aye aye, sir."

He turned back to the binnacle.

"Port fifteen. Midships. Steady."

Looking under his arm he saw Nathaniel pass the bridge messenger in the waist. Seen thus, he was a bat hanging upside down from the roof of a cave. Nat passed on, walking and lurching till the break of the fo'castle hid him.

107

He found he was cursing an invisible Nat, cursing him for Mary, for the contempt in old Gin-soak's face. The centre, looking in this reversed world over the binnacle, found itself beset by a storm of emotions, acid and inky and cruel. There was a desperate amazement that anyone so good as Nat, so unwillingly loved for the face that was always rearranged from within, for the serious attention, for love given without thought, should also be so quiveringly hated as though he were the only enemy. There was amazement that to love and to hate were now one thing and one emotion. Or perhaps they could be separated. Hate was as hate had always been, an acid, the corroding venom of which could be borne only because the hater was strong.

"I am a good hater."

He looked quickly at the deck watch, across at *Wildebeeste* and gave orders for the new course.

And love? Love for Nat? That was this sorrow dissolved through the hate so that the new solution was a deadly thing in the chest and the bowels.

He muttered over the binnacle.

"If I were that glass toy that I used to play with I could float in a bottle of acid. Nothing could touch me then."

Zag.

"That's what it is. Ever since I met her and she interrupted the pattern coming at random, obeying no law of life, facing me with the insoluble, unbearable problem of her existence the acid's been chewing at my guts. I can't

108

even kill her because that would be her final victory over me. Yet as long as she lives the acid will eat. She's there. In the flesh. In the not even lovely flesh. In the cheap mind. Obsession. Not love. Or if love, insanely compounded of this jealousy of her very being. *Odi et amo.* Like that thing I tried to write."

There were lace curtains in decorous curves either side of the oak occasional table with its dusty fern. The round table in the centre of the almost unused parlour smelt of polish—might one day support a coffin in state, but until then, nothing. He looked round at the ornaments and plush, took a breath of the air that was trapped this side of the window, smelt of last year and varnish like the vilest cooking sherry. The room would suit her. She would fit it, she was the room at all points except for the mania.

He looked down at the writing-pad on his knee.

Zig.

"And that wasn't the half of it. And the acid still eats. Who could ever dream that he would fall in love—or be trapped—by a front parlour on two feet?"

He began to pace backward and forward on the bridge.

"As long as she lives the acid will eat. There's nothing that can stand that. And killing her would make it worse."

He stopped. Looked back along the deck at the quarter-deck and the empty, starboard rail.

"Christ! Starboard twenty——"

There was a sense in which she could be—or say that the acid flow could be checked. Not to pass Petty Officer

Roberts' message on was one thing—but that merely acquiesced in the pattern. But say one nudged circumstances —not in the sense that one throttled with the hands or fired a gun—but gently shepherded them the way they might go? Since it would be a suggestion to circumstances only it could not be considered what a strict moralist might call it——

"And who cares anyway?"

This was to run with a rapier at the arras without more than a hope of success.

"He may never sit there again."

Then the officer of the watch in the execution of his duty gives a helm order to avoid floating wreckage or a drifting mine and no one is any the worse.

"But if he sits there again——"

The corrosive swamped him. A voice cried out in his belly—I do not want him to die! The sorrow and hate bit deep, went on biting. He cried out with his proper voice.

"Does no one understand how I feel?"

The look-outs had turned on their perches. He scowled at them and felt another warmth in his face. His voice came out savagely.

"Get back to your sectors."

He leaned over the binnacle and felt how his body shook.

"I am chasing after—a kind of peace."

Barmaid's blush with hair that was coarse even for a barmaid. He looked at the ledges of rock.

"A kind of peace."

Coral growth.

He shook his head as though he were shaking water out of his hair.

"I came down here for something."

But there was nothing, only weed and rock and water.

He climbed back to the Red Lion, gathered some of the uneaten mussels that he had left from the morning and went up the High Street to the Look-out. He sat under the south side of the winking Dwarf and opened them with his knife. He ate with long pauses between each mouthful. When he had finished the last one he lay back.

"Christ."

They were no different from the mussels of yesterday but they tasted of decay.

"Perhaps I left them too long in the sun."

But they hang in the sun between tides for hours!

"How many days have I been here?"

He thought fiercely, then made three scratches on the rock with his knife.

"I must not let anything escape that would reinforce personality. I must make decisions and carry them out. I have put a silver head on the Dwarf. I have decided not to be tricked into messing about with the water-hole. How far away is the horizon? Five miles? I could see a crow's-nest at ten miles. I can advertise myself over a circle twenty miles in diameter. That's not bad.

The Atlantic is about two thousand miles wide up here. Twenty into two thousand goes a hundred."

He knelt down and measured off a line ten inches in length as near as he could judge.

"That makes it a tenth of an inch."

He put the blade of his knife on the line at about two inches from the end and rotated the haft slowly till the point made a white mark in the grey rock. He squatted back on his heels and looked at the diagram.

"With a really big ship I could be seen at fifteen miles."

He put the point of the knife back on the mark and enlarged it. He paused, then went on scraping till the mark was the size of a silver threepenny-bit. He put out his foot and scuffed the seaboot stocking over the mark until it was grey and might have been there since the rock was made.

"I shall be rescued today."

He stood up and looked into the silver face. The sun was still shining back at him. He traced mental lines from the sun to the stone, bounced them out at this part of the horizon and that. He went close to the Dwarf and looked down at the head to see if he could find his face reflected there. The sunlight bounced up in his eyes. He jerked upright.

"The air! You fool! You clot! They ferry planes and they must use this place for checking the course—and Coastal Command, looking for U-boats——"

He cupped his hands at his eyes and turned slowly

112

round, looking at the sky. The air was dense blue and interrupted by nothing but the sun over the south sea. He flung his hands away and began to walk hastily up and down by the Look-out.

"A thinking day."

The Dwarf was all right for ships—they were looking across at a silhouette. They would see the Dwarf or perhaps the gleam of the head. But to a plane, the Dwarf would be invisible, merged against the rock, and the glint from the silver might be a stray crystal of quartz. There was nothing about the rock to catch the eye. They might circle at a few thousand feet—a mile, two miles—and see nothing that was different. From above, the stone would be a tiny grey patch, that was eye-catching only by the surf that spread round in the sea.

He looked quickly and desperately up, then away at the water.

A pattern.

Men make patterns and superimpose them on nature. At ten thousand feet the rock would be a pebble; but suppose the pebble were striped? He looked at the trenches. The pebble was striped already. The upended layers would be grey with darker lines of trench between them.

He held his head in his hands.

A chequer. Stripes. Words. S.O.S.

"I cannot give up my clothes. Without them I should freeze to death. Besides if I spread them out they would still be less visible than this guano."

113

He looked down the High Street between his hands.

"Pare away here and here and there. Make all smooth. Cut into a huge, shadowed S.O.S."

He dropped his hands and grinned.

"Be your age."

He squatted down again and considered in turn the material he had with him. Cloth. Small sheets of paper. A rubber lifebelt.

Seaweed.

He paused, lifted his hands and cried out in triumph.

"Seaweed!"

8

There were tons of the stuff hanging round the rock, floating or coiled down under water by Prospect Cliff.

"Men make patterns."

Seaweed, to impose an unnatural pattern on nature, a pattern that would cry out to any rational beholder —Look! Here is thought. Here is man!

"The best form would be a single indisputable line drawn at right angles to the trenches, piled so high that it will not only show a change of colour but even throw a shadow of its own. I must make it at least a yard wide and it must be geometrically straight. Later I will fill up one of the trenches and turn the upright into a cross. Then the rock will become a hot cross bun."

Looking down towards the three Rocks he planned the line to descend across the trenches, parallel more or less to the High Street. The line would start at the Red Lion and come up to the Dwarf. It would be an operation.

He went quickly down the High Street: and now that he had found a job with point, he was muttering without knowing why.

"Hurry! Hurry!"

Then his ears began to fill with the phantom buzzing of planes. He kept looking up and fell once, cutting himself. Only when he was already pulling at the frondy weed by Food Cliff did he pause.

"Don't be a fool. Take it easy. There's no point in looking up because you can do nothing to attract attention. Only a clot would go dancing and waving his shirt because he thought there was a plane about five miles up."

He craned back his head and searched the sky but found nothing besides blueness and sun. He held his breath and listened and heard nothing but the inner, mingled humming of his own life, nothing outside but the lap and gurgle of water. He straightened his neck and stood there thinking. He went back to the crevice. He stripped naked and spread his clothing in the sun. He arranged each item carefully to one side of where the line of seaweed would lie. He went back to the Red Lion and looked down at the space between the Red Lion and the three rocks. He turned round and lowered himself over the edge. The water was colder than he remembered, colder than the fresh water that he drank. He ground his teeth and forced himself down and the rock was so sharp against his knees that he reopened the wounds of the first day. His waist was on the rock between his hands and he was groaning. He could not feel bottom and the weed round his calves was colder than the water. The cold squeezed as the water had done in the open sea, so that he was panic-stricken

116

at the memory. He made a high, despairing sound, pushed himself clear of the rock and fell. The water took him with a freezing hand. He opened his eyes and weed was lashing before them. His head broke the surface and he struck out frantically for the rock. He hung there, shivering.

"Take a grip."

There was whiteness under the weed. He pushed off and let his feet sink. Under the weed, caught between his own rock and the three others were boulders, quartz perhaps, stacked and unguessable. He stood, crouched in the water, half-supporting his weight with swimming movements of the arms and felt round him with his feet. Carefully he found foothold and stood up. The water reached to his chest and the weed dragged at him. He took a breath and ducked. He seized weed and tried to tear off fronds but they were very tough and he could win no more than a handful before he had to surface again. He began to collect weed without ducking, reaping the last foot of the crop. Sometimes when he pulled there would be a stony turn and slight shock, or the water-slowed movements of readjustment. He threw weed up on the rock and the fronds flopped down over the edge, dripping.

Suddenly the weed between his feet tugged and something brushed over his toes. A line of swift and erratic movement appeared in the weed, ceased. He clawed at the cliff and hung there, drawing his legs up.

The water lapped.

"Crab. Lobster."

117

He kneed his painful way to the Red Lion and lay down by the weed till his heart steadied.

"I loathe it."

He crawled to the edge of the cliff and looked down. At once, as if his eye had created it, he saw the lobster among the weed, different in dragon-shape, different in colour. He knelt, looking down, mesmerized while the worms of loathing crawled over his skin.

"Beast. Filthy sea-beast."

He picked up a mussel shell and threw it with all his strength into the water. At the smack, the lobster clenched like a fist and was gone.

"That line of seaweed's going to take a devil of a time to build."

He shook himself free of the worms on his skin. He lowered himself over Prospect Cliff. The bottom four or five feet was covered with a hanging mass of strap-weed. At the surface of the water, weed floated out so that the sea seemed solid.

"Low water."

He climbed along the rock and began to tug at the weed but it would not come off. The roots clung to the rock with suckers more difficult to remove than limpets or mussels. Some of the weeds were great bushes that ended in dimpled bags full of jelly. Others were long swords but with a fluted and wavered surface and edge. The rest was smooth brown leather like an assembly of sword belts for all the officers in the world. Under the weed the rock was furry with coloured

118

growths or hard and decorative with stuff that looked like uncooked batter. There was also Barmaid's Blush. There were tiny bubblings and pips and splashes.

He tugged at a bunch of weed with one hand while he hung on to the rock with the other. He cursed and climbed back up the rock, walked up the High Street to the Lookout and stood looking at the sea and sky.

He came to with a jump.

"Don't waste time. Be quick."

He went to the crevice, slung the knife round his neck by its lanyard and picked up the lifebelt. He unscrewed the mouth of the tit, let the air out and climbed down the rock. He slung the lifebelt over his arm and went at the weedroots with the knife. They were not only hard as hard rubber but slippery. He had to find a particular angle and a particular careful sobriety of approach before he could get the edge of his knife into them. He wore the weed like firewood over his shoulder. He held the lifebelt in his teeth and drew fronds of weed through between the lifebelt and the tape. He reversed his position, holding on with his left arm and gathering with his right. The weed made a great bundle on his shoulder that draped down and fell past his knees in a long, brown smear.

He climbed to the Red Lion, and flung down the weed. At a distance of a few feet from him it looked like a small patch. He laid out the separate blades, defining the straight line that would interrupt the trenches. In the trenches themselves the weed had no support.

119

"I must fill the trenches flush with the wall where the weed crosses them."

When he had used up all the weed the load stretched from the Red Lion to the Look-out. On the average the line was two inches wide.

He went back to Prospect Cliff and got more weed. He squatted in the Red Lion with his forehead corrugated. He shut one eye and considered his handiwork. The line was hardly visible. He climbed round to the cliff again.

There was a sudden plop in the water by the farthest of the three rocks, so that he sprang round. Nothing. No foam, only a dimpled interruption in the pattern of wavelets.

"I ought to catch fish."

He gathered himself another load of weed. The jellied bags burst when he pressed them, and he put one of the bags to his lips but the taste was neutral. He carried another load to the Red Lion and another. When he piled the weed in the first trench it did not come within a foot of the top.

He stood in the trench, looking down at the red and brown weed and felt suddenly listless.

"Twelve loads? Twenty? And then the line to thicken after that——"

Intelligence sees so clearly what is to be done and can count the cost beforehand.

"I will rest for a while."

He went to the Dwarf and sat down under the empty sky. The seaweed stretched away across the rock like a trail.

120

"Harder than ever in my life before. Worn out for to-day."

He put his head on his knees and muttered to the ghost of a diagram—a line with a grey blob on it.

"I haven't had a crap since we were torpedoed."

He sat motionless and meditated on his bowels. Presently he looked up. He saw that the sun was on the decline and made a part of the horizon particularly clear and near. Squinting at it he thought he could even see the minute distortions that the waves made in the perfect curve of the world.

There was a white dot sitting between the sun and Safety Rock. He watched closely and saw that the dot was a gull sitting in the water, letting itself drift. All at once he had a waking vision of the gull rising and flying east over the sea's shoulder. To-morrow morning it could be floating among the stacks and shields of the Hebrides or following the plough on some Irish hill-side. As an intense experience that interrupted the bright afternoon before him he saw the ploughman in his cloth cap hitting out at the squawking bird.

"Get away from me now and the bad luck go with you!"

But the bird would not perch on the boundary-stone, open its bill and speak as in all folk lore. Even if it were more than a flying machine it could not pass on news of the scarred man sitting on a rock in the middle of the sea. He got up and began to pace to and fro on the Look-out. He took the thought out and looked at it.

121

I may never get away from this rock at all.

Speech is identity.

"You are all a machine. I know you, wetness, hardness, movement. You have no mercy but you have no intelligence. I can outwit you. All I have to do is to endure. I breathe this air into my own furnace. I kill and eat. There is nothing to——"

He paused for a moment and watched the gull drifting nearer; but not so near that the reptile under the white was visible.

"There is nothing to fear."

The gull was being carried along by the tide. Of course the tide operated here too, in mid-Atlantic, a great wave that swept round the world. It was so great that it thrust out tongues that became vast ocean currents, sweeping the water in curves that were ten thousand miles long. So there was a current that flowed past this rock, rising, pausing, reversing and flowing back again eternally and pointlessly. The current would continue to do so if life were rubbed off the skin of the world like the bloom off a grape. The rock sat immovable and the tide went sweeping past.

He watched the gull come floating by Prospect Cliff. It preened its feathers and fluttered like a duck in a pond.

He turned abruptly away and went quickly down to Prospect Cliff. Half the hanging seaweed was covered.

To-morrow.

"Exhausted myself. Mustn't overdo it."

Plenty to do on a rock. Never a dull moment.

He considered the mussels with positive distaste and switched his mind instead to the bags of jelly on the seaweed. He had a vague feeling that his stomach was talking to him. It disliked mussels. As for anemones—the bare thought made the bag contract and send a foul taste to his mouth.

"Overwork. Exposure. Sunburn, perhaps. I mustn't overdo it."

He reminded himself seriously that this was the day on which he was going to be rescued but could not rediscover conviction.

"Dress."

He put on his clothes, walked round the Dwarf then sat down again.

"I should like to turn in. But I mustn't as long as there's light. She might come close for a look, blow her siren and go away again if I didn't show myself. But I thought to some purpose today. To-morrow I must finish the seaweed. She may be just below the horizon. Or up so high I can't see her. I must wait."

He hunched down by the Dwarf and waited. But time had infinite resource and what at first had been a purpose became grey and endless and without hope. He began to look for hope in his mind but the warmth had gone or if he found anything it was an intellectual and bloodless ghost.

He muttered.

"I shall be rescued. I shall be rescued."

123

*

At an end so far from the beginning that he had forgotten everything he had thought while he was there, he lifted his chin and saw that the sun was sinking. He got up heavily, went to the water-hole and drank. The stain of red round the nearer edge was wider.

He echoed.

"I must do something about water."

He dressed as for bed and wrapped the grey sweater round his feet. It made a muffling between them and the rock like the cathedral carpets over stone. That was a particular sensation the feet never found anywhere else particularly when they wore those ridiculous medieval shoes of Michael's all fantasticated but with practically no sole. Beside the acoustics were so bad—wah, wah, wah and then a high whine up among the barrel vault to which one added with every word one spoke as though one were giving a little periodic momentum to a pendulum——

"Can't hear you, old man, not a sausage. Up a bit. Give. I still can't hear you——"

"More? Slower?"

"Not slower for God's sake. Oh, turn it up. That's all for today boys and girls. Wait a bit, Chris. Look, George, Chris isn't coming off here at all——"

"Give him a bit more time, old man. Not your pitch is it, Chris?"

"I can manage, George."

"He'll be better in the other part, old man. Didn't you

124

see the rehearsal list, Chris? You're doubling—but of course——"

"Helen never said——"

"What's Helen got to do with it?"

"She never said——"

"I make out my own lists, old man."

"Of course, Pete, naturally."

"So you're doubling a shepherd and one of the seven deadly sins, old man. Eh, George, don't you think? Chris for one of the seven deadly sins?"

"Definitely, old man, oh, definitely."

"Well, I do think, Pete, after the amount of work I've done for you, I shouldn't be asked to——"

"Double, old man? Everybody's doubling. I'm doubling. So you're wanted for the seven sins, Chris."

"Which one, Pete?"

"Take your pick, old man. Eh, George? We ought to let dear old Chris pick his favourite sin, don't you, think?"

"Definitely, old boy, definitely."

"Prue's working on them in the crypt, come and look, Chris——"

"But if we've finished until tonight's house——"

"Come along, Chris. The show must go on. Eh, George? You'd like to see which mask Chris thinks would suit him?"

"Well—yes. Yes by God, Pete. I would. After you, Chris."

"I don't think I——"

125

"After you, Chris."

"Curious feeling to the feet this carpet over stone, George. Something thick and costly, just allowing your senses to feel the basic stuff beneath. There they are Chris, all in a row. What about it?"

"Anything you say, old man."

"What about Pride, George? He could play that without a mask and just stylized make-up, couldn't he?"

"Look, Pete, if I'm doubling I'd sooner not make——"

"Malice, George?"

"Envy, Pete?"

"I don't mind playing Sloth, Pete."

"Not Sloth. Shall we ask Helen, Chris? I value my wife's advice."

"Steady, Pete."

"What about a spot of Lechery?"

"Pete! Stop it."

"Don't mind me Chris, old, man. I'm just a bit wrought-up that's all. Now here's a fine piece of work, ladies and gentleman, guaranteed unworn. Any offers? Going to the smooth-looking gentleman with the wavy hair and profile. Going! Going——"

"What's it supposed to be, old man?"

"Darling, it's simply *you*! Don't you think, George?"

"Definitely, old man, definitely."

"Chris-Greed. Greed-Chris. Know each other."

"Anything to please you, Pete."

"Let me make you two better acquainted. This painted

126

bastard here takes anything he can lay his hands on. Not food, Chris, that's far too simple. He takes the best part, the best seat, the most money, the best notice, the best woman. He was born with his mouth and his flies open and both hands out to grab. He's a cosmic case of the bugger who gets his penny and someone else's bun. Isn't that right, George?"

"Come on, Pete. Come and lie down for a bit."

"Think you can play Martin, Greed?"

"Come on, Pete. He doesn't mean anything, Chris. Just wrought-up. A bit over-excited, eh, Pete?"

"That's all. Yes. Sure. That's all."

"I haven't had a crap for a week."

The dusk came crowding in and the sea-gulls. One sat on the Dwarf and the silver head rocked so that the sea-gull muted and flapped away. He went down to the crevices blew up the lifebelt, tied the tapes and put it under his head. He got his hands tucked in. Then his head felt unprotected, although he was wearing the balaclava, so that he wriggled out and fetched his sou'wester from the Red Lion. He went through the business of insertion again.

"Good God!"

He hauled himself out.

"Where the hell's my oilskin?"

He went scrambling over the rocks to the Red Lion, the water-hole, the Prospect Cliff——

127

"It can't be by the Dwarf because I never——"

In and out of the trenches, stinking seaweed, clammy, is it underneath?

He found his oilskin where he had left it by the Dwarf. There were white splashes on in. He put his oilskin over his duffle and inserted himself again.

"That's what they can never tell you, never give you any idea. Not the danger or the hardship but the niggling little idiocies, the damnable repetitions, the days dripping away in a scrammy-handed flurry of small mistakes you wouldn't notice if you were at work or could drop into the Red Lion or see your popsie—Where's my knife? Oh, Christ!"

But the knife was present, had swung round and was a rock-like projection under his left ribs. He worked it free and cursed.

"I'd better do my thinking now. I was wrong to do it when I could have worked. If I'd thought last night instead I could have treated the day methodically and done everything.

Now: problems. First I must finish that line of weed. Then I must have a place for clothes so that I never get into a panic again. I'd better stow them here so that I never forget. Second. No third. Clothes were second. First clothes in the crevice, then more weed until the line is finished. Third, water. Can't dig for it. Must catch it when it comes. Choose a trench below guano level and above spray. Make a catchment area."

128

He worked his lower jaw sideways. His bristles were very uncomfortable in the wool of the balaclava. He could feel the slight freezing, prickling sensation of sunburn on his arms and legs. The unevennesses of the rock were penetrating again.

"It'll soon rain. Then I'll have too much water. What shall I do about this crack? Musn't get my clothes wet. I must rig a tent. Perhaps to-morrow I'll be rescued."

He remembered that he had been certain of rescue in the morning and that made his heart sink unaccountably as though someone had broken his sworn word. He lay, looking up into the stars and wondering if he could find a scrap of wood to touch. But there was no wood on the rock, not even the stub of a pencil. No salt to throw over the left shoulder. Perhaps a splash of sea-water would be just as effective.

He worked his hand down to his right thigh. The old scar must have caught the sun too, for he could feel the raised place burning gently—a not unpleasant feeling but one that took the attention. The bristles in the balaclava made a scratching sound when he grimaced.

"Four. Make the knife sharp enough to shave with. Five. Make sure I'm not egg-bound to-morrow."

The sunburn pricked.

"I am suffering from reaction. I went through hell in the sea and in the funnel, and then I was so pleased to be safe that I went right over the top. And that is followed by a set-back. I must sleep, must keep quite still

129

and concentrate on the business of sleeping."

The sunburn went on pricking, the bristles scratched and scraped and the unevennesses of the rock lit their slow, smouldering fires. They stayed there like the sea. Even when consciousness was modified they insisted. They became a luminous landscape, they became a universe and he oscillated between moments of hanging in space, observing them and of being extended to every excruciating corner.

He opened his eyes and looked up. He shut them again and muttered to himself.

"I am dreaming."

He opened his eyes and the sunlight stayed there. The light lulled the fires to a certain extent because the mind could at last look away from them. He lay, looking at the daylight sky and trying to remember the quality of this time that had suddenly foreshortened itself.

"I wasn't asleep at all!"

And the mind was very disinclined to hutch out of the crevice and face what must be done. He spoke toneless words into the height of air over him.

"I shall be rescued today."

He hauled himself out of the crevice and the air was warm so that he undressed to trousers and sweater. He folded his clothes carefully and put them in the crevice. When he hutched forward in the water-hole the red deposit made a mark across his chest. He drank a great deal

130

of water and when he stopped drinking he could see that there was a wider space of darkness between the water and the window.

"I must get more water."

He lay still and tried to decide whether it was more important to arrange for catching water or to finish the line of weed. That reminded him how quickly time could pass if you let it out of your sight so he scrambled back to the Look-out. This was a day of colour. The sun burned and the water was deep blue and sparkled gaily. There was colour spilt over the rocks, shadows that were deep purple until you looked straight at them. He peered down the High Street and it was a picture. He shut his eyes and then opened them again but the rock and the sea seemed no more real. They were a pattern of colour that filled the three lights of his window.

"I am still asleep. I am shut inside my body."

He went to the Red Lion and sat by the sea.

"What did I do that for?"

He frowned at the water.

"I mean to get food. But I'm not hungry. I must get weed."

He fetched the lifebelt and knife from the crevice and went to Prospect Cliff. He had to climb farther along the ledges for weed because the nearer part of the cliff was stripped already. He came to a ledge that was vaguely familiar and had to think.

"I came here to get stones for the Dwarf. I tried to

131

shift that stone there but it wouldn't move although it was cracked."

He frowned at the stone. Then he worked his way down until he was hanging on the cliff by it with both hands and the crack was only a foot from his face. Like all the rest of the cliff where the water could reach it was cemented with layers of barnacles and enigmatic growths. But the crack was wider. The whole stone had moved and skewed perhaps an eighth of an inch. Inside the crack was a terrible darkness.

He stayed there, looking at the loose rock until he forgot what he was thinking. He was envisaging the whole rock as a thing in the water, and he was turning his head from side to side.

"How the hell is it that this rock is so familiar? I've never been here before——"

Familiar, not as a wartime acquaintance whom one knows so quickly because one is forced to live close to him for interminable stretches of hours but familiar as a relative, seldom seen, but to be reckoned with, year after year, familiar as a childhood friend, a nurse, some acquaintance with a touch of eternity behind him; familiar now, as the rocks of childhood, examined and reapprized holiday after holiday, remembered in the darkness of bed, in winter, imagined as a shape one's fingers can feel in the air——

There came a loud plop from the three rocks. He scrambled quickly to the Red Lion but saw nothing.

"I ought to fish."

The seaweed in the trenches stank. There came another plop from the sea and he was in time to see the ripples spreading. He put his hands on either cheek to think but the touch of hair distracted him.

"I must have a beard pretty well. Bristles, anyway. Strange that bristles go on growing even when the rest of you is——"

He went quickly to Prospect Cliff and got a load of weed and dumped it in the nearest trench. He went slowly up the High Street to the Look-out and sat down, his opened hands on either side of him. His head sank between his knees. The lap lap of water round Safety Rock was very quieting and a gull stood on the Look-out like an image.

The sounds of the inside body spread. The vast darkness was full of them as a factory is full of the sound of machinery. His head made a tiny bobbing motion each time his heart beat.

He was jerked out of this state by a harsh scream. The gull had advanced across the rock, its wings half-open, head lowered.

"What do you want?"

The feathered reptile took two steps sideways then shuffled its wings shut. The beak preened under the wing.

"If I had a crap I'd feel better."

He heaved himself round and looked at the Dwarf who winked at him with a silver eye. The line of the horizon was hard and near. Again he thought he could see indentations in the curve.

133

The trouble was there were no cushions on the rock, no tussocks. He thought for a moment of fetching his duffle and folding the skirt as a seat but the effort seemed too great.

"My flesh aches inside as though it were bruised. The hardness of the rock is wearing out my flesh. I will think about water."

Water was insinuating, soft and yielding.

"I must arrange some kind of shelter. I must arrange to catch water."

He came to a little, felt stronger and worried. He frowned at the tumbled rocks that were so maddeningly and evasively familiar and followed with his eye the thin line of weed. It shone in places. Perhaps the weed would appear from the air as a shining strip.

"I could catch water in my oilskin. I could make the wall of a trench into a catchment area."

He stopped talking and lay back until the unevenness of the Dwarf as a chair-back made him lean forward again. He sat, hunched up and frowning.

"I am aware of——"

He looked up.

"I am aware of a weight. A ponderous squeezing. Agoraphobia or anyway the opposite of claustrophobia. A pressure."

Water catchment.

He got to his feet and climbed back down the High Street. He examined the next trench to his sleeping crevice.

"Prevailing wind. I must catch water from an area facing south west."

He took his knife and drew a line sloping down across the leaning wall. It ended in a hollow, set back to the depth of his fist where the wall met the bottom of the trench. He went to the Dwarf, carefully extracted a white potato and brought it back. On the end of the clasp knife was a projection about a quarter of an inch long which was intended as a screwdriver. He placed this against the rock about an inch above the slanting line and tapped the other end of his knife with the stone. The rock came away in thin flakes. He put the screwdriver in the slanting line and tapped till the line sank in. Soon he had made a line perhaps an eighth of an inch deep and a foot long. He went to the bottom end of the line.

"Begin at the most important end of the line. Then no matter how soon the rain comes I can catch some of it."

The noise of the taps was satisfactorily repeated in the trench and he felt enclosed as though he were working in a room.

"I could spread my duffle or oilskin over this trench and then I should have a roof. That ponderous feeling is not so noticeable here. That's partly because I am in a room and partly because I am working."

His arms ached but the line rose away from the floor and he could work in an easier position. He made a dreamy calculation to see whether increasing ease would overtake tiredness and found that it would not. He sat on the floor

135

with his face a few inches from the rock. He leaned his forehead on stone. His hand fell open.

"I could go to the crevice and lie down for a bit. Or I could roll up in my duffle by the Dwarf."

He jerked his head away from the rock and set to work again. The cut part of the line lengthened. This part met the part he had cut first and he sat back to examine it.

"I should have cut it back at a slant. Damn."

He grimaced at the rock and went back over the cut so that the bottom of the groove trended inward.

"Make it deeper near the end."

Because the amount of water in the cut—but he changed his mind and did the calculation out loud.

"The amount of water in any given length of the cut will consist of all the water collected higher up, and also will be proportional to the area of rock above."

He tapped at the rock and the flakes fell. His hands gave out and he sat on the floor of the trench, looking at his work.

"After this I shall do a real engineering job. I shall find a complex area round a possible basin and cut a network of lines that will guide the water to it. That will be rather interesting. Like sand-castles."

Or like Roman emperors, bringing water to the city from the hills.

"This is an aqueduct. I call it the Claudian."

He began to flake again, imposing purpose on the senseless rock.

136

"I wonder how long I've been doing that?"

He lay down in the trench and felt his back bruise. The Claudian was a long, whitish scar.

"There is something venomous about the hardness of this rock. It is harder than rock should be. And—familiar."

The ponderous weight squeezed down. He struggled up to a sitting position.

"I should have dried seaweed and lined the crevice. But there are too many things to do. I need another hand on this job of living and being rescued. Perhaps I could find another place to sleep. In the open? I feel warm enough."

Too warm.

"My flesh is perceptible inside—as though it were bruised everywhere to the bone. And big. Tumescent."

The globe of darkness turned a complicated window towards the sky. The voice evaporated at the gate like escaping steam on a dry day.

"I'm working too hard. If I don't watch out I shall exhaust myself. Anyway I'll hand it to you, Chris. I don't think many people would——"

He stopped suddenly, then began again.

"Chris. Christopher! Christopher Hadley Martin——"

The words dried up.

There was an instrument of examination, a point that knew it existed. There were sounds that came out of the lower part of a face. They had no meaning attached to them. They were useless as tins thrown out with the lids buckled back.

137

"Christopher. Christopher!"

He reached out with both arms as though to grab the words before they dried away. The arms appeared before the window and in complete unreason they filled him with terror.

"Oh, my God."

He wrapped his arms round him, hugged himself close, rocked from side to side. He began to mutter.

"Steady. Steady. Keep calm."

9

He got up and sat gingerly on the side of the trench. He could feel the separate leaves of rock and their edges through his trousers and pants. He shifted farther down the trench to a place where the leaves were smoothly cut but his backside seemed to fare no better.

"I am who I was."

He examined the shape of his window and the window-box of hair that was flourishing between his two noses. He turned the window down and surveyed all that he could see of himself. The sweater was dragged out into tatters and wisps of wool. It lay in folds beneath his chest and the sleeves were concertina'd. The trousers beneath the sweater were shiny and grey instead of black and beneath them the seaboot stockings drooped like the wads of waste that a stoker wipes his hands on. There was no body to be seen, only a conjunction of worn materials. He eyed the peculiar shapes that lay across the trousers indifferently for a while until at last it occurred to him how strange it was that lobsters should sit there. Then he was suddenly seized with a terrible loathing for lobsters and flung them

139

away so that they cracked on the rock. The dull pain of the blow extended him into them again and they became his hands, lying discarded where he had tossed them.

He cleared his throat as if about to speak in public.

"How can I have a complete identity without a mirror? That is what has changed me. Once I was a man with twenty photographs of myself—myself as this and that with the signature scrawled across the bottom right-hand corner as a stamp and seal. Even when I was in the Navy there was that photograph in my identity card so that every now and then I could look and see who I was. Or perhaps I did not even need to look, but was content to wear the card next to my heart, secure in the knowledge that it was there, proof of me in the round. There were mirrors too, triple mirrors, more separate than the three lights in this window. I could arrange the side ones so that there was a double reflection and spy myself from the side or back in the reflected mirror as though I were watching a stranger. I could spy myself and assess the impact of Christopher Hadley Martin on the world. I could find assurance of my solidity in the bodies of other people by warmth and caresses and triumphant flesh. I could be a character in a body. But now I am this thing in here, a great many aches of bruised flesh, a bundle of rags and those lobsters on the rock. The three lights of my window are not enough to identify me however sufficient they were in the world. But there were other people to describe me to myself—they fell in love with me, they applauded me, they caressed this body, they defined it for me. There were

140

the people I got the better of, people who disliked me, people who quarrelled with me. Here I have nothing to quarrel with. I am in danger of losing definition. I am an album of snapshots, random, a whole show of trailers of old films. The most I know of my face is the scratch of bristles, an itch, a sense of tingling warmth."

He cried out angrily.

"That's no face for a man! Sight is like exploring the night with a flashlight. I ought to be able to see all round my head——"

He climbed down to the water-hole and peered into the pool. But his reflection was inscrutable. He backed out and went down to the Red Lion among the littered shells. He found a pool of salt water on one of the sea rocks. The pool was an inch deep under the sun with one green-weeded limpet and three anemones. There was a tiny fish, less than an inch long, sunning itself on the bottom. He leaned over the pool, looked through the displayed works of the fish and saw blue sky far down. But no matter how he turned his head he could see nothing but a patch of darkness with the wild outline of hair round the edge.

"The best photograph was the one of me as Algernon. The one as Demetrius wasn't bad, either—and as Freddy with a pipe. The make-up took and my eyes looked really wide apart. There was the Night Must Fall one. And that one from The Way of the World. Who was I? It would have been fun playing opposite Jane. That wench was good for a tumble."

141

The rock hurt the scar on the front of his right thigh. He shifted his leg and peered back into the pool. He turned his head sideways again, trying to catch the right angle for his profile—the good profile, the left one, elevated a little and with a half-smile. But first a shadowy nose and then the semicircle of an eye socket got in the way. He turned back to inquire of his full face but his breathing ruffled the water. He puffed down and the dark head wavered and burst. He jerked up and there was a lobster supporting his weight at the end of his right sleeve.

He made the lobster into a hand again and looked down at the pool. The little fish hung in sunshine with a steady trickle of bubbles rising by it from the oxygen tube. The bottles at the back of the bar loomed through the aquarium as cliffs of jewels and ore.

"No, thanks, old man, I've had enough."

"He's had enough. Ju hear that, George? Ju hear?"

"Hear what, Pete?"

"Dear ol' Chris has had enough."

"Come on, Chris."

"Dear ol' Chris doesn't drink 'n doesn't smoke."

"Likes company, old man."

"Likes company. My company. I'm disgusted with myself. Yur not goin' to say 'Time, Gentlemen, please', miss, are you, gentlemen? He promised his old mother. He said. She said. She said, Chris, my child, let the ten commandments look after themselves she said. But don't

142

drink and don't smoke. Only foke, I beg your pardon, miss, had I known such an intemperate word would have escaped the barrier of my teeth I would have taken steps to have it indictated in the sex with an obelisk or employed a perifris."

"Come on, Pete. Take his other arm, Chris."

"Unhand me, Gentlemen. By heaven I'll make a fish of him that lets me. I am a free and liberal citizen of this company with a wife and child of indifferent sex."

"It's a boy, old man."

"Confidently, George, it's not the sex but the wisdom. Does it know who I am? Who we are? Do you love me, George?"

"You're the best producer we've ever had, you drunken old soak."

"I meant soak, miss. George, you're the most divinely angelic director the bloody theatre ever had and Chris is the best bloody juvenile, aren't you, Chris?"

"Anything you say, eh, George?"

"Definitely, old man, definitely."

"So we all owe everything to the best bloody woman in the world. I love you, Chris. Father and mother is one flesh. And so my uncle. My prophetic uncle. Shall I elect you to my club?"

"How about toddling home, now, Pete?"

"Call it the Dirty Maggot Club. You member? You speak Chinese? You open sideways or only on Sundays?"

"Come on, Pete."

143

"We maggots are there all the week. Y'see when the Chinese want to prepare a very rare dish they bury a fish in a tin box. Presently all the lil' maggots peep out and start to eat. Presently no fish. Only maggots. It's no bloody joke being a maggot. Some of 'em are phototropic. Hey, George—phototropic!"

"What of it, Pete?"

"Phototropic. I said phototropic, miss."

"Finish your maggots, Pete and let's go."

"Oh, the maggots. Yes, the maggots. They haven't finished yet. Only got to the fish. It's a lousy job crawling round the inside of a tin box and Denmark's one of the worst. Well, when they've finished the fish, Chris, they start on each other."

"Cheerful thought, old man."

"The little ones eat the tiny ones. The middle-sized ones eat the little ones. The big ones eat the middle-sized ones. Then the big ones eat each other. Then there are two and then one and where there was a fish there is now one huge, successful maggot. Rare dish."

"Got his hat, George?"

"Come on, Pete! Now careful——"

"I love you, Chris, you lovely big hunk. Eat me."

"Get his arm over your shoulder."

"There's nearly half of me left'n, I'm phototropic. You eat George yet? 'N when there's only one maggot left the Chinese dig it up——"

"You can't sit down here, you silly sot!"

144

"Chinese dig it up——"

"For Christ's sake, stop shouting. We'll have a copper after us."

"Chinese dig it up——"

"Snap out of it, Pete. How the hell do the Chinese know when to dig it up?"

"They know. They got X-ray eyes. Have you ever heard a spade knocking on the side of a tin box, Chris? Boom! Boom! Just like thunder. You a member?"

There was a round of ripples by the three rocks. He watched them intently. Then a brown head appeared by the rocks, another and another. One of the heads had a silver knife across its mouth. The knife bent, flapped and he saw the blade was a fish. The seal heaved itself on to the rock while the others dived, leaving dimpled water and circles. The seal ate, calmly in the sun, rejected the head and tail and lay quiet.

"I wonder if they know about men?"

He stood up slowly and the seal turned its head towards him so that he found himself flinching from an implacable stare. He raised his arms suddenly in the gesture of a man who points a gun. The seal heaved round on the rock and dived. It knew about men.

"If I could get near I could kill it and make boots and eat the meat——"

The men lay on the open beach, wrapped in skins. They endured the long wait and the stench. At dusk, great

145

beasts came out of the sea, played round them, then lay down to sleep.

"An oilskin rolled up would look enough like a seal. When they were used to it I should be inside."

He examined the thought of days. They were a recession like repeated rooms in mirrors hung face to face. All at once he experienced a weariness so intense that it was a pain. He laboured up to the Look-out through the pressure of the sky and all the vast quiet. He made himself examine the empty sea in each quarter. The water was smoother to-day as though the dead air were flattening it. There was shot silk in swathes, oily-looking patches that became iridescent as he watched, like the scum in a ditch. But the wavering of this water was miles long so that a molten sun was elongated, pulled out to nothing here to appear there in a different waver with a sudden blinding dazzle.

"The weather changed while I was in the Red Lion with George and Pete."

He saw a seal head appear for a moment beyond the three rocks and had a sudden wild sight of himself riding a seal across the water to the Hebrides.

"Oh, my God!"

The sound of his voice, flat, yet high and agonized, intimidated him. He dropped his arms and huddled down in his body by the Dwarf. A stream of muttered words began to tumble through the hole under his window.

"It's like those nights when I was a kid, lying awake

thinking the darkness would go on for ever. And I couldn't go back to sleep because of the dream of the whatever it was in the cellar coming out of the corner. I'd lie in the hot, rumpled bed, hot burning hot, trying to shut myself away and know that there were three eternities before the dawn. Everything was the night world, the other world where everything but good could happen, the world of ghosts and robbers and horrors, of things harmless in the daytime coming to life, the wardrobe, the picture in the book, the story, coffins, corpses, vampires, and always squeezing, tormenting darkness, smoke thick. And I'd think of anything because if I didn't go on thinking I'd remember whatever it was in the cellar down there, and my mind would go walking away from my body and go down three stories defenceless, down the dark stairs past the tall, haunted clock, through the whining door, down the terrible steps to where the coffin ends were crushed in the walls of the cellar—and I'd be held helpless on the stone floor, trying to run back, run away, climb up——"

He was standing, crouched. The horizon came back.

"Oh, my God!"

Waiting for the dawn, the first bird cheeping in the eaves or the tree-tops. Waiting for the police by the smashed car. Waiting for the shell after the flash of the gun.

The ponderous sky settled a little more irresistibly on his shoulders.

"What's the matter with me? I'm adult. I know what's what. There's no connection between me and the kid in

147

the cellar, none at all. I grew up. I firmed my life. I have it under control. And anyway there's nothing down there to be frightened of. Waiting for the result. Waiting for that speech—not the next one after this, I know that, but where I go across and take up the cigarette-box. There's a black hole where that speech ought to be and he said you fluffed too much last night, old man. Waiting for the wound to be dressed. This will hurt a little. Waiting for the dentist's chair.

"I don't like to hear my voice falling dead at my mouth like a shot bird."

He put a hand up to either side of his window and watched two black lines diminish it. He could feel the roughness of bristles under either palm and the heat of cheeks.

"What's crushing me?"

He turned his sight round the horizon and the only thing that told him when he had completed the circle was the brighter waver under the sun.

"I shall be rescued any day now. I must not worry. Trailers out of the past are all right but I must be careful when I see things that never happened, like—I have water and food and intelligence and shelter."

He paused for a moment and concentrated on the feeling in the flesh round his window. His hands and skin felt lumpy. He swivelled his eyes sideways and saw that there might indeed be a slight distortion of the semicircle of the eye-hollows.

"Heat lumps? When it rains I shall strip and have a bath. If I haven't been rescued by then."

He pressed with the fingers of his right hand the skin round his eyes. There were heat lumps on the side of his face, that extended down beneath the bristles. The sky pressed on them but they knew no other feeling.

"I must turn in. Go to bed. And stay awake."

The day went grey and hot. Dreary.

"I said I should be sick. I said I must watch out for symptoms."

He went down to the water-hole and crawled in. He drank until he could hear water washing about in his belly. He crawled out backwards and dimensions were mixed up. The surface of the rock was far too hard, far too bright, far too near. He could not gauge size at all.

There was no one else to say a word.

You're not looking too good, old man.

"How the hell can I tell how I look?"

He saw a giant impending and flinched before he could connect the silver head with his chocolate paper. He felt that to stand up would be dangerous for a reason he was not able to formulate. He crawled to the crevice and arranged the clothing. He decided that he must wear everything. Presently he lay with his head out of the crevice on an inflated lifebelt. The sky was bright blue again but very heavy. The opening under his bristles dribbled on.

"Care Charmer Sleep. Cracker mottoes. Old tags. Rag bag of a brain. But don't sleep because of the cellar. How

149

sleep the brave. Nat's asleep. And old gin-soak. Rolled along the bottom or drifting like an old bundle. This is high adventure and anyone can have it. Lie down, rat. Accept your cage. How much rain in this month? How many convoys? How many planes? My hands are larger. All my body is larger and tenderer. Emergency. Action stations. I said I should be ill. I can feel the old scar on my leg tingling more than the rest. Salt in my trousers. Ants in my pants."

He hutched himself sideways in the crevice and withdrew his right hand. He felt his cheek with it but the cheek was dry.

"The tingling can't be sweat, then."

He got his hand back and scratched in his crutch. The edge of the duffle was irritating his face. He remembered that he ought to be wearing the balaclava but was too exhausted to find it. He lay still and his body burned.

He opened his eyes and the sky was violet over him. There was an irregularity in the eye sockets. He lay there, his eyes unfocused and thought of the heat lumps on his face. He wondered if they would close the sockets altogether.

Heat lumps.

The burnings and shiverings of his body succeeded each other as if they were going over him in waves. Suddenly they were waves of molten stuff, solder, melted lead, heated acid, so thick that it moved like oil. Then he was fighting and crying to get out of the crevice.

150

He knelt, shaking on the rock. He put his hands down and they hurt when he leaned his weight on them. He peered down at them first with one eye then the other. They swelled and diminished with a slow pulsing.

"That's not real. Thread of Life. Hang on. That's not real."

But what was real was the mean size of the hands. They were too big even on the average, butcher's hands so full of blood that their flesh was pulpy and swollen. His elbows gave way and he fell between his hands. His cheek was against the uniquely hard rock, his mouth open and he was looking blearily back into the crevice. The waves were still in his body and he recognized them. He gritted his teeth and hung on to himself in the centre of his globe.

"That must mean I'm running a temperature of well over a hundred. I ought to be in hospital."

Smells. Formalin. Ether. Meth. Idioform. Sweet chloroform. Iodine.

Sights. Chromium. White sheets. White bandages. High windows.

Touches. Pain, Pain, Pain.

Sounds. Forces programme drooling like a cretin in the ears from the headphones hitched under the fever chart.

Tastes. Dry lips.

He spoke again with intense solemnity and significance.

"I must go sick."

He lugged the clothes off his body. Before he had got down to his vest and pants the burning was intolerable so

151

that he tore off his clothes and threw them anywhere. He stood up naked and the air was hot on his body, but the action of being naked seemed to do something, for his body started to shiver. He sat painfully on the wall by the white scar of the Claudian and his teeth chattered.

"I must keep going somehow."

But the horizon would not stay still. Like his hands, the sea pulsed. At one moment the purple line was so far away that it had no significance and the next, so close that he could stretch out his arm and lay hold.

"Think. Be intelligent."

He held his head with both hands and shut his eyes.

"Drink plenty of water."

He opened his eyes and the High Street pulsed below him. The rock was striped with lines of seaweed that he saw presently were black shadows cast by the sun and not seaweed at all. The sea beyond the High Street was dead flat and featureless so that he could have stepped down and walked on it, only his feet were swollen and sore. He took his body with great care to the water-hole and pulled himself in. At once he was refrigerated. He put his face in the water and half-gulped, half-ate it with chattering teeth. He crawled away to the crevice.

"The squeezing did it, the awful pressure. It was the weight of the sky and the air. How can one human body support all that weight without bruising into a pulp?"

He made a little water in the trench. The reptiles were floating back to the sea round the rock. They said nothing

152

but sat on the flat sea with their legs hidden.

"I need a crap. I must see about that. Now I must wear everything and sweat this heat out of my body."

By the time he had pulled on all his clothing dusk was come and he felt his way into the crevice with his legs. The crevice enlarged and became populous. There were times when it was larger than the rock, larger than the world, times when it was a tin box so huge that a spade knocking at the side sounded like distant thunder. Then after that there was a time when he was back in rock and distant thunder was sounding like the knocking of a spade against a vast tin box. All the time the opening beneath his window was dribbling on like the Forces Programme, cross-talking and singing to people whom he could not see but knew were there. For a moment or two he was home and his father was like a mountain. The thunder and lightning were playing round the mountain's head and his mother was weeping tears like acid and knitting a sock without a beginning or end. The tears were a kind of charm for after he had felt them scald him they changed the crevice into a pattern.

The opening spoke.

"She is sorry for me on this rock."

Sybil was weeping and Alfred. Helen was crying. A bright boy face was crying. He saw half-forgotten but now clearly remembered faces and they were all weeping.

"That is because they know I am alone on a rock in the middle of a tin box."

153

They wept tears that turned them to stone faces in a wall, masks hung in rows in a corridor without beginning or end. There were notices that said No Smoking, Gentlemen, Ladies, Exit and there were many uniformed attendants. Down there was the other room, to be avoided, because there the gods sat behind their terrible knees and feet of black stone, but here the stone faces wept and had wept. Their stone cheeks were furrowed, they were blurred and only recognizable by some indefinite mode of identity. Their tears made a pool on the stone floor so that his feet were burned to the ankles. He scrabbled to climb up the wall and the scalding stuff welled up his ankles to his calves, his knees. He was struggling, half-swimming, half-climbing. The wall was turning over, curving like the wall of a tunnel in the underground. The tears were no longer running down the stone to join the burning sea. They were falling freely, dropping on him. One came, a dot, a pearl, a ball, a globe, that moved on him, spread. He began to scream. He was inside the ball of water that was burning him to the bone and past. It consumed him utterly. He was dissolved and spread throughout the tear an extension of sheer, disembodied pain.

He burst the surface and grabbed a stone wall. There was hardly any light but he knew better than to waste time because of what was coming. There were projections in the wall of the tunnel so that though it was more nearly a well than a tunnel he could still climb. He laid hold, pulled himself up, projection after projection. The light

154

was bright enough to show him the projections. They were faces, like the ones in the endless corridor. They were not weeping but they were trodden. They appeared to be made of some chalky material for when he put his weight on them they would break away so that only by constant movement upward was he able to keep up at all. He could hear his voice shouting in the well.

"I am! I am! I am!"

And all the time there was another voice that hung in his ears like the drooling of the Forces Programme. Nobody paid any attention to this voice but the nature of the cretin was to go on talking even though it said the same thing over and over again. This voice had some connection with the lower part of his own face and leaked on as he climbed and broke the chalky, convenient faces.

"Tunnels and wells and drops of water all this is old stuff. You can't tell me. I know my stuff just sexual images from the unconscious, the libido, or is it the id? All explained and known. Just sexual stuff what can you expect? Sensation, all tunnels and wells and drops of water. All old stuff, you can't tell me. I know."

10

A tongue of summer lightning licked right inside the inner crevice so that he saw shapes there. Some were angled and massive as the corners of corridors and between them was the light falling into impenetrable distances. One shape was a woman who unfroze for that instant and lived. The lightning created or discovered her in the act of breathing in; and so nearly was that breath finished that she seemed only to check and breathe out again. He knew without thinking who she was and where she was and when, he knew why she was breathing so quickly, lifting the silk blouse with apples, the forbidden fruit, knew why there were patches of colour on either cheek-bone and why the flush had run as it so uniquely did into the nose. Therefore she presented to him the high forehead, the remote and unconquered face with the three patches of pink arranged across the middle. As for the eyes, they fired an ammunition of contempt and outrage. They were eyes that confirmed all the unworded opinions of his body and fevered head. Seen as a clothed body or listened to, she was common and undistinguished. But the eyes belonged to some other person for they had nothing to do with the irregularity of the face or the aspirations, prudish and social, of the voice. There was the individual, Mary, who was nothing but the intersection of influences from the cradle up, the Mary gloved and hatted for church, she Mary who ate with such maddening refinement, the Mary who carried, poised on her two little feet, a treasure of demoniac and musky attractiveness that was all the more terrible because she was almost unconscious of it. This intersection was so inevitably constructed that its every word and action could be predicted. The intersection would choose the ordinary rather than the exceptional; would fly to what was respectable as to a magnet. It was a fit companion for the pursed-up mouth, the too high forehead, the mousey hair. But the eyes—they had nothing in common with the mask of flesh that nature had fixed on what must surely be a real and invisible face. They were one with the incredible smallness of the waist and the apple breasts, the transparency of the flesh. They were large and wise with a wisdom that never reached the surface to be expressed in speech. They gave to her many silences—so explicable in terms of the intersection—a mystery that was not there. But combined with the furious musk, the little guarded breasts, the surely impregnable virtue, they were the death sentence of Actaeon. They made her occupy as by right, a cleared space in the world behind the eyes that was lit by flickers of summer lightning. They made her a madness, not so much in the loins as in the pride, the need to assert and break, a blight in the growing point of life.

157

They brought back the nights of childhood, the hot, eternal bed with seamed sheets, the desperation. The things she did became important though they were trivial, the very onyx she wore became a talisman. A thread from her tweed skirt—though she had bought it off the hook in a shop where identical skirts hung empty and unchanged—that same thread was magicked into power by association. Her surname—and he thumped rock with lifted knees—her surname now abandoned to dead Nathaniel forced him to a reference book lest it should wind back to some distinction that would set her even more firmly at the centre than she was. By what chance, or worse what law of the universe was she set there in the road to power and success, unbreakable yet tormenting with the need to conquer and break? How could she take this place behind the eyes as by right when she was nothing but another step on which one must place the advancing foot? Those nights of imagined copulation, when one thought not of love nor sensation nor comfort nor triumph, but of torture rather, the very rhythm of the body reinforced by hissed ejaculations—take that and that! That for your pursed mouth and that for your pink patches, your closed knees, your impregnable balance on the high, female shoes—and that if it kills you for your magic and your isled virtue!

How can she so hold the centre of my darkness when the only real feeling I have for her is hate?

Pale face, pink patches. The last chance and I know what she is going to say, inevitably out of the intersection.

158

And here it comes quickly, with an accent immediately elevated to the top drawer.

"No."

There are at least three vowels in the one syllable.

"Why did you agree to come here with me, then?"

Three patches.

"I thought you were a gentleman."

Inevitably.

"You make me tired."

"Take me home, please."

"Do you really mean that in the twentieth century? You really feel insulted? You don't just mean 'No, I'm sorry, but no'?"

"I want to go home."

"But look——"

I must, I must, don't you understand you bloody bitch?

"Then I'll take a bus."

One chance. Only one.

"Wait a minute. Our language is so different. Only what I'm trying to say is—well, it's difficult. Only don't you understand that I—Oh Mary, I'll do anything to prove it to you!"

"I'm sorry. I just don't care for you in that way."

And then he, compelled about the rising fury to tread the worn path:

"Then it's still—no?"

Ultimate insult of triumph, understanding and compassion.

"I'm sorry, Chris. Genuinely sorry."

"You'll be a sister to me, I know."

But then the astonishing answer, serenely, brushing away the sarcasm.

"If you like."

He got violently to his feet.

"Come on. Let's get out of here for Christ's sake."

Wait, like a shape in the driving seat. Does she know nothing of me at all? She comes from the road house, one foot swerved in front of the other as in the photographs, walking an invisible tight-rope across the gravel, bearing proudly the invincible banner of virginity.

"That door's not properly shut. Let me."

Subtle the scent, the touch of the cheap, transmuted tweed, hand shaking on the gear, road drawing back, hooded wartime lights, uncontrollable summer lightning ignoring the regulations from beyond that hill to away south in seven-league boots, foot hard down, fringes of leaves jagged like a painted drop, trees touched, brought into being by sidelights and bundled away to the limbo of lost chances.

"Aren't you driving rather fast?"

Tilted cheek, pursed mouth, eyes under the foolish hat, remote, blacked out. Foot hard down.

"Please drive slower, Chris!"

Tyre-scream, gear-whine, thrust and roar——

"Please——!"

Rock, sway, silk hiss of skid, scene film-flicking.

160

Power.

"Please! Please!"

"Let me, then. Now. Tonight, in the car."

"Please!"

Hat awry, road unravelled, tree-tunnel drunk up——

"I'll kill us."

"You're mad—oh, please!"

"Where the road forks at the whitewashed tree, I'll hit it with your side. You'll be burst and bitched."

"Oh God, oh God."

Over the verge, clout on the heap of dressing, bump, swerve back, eating macadam, drawing it in, pushing it back among the lost chances, pushing it down with time back to the cellar——

"I'm going to faint."

"You'll let me make love to you? Love to you?"

"Please stop."

On the verge, trodden with two feet to a stop, with dead engine and lights, grabbing a stuffed doll, plundering a doll that came to life under the summer lightning, knees clapped together over the hoarded virginity, one hand pushing down the same tweed skirt, one to ward off, finding with her voice a protection for the half-naked breast——

"I shall scream!"

"Scream away."

"You filthy, beastly——"

Then the summer lightning over a white face with two

161

staring eyes only a few inches away, eyes of the artificial woman, confounded in her pretences and evasion, forced to admit her own crude, human body—eyes staring now in deep and implacable hate.

Nothing out of the top drawer now. Vowels with the burr of the country on them.

"Don't you understand, you swine? You can't——"

The last chance. I must.

"I'll marry you then."

More summer lightning.

"Chris. Stop laughing. D'you hear? Stop it! I said stop it!"

"I *loathe* you. I never want to see you or hear of you as long as I live."

Peter was riding behind him and they were flat out. It was his new bike under him but it was not as good as Peter's new one. If Peter got past with that new gear of his he'd be uncatchable. Peter's front wheel was overlapping his back one in a perfect position. He'd never have done that if he weren't deadly excited. The road curves here to the right, here by the pile of dressing. They are built up like rock—a great pile of stones for mending the road down to Hodson's Farm. Don't turn, go straight on, keep going for the fraction of a second longer than he expects. Let him turn, with his overlapping wheel. Oh clever, clever, clever. My leg, Chris, my leg—I daren't look at my leg. Oh Christ.

162

The cash-box. Japanned tin, gilt lines. Open empty. What are you going to do about it, there was nothing written down. Have a drink with me some time.

She's the producer's wife, old boy.

Oh clever, clever, clever power, then you can bloody well walk home; oh clever, real tears break down triumph, clever, clever, clever.

Up stage. Up stage. Up stage. I'm a bigger maggot than you are. You can't get any further up stage because of the table, but I can go all the way up to the french window.

"No, old man. I'm sorry, but you're not essential."

"But George—we've worked together! You know me——"

"I do, old man. Definitely."

"I should be wasted in the Forces. You've seen my work.

"I have, old man."

"Well then——"

The look up under the eyebrows. The suppressed smile. The smile allowed to spread until the white teeth were reflected in the top of the desk.

"I've been waiting for something like this. That's why I didn't kick you out before. I hope they mar your profile, old man. The good one."

There were ten thousand ways of killing a man. You

163

could poison him and watch the smile turn into a rictus. You could hold his throat until it was like a hard bar.

She was putting on a coat.

"Helen——"

"My sweet."

The move up, vulpine, passionate.

"It's been so long."

Deep, shuddering breath.

"Don't be corny, dear."

Fright.

"Help me, Helen, I must have your help."

Black maggot eyes in a white face. Distance. Calculation. Death.

"Anything my sweet, but of course."

"After all you're Pete's wife."

"So crude, Chris."

"You could persuade him."

Down close on the settee, near.

"Helen——"

"Why don't you ask Margot, my sweet, or that little thing you took out driving?"

Panic. Black eyes in a white face with no more expression than hard, black stones.

Eaten.

Nathaniel bubbling over in a quiet way—not a bubble over, a simmer, almost a glow.

"I have wonderful news for you, Chris."

"You've met an aeon at last."

Nat considered this, looking up at the reference library. He identified the remark as a joke and answered it with the too profound tones he reserved for humour.

"I have been introduced to one by proxy."

"Tell me your news. Is the war over? I can't wait."

Nathaniel sat down in the opposite armchair but found it too low. He perched himself on the arm, then got up and rearranged the books on the table. He looked into the street between the drab black-out curtains.

"I think finally, I shall go into the Navy."

"You!"

Nodding, still looking out of the window:

"If they'd have me, that is. I couldn't fly and I shouldn't be any use in the Army."

"But you clot! You don't have to go, do you?"

"Not—legally."

"I thought you objected to war."

"So I do."

"Conchie."

"I don't know. I really don't know. One thinks this and that—but in the end, you know, the responsibility of deciding is too much for one man. I ought to go."

"You've made your mind up?"

"Mary agrees with me."

"Mary Lovell? What's she got to do with it?"

"That's my news."

Nathaniel turned with a forgotten book in his hands.

165

He came towards the fire, looked at the armchair, remembered the book and put it on the table. He took a chair, drew it forward and perched on the edge.

"I was telling you after the show last night. You remember? About how our lives must reach right back to the roots of time, be a trail through history?"

"I said you were probably Cleopatra."

Nat considered this gravely.

"No, I don't think so. Nothing so famous."

"Henry the Eighth, then. Is that your news?"

"One constantly comes across clues. One has—flashes of insight—things given. One is——" The hands began to spread sideways by the shoulders as though they were feeling an expansion of the head—"One is conscious when meeting people that they are woven in with one's secret history. Don't you think? You and I, for example. You remember?"

"You used to talk an awful lot of cock."

Nathaniel nodded.

"I still do. But we are still interwoven and the same things hold good. Then when you introduce me to Mary—you remember? You see how we three act and re-act. There came that sudden flash, that—stab of knowledge and certainty that said, 'I have known you before.'"

"What on earth are you talking about?"

"She felt it too. She said so. She's so—wise, you know! And now we are both quite certain. These things are written in the stars, of course, but under them, Chris, we have

166

to thank you for bringing us together."

"You and Mary Lovell?"

"Of course these things are never simple and we've meditated apart from each other and together——"

An enchantment was filling the room. Nat's head seemed to grow large and small with it.

"And I should be awfully pleased, Chris, if you'd be best man for me."

"You're going to marry! You and——"

"That was the joyous news."

"You can't!"

He heard how anguished his voice was, found he was standing up.

Nat looked past him into the fire.

"I know it's sudden but we've meditated. And you see, I shall be going into the Navy. She's so good and brave. And you, Chris—I knew you would bring your whole being to such a decision."

He stood still, looking down at the tousled black hair, the length of limb. He felt the bleak recognition rising in him of the ineffable strength of these circumstances and this decision. Not where he eats but where he is eaten. Blood rose with the recognition, burning in the face, power to break. Pictures of her fell through his mind like a dropped sheaf of snapshots—Mary in the boat, carefully arranging her skirt; Mary walking to church, reeking of it, the very placing of her feet and carriage of her little bum an insolence; Mary struggling, knees clapped

167

together over the hoarded virginity, trying with one hand to pull down her skirt, with the other to ward off, the voice finding the only protection for her half-naked breast——

"I shall scream!"

Nat looked up, his mouth open.

"I'm not being a fool this time you know. You needn't worry."

The snapshots vanished.

"I was—I don't know what I was saying, Nat—quoting from some play or other."

Nat spread his hands and smiled diffidently.

"The stars can't be thwarted."

"Especially if they happen to agree with what you want."

Nat considered this. He reddened a little and nodded gravely.

"There is that danger."

"Be careful, Nat, for God's sake."

But not known, not understood—what is he to be careful of? Of staying near me? Of standing with her in the lighted centre of my darkness?

"You'll be here to look after her, Chris, when I've gone."

There is something in the stars. Or what is this obscure impulse that sets my words at variance with my heart?

"Only be careful. Of me."

"Chris!"

Because I like you, you fool and hate you. And now I hate you.

"All right, Nat, forget it."

"There's something the matter."

An impulse gone, trodden down, kicked aside.

"I shall be in the Navy, too."

"But the theatre!"

Gone down under calculation and hate.

"One has one's better feelings."

"My dear man!" Nat was standing and beaming. "Perhaps we can be in the same ship."

Drearily and with the foreknowledge of a chosen road.

"I'm sure we shall be. That's in our stars."

Nat nodded.

"We are connected in the elements. We are men for water."

"Water. Water."

The clothes bound him like a soggy bundle. He hauled himself out into the sun. He lay there feeling that he spread like seaweed. He got his hands up and plucked at the toggles of his duffle while the snapshots whirled and flew like a pack of cards. He got the toggles free and plucked at the rest of his clothing. When he had only vest and pants on he crawled away, yards over the rock to the water-hole. He crawled up the High Street and lay down by the Dwarf.

"If I am not delirious this is steam rising from my clothes. Sweat."

He propped his back against the Dwarf.

"Be intelligent."

His legs before him were covered with white blotches. There were more on his stomach when he lifted his vest, on his arms and legs. They were deformations at the edge of the eye-sockets.

"Stay alive!"

Something fierce pushed out of his mind.

"I'll live if I have to eat everything else on this bloody box!"

He looked down at his legs.

"I know the name for you bloody blotches. Urticaria. Food poisoning."

He lay quiet for a time. The steam rose and wavered. The blotches were well-defined and of a dead whiteness. They were raised so that even swollen fingers could feel their outline.

"I said I should be ill and I am."

He peered hazily round the horizon but it had nothing to give. He looked back at his legs and decided that they were very thin for all the blotches. Under his vest he could feel the trickle of water that found its way down from blotch to blotch.

The pressure of the sky and air was right inside his head.

11

A thought was forming like a piece of sculpture behind the eyes but in front of the unexamined centre. He watched the thought for a timeless interim while the drops of sweat trickled down from blotch to blotch. But he knew that the thought was an enemy and so although he saw it he did not consent or allow it to become attached to him in realization. If the slow centre had any activity now it brooded on its identity while the thought stayed there like an ignored monument in a park. Christopher and Hadley and Martin were separate fragments and the centre was smouldering with a dull resentment that they should have broken away and not be sealed on the centre. The window was filled with a pattern of colour but in this curious state the centre did not think of the pattern as exterior. It was the only visible thing in a dark room, like a lighted picture on the wall. Below it was the sensation of water trickling and discomfort of a hard surface. The centre for a time was sufficient. The centre knew self existed, though Christopher and Hadley and Martin were fragments far off.

A curtain of hair and flesh fell over the picture on

171

the wall and there was nothing to be examined but the thought. It became known. The terror that swept in with the thought shocked him into the use of his body. There was a flashing of nerves, tensing of muscles, heaves, blows, vibration; and the thought became words that tumbled out of his mouth.

"I shall never get away from this rock."

The terror did more. It straightened the hinged bones and stood him up, sent him reeling round the Look-out in the pressure of the sky till he was clinging to the Dwarf and the stone head was rocking gently, rocking gently, and the sun was swinging to and fro, up and down in the silver face.

"Get me off this rock!"

The Dwarf nodded its silver head, gently, kindly.

He crouched down by a whitish trench and the pattern of colour was sight again.

Christopher and Hadley and Martin came part way back. He forced the pattern to fit everywhere over the rock and the sea and the sky.

"Know your enemy."

There was illness of the body, effect of exposure. There was food-poisoning that made the world a mad place. There was solitude and hope deferred. There was the thought; there were the other thoughts, unspoken and un-admitted.

"Get them out. Look at them."

Water, the only supply, hung by a hair, held back by the slimy tamping; food that grew daily less; pressure, inde-

172

scribable pressure on the body and the mind; battle with the film-trailers for sleep. There was——

"There was and is——"

He crouched on the rock.

"Take it out and look at it.

"There is a pattern emerging. I do not know what the pattern is but even my dim guess at it makes my reason falter."

The lower half of his face moved round the mouth till the teeth were bare.

"Weapons. I have things that I can use."

Intelligence. Will like a last ditch. Will like a monolith. Survival. Education, a key to all patterns, itself able to impose them, to create. Consciousness in a world asleep. The dark, invulnerable centre that was certain of its own sufficiency.

He began to speak against the flat air, the blotting-paper.

"Sanity is the ability to appreciate reality. What is the reality of my position? I am alone on a rock in the middle of the Atlantic. There are vast distances of swinging water round me. But the rock is solid. It goes down and joins the floor of the sea and that is joined to the floors I have known, to the coasts and cities. I must remember that the rock is solid and immovable. If the rock were to move then I should be mad."

A flying lizard flapped overhead, and dropped down out of sight.

173

"I must hang on. First to my life and then to my sanity. I must take steps."

He dropped the curtains over the window again.

"I am poisoned. I am in servitude to a coiled tube the length of a cricket pitch. All the terrors of hell can come down to nothing more than a stoppage. Why drag in good and evil when the serpent lies coiled in my own body?"

And he pictured his bowels deliberately, the slow, choked peristaltic movement, change of the soft food to a plug of poison.

"I am Atlas. I am Prometheus."

He felt himself loom, gigantic on the rock. His jaws clenched, his chin sank. He became a hero for whom the impossible was an achievement. He knelt and crawled remorselessly down the rock. He found the lifebelt in the crevice, took his knife and sawed the metal tit away from the tube. He crawled on down towards the Red Lion and now there was background music, snatches of Tchaikovsky, Wagner, Holst. It was not really necessary to crawl but the background music underlined the heroism of a slow, undefeated advance against odds. The empty mussel shells cracked under his bones like potsherds. The music swelled and was torn apart by brass.

He came to the pool on the rock with the one weedy limpet and three prudish anemones. The tiny fish still lay in the water but on a different part of the rock. He pushed the lifebelt under the surface of the water so that the fish flicked desperately from side to side. A string of bubbles

174

came out of the tube. He collapsed the long bladder and then began to pull it open again. Little spits of water entered the tit and worked down between more bubbles. Strings only, now, deep. He lifted the whole lifebelt out and hefted the bag. There was a washing sound from the bladder. He sank it in the pool again and went on working. The strings were working too, and woodwind was added and a note or two of brass. Presently, and soon there would come the suspended chord that would stand the whole orchestra aside for the cadenza. The weedy top of the limpet was above the surface. The tiny fish, tricked by this unnatural ebb was lying on wet rock in the sun and trying to wriggle against the surface tension. The anemones had shut their mouths even tighter. The bladder of the lifebelt was two-thirds full.

He hutched himself back against a rock with his legs sprawled apart. The music rose, the sea played and the sun. The universe held its breath. Grunting and groaning he began to work the rubber tube into his backside. He folded the two halves of the long bladder together and sat on it. He began to work at the bladder with both hands, squeezing and massaging. He felt the cold trickle of the sea water in his bowels. He pumped and squeezed until the bladder was squashily flat. He extracted the tube and crept carefully to the edge of the rock while the orchestra thundered to a pause.

And the cadenza was coming—did come. It performed with explosive and triumphant completeness of technique

175

into the sea. It was like the bursting of a dam, the smashing of all hindrance. Spasm after spasm with massive chords and sparkling arpeggios, the cadenza took of his strength till he lay straining and empty on the rock and the orchestra had gone.

He turned his face on the rock and grunted at the antagonist.

"Are you beaten yet? I'm not."

The hand of the sky fell on him. He got up and knelt among the mussel shells.

"Now I shall be sane and no longer such a slave to my body."

He looked down at the dead fish. He pushed the body with his finger to the mouth of an anemone. Petals emerged and tried to take hold.

"Stings. Poison. Anemones poisoned me. Perhaps mussels are all right after all."

He felt a little stronger and no longer so heroic that he need crawl. He went slowly back to the Look-out.

"Everything is predictable. I knew I shouldn't drown and I didn't. There was a rock. I knew I could live on it and I have. I have defeated the serpent in my body. I knew I should suffer and I have. But I am winning. There is a certain sense in which life begins anew now, for all the blotting-paper and the pressure."

He sat down by the Dwarf and drew up his knees. His sight was right on the outside and he lived in the world.

"I believe I'm hungry."

And why not, when life begins again?

"Food on a plate. Rich food in comfort. Food in shops, butchers' shops, food, not swimming, shutting like a fist and vanishing into a crevice but dead on a slab, heaped up, all the sea's harvest——"

He examined the sea. The tide was running and glossy streaks were tailing away from the three rocks.

"Optical illusion."

For of course the rock was fixed. If it seemed to move slowly forward in the tide that was because the eye had nothing else as a point of reference. But over the horizon was a coast and that remained at a constant distance while the water flowed. He smiled grimly.

"That wasn't a bad trick. It might have caught most people."

Like the train that seems to move backwards when the other one steams away from beside it. Like hatched lines with one across.

"For of course the rock is still and the water moves. Let me work it out. The tide is a great wave that sweeps round the world—or rather the world turns inside the tide, so I and the rock are——"

Hastily he looked down at the rock between his feet.

"So the rock is still."

Food. Heaped on a slab, not swimming free but piled up, all the spoils of the sea, a lobster, not shutting like a fist and shooting back into a crevice but——

He was on his feet. He was glaring down at the place

177

where the weed grew under water by the three rocks. He cried out.

"Whoever saw a lobster like that swimming in the sea? A red lobster?"

Something was taken away. For an instant he felt himself falling; and then there came a gap of darkness in which there was no one.

Something was coming up to the surface. It was uncertain of its identity because it had forgotten its name. It was disorganized in pieces. It struggled to get these pieces together because then it would know what it was. There was a rhythmical noise and disconnection. The pieces came shakily together and he was lying sideways on the rock and a snoring noise was coming from his mouth. There was a feeling of deep sickness further down the tunnel. There was a separation between now, whenever now was, and the instant of terror. The separation enabled him to forget what had caused that terror. The darkness of separation was deeper than that of sleep. It was deeper than any living darkness because time had stopped or come to an end. It was a gap of not-being, a well opening out of the world and now the effort of mere being was so exhausting that he could only lie sideways and live.

Presently he thought.

"Then I was dead. That was death. I have been frightened to death. Now the pieces of me have come together and I am just alive."

178

The view was different too. The three rocks were nearer and there were sharp things—mussel shells, he thought, brilliantly—cutting his cheek.

"Who carried me down here?"

There came a little pain with the words which he traced to his tongue. The tip was swollen, and aching, and there was salt in his mouth. He could see a pair of empty trousers lying near him and curious marks on the rock. These marks were white and parallel. There was blood in them and traces of froth.

He attended to the rest of his body. He identified a hard, bar-like object as his right arm, twisted back. That led him to the pain in the joints. He eased over so that his arm was free and gazed at the hand on the end.

Now he saw that he was not wearing his pants because they were out there in his right hand. They were torn and there was blood on them.

"I've been in a fight."

He lay, considering things dully.

"There is someone else on the rock with me. He crept out and slugged me."

The face twisted.

"Don't be a fool. You're all alone. You've had a fit."

He felt for his left hand and found it with a grunt of pain. The fingers were bitten.

"How long was I? Is it today or yesterday?"

He heaved himself up on hands and knees.

"Just when I was myself again and victorious, there

179

came a sort of something. A Terror. There was a pattern emerging from circumstances."

Then the gap of not-being.

"This side of the gap is different from the other. It's like when you've finished a lights rehearsal and they cut. Then where there was bright, solid scenery is now only painted stuff, grey under the pilot light. It's like chess. You've got an exultant attack moving but overlooked a check and now the game is a fight. And you're tied down."

Bright rock and sea, hope, though deferred, heroics. Then in the moment of achievement, the knowledge, the terror like a hand falling.

"It was something I remembered. I'd better not remember it again. Remember to forget. Madness?"

Worse than madness. Sanity.

He heaved himself on his hands and knees and laboured to trace his fit, by the scattered clothing and the marks on the rock, back to where he had begun. He stopped by the Dwarf, looking down at rock with a pattern scratched on it—a pattern now crossed by the gritted mark of teeth.

"That was to be expected. Everything is to be expected. The world runs true to form. Remember that."

He looked thoughtfully down at the streaks that the rock was leaving behind in the sea.

"I must not look at the sea. Or must I? Is it better to be sane or mad? It is better to be sane. I did not see what I thought I saw. I remembered wrongly."

Then he had an important idea. It set him at once

180

searching the rock, not in a casual way but inch by inch. Only after an eternity of searching, of cracks and bumps and roughnesses did he remember that he was foolish to search for a piece of wood to touch because there was none.

His pants were still trailing from his hand and he had a sudden thought that he could put them on. When he had done this his head cleared of all the mists except the pain. He put his hand up to the pain and found that there was a lump under the hair and the hair was stuck with blood. He examined his legs. The white blotches were smaller and no longer important. He remembered a custom and clambered into the water-hole. When he was in there he noticed a sudden, bright light in the opening over the far end and some deep seat of rationality drove him back to the Look-out; and he knew what the light and the noise that had come after it portended.

The sun was still shining but there was a change over a part of the horizon. He knelt to look at this change and it was divided again by a vertical jab of light. This light left a token in each eye that made seeing a divided business. He peered round the green streak that the light left and saw that the darkness made a definite line on the surface of the sea. It was coming nearer. Instantly he was in his body and knew where he was.

"Rain!"

Of course.

"I said there would be rain!"

181

Let there be rain and there was rain.

He scrambled down the High Street, got his sou'wester and arranged it in the lay-back under the end of the Claudian. He pulled off what clothes he was wearing and thrust them into the crevice. He was aware of bright lights and noise. He put his oilskin in a trench and ducked the body into a basin. He went almost upright to the Look-out and heard the hiss of the rain as the edge of the curtain fell on the Safety Rock. It hit him in the face sprang in foot-high leaps from the Dwarf and the surface of the look-out. He glistened and streamed from head to foot in a second.

There was a merciless flash-bang from the curtain and then he was stumbling down to the crevice and burrowing in head first while the thunder trampled overhead. Even in the depth of the crevice he saw a livid light that hurt his ears; and then there was the cessation of all noises but a high, singing note. This was so intimate to the head that it took the place of the thunder. His feet were being bastinadoed. His mouth said things but he could not hear them so did not know what they were. There was water running in the crevice, under his face, dripping from the rock, water running round his loins, water. He made his body back out of the crevice and was under a waterfall. He stumbled into a trench and found his sou'wester full and spilling. There was a tap of water running from the end of the Claudian and he took up the heavy sou'wester and poured water into his mouth. He put the sou'wester back and went to his oilskin. There was a bath ready for him but the rain was washing over him like a shower. He went back to the sou'wester, watched it fill and took it to the water-hole. He could hear the running click and trickle under the rock now—water running down, seaping through in unguessed crannies, falling with a multitudinous chattering into the hollow. Already the stretch of red clay was narrower.

"I said it would rain, and it has."

He waited, shivering in the chilly cave, waited for the satisfaction that ought to come with the fulfilled prediction. But it would not come.

He crouched there, no longer listening to the water but frowning down at his shadow.

"What piece have I lost in my game? I had an attack, I was doing well, and then——" And then, the gap of dark, dividing that brighter time from this. On the other side of the gap was something that had happened. It was something that must not be remembered; but how could you control if you deliberately forgot? It was something about a pattern that was emerging.

"Inimical."

He considered the word that his mouth had spoken. The word sounded harmless unless the implications were attached. To avoid that, he deliberately bent the process of thought and made his mouth do as he bid.

"How can a rock be inimical?"

He crawled away quickly into a rain that fell more

lightly. The storm had hurried away over the three rocks and dulled the motion of the water. The clouds had dulled everything. They had left a grey, drizzly sea over which the air moved, pushed at the rock in a perceptible wind.

"That was a subsidiary thunder-storm on the edge of a cyclone. Cyclones revolve anti-clockwise in the northern hemisphere. The wind is southerly. Therefore we are on the eastern edge of a cyclone that is moving east. Since I can foretell the weather I can be armed against it. The problem will be now to cope with too much water, not too little."

He paid only half-attention to his mouth. It lectured on reassuring nothing but itself. But the centre of the globe was moving and flinching from isolated outcrops of knowledge. It averted attention from one only to discover another. It attempted to obliterate each separate outcrop when it found that they could not be ignored.

"The whole problem of insanity is so complex that a satisfactory definition, a norm, has never been established."

Far out from the centre, the mouth quacked on.

"Where, for example, shall we draw the line between the man whom we consider to be moody or excitable, and the genuine psychopathic manic-depressive?"

The centre was thinking, with an eye lifted for the return of the storm of terror, about how difficult it was to distinguish between sleeping and waking when all one experienced was a series of trailers.

"A recurrent dream, a neurosis? But surely the normal child in its cot goes through all the symptoms of the neurotic?"

If one went step by step—ignoring the gap of dark and the terror on the lip—back from the rock, through the Navy, the stage, the writing, the university, the school, back to bed under the silent eaves, one went down to the cellar. And the path led back from the cellar to the rock.

"The solution lies in intelligence. That is what distinguishes us from the helpless animals that are caught in their patterns of behaviour, both mental and physical."

But the dark centre was examining a thought like a monument that had replaced the other in the dreary park.

Guano is insoluble.

If guano is insoluble, then the water in the upper trench could not be a slimy wetness, the touch of which made a flaming needle nag at the corner of an eye.

His tongue felt along the barrier of his teeth—round to the side where the big ones were and the gap. He brought his hands together and held his breath. He stared at the sea and saw nothing. His tongue was remembering. It pried into the gap between the teeth and re-created the old, aching shape. It touched the rough edge of the cliff, traced the slope down, trench after aching trench, down towards the smooth surface where the Red Lion was, just above the gum—understood what was so hauntingly familiar and painful about an isolated and decaying rock in the middle of the sea.

185

12

Now there was nothing to do but protect normality. There was the centre wielding the exterior body as by strings. He made the body go down from the Look-out to the crevice. He found damp clothes and put them on until he could see extensions of clothing and seaboot stockings like piles of waste. The body and the clothing were ungainly as a diving dress. He went to Food Cliff and gathered mussels, made his mouth receive them. He did not look outwards but down where the water danced alongside the rock. The sea was ruffled and there were wavelets each carrying smaller wavelets on its back so that the depth was obscured and the water grave and chilly. As his jaws worked he sat still with two lobsters lying on the rock beside him. The meal went on under pricking rain, a stirring of wind and scuds of dimples across the surface of the water. He took morsels of food with one lobster and brought them to his face. The lobsters wore armour to protect them from the enormous pressure of the sky.

Between mouthfuls his voice quacked, veering in towards reason and truth and then skating away.

"I have no armour and that is why I am being squeezed thin. It has marred my profile too. My mouth sticks out such a long way and I have two noses."

But the centre thought of other things.

"I must be careful when I look round at the wind. I don't want to die again."

Meanwhile there were many mussels and one could make the mouth perform and obliterate the other possibilities.

"I was always two things, mind and body. Nothing has altered. Only I did not realize it before so clearly."

The centre thought of the next move. The world could be held together by rivets driven in. Flesh could be mended by the claws of ants as in Africa. The will could resist.

And then there were no more mussels within reach. He made the lobster mime eating but the sensations in the mouth were not the same.

"Have to do it."

He turned himself on all fours. He held his breath and looked up and there was the old woman from the corner of the cellar standing on the skyline.

"She is the Dwarf. I gave her a silver head."

Wind pushed in his face and a touch of rain. The old woman nodded with her face of dulled silver.

"It is lucky I put a silver mask over the other face. She is the Dwarf. That is not the next move."

He worked his way back towards the Look-out, carried his body near the Dwarf and made it kneel down. Above

187

him the Dwarf nodded gently with a face of dulled silver.

There was something in the topmost trench that was different. Immediately he flinched back and looked warily. The white stuff in the bottom was broken up and scattered because a chunk of rockleaf had fallen from the side of the trench. He crept forward and examined the chunk. On one edge the leaves were worn and ancient but on the other three they were white as muck and freshly broken. The chunk was about a yard each way and six inches thick. It was a considerable book and there was a strange engraving in the white cover. For a while his eye liked the engraving because it made a pattern and was not words, which would have killed him immediately. His eye followed the indented and gouged lines again and again as his mouth had eaten mussels. By the edge of the book was the recess from which it had come.

There was an engraving in the recess too. It was like a tree upside down and growing down from the old edge where the leaves were weathered by wind and rain. The trunk was a deep, perpendicular groove with flaky edges. Lower down, the trunk divided into three branches and these again into a complication of twigs like the ramifications of bookworm. The trunk and the branches and the twigs were terrible black. Round the twigs was an apple blossom of grey and silver stain. As he watched, drops of water dulled the stain and lay in the branches like tasteless fruit.

His mouth quacked.

188

"Lightning!"

But the dark centre was shrunk and dreadful and knowing. The knowing was so dreadful that the centre made the mouth work deliberately.

"Black lightning."

There was still a part that could be played—there was the Bedlamite, Poor Tom, protected from knowledge of the sign of the black lightning.

He grabbed the old woman with her nodding silver head.

"Help me, my sweet, I must have your help!"

The mouth took over.

"If you let him go on doing that, my sweet, he'll knock the whole bloody rock apart and we shall be left swimming."

Swimming in what?

The mouth went frantic.

"There was that rock round by Prospect Cliff, my sweet, that one moved, the water moved it. I wouldn't ask anyone but you because the rock is fixed and if he'll only let it alone it'll last for ever. After all, my sweet, you're his wife."

Out of bed on the carpet with no shoes. Creep through the dark room not because you want to but because you've got to. Pass the door. The landing, huge, the grandfather clock. No safety behind me. Round the corner now to the stairs. Down, pad. Down, pad. The hall, but grown. Darkness sitting in every corner. The banisters high up, can

189

just reach them with my hand. Not for sliding down now. Different banisters, everything different, a pattern emerging, forced to go down to meet the thing I turned my back on. Tick, tock, shadows pressing. Past the kitchen door. Draw back the bolt of the vault. Well of darkness. Down pad, down. Coffin ends crushed in the wall. Under the churchyard back through the death door to meet the master. Down, pad, down. Black lumps piled, smell damp. Shavings from coffins.

"A man must be mad when he sees a red lobster swimming in the sea. And guano is insoluble. A madman would see the gulls as flying lizards, he would connect the two things out of a book and it would come back to him when his brain turned no matter how long ago and forgotten the time when he read that—wouldn't he, my sweet? Say he would! Say he would!"

The silver face nodded on gently and the rain spattered.

Kindling from coffins, coal dust, black as black lightning. Block with the axe by it, not worn for firewood but by executions.

"Seals aren't inimical and a madman wouldn't sleep properly. He would feel the rock was too hard, too real; he would superimpose a reality, especially if he had too much imagination. He would be capable of seeing the engraving as a split into the whole nature of things—wouldn't he?"

And then fettered in the darkness by the feet, trying to lift one and finding a glue, finding a weakness where there should be strength now needed because by nature there

190

was nothing to do but scream and try to escape. Darkness in the corner doubly dark, thing looming, feet tied, near, an unknown looming, an opening darkness, the heart and being of all imaginable terror. Pattern repeated from the beginning of time, approach of the unknown thing, a dark centre that turned its back on the thing that created it and struggled to escape.

"Wouldn't he? Say he would!"

There was a noise by his left arm and water scattered across the Look-out. He made the exterior face turn into the wind and the air pushed against the cheeks. The water on the Dwarf now was not rain but spray. He crept to the edge of the cliff and looked down the funnel. The water was white round Safety Rock and as he looked a dull sound in the funnel was followed by a plume of spray.

"This weather has been investigated before but from a lower level. He climbed there and the limpets held on."

There was a gathering rhythm in the sea. The Safety Rock tripped the waves and shot them at the cleft below the funnel. Nine times out of ten these waves would meet a reflection coming back and spurt up a line of spray like a fuse burning—a fast fuse that whipped over the water. But the tenth time the wave would find the way clear because the ninth wave had been a very small one. So the tenth wave would come wheeling in, the cleft would squeeze the water so that it speeded up and hit the back of the angle—bung! and a feather of spray would flicker in the funnel. If the tenth wave was big the feather would

191

become a plume and the wind would catch a handful from the top and sling shot across the Dwarf to go scattering down the High Street.

To watch the waves was like eating mussels. The sea was a point of an attention that could be prolonged even more than eating. The centre concentrated and left the mouth to itself.

"Of course a storm has to come after a time. That was to be expected. And who could invent all that complication of water, running true to form, obeying the laws of nature to the last drop? And of course a human brain must turn in time and the universe be muddled. But beyond the muddle there will still be actuality and a poor mad creature clinging to a rock in the middle of the sea."

There is no centre of sanity in madness. Nothing like this "I" sitting in here, staving off the time that must come. The last repeat of the pattern. Then the black lightning.

The centre cried out.

"I'm so alone! Christ! I'm so alone!"

Black. A familiar feeling, a heaviness round the heart, a reservoir which any moment might flood the eyes now and for so long, strangers to weeping. Black, like the winter evening through which the centre made its body walk—a young body. The window was diversified only by a perspective of lighted lamps on the top of the street lamp-posts. The centre was thinking—I am alone; so alone! The reservoir overflowed, the lights all the way

192

along to Carfax under Big Tom broke up, put out rainbow wings. The centre felt the gulping of its throat, sent eyesight on ahead to cling desperately to the next light and then the next—anything to fasten the attention away from the interior blackness.

Because of what I did I am an outsider and alone.

The centre endured a progress through an alley, across another road, a quadrangle, climbed bare wooden stairs. It sat by a fire and all the bells of Oxford tolled for the reservoir that overflowed and the sea roared in the room.

The centre twisted the unmanliness out of its face but the ungovernable water ran and dripped down the cheeks.

"I am so alone. I am *so* alone!"

Slowly, the water dried. Time stretched out, like the passage of time on a rock in the middle of the sea.

The centre formulated a thought.

Now there is no hope. There is nothing. If they would only look at me, or speak—if I could only be a part of something——

Time stretched on, indifferently.

There was the sound of feet on the stairs, two stories down. The centre waited without hope, to hear which room they would visit. But they came on, they climbed, were louder, almost as loud as the heart-beats so that when they stopped outside the door he was standing up and his hands were by his chest. The door opened a few inches and a shock of black curls poked round by the very top.

193

"Nathaniel!"

Nathaniel bowed and beamed his way into the room and stood looking down at the window.

"I thought I might catch you. I'm back for the week-end." Then as an afterthought: "Can I come in?"

"My dear man!"

Nathaniel operated on his great-coat, peered round solemnly as though the question of where to put it was a major one.

"Here. Let me take that for you—sit down—I'm—my dear man!"

Nathaniel was grinning too.

"It's good to see you, Christopher."

"And you can stay? You don't have to rush away?"

"I've come up to give a lecture to the——"

"But not this evening?"

"No. I can stay this evening."

The centre sat opposite, right on the outside of its window—right out in the world.

"We'll talk. Let's talk, Nat."

"How's the social whirl?"

"How's London?"

"Doesn't like lectures on heaven."

"Heaven?"

Then the body was laughing, louder and louder and the water was flowing again. Nat was grinning and blushing too.

"I know. But you don't have to make it worse."

194

He smeared away the water and hiccupped.

"Why heaven?"

"The sort of heaven we invented for ourselves after death, if we aren't ready for the real one."

"You would—you curious creature!"

Nathaniel became serious. He peered upwards, raised an index finger and consulted a reference book beyond the ceiling.

"Take us as we are now and heaven would be sheer negation. Without form and void. You see? A sort of black lightning, destroying everything that we call life——"

The laughter came back.

"I don't see and I don't much care but I'll come to your lecture. My dear Nat—you've no idea how glad I am to see you!"

The burning fuse whipped through Nathaniel's face and he was gone. The centre remained looking down into the funnel. His mouth was open in astonishment and terror.

"And I liked him as much as that!"

Black and feeling one's way to the smooth steel ladder that glinted only faintly in the cloud light. The centre tried to resist, like a child trying to resist a descent into the midnight cellar but its legs bore it on. Up and up, from the waist to the level of the fo'c'sle, up past B gun. Shall I meet him? Will he stand there tonight?

195

And there, sketched against the clouds in Indian ink, random in limb and gesture, an old binder by a rick, was Nathaniel, swaying and grabbing at a midnight salute. Wotcher, Nat, rose in his throat and he swallowed it. Pretend not to see. Be as little connected as possible. Fire a fuse from the bridge that will blow him away from her body and clear the way for me. We are all past the first course, we have eaten the fish.

And it may not work. He may not bother to lay aft and pray to his aeons. Good-bye, Nat, I loved you and it is not in my nature to love much. But what can the last maggot but one do? Lose his identity?

Nathaniel stood swaying and spread-eagled in the dark, understanding obediently that he had not been seen. Instead he stood away from the officer's approach and fumbled on down the ladder.

Everything set, the time, the place, the loved one.

"You're early for once, thank God. Course o-four-five, speed twenty-eight knots. Nothing in sight and we press on for another hour."

"Anything new?"

"Same as was. We're thirty miles north of the convoy, all on our own, going to send off the signal in an hour's time. The old man'll be up for that. There you are. No zigzag. Dead easy. Oh—the moon'll be up in ten minutes' time and we'd make quite a target if we tripped over a U-boat. Pass it on. Nighty night."

"Sweet dreams."

He heard the steps descending. He crossed to the starboard side of the bridge and looked aft. There was engine-noise, outline of the funnel. The wake spread out dull white astern and a secondary wave fanned out from midships. The starboard side of the quarter-deck was just visible in outline but the surface was dark by contrast and all the complications of the throwers, the depth-charges, the sweeps and lifted gun made it very difficult to see whether there was a figure leaning on the rail among them. He stared down and wondered whether he saw or created in his mind, the mantis shape with forelegs lifted to the face.

It is not Nathaniel leaning there, it is Mary.

I must. I must. Don't you understand, you bloody bitch?

"Messenger!"

"Sir."

"Get me a cup of cocoa."

"Aye aye, sir!"

"And messenger—never mind."

Feet descending the ladder. Darkness and the wind of speed. Glow over to starboard like a distant fire from a raided city. Moonrise.

"Port look-out!"

"Sir?"

"Nip down to the wheel-house and get me the other pair of night-glasses. I think these need overhauling. You'll find them in the rack over the chart table."

197

"Aye aye, sir!"

"I'll take over your sector while you're gone."

"Aye aye, sir!"

Feet descending the ladder.

Now.

Ham it a bit. Casual saunter to the port side. Pause.

Now. Now. Now.

Scramble to the binnacle, fling yourself at the voice pipe, voice urgent, high, sharp, frightened——

"Hard a-starboard for Christ's sake!"

A destroying concussion that had no part in the play. Whiteness rising like a cloud, universe spinning. The shock of a fall somewhere, shattering, mouth filled—and he was fighting in all directions with black impervious water.

His mouth screamed in rage at the whiteness that rose out of the funnel.

"And it was the right bloody order!"

Eaten.

He was no longer able to look at the waves, for every few minutes they were hidden by the rising whiteness. He made his sight creep out and look at his clothed body. The clothes were wringing wet and the seaboot stockings smeared like mops. His mouth said something mechanical.

"I wish I hadn't kicked off my seaboots when I was in the water."

198

The centre told itself to pretend and keep on pretending.

The mouth had its own wisdom.

"There is always madness, a refuge like a crevice in the rock. A man who has no more defence can always creep into madness like one of those armoured things that scuttle among weed down where the mussels are."

Find something to look at.

"Madness would account for everything, wouldn't it, my sweet?"

Do, if not look.

He got up and staggered in the wind with the rain and spray pelting him. He went down the High Street and there was his oilskin made into a basin and full of water. He took his sou'wester and began to bail out the oilskin and take the water to the water-hole. He concentrated on the laws of water, how it fell or lay, how predictable it was and manageable. Every now and then the rock shook, a white cloud rose past the Look-out and there were rivulets of foam in the upper trenches. When he had emptied his oilskin he held it up, drained it and put it on. Fooling with buttons the centre could turn away from what was to come. While he did this he was facing the Claudian where the foam now hung in gobs and the oilskin thrust him against the cut. As he stood pinned, he was struck a blow in the back and bucketfuls of water fell in the trench. It washed round then settled scummily in the bottom. He felt his way along the Claudian to the crevice and backed

199

himself in. He put on his sou'wester and laid his forehead on his arms. The world turned black and came to him through sound.

"If a madman heard it he would think it was thunder and of course it would be. There is no need to listen like that. It will only be thunder over the horizon where the ships are passing to and fro. Listen to the storm instead. It is going to flail on this rock. It is going to beat a poor wretch into madness. He does not want to go mad only he will have to. Think of it! All you people in warm beds, a British sailor isolated on a rock and going mad not because he wants to but because the sea is a terror—the worst terror there is, the worst imaginable."

The centre co-operated but with an ear cocked. It concentrated now on the words that spilt out of the mouth because with the fringes of flesh and hair lowered over the window the words could be examined as the thoughts had been. It provided background music.

"Oh help, help! I am dying of exposure. I am starving, dying of thirst. I lie like driftwood caught in a cleft. I have done my duty for you and this is my reward. If you could only see me you would be wrung with pity. I was young and strong and handsome with an eagle profile and wavy hair; I was brilliantly clever and I went out to fight your enemies. I endured in the water, I fought the whole sea. I have fought a rock, and gulls and lobsters and seals and a storm. Now I am thin and weak. My joints are like knobs and my limbs like sticks. My face is fallen in with age and my hair is white with salt and suffering. My eyes are dull stones——"

The centre quivered and dwindled. There was another noise beyond the storm and background music and sobbed words from the mouth.

"—my chest is like the ribs of a derelict boat and every breath is an effort——"

The noise was so faint in comparison with the uproar of the wind and rain and waves that it caught and glued attention. The mouth knew this too and tried harder.

"I am going mad. There is lightning playing on the skirts of a wild sea. I am strong again——"

And the mouth sang.

The centre still attended through the singing, the background music, the uproar from outside. The noise came again. The centre could confuse it for a while with thunder.

"Hoé, hoé! Thor's lightning challenges me! Flash after flash, rippling spurts of white fire, bolts flung at Prometheus, blinding white, white, white, searing, the aim of the sky at the man on the rock——"

The noise, if one attended as the centre was forced to attend was dull and distant. It might have been thunder or gun-fire. It might have been the sound of a drum and the mouth seized on that.

"Rata tat tat tat! The soldiers come, my Emperor is taken! Rat a tat!"

It might have been the shifting of furniture in an upper room and the mouth panicked after that thought with the automatic flick of an insect.

"Put it down here. Roll back that corner of the carpet and then you can get the table out. Shall we have it next to the radiogram? Take that record off and put on something rocklike and heroic——"

It might have been flour-sacks slid down an iron ladder to resound on the steel deck.

"Hard a-starboard! Hard a-starboard!"

It might have been the shaking of the copper sheet in the wings.

"I must have the lead or I shall leave the coal flat——"

The cellar door swinging to behind a small child who must go down, down in his sleep to meet the thing he turned from when he was created.

"Off with his head! Down on the block among the kindling and coal-dust!"

But the centre knew. It recognized with a certainity that made the quacking of the mouth no more help than hiccups. The noise was the grating and thump of a spade against an enormous tin box that had been buried.

13

"Mad," said the mouth, "raving mad. I can account for everything, lobsters, maggots, hardness, brilliant reality, the laws of nature, film-trailers, snapshots of sight and sound, flying lizards, enmity—how should a man not be mad? I will tell you what a man is. He goes on four legs till Necessity bends the front end upright and makes a hybrid of him. The finger-prints of those hands are about his spine and just above the rump for proof if you want it. He is a freak, an ejected foetus robbed of his natural development, thrown out in the world with a naked covering of parchment, with too little room for his teeth and a soft bulging skull like a bubble. But nature stirs a pudding there and sets a thunderstorm flickering inside the hardening globe, white, lambent lightning a constant flash and tremble. All your lobsters and film-trailers are nothing but the random intersections of instant bushes of lightning. The sane life of your belly and your cock are on a simple circuit, but how can the stirred pudding keep constant? Tugged at by the pill of the earth, infected by the white stroke that engraved the book, furrowed, lines

203

burned through it by hardship and torment and terror-unbalanced, brain-sick, at your last gasp on a rock in the sea, the pudding has boiled over and you are no worse than raving mad."

Sensations. Coffee. Hock. Gin. Wood. Velvet. Nylon. Mouth. Warm, wet nakedness. Caves, slack like a crevice or tight like the mouth of a red anemone. Full of stings. Domination, identity.

"You are the intersections of all the currents. You do not exist apart from me. If I have gone mad then you have gone mad. You are speaking, in there, you and I are one and mad."

The rock shook and shook again. A sudden coldness struck his face and washed under him.

To be expected.

"Nathaniel!"

Black centre, trying to stir itself like a pudding.

The darkness was shredded by white. He tumbled over among the sensations of the crevice. There was water everywhere and noise and his mouth welcomed both. It spat and coughed. He heaved himself out amid water that swirled to his knees and the wind knocked him down. The trench was like a little sea, like the known and now re-membered extravagances of a returning tide among rocks. What had been a dry trench was half-full of moving water on which streaks of foam were circling and interlacing. The wind was like an express in a tunnel and every-where there was a trickling and washing and pouring.

He scrambled up in the trench, without hearing what his mouth said and suddenly he and his mouth were one.

"You bloody great bully!"

He got his face above the level of the wall and the wind pulled the cheeks in like an airman's. Bird-shot slashed. Then the sky above the old woman jumped. It went white. An instant later the light was switched off and the sky fell on him. He collapsed under the enormous pressure and went down in the water of the trench. The weight withdrew and left him struggling. He got up and the sky fell on him again. This time he was able to lurch along the trench because the weight of water was just not sufficient to break him and the sea in the trench was no higher than his knees. The world came back, storm-grey and torn with flying streamers, and he gave it storm-music, crash of timpany, brass blared and a dazzle of strings. He fought a hero's way from trench to trench through water and music, his clothes shaking and plucked, tattered like the end of a windsock, hands clawing. He and his mouth shouted through the uproar.

"Ajax! Prometheus!"

The old woman was looking down at him as he struggled through bouts of white and dark. Then her head with its silver mask was taken by a whiteness and she hunched against the sky with her headless shoulders. He fell in the white trench over the book with his face against the engraving and the insoluble muck filled his mouth. There came a sudden pressure and silence. He was lif-

205

ted up and thrown down again, struck against rock. For a moment as the water passed away he saw the Look-out against the sky now empty of the old woman but changed in outline by scattered stones.

"She is loose on the rock. Now she is out of the cellar and in daylight. Hunt her down!"

And the knife was there among all the other sensations, jammed against his ribs. He got it in his hands and pulled the blade open. He began to crawl and hunt and swim from trench to trench. She was leaning over the rail but vanished and he stole after her into the green room. But she was out by the footlights and when he crouched in the wings he saw that he was not dressed properly for the part. His mouth and he were one.

"Change your clothes! Be a naked madman on a rock in the middle of a storm!"

His claws plucked at the tatters and pulled them away. He saw a glimpse of gold braid and an empty seaboot stocking floating away like a handful of waste. He saw a leg, scarred, scaly and stick thin and the music mourned for it.

He remembered the old woman and crawled after her down the High Street to the Red Lion. The back wash of the waves was making a welcome confusion round the three rocks and the confusion hid the place where the red lobster had been. He shouted at the rocks but the old woman would not appear among them. She had slipped away down to the cellar. Then he glimpsed her lying huddled in the crevice

206

and he struggled up to her. He fell on her and began to slash with his knife while his mouth went on shouting.

"That'll teach you to chase me! That'll teach you to chase me out of the cellar through cars and beds and pubs, you at the back and me running, running after my identity disc all the days of my life! Bleed and die."

But he and his voice were one. They knew the blood was sea water and the cold, crumpling flesh that was ripped and torn nothing but oilskin.

Now the voice became a babble, sang, swore, made meaningless syllables, coughed and spat. It filled every tick of time with noise, jammed the sound so that it choked; but the centre began to know itself as other because every instant was not occupied by noise. The mouth spat and deviated into part sense.

"And last of all, hallucination, vision, dream, delusion will haunt you. What else can a madman expect? They will appear to you on the solid rock, the real rock, they will fetter your attention to them and you will be nothing worse than mad."

And immediately the hallucination was there. He knew this before he saw it because there was an awe in the trench, framed by the silent spray that flew over. The hallucination sat on the rock at the end of the trench and at last he faced it through his blurred window. He saw the rest of the trench and crawled along through water that was gravely still unless a gust struck down with a long twitch and shudder of the foamy scum. When he was near,

207

he looked up from the boots, past the knees, to the face and engaged himself to the mouth.

"You are a projection of my mind. But you are a point of attention for me. Stay there."

The lips hardly moved in answer.

"You are a projection of my mind."

He made a snorting sound.

"Infinite regression or better still, round and round the mulberry bush. We could go on like that for ever."

"Have you had enough, Christopher?"

He looked at the lips. They were clear as the words. A tiny shred of spittle joined them near the right corner.

"I could never have invented that."

The eye nearest the Look-out was bloodshot at the outer corner. Behind it or beside it a red strip of sunset ran down out of sight behind the rock. The spray still flew over. You could look at the sunset or the eye but you could not do both. You could not look at the eye and the mouth together. He saw the nose was shiny and leathery brown and full of pores. The left cheek would need a shave soon, for he could see the individual bristles. But he could not look at the whole face together. It was a face that perhaps could be remembered later. It did not move. It merely had this quality of refusing overall inspection. One feature at a time.

"Enough of what?"

"Surviving. Hanging on."

The clothing was difficult to pin down too so that he

208

had to examine each piece. There was an oilskin—belted, because the buttons had fetched away. There was a woollen pullover inside it, with a roll-neck. The sou'wester was back a little. The hands were resting one on either knee, above the seaboot stockings. Then there were seaboots, good and shiny and wet and solid. They made the rock behind them seem like cardboard, like a painted flat. He bent forward until his bleared window was just above the right instep. There was no background music now and no wind, nothing but black, shiny rubber.

"I hadn't considered."

"Consider now."

"What's the good? I'm mad."

"Even that crevice will crumble."

He tried to laugh up at the bloodshot eye but heard barking noises. He threw words in the face.

"On the sixth day he created God. Therefore I permit you to use nothing but my own vocabulary. In his own image created he Him."

"Consider now."

He saw the eye and the sunset merge. He brought his arms across his face.

"I won't. I can't."

"What do you believe in?"

Down to the black boot, coal black, darkness of the cellar, but now down to a forced answer.

"The thread of my life."

"At all costs."

209

Repeat after me:

"At all costs."

"So you survived."

"That was luck."

"Inevitability."

"Didn't the others want to live then?"

"There are degrees."

He dropped the curtains of flesh and hair and blotted out the boots. He snarled.

"I have a right to live if I can!"

"Where is that written?"

"Then nothing is written."

"Consider."

He raged on the cardboard rock before the immovable, black feet.

"I will not consider! I have created you and I can create my own heaven."

"You have created it."

He glanced sideways along the twitching water, down at his skeleton legs and knees, felt the rain and spray and the savage cold on his flesh.

He began to mutter.

"I prefer it. You gave me the power to choose and all my life you led me carefully to this suffering because my choice was my own. Oh yes! I understand the pattern. All my life, whatever I had done I should have found myself in the end on that same bridge, at that same time, giving that same order—the right order, the wrong order. Yet, suppose I climbed away from the cellar over the bodies of used and defeated people, broke them to make steps on the road away from you, why should you torture me? If I ate them, who gave me a mouth?"

"There is no answer in your vocabulary."

He squatted back and glared up at the face. He shouted. "I have considered. I prefer it, pain and all."

"To what?"

He began to rage weakly and strike out at the boots.

"To the black lightning! Go back! Go back!"

He was bruising skin off his hands against the streaming rock. His mouth quacked and he went with it into the last crevice of all.

"Poor mad sailor on a rock!"

He clambered up the High Street.

> *Rage, roar, spout!*
> *Let us have wind, rain, hail, gouts of blood,*
> *Storms and tornadoes . . .*

He ran about on the Look-out, stumbling over scattered stones.

> *. . . hurricanes and typhoons . . .*

There was a half-light, a storm-light. The light was ruled in lines and the sea in ridges and valleys. The monstrous waves were making their way from east to west

211

in an interminable procession and the rock was a trifle among them. But it was charging forward, searing a white way through them, careless of sinking, it was thrusting the Safety Rock forward to burst the ridges like the prow of a ship. It would strike a ridge with the stone prow and burst water into a smother that washed over the fo'c'sle and struck beneath the bridge. Then a storm of shot would sweep over the bridge and strike sense and breath away from his body. He flung himself on a square stone that lay where the old woman had stood with her masked head. He rode it astride, facing into the wind and waves. And again there was background music and a mouth quacking.

"Faster! Faster!"

His rock bored on. He beat it with his heels as if he wore spurs.

"Faster!"

The waves were each an event in itself. A wave would come weltering and swinging in with a storm-light running and flickering along the top like the flicker in a brain. The shallow water beyond the safety rock would occur, so that the nearer part of the wave would rise up, tripped and angry, would roar, swell forward. The Safety Rock would become a pock in a whirlpool of water that spun itself into foam and chewed like a mouth. The whole top of the wave for a hundred yards would move forward and fall into acres of lathering uproar that was launched like an army at the rock.

"Faster!"

His hand found the identity disc and held it out.

The mouth screamed out away from the centre.

"I spit on your compassion!"

There was a recognizable noise away beyond the waves and in the clouds. The noise was not as loud as the sea or the music or the voice but the centre understood. The centre took the body off the slab of rock and bundled it into a trench. As it fell the eye glimpsed a black tendril of lightning that lay across the western sky and the centre screwed down the flaps of flesh and hair. Again there came the sound of the spade against the tin box.

"Hard a-starboard! I'll kill us both, I'll hit the tree with that side and you'll be burst and bitched! There was nothing in writing!"

The centre knew what to do. It was wiser than the mouth. It sent the body scrambling over the rock to the water-hole. It burrowed in among the slime and circling scum. It thrust the hands forward, tore at the water and fell flat in the pool. It wriggled like a seal on a rock with the fresh water streaming out of its mouth. It got at the tamping at the farther end and heaved at the stones. There was a scraping and breaking sound and then the cascade of falling stones and water. There was a wide space of storm-light, waves. There was a body lying in the slimy hollow where the fresh water had been.

"Mad! Proof of madness!"

It made the body wriggle back out of the hole, sent it

up to the place where the Look-out had been.

There were branches of the black lightning over the sky, there were noises. One branch ran down into the sea, through the great waves, petered out. It remained there. The sea stopped moving, froze, became paper, painted paper that was torn by a black line. The rock was painted on the same paper. The whole of the painted sea was tilted but nothing ran downhill into the black crack which had opened in it. The crack was utter, was absolute, was three times real.

The centre did not know if it had flung the body down or if it had turned the world over. There was rock before its face and it struck with lobster claws that sank in. It watched the rock between the claws.

The absolute lightning spread. There was no noise now because noise had become irrelevant. There was no music, no sound from the tilted, motionless sea.

The mouth quacked on for a while then dribbled into silence.

There was no mouth.

Still the centre resisted. It made the lightning do its work according to the laws of this heaven. It perceived in some mode of sight without eyes that pieces of the sky between the branches of black lightning were replaced by pits of nothing. This made the fear of the centre, the rage of the centre vomit in a mode that required no mouth. It screamed into the pit of nothing voicelessly, wordlessly.

"I shit on your heaven!"

214

The lines and tendrils felt forward through the sea. A segment of storm dropped out like a dead leaf and there was a gap that joined sea and sky through the horizon. Now the lightning found reptiles floating and flying motionlessly and a tendril ran to each. The reptiles resisted, changing shape a little, then they too, dropped out and were gone. A valley of nothing opened up through Safety Rock.

The centre attended to the rock between its claws. The rock was harder than rock, brighter, firmer. It hurt the serrations of the claws that gripped.

The sea twisted and disappeared. The fragments were not visible going away, they went into themselves, dried up, destroyed, erased like an error.

The lines of absolute blackness felt forward into the rock and it was proved to be as insubstantial as the painted water. Pieces went and there was no more than an island of papery stuff round the claws and everywhere else there was the mode that the centre knew as nothing.

The rock between the claws was solid. It was square and there was an engraving on the surface. The black lines sank in, went through and joined.

The rock between the claws was gone.

There was nothing but the centre and the claws. They were huge and strong and inflamed to red. They closed on each other. They contracted. They were outlined like a night sign against the absolute nothingness and they gripped their whole strength into each other.

The serrations of the claws broke. They were lambent and real and locked.

The lightning crept in. The centre was unaware of anything but the claws and the threat. It focused its awareness on the crumbled serrations and the blazing red. The lightning came forward. Some of the lines pointed to the centre, waiting for the moment when they could pierce it. Others lay against the claws, playing over them, prying for a weakness, wearing them away in a compassion that was timeless and without mercy.

14

The jetty, if the word would do for a long pile of boulders, was almost under the tide at the full. The drifter came in towards it, engine stopped, with the last of her way and the urging of the west wind. There was a wintry sunset behind her so that to the eyes on the beach she seemed soon a black shape from which the colour had all run away and been stirred into the low clouds that hung just above the horizon. There was a leaden tinge to the water except in the path of the drifter—a brighter valley of red and rose and black that led back to the dazzling horizon under the sun.

The watcher on the beach did not move. He stood, his seaboots set in the troughs of dry sand that his last steps had made, and waited. There was a cottage at his back and then the slow slope of the island.

The telegraph rang astern in the drifter and she checked her way with a sudden swirl of brighter water from the screws. A fender groaned against stone. Two men jumped on to the jetty and sought about them for the bollards that were not there. An arm gesticulated from the wheel-house. The men caught their ropes round boulders and stood, holding on.

An officer stepped on to the jetty, came quickly towards the beach and jumped down to the dry sand. The wind ruffled papers that he held in his hand so that they chattered like the dusty leaves of late summer. But here they were the only leaves. There was sand, a cottage, rocks and the sea. The officer laboured along in the dry sand with his papers chattering and came to a halt a yard from the watcher.

"Mr. Campbell?"

"Aye. You'll be from the mainland about the——?"

"That's right."

Mr. Campbell removed his cloth cap and put it back again.

"You've not been over-quick."

The officer looked at him solemnly.

"My name's Davidson, by the way. Over-quick. Do you know, Mr. Campbell, that I do this job, seven days a week?"

Mr. Campbell moved his seaboots suddenly. He peered forward into Davidson's grey and lined face. There was a faint, sweet smell on the breath and the eyes that did not blink were just a fraction too wide open.

Mr. Campbell took off his cap and put it on again.

"Well now. Fancy that!"

The lower part of Davidson's face altered to the beginnings of a grin without humour.

"It's quite a widespread war, you know."

Mr. Campbell nodded slowly.

"I'm sorry that I spoke. A sad harvest for you, Captain. I do not know how you can endure it."

The grin disappeared.

"I wouldn't change."

Mr. Campbell tilted his head sideways and peered into Davidson's face.

"No? I beg your pardon, sir. Come now and see where we found it."

He turned and laboured away along the sand. He stopped and pointed down to where an arm of water was confined by a shingly spit.

"It was there, still held by the lifebelt. You'll see, of course. There was a broken orange-box and a tin. And the lineweed. When we have a nor'wester the lineweed gets caught there—and anything else that's floating."

Davidson looked sideways at him.

"It seems important to you, Mr. Campbell, but what I really want is the identity disc. Did you remove that from the body?"

"No. No. I touched—as little as possible."

"A brown disc about the size of a penny, probably worn round the neck?"

"No. I touched nothing."

Davidson's face set grim again.

"One can always hope, I suppose."

Mr. Campbell clasped his hands, rubbed them restlessly,

cleared his throat.

"You'll take it away tonight?"

Now Davidson peered in his turn.

"Dreams?"

Mr. Campbell looked away at the water. He muttered.

"The wife——"

He glanced up at the too-wide eyes, the face that seemed to know more than it could bear. He no longer evaded the meeting but shrank a little and answered with sudden humility.

"Aye."

Davidson nodded, slowly.

Now two ratings were standing on the beach before the cottage. They bore a stretcher.

Mr. Campbell pointed.

"It is in the lean-to by the house, sir. I hope there is as little to offend you as possible. We used paraffin."

"Thank you."

Davidson toiled back along the beach and Mr. Campbell followed him. Presently they stopped. Davidson turned and looked down.

"Well——"

He put his hand to the breast pocket of his battledress and brought out a flat bottle. He looked Mr. Campbell in the eye, grinned with the lower part of his face, pulled out the cork and swigged, head back. The ratings watched him without comment.

"Here goes, then."

Davidson went to the lean-to, taking a torch from his trouser pocket. He ducked through the broken door and disappeared.

The ratings stood without movement. Mr. Campbell waited, silently, and contemplated the lean-to as though he were seeing it for the first time. He surveyed the mossed stones, the caved-in and lichenous roof as though they were a profound and natural language that men were privileged to read only on a unique occasion.

There was no noise from inside.

Even on the drifter there was no conversation. The only noises were the sounds of the water falling over on the little beach.

Hush. Hush.

The sun was a half-circle in a bed of crimson and slate.

Davidson came out again. He carried a small disc, swinging from a double string. His right hand went to the breast pocket. He nodded to the ratings.

"Go on, then."

Mr. Campbell watched Davidson fumble among his papers. He saw him examining the disc, peering close, transferring details carefully to a file. He saw him put the disc away, crouch, rub his hands backwards and forwards in the dry, clean sand. Mr. Campbell spread his arms wide in a gesture of impotence and dropped them.

"I do not know, sir. I am older than you but I do not know."

Davidson said nothing. He stood up again and took out

221

his bottle.

"Don't you have second sight up here?"

Mr. Campbell looked unhappily at the lean-to.

"Don't joke, sir. That was unworthy of you."

Davidson came down from his swig. Two faces approached each other. Campbell read the face line by line as he had read the lean-to. He flinched from it again and looked away at the place where the sun was going down—seemingly for ever.

The ratings came out of the lean-to. They carried a stretcher between them that was no longer empty.

"All right, lads. There's a tot waiting for you. Carry on."

The two sailors went cautiously away through the sand towards the jetty. Davidson turned to Mr. Campbell.

"I have to thank you, Mr. Campbell, in the name of this poor officer."

Mr. Campbell took his eyes away from the stretcher.

"They are wicked things, those lifebelts. They give a man hope when there is no longer any call for it. They are cruel. You do not have to thank me, Mr. Davidson."

He looked at Davidson in the gloom, carefully, eye to eye. Davidson nodded.

"Maybe. But I thank you."

"I did nothing."

The two men turned and watched the ratings lifting the stretcher to the low jetty.

"And you do this every day."

"Every day."

222

"Mr. Davidson——"

Mr. Campbell paused so that Davidson turned towards him again. Mr. Campbell did not immediately meet his eye.

"—we are the type of human intercourse. We meet here, apparently by chance, a meeting unpredictable and never to be repeated. Therefore I should like to ask you a question with perhaps a brutal answer."

Davidson pushed his cap back on his head and frowned. Mr. Campbell looked at the lean-to.

"Broken, defiled. Returning to the earth, the rafters rotted, the roof fallen in—a wreck. Would you believe that anything ever lived there?"

Now the frown was bewildered.

"I simply don't follow you, I'm afraid."

"All those poor people——"

"The men I——?"

"The harvest. The sad harvest. You know nothing of my—shall I say—official beliefs, Mr. Davidson; but living for all these days next to that poor derelict—Mr. Davidson. Would you say there was any—surviving? Or is that all? Like the lean-to?"

"If you're worried about Martin—whether he suffered or not——"

They paused for a while. Beyond the drifter the sun sank like a burning ship, went down, left nothing for a reminder but clouds like smoke.

Mr. Campbell sighed.

223

"Aye," he said, "I meant just that."

"Then don't worry about him. You saw the body. He didn't even have time to kick off his seaboots."

Afterword by Philippa Gregory

This is an afterword, rather than a foreword, because any study of this extraordinary novel has to consider the ending: the most important section in this novel. Read at their simplest, the final pages are a 'twist in the tail' like the playful reverse of a traditional short story, but these pages are far more than this: they are a shocking revelation to the reader that the whole novel has been an illusion of the narrator Pincher Martin. In place of the illusion we suddenly see a snapshot of the real world, and a suggestion of what has really taken place.

The 'twist' is the total inversion of the story. We readers thought that we were reading a story about survival, in which the survival of the material world, of the mind and body of a profoundly materialistic man whose very nickname, 'Pincher', implies grabbing, is the drama and chief concern. It seems to be a novel rather like one of the earliest novels ever written: *Robinson Crusoe* – a novel about marooning and survival. Shockingly, in the last pages we learn in a few brutal phrases that the story was not, as we thought, about life, but was all along about dying a death so

225

fast that the narrator did not even have time to kick off his seaboots and swim, but was dragged down to drown, and the story which we have followed was nothing more than his last anguished thoughts, as drowning men are said to have.

This is much more profound and thought-provoking than a mere 'twist in the tail' trick. It means that we the reader have been like Pincher, fretting about water and anemones, rocks, seals and seagulls, and it has all been the last illusion of a dying consciousness. Our reading experience is further devalued because Pincher slowly reveals himself as a wicked man – a rapist and a murderer. This novel, on which we have spent some hours of our time, is the final misunderstanding of a man who has made many mistakes. Not until the very last moment does he begin to learn – the turbulent condition of the island is the turmoil of his drowning, but he never knows this, just as he never knows his own nature, his love for Nat, the beauty of Mary, or the wisdom that Nat would have volunteered. It is only at the moment of his death that he sees truly at last – and all he sees, all he can see, is a dark lightning.

Our reading experience of this novel makes us reflect on reading in general. In all novels the narrator persuades us of a reality and we volunteer to be drawn in. Golding exposes the whole complicit delusion of reading any novel when the Pincher Martin narrator, that we have believed and trusted, turns out to have been dead all along. With the outstanding confidence of a great novelist, Golding

226

at once sets another scene: another island, another naval crew, which we are again supposed to read as a reality. Some parts of this new story are told in conversation, but overall the story is described by an omniscient narrator who – once again – we trust. It is no accident that the last lines of dialogue, the only 'live' dialogue of the novel, are a misunderstanding, when Mr Campbell asks the officer Mr Davidson if there is any sort of afterlife, if the corpse had 'lived' among the decay of the lean-to; and the naval officer replies that the death was too quick for suffering. In this layered world that Golding has created, there are illusions and misunderstandings, but nothing is certain.

Nothing is certain and nothing is clear! I love this novel dearly; but it has puzzled many readers, and there was much that I did not understand at a first reading, nor still now after many re-readings. I confess too that I had to read criticism of the book to learn that the island with its meticulous description of the detail is Pincher's own mouth, his missing tooth. His egoism is such that when he is trying to imagine his survival, he imagines his own body; his illusions are random facts that he can remember. This is not an easy book to read in any way, not for comprehension, not for entertainment.

So why do I like it so much? Firstly, I think this is a novel by an author at the peak of his ability, uncompromising in the pursuit of the story he wants to tell. It is absolutely convincing even when it is describing the wildest of delusions. The collapse of Pincher's consciousness is meticulously

227

mapped. It would be hard to imagine a more powerful study of a single mind under pressure. The terror of madness is always a powerful motif in a novel, since the novel itself is a sort of madness: the reader enters into an imaginary world and experiences profound emotions about things that are not real. Many novels that describe a narrator's slide into madness do so by studying an individual entrapped by intensely described others. But in this novel there are very few characters at all, and they are seen only and exclusively through the darkness of Pincher's vision, they are symptoms more than characters. Mary, the woman he desires, is viciously caricatured and her struggle against his assault shown in the most unsympathetic light. The friend that he deeply loves, Nat, is introduced to the reader as a fool, described as an insect. In one of the rare honest declarations, Pincher knows that he loves and hates Nat.

Many readers find Pincher easy to dislike, and it is a triumph by the author to have us stay in the company of a hateful and untrustworthy narrator. Only in his descriptions of his childhood is he a sympathetic character. He is never clear about his suffering at the hands of his mother, but Golding tells us enough to suggest that the dangerous man was a damaged child. Only at the end of the novel, as a vital part of the inversion of the story, does Golding show us Christopher Martin – as his identity disc names him – not Pincher, of the greedy claw hands. We see Christopher as a body worth recovering, not a murderer marooned on a barren rock. We see the young man who gave his life for his country and not the actor who tried to cheat his way out of service, and we see other men also damaged by war: the naval officer who does his work with the help of drink, his men who are promised a measure of rum for carrying the corpse, and the crofter who has had nightmares since the body was washed ashore.

The end of the novel offers us a hard spiritual truth. Mr Campbell asks if there is any 'surviving' – he seems to mean is Christopher Martin as dead and decaying as his last home, the collapsing lean-to? Mr Davidson answers in terms of suffering and says that the death was so quick that Christopher Martin drowned before he could kick off his boots. We the reader, know better. We know that in those seconds there was great suffering, a suffering that seemed to Christopher to go on for days, in which he reviewed his life and understood some of it. His last moments as he realized that the dark lightning that had come for him, was Nat's earlier description of heaven:

Take us as we are now and heaven would be sheer negation ... A sort of black lightning destroying everything that we call life.

What Nat describes is not easy to understand, but it is – as he says – what heaven must be for sinners. Martin cannot see heaven, but he can see a compassionate end to the terrible ego that is himself. Martin knew at the end that

229

though he hated Nat, he loved him too, and his final vision was that the dark lightning had come for him 'in a compassion that was timeless and without mercy'.

The novels of William Golding

ff

Lord of the Flies

A plane crashes on a desert island and the only survivors, a group of schoolboys, assemble on the beach and wait to be rescued. By day they inhabit a land of bright fantastic birds and dark blue seas, but at night their dreams are haunted by the image of a terrifying beast. As the boys' delicate sense of order fades, so their childish dreams are transformed into something more primitive, and their behaviour starts to take on a murderous, savage significance.

ff

The Inheritors

This was a different voice; not the voice of the people.
It was the voice of other.

When the spring came the people moved back to their familiar home. But this year strange things were happening – inexplicable sounds and smells; unexpected acts of violence; and new, unimaginable creatures half glimpsed through the leaves. Seen through the eyes of a small tribe of Neanderthals whose world is hanging in the balance, *The Inheritors* explores the emergence of a new race, *Homo sapiens*, whose growing dominance threatens an entire way of life.

ff

Free Fall

Somehow, somewhere, Sammy Mountjoy lost his freedom, the faculty of freewill 'that cannot be debated but only experienced, like a colour or the taste of potatoes'. As he retraces his life in an effort to discover why he no longer has the power to choose and decide for himself, the narrative moves between England and a prisoner-of-war camp in Germany. In *Free Fall*, his fourth novel, William Golding has created a poetic fiction, and an allegory, as moving as it is unforgettable.

ff

The Spire

Dean Jocelin has a vision: that God has chosen him to erect a great spire on his cathedral. His mason anxiously advises against it, for the old cathedral was built without foundations. Nevertheless, the spire rises octagon upon octagon, pinnacle by pinnacle, until the stone pillars shriek and the ground beneath it swims. Its shadow falls ever darker on the world below, and on Dean Jocelin in particular.

ff

The Pyramid

Oliver is eighteen, and wants to enjoy himself before going to university. But this is the 1920s, and he lives in Stilbourne, a small English country town, where everyone knows what everyone else is getting up to, and where love, lust and rebellion are closely followed by revenge and embarrassment. Written with great perception and subtlety, *The Pyramid* is William Golding's funniest and most light-hearted novel, which probes the painful awkwardness of the late teens, the tragedy and farce of life in a small community and the consoling power of music.

ff

The Scorpion God

Three short novels show Golding at his subtle, ironic, mysterious best. In *The Scorpion God* we see the world of ancient Egypt at the time of the earliest pharaohs. *Clonk Clonk* is a graphic account of a crippled youth's triumph over his tormentors in a primitive matriarchal society. And *Envoy Extraordinary* is a tale of Imperial Rome where the emperor loves his illegitimate grandson more than his own arrogant, loutish heir.

ff

Darkness Visible

Darkness Visible opens at the height of the London Blitz, when a naked child steps out of an all-consuming fire. Miraculously saved but hideously scarred, soon tormented at school and at work, Matty becomes a wanderer, a seeker after some unknown redemption. Two more lost children await him, twins as exquisite as they are loveless. Toni dabbles in political violence; Sophy, in sexual tyranny. As Golding weaves their destinies together, his book reveals both the inner and outer darkness of our world.

ff

The Paper Men

Fame, success, fortune, a drink problem slipping over the edge into alcoholism, a dead marriage, the incurable itches of middle-aged lust. For Wilfred Barclay, novelist, the final unbearable irritation is Professor Rick L. Tucker, implacable in his determination to become The Barclay Man. Locked in a lethal relationship they stumble across Europe, shedding wives, self-respect and illusions. The climax of their odyssey, when it comes, is as inevitable as it is unexpected.

ff

The Double Tongue

Golding's final novel, left in draft at his death, tells the story of a priestess of Apollo. Arieka is one of the last to prophesy at Delphi, in the shadowy years when the Romans were securing their grip on the tribes and cities of Greece. The plain, unloved daughter of a local grandee, she is rescued from the contempt and neglect of her family by her Delphic role. Her ambiguous attitude to the god and her belief in him seem to move in parallel with the decline of the god himself – but things are more complicated than they appear.

ff

Rites of Passage

Sailing to Australia in the early years of the nineteenth century, Edmund Talbot keeps a journal to amuse his godfather back in England. Full of wit and disdain, he records the mounting tensions on the ancient, sinking warship where officers, sailors, soldiers and emigrants jostle in the cramped spaces below decks. Then a single passenger, the obsequious Reverend Colley, attracts the animosity of the sailors, and in the seclusion of the fo'castle something happens to bring him into a 'hell of degradation', where shame is a force deadlier than the sea itself.

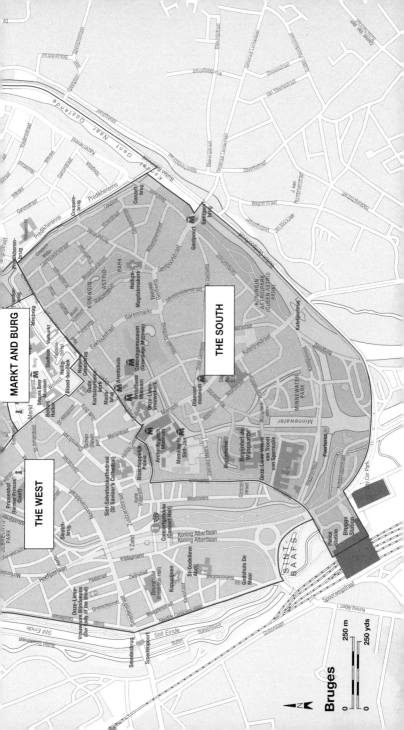

Bruges

MARKT AND BURG

THE WEST

THE SOUTH

Left: cruising the waterways is a relaxing way to enjoy the historic sights.

Atlas

Below: stained glass in Sint-Salvatorskathedraal.

Bruges

Bruges is a Gothic gem of a city that has seen good and bad times, and lived to tell the tale. Its glittering years as a commercial hotspot – from 1200 to 1400 – were followed by decline after its sea route silted up. Disaster back then has brought riches today: having lain untouched for centuries it has become a living museum; a symbol of the modern Flemish renaissance.

Bruges Fact and Figures
Population: Central Bruges 20,000 (entire municipal area including suburbs, villages and Zeebrugge: 117,000)
Area: 4.3 sq km (municipal area: 138.4 sq km)
Population density: 5,000 inhabitants per sq km
Number of nationalities resident in Bruges: 136
Visitors staying overnight in central Bruges: 5 million per year
No. of hotel rooms: over 2,000
No. of World Heritage Sites: 3 (entire city centre, Belfry and Begijnhof)
No. of museums: 28
No. of bridges: 40
No. of churches: 18
No. of restaurants with Michelin stars: 6

Geography

Bruges – *Brugge* to its residents – is situated where the polders of the maritime plain meet the sandy interior of Flanders. It is capital of West Flanders, one of Belgium's 10 provinces, bordered by the Netherlands, France, the North Sea (it contains the entire Belgian coastline), the Walloon province of Hainaut and the Flemish province of East Flanders.

Its egg-shaped historic centre is contained by a 7km-long 'ring canal', which traces the route of the former defensive outer ramparts. Within this boundary are all the visitor attractions and most tourist accommodation. A ring road follows this perimeter boundary and keeps most traffic well away from the centre, which has a traffic management policy (one-way streets) designed to discourage motorists, and where most people move around on foot or by bicycle.

The city suburbs are named after parishes outside the old walls (Sint-Michiels, Sint-Andries, Sint-Jozef, Sint-Pieters, Sint-Kruis and so on). The municipal district of Bruges includes these outskirts, as well as a stretch of land between Bruges and the coast, encompassing the historic village of Lissewege and the port-town of Zeebrugge, which is linked to the city by canal.

Rivers and Canals

The renown of Bruges is rooted deep in its waterways. The city grew up from a Gallo-Roman settlement on the banks of the rivers Dijver and Reie. It is first mentioned by name in 864, when the name *Bruggia* – meaning 'landing stage', or 'port' – appears on coins.

Until the 11th century, ships could sail right into the city along the River Reie. By that time, the development of the cloth industry had made the city an international trading hub. Silting closed access by the end of the century, but a new channel was created by a coastal flood in 1134. This channel – Het Zwin – reopened a sea route as far as Damme, north-east of Bruges. A canal was dug to

Below: a horse-drawn tour of the Markt.

Damme, and this became the city's commercial outpost.

The Zwin outlet silted up again from the early 16th century, sealing the end of the city's golden age, but the remaining canal network has cemented Bruge's reputation, and explains the oft-heard title, 'the Venice of the North'.

From Hunger to Tourism

If it rose to prominence thanks to its weaving and waters, Bruges retains its pristine condition thanks to early tourists. The advent of the railway connecting Ostend, Bruges, Ghent and Brussels reversed the poverty-stricken town's fortunes, as Britons en route to visit the Waterloo battlefields 'discovered' a city preserved in time. Word spread and tentative

conservation efforts were begun. Now the town is a pocket-sized museum piece, peopled by camera-wielding visitors.

Population

The West Flemish are famously unfriendly, and speak a dialect that even other Flemings find hard to understand, yet they are intensely proud of their provincial capital and lay on a fine spread for the thousands of tourists who come to visit each day. As the Flemish economy thrives, and Bruges scrubs its bricks cleaner with every passing year, valiant efforts are being made to strike a balance between the 21st century city, as represented by the daring Concertgebouw, and the time capsule on which its current fortune depends.

Highlights

▲ **Groeningemuseum** The provincial city art gallery with a world-class reputation.
▶ **Memling in Sint-Jan** Jewel-like colours and the finest detail characterise the Memling masterpieces.

▲ **Burg** The city grew from this original square, now a panorama of architectural history that includes the revered Holy Blood basilica.

▶ **Belfort and Hallen** The great Belfry and Market Hall, built in the 13th century and as impressive now as they were then.

▲ **Begijnhof de Wijngaarde** Maybe the best surviving example of a beguinage, dating from medieval times.
▶ **Canals** The lifeblood of the city and magnetic in their attraction.

Markt and Burg

The energy of Bruges comes from its two central squares, the Markt and the Burg, representing the historic city's dual strengths: trade and nobility. The Burg is older and grander: a fortified castle was built here in the 9th century and the city grew up around it. It remained the seat of the Counts of Flanders until the dukes of Burgundy decamped to Prinsenhof palace in the 15th century, and the square is still full of architectural treasures. The Markt was the heart of commercial activity: goods were traded in the Hallen; and the trades' guildhouses – now busy pavement cafés – surround the square. There is a food market here every Wednesday.

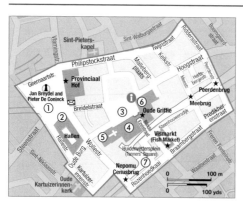

The Markt ①

The Markt has been the hub of daily life in Bruges for over 1,000 years, having served as a marketplace since 958. It is still the focal point of commercial activity, and hosts markets, festivities and street entertainment. Buses and cyclists rattle across the cobbles, and horse-drawn carriage tours depart from here.

Dominating the square is the 13th-century brick complex of the **Belfort-Hallen** ②, the Belfry from which a carillon chimes every quarter-hour. The former cloth halls around its base are where merchants would come to trade their wares.

On the east side of the square stand the city's main

post office and the neo-Gothic **Provinciaal Hof**, the seat of the provincial government of West Flanders. This was previously the site of the Waterhalle (Water Hall), which covered a central canal dock and large quaysides. Cargo would be loaded and unloaded from small boats, which arrived heavily laden from Damme, the city's former sea-port 7km (4 miles) north-east of Bruges. The canal was later truncated to end at Jan Van Eyckplein.

The **statue** at the centre of the Markt honours two heroes of the Flemish rebellion against the French at the Battle of the Golden Spurs in 1302, named Jan Breydel and Pieter De Coninck.
See also Monuments, p.78

The Burg ③

The most historic square in Bruges, referred to in manuscripts from the 9th century, the Burg was the centre of civic and religious life, leaving the grubby business of commerce to the Markt. It takes its name from the fortress or 'burg' that was built here in 865 by Baldwin Iron Arm, the first Count of Flanders, as a defence against Norman invasion, and around which a village developed. Popular events, including burnings at the stake and beheadings, were often held in the Burg. Today, you are more likely to see an outdoor concert.

Pride of place goes to the graceful, triple-turreted Gothic **Stadhuis** ④ (City

Below: Justice holds her scales atop the Proosdij in the Burg.

6

the Vismarkt (fish market) – the current structure built in 1821 and still partly occupied by fresh fish stalls each morning except Sunday. Next to it are the Huidenvettersplein (Tanners' Square), which was surrounded by the tanners' guildhouse (built in 1523 and turreted) and the Fishmongers' Corporation House (beside the boat trip booth and jetty; note the fishy coat of arms above the door, *see picture* below). Crossing Tanners' Square diagonally, you reach **Rozenhoedkaai** ⑦ (Rosary Quay), where the low canal wall provides ample room to enjoy one of the most popular viewpoints in Bruges: across a broad sweep of canal and a cluster of tiled rooftops to the Belfry.

SEE ALSO CANALS AND BRIDGES, P.38

Groenerei

A left turn at the Vismarkt takes you along the lovely Groenerei canalside, where two pretty bridges, the Meebrug and Peerdenbrug, offer a view back to the rear of the Stadhuis and the tower of Sint-Salvatorskathedraal.

Hall), on the south side of the square. This late 14th-century building was built on the site of a former prison. In the south-west corner of the Burg is the **Heilig Bloedbasiliek** ⑤ (Basilica of the Holy Blood), two chapels one atop of the other built in honour of a sacred relic: a phial alleged to contain Christ's blood, brought back from the Holy Land in the 12th century. On the other side of the Stadhuis are the **Oude Griffie** (1537), the old county records office now occupied by law courts.

Next door, in the south-east corner of the square, stands the large neoclassical **Paleis van Het Brugse Vrije** ⑥ (Liberty of Bruges Palace), seat of an autonomous administrative district (the Brugse Vrije) created in the 12th century, which included much of Flanders but not Bruges. The Palace was rebuilt in the 18th century on the site of the 1520s original, parts of which can be seen from the canalside of the building.

SEE ALSO ARCHITECTURE, P.25;
CHURCHES, P.46; MONUMENTS, P.81;
MUSEUMS AND GALLERIES, P.82

Below: coat of arms on the former Fishmongers' Corporation House.

Horse-and-carriage tours of Bruges leave from the Markt every day from 9.30am–5.30pm, except during the Wednesday street market, when the carriages redeploy to the Burg, and during icy weather. A tour lasts around 35 minutes and costs €44 for up to five adults.

Vismarkt and Huidenvettersplein

Along Blinde Ezelstraat and across the canal you are transported from the rarefied realm of nobles and religious relics to daily life in medieval Bruges. Across the canal, which would have served as an open drain, is

South

Bruges is at its most seductive in the lush south of the city. The district south of the Dijver feels far removed from the outside world and its commercial imperatives, and the treasures in its museums and churches seem to stand aloof from the wealth that brought them into being. Some of the world's greatest artworks are here: Van Dycks in the Groeninge-museum, Memlings in the former hospital of Sint-Jan, and a Michelangelo in the Onze-Lieve-Vrouwekerk. Further south is the Begijnhof, a medieval community for women, and the Minnewater park with its lake and swans, where you could be forgiven for imagining that you are on a film set.

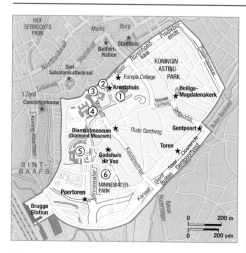

concession on beer itself. Its leading light was Lodewijk van Gruuthuse (c. 1427–92), counsellor to the Burgundian dukes Philip the Good and Charles the Bold, whose equestrian statue stands sentinel above the entrance. Today it is a museum of decorative arts (closed for renovation until late 2017).
SEE ALSO MUSEUMS AND GALLERIES, P.86

Onze-Lieve-Vrouwekerk ③

Abutting the palace is the **Onze-Lieve-Vrouwekerk** (Church of Our Lady), whose vast brick tower and spire – the second highest in Belgium – dominates the city beneath. First mentioned in records in 1089, it once

Groeningemuseum ①

Built in 1929 on the site of a former Augustinian monastery, and restored in 2002–3, the city's most important – and moderately sized – museum was designed to house works which had formerly been displayed in the Bruges Academy of Fine Arts. Many of the older works date from the Golden Age of Bruges, and were commissioned by the city's wealthy burghers, merchants and clerics, several of whom appear in the biblical scenes depicted. An extension of the museum, used for temporary exhibitions and to

house the city's collection of works by Belgo-British artist Frank Brangwyn, is in the **Arentshuis**, an 18th-century mansion across the cobbled lane (called Groeninge).
SEE ALSO MUSEUMS AND GALLERIES, P.83, 85

Gruuthuse Museum ②

Further along the Dijver past the Arentshuis is the lavish 15th-century Palace of the Lords of Gruuthuse, built by a family who had a lucrative monopoly on the sale of *gruut* (a mixture of herbs for improving the flavour of beer), and later held the tax

Below: the Groeninge-museum is housed in a former monastery.

8

Left: romantic Minnewater with its Lake of Love.

Begijnhof De Wijngaarde

South down the canal from Sint-Janshospitaal, following the winding streets, is the enclosure of the **begijnhof** ⑤, a grassy tree-shaded courtyard surrounded by white-washed houses that were occupied by women (beguines) who renounced wealth but did not take holy orders. The last beguine left in 1927, and the site is now owned by a Benedictine convent whose nuns wear habits similar to those worn by the beguines. Many of the houses are now occupied by lay people, but the convent maintains a guest house for those on spiritual visits.
SEE ALSO BEGUINAGES, P.29; MUSEUMS AND GALLERIES, P.84

Next door to the Groeninge-museum is the main building of the College of Europe, an elite post-university establishment founded in 1949 to drive the unification of Europe. Today, around 420 graduates, who must be conversant in French and English, follow one-year Masters programmes in law, economics or political science, in preparation for a high-flying career in the European institutions or international business. The college also has a campus in Warsaw (Natolin), opened in 1992 (www.coleurope.eu).

served as a kind of inland lighthouse for ships on their way to Bruges. The church's main attractions are a Michel-angelo sculpture and the tombs of Mary of Burgundy, who died in 1482, and her father, Charles the Bold, who died in 1477. It was in this church that Mary married Maximilian of Austria in 1477,

joining the house of Burgundy to the Habsburgs, in a cere-mony noted for its lavishness and for the fact that the bride and groom could not speak each other's language.
SEE ALSO CHURCHES, P.47; MUSEUMS AND GALLERIES, P.86

Memling in Sint-Jan ④

The floor level is a metre below the road behind the Gothic doorway of the **Mem-ling in Sint-Jan** museum, showing how the street level has risen over the centuries. The museum contains price-less works by German artist Hans Memling, who came to Bruges aged 25 and made his fortune, becoming one of the richest men in the city by the time he died here in 1494. Six of his paintings can be seen in the former chapel of the **Sint-Janshospitaal** (St John's hospital), founded in the 12th century. It is now a fascinating hospital museum.
SEE ALSO MUSEUMS AND GALLERIES, P.87

Parks

Two of the city's largest green spaces are south: the pretty **Minnewater park** ⑥, with its large lake (the so-called 'Lake of Love'), and east, the landscaped former botanical garden of **Koningin Astrid-park** (Queen Astrid Park).
SEE ALSO PARKS AND GARDENS, P.105

Below: tranquility in the courtyard of the begijnhof.

9

West

The Burgundian dukes made this district their home in the 15th century. Nearby Sint-Jakobskerk did well out of it, as princes and merchants sought to out-do each other in generosity to their parish church. Later, the cathedral of Bruges moved to the west, after the original in the Burg was destroyed. Today, the area is mainly visited for the two long shopping streets that run parallel to each other from the Markt to the 't Zand square, site of a former railway station and now dominated by the city's new concert hall. Beyond that lies a quiet district of respectable terraced houses, including a pretty street lined with typical almshouses.

Prinsenhof ①

The Dukes' Palace luxury hotel occupies the site of the former Burgundian palace, the **Prinsenhof** (Princes' Court), built for the dukes of Burgundy to replace their damp and draughty 11th-century wooden residence on the Burg. The original palace – what survives is a largely rebuilt, neo-Gothic copy –

> A delicate statue of Mary of Burgundy riding side-saddle on a horse, *Flandria Nostra*, is situated on Muntplein, not far from the Prinsenhof.

was vast: it would have been surrounded by high walls and battlements and stretched from Noordzandstraat to the parallel Moerstraat.

Philip the Good married Isabella of Portugal here in 1430, and founded the Order of the Golden Fleece to mark the event. The wedding banquet was held in a hall decorated with tapestries made of gold thread specially for the occasion. Every dish was delivered on a gold platter, to the sound of trumpets, while jousting entertained the guests outside. Philip's son Duke Charles the Bold married Margaret of York here in 1468, again with the kind of banquet that has made the term 'Burgundian' a byword for excess. Sorrow began to

shroud the palace after the violent death of Charles the Bold, in 1477. Just five years later, Charles' daughter Mary, Duchess of Burgundy, died in the palace as a result of injuries sustained during a riding accident. She was just 25. Her death led to widespread mourning, and the building never recovered its former glory. The Habsburgs put it up for sale in 1631, and it passed into the hands of a Franciscan order, before being largely destroyed under French rule at the end of the 18th century.

Sint-Jakobskerk ②

The 13th-century church was enlarged due to gifts from the dukes of Burgundy and then packed with valuable artworks by wealthy donors; it

Below: bronze sculpture of bathing women on the 't Zand.

Left: hanging out by the fountain on the 't Zand.

From 1424 until his death in 1441, painter Jan Van Eyck was in the pay of Philip the Good, Duke of Burgundy. A member of the diplomatic mission sent to Lisbon in 1428 to beg the hand of Isabella of Portugal, it is said that his portrait of her helped confirm the duke's choice of wife. He undertook a number of secret missions for the duke, for which he was handsomely rewarded.

by funfairs and a Saturday market, and lined with cafés and brasseries frequented more by locals than tourists. The vista is now dominated by the remarkable modern **Concertgebouw** ⑤ (concert hall), created in 2002 for the city's year as European Capital of Culture.
SEE ALSO ARCHITECTURE, P.24

Almshouses

West of 't Zand is a calm, residential neighbourhood with a number of *godshuizen* (almshouses), particularly along Boeveriestraat, where the tiny whitewashed homes have been undergoing renovation for 21st century occupants: the **Godshuis De Moor** was founded in 1480 for aged stonemasons, carpenters and coopers; while **Godshuis Van Volden** occupies the site of a medieval hospital for foundlings and mentally ill children. A little to the north, clustered around the chapel of **Onze-Lieve-Vrouw-van-Blindekens** ⑥ (Our Lady of the Blind) on Kreupelstraat, are almshouses for the blind: named Van Pamel, Marius Voet and Laurentia Soutieu.
SEE ALSO CHURCHES, P.48; PALACES AND HOUSES, P.101

Although the chapel buildings date from the 17th century, Onze-Lieve-Vrouw-van-Blindekens (Our Lady of the Blind) was built to honour a promise made at the battle of Mons-en-Pévèle in 1304 against the French (which resulted in a treaty granting Flemish independence). The chapel is the departure point for the annual Feast of the Assumption procession held on 15 August, which makes its way from here to Onze-Lieve-Vrouw van de Potterie (Our Lady of the Pottery), on Potterierei.

has an internal harmony lacking in many Bruges churches and is lit by a pale pink light when the sun shines.
SEE ALSO CHURCHES, P.48

Sint-Salvatorskathedraal

During the Burgundian era, **Sint-Salvatorskathedraal** ③ was just St Saviour's, another parish church, albeit the old-

est in Bruges, dating from the 9th century. When Bruges found itself a cathedral-free zone, after French occupation forces demolished St Donatian's Cathedral in the Burg, St Saviour's was pressed into service in 1834 as a replacement seat for the Bishop of Bruges. The **museum** in its treasury contains valuable artworks, and the 15th-century wooden choir stalls flanking the altar bear a complete set of escutcheons of the Knights of the Order of the Golden Fleece, who held a chapter meeting here in 1478.
SEE ALSO CHURCHES, P.49; MUSEUMS AND GALLERIES, P.88

't Zand ④

Major transformations on the **'t Zand** in recent years have given a new burst of life to this once dreary square, left vacant when the city's first railway station moved south. The ring road passes under the square, which is cheered

North

Northern Bruges was historically the city's gateway to the outside world, via the canal to Damme and the Zwin inlet. Merchants from all over Europe set up trading posts locally, and their legacy lives on in street names like Spanjaardstraat (Spanish Street), Engelsestraat (English Street) and Oosterlingenplein (Easterners' Square), which referred to the German traders based here. Beyond this distinctly grand quarter, and the other side of a wonderful stretch of canal, is the old artists' neighbourhood of Sint-Gillis (Saint Giles). It is centred around the Gothic church of Sint Gillis and pleasantly removed from the tourist frenzy of other areas.

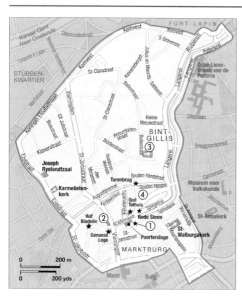

in Bruges to win renovation funding in the 19th century, marking the start of efforts to preserve the city's medieval character.

The two quays flanking the canal along Spiegelrei and Spinolarei were used as mooring points for boats arriving in the city, and mansions were built to house merchants and courtiers from other trading nations; many of the houses had vaulted cellars for storage, some of which can still be seen.
SEE ALSO MONUMENTS, P.79

Huis Ter Beurze ②
At Vlamingstraat 35 is **Huis Ter Beurze** (Ter Beurze House), with a plaque noting the year 1453 on the facade. It used to be an inn and money-changing operation run by the Van den Beurze family, and was frequented by so many foreign merchants and bankers that the surroundings became known as the Beursplein. It is from this that the word 'Bourse', the common international name for a stock exchange, comes.

Several houses were occupied by Italian merchants: the **Genuese loge** (Genoese lodge) at Vlamingstraat 33 (1399), now the Friet Museum, has the city's

Jan Van Eyckplein ①
During the Middle Ages, when Bruges was a key member of the powerful Baltic-based Hanseatic League trading alliance, hosting the most important of the league's principal *kontore* (foreign outposts), this square was a busy place. On the west side is the slender-towered **Poortersloge** (Burghers' Lodge), something of an elite gentlemen's club in the 15th century, now home

to the town archives. On the north side of the square is the **Oud Tolhuis** (Customs House), where taxes were levied on imported goods, and next to it the tiny *pijnders* (porters) lodge. The two buildings are now part of the provincial library, and house hundreds of Gothic manuscripts. The **Rode Steen** house on the east of the square (Jan van Eyckplein 8) dates from the 13th–18th century; it was the first house

12

Left: Hans Memling looking down on Woensdagmarkt.

Miraelstraat and was buried in **Sint-Gilliskerk** ③ in 1494. Lancelot Blondeel and Pieter Pourbus lived on the same street, while Gerard David and Antoon Claeissens lived on Sint-Jorisstraat. Jan van Eyck entertained guests in his home and studio at the junction of Torenbrug and Gouden-Handstraat, overlooking the attractive stretch of canal along **Gouden-Handrei** ④.

The neighbourhood later became something of an English colony. An orphanage on Sint-Jorisstraat was run by an English family until World War I and an English seminary was located on Gouden Handstraat. The house on the corner of Sint-Jorisstraat and Clarastraat was owned by English art historian James Weale (1832–1917), who, together with poet Guido Gezelle, launched a magazine and is credited with rediscovering and identifying the works of Hans Memling and many other **Flemish Primitives**.

SEE ALSO PAINTING AND SCULPTURE, P.96

Bruges' early prosperity was a result of its role as the chief port of Flanders, a hub of English and Scandinavian trade. From the Roman period to the 11th century, ships sailed right into the centre on the River Reie; later, sea-going ships sailed into Damme, while smaller vessels ferried goods along the canal from Damme to Bruges. In addition to being a major hub, Bruges was one of the important textile centres in north-west Europe.

Sint-Gillis

North of the canal that loops around this central northern area are the humble terraced streets of Sint-Gillis (St Giles) and Sint-Joris (St George), once home to the greatest names in Flemish painting. **Hans Memling** owned two houses on Jan

coat of arms above the side door; there was also the **Venetian consulate** at No. 37; and the **Florentine Lodge** at Academiestraat 1, now De Florentijnen restaurant. An engraving on the facade quotes a passage from Dante's *Divine Comedy* referring to Bruges. Not far away, the **Hof Bladelin** at Naaldenstraat 19 was home to Medici bank officials.

Below: peaceful stretch of water at Gouden Handrei.

13

East

The Sint-Anna district to the north-east of Bruges has a less worldly air than the rest of the city, its streets disturbed only by the sounds of bicycle bells, windmill sails or the lick of a paintbrush as the area completes its renovation. The museums here deal more with matters of everyday life – medicine in medieval Bruges, schooling and local crafts, lace-making and literature – while an unusual church recreates a corner of the Holy Land in Bruges. At the area's perimeter, the grassy banks of the canal ring – from the Coupure canal in the south-east to the Dampoort in the north – are popular with joggers, cyclists and dog-walkers.

Above: coat-of-arms finely crafted in lace.

Annakerk ① (Church of St Anne), with lavish decoration, is a 1624 Baroque replacement for the Gothic church demolished in 1561.

The striking **Jeruzalem-kerk** ② (Jerusalem Church) was built in 1428 by a wealthy Bruges family and modelled on the Church of the Holy Sepulchre in Jerusalem. Even stranger inside than out, the church is still privately owned. Next door is a row of 15th-century almshouses founded by the Adornes family.

The **Bruggemuseum-Volkskunde** ③ (Folklore Museum) recreates typical 19th-century interiors in a row of almshouses along Bal-straat, including workshops of various trades and craft-speople, a schoolroom and a tavern. At No. 16 lies the **Kantcentrum** (Lace Centre). SEE ALSO CHILDREN, P.44; CHURCHES, P.50–1; MUSEUMS AND GALLERIES, P.89, 90–1.

Sint-Anna

Home in the 19th century to the poorest citizens, the streets around Sint-Annakerk were rediscovered by artists and, later, young profession-als, who have restored the rows of terraced houses. There are few shops in the tranquil neighbourhood, which has something of a village atmosphere. The **Sint-**

Around the Windmills

Out towards the ring canal are just four wooden-stilt **windmills** remaining of the 29 that once ringed the city ramparts. Two of them are open to the public in sum-mer: regular demonstrations of the miller's craft prove that they are still in working order.

Lace-making was an industry which at its peak in the 1840s provided steady employment – and low wages – for 10,000 local women and girls (nearly a quarter of the population). Handmade lace is expensive, and most of the lace sold today is machine-made and imported. The most popular kind made here is bobbin lace, created using a technique where threads of silk, linen or cotton on as many as 700 bobbins are crossed and braided around a framework of pins.

Nearby are the homes of two exclusive sporting clubs dating from the 16th century: the **Schuttersgilde Sint-Joris** and **Sint-Sebastiaan** (St George and St Sebastian Archers' Guilds), the first is for the crossbow, the second

14

Left: 19th-century windmill Sint-Janshuismolen.

Dampoort, where the canal from Damme enters the city. This was the route by which trading vessels arrived in the Middle Ages. Today, pleasure cruisers and working barges wait here for the road-bridge to lift. After the route via the Zwin inlet and Damme silted up, a canal was built to Ostend, opened in 1622. Large vessels today generally take the Boudewijnkanaal to the sea port of Zeebrugge.

The canal snakes its way from here to the city centre along the tree-lined Potterierei, named after the chapel of the potters' guild, the **Onze-Lieve-Vrouw ter Potterie** ⑤ (Our Lady of the Pottery), and its adjacent hospice, dating from 1276 and functioning until the 17th century. Parts of the former hospice now house the **Potterie-museum**, dedicated to the history of medical treatment, as well as furniture, paintings and religious artefacts.

A little further down the canal is the Baroque church and college of the **Groot Seminarie**, the episcopal seminary, which occupies the former Duinen Abdij (Abbey of the Dunes).

SEE ALSO CHURCHES, P.51; MONUMENTS, P.81; MUSEUMS AND GALLERIES, P.91

Fluent in English, the poet and priest Guido Gezelle translated several English works into Dutch. He also catalogued around 150,000 words, phrases and proverbial sayings from the old Netherlandic dialect and wrote poetry that aimed to recreate the 'golden age' of Flanders' rural and devoutly Catholic society.

for the longbow. Still with an elite – and all male – membership, they occupy historic buildings with fine gardens.

Between the clubs, on Rolweg, the **Bruggemuseum-Gezelle** ④ honours the work of the Bruges poet and priest (1830–99) in the house where he grew up. Gezelle was one of the principal 19th-century Flemish men of letters, and founder of the Flemish Academy of Language and Literature. He died in the **Engels Klooster** (English Convent) in the par-

allel street, Carmersstraat. The convent was one of the focal points of the English Colony, which in the 1860s numbered 1,200.

SEE ALSO MONUMENTS, P.80; MUSEUMS AND GALLERIES, P.90

Potterierei and Dampoort

The northernmost windmill, **Koeleweimolen** (Cool Meadow Mill), is up near the

Below: handsome buildings along the Potterierei.

Around Langestraat

The neighbourhood south of Langestraat, bordered to the west by the **Coupure** canal, was until recently a forgotten corner of the city. Gentrification has recently arrived, and the streets are newly cobbled and dotted with quiet bed and breakfast places. The quayside along **Predikherenrei** is a mooring spot for houseboats.

SEE ALSO CANALS AND BRIDGES, P.38

15

Around Bruges

Attractions outside central Bruges vary from the pretty villages of Damme and Lissewege to the north-east and north, the Boudewijn theme park with dolphinarium to the south and two country estates, Beisbroek and Tudor City Park in the south-west, the first of which has an observatory and planetarium. Also to the south are a 14th-century moated castle at Tillegem and a feudal farm, the Zeven Torentjes (Seven Towers). Further afield (but accessible by rail or bus tour) is the rebuilt town of Ieper (Ypres), once a flourishing medieval cloth town but best known as the centre of Flanders Fields during World War I.

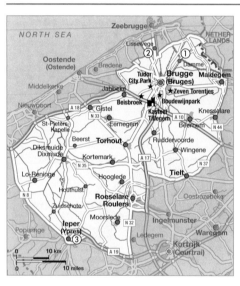

Above: attractive whitewashed buildings in Lissewege.

Damme and Lissewege

Damme ① is accessible from Bruges via bus, paddle-steamer (the *Lamme Goedzak* moors at Noorweegse Kaai near Dampoort) or bike on a 7km (4-mile) ride alongside the canal. This genteel village was once the sea-port of Bruges and quite a large town. It retains an air of medieval prosperity, with a 15th-century town hall, a hospital for the poor, Sint-Janshospitaal, and a partly ruined church, Onze-Lieve-

Vrouwekerk (Church of Our Lady), built in 1340 over a chapel dating from 1225.

The village has made much of its literary connections. In front of the Town Hall stands a statue of the scholar-poet Jacob van Maerlant (1230–96), the 'father of Dutch poetry', who lived in Damme from around 1270, writing his most important works there. It has also adopted 14th-century German folk-tale character Tijl Uilenspiegel, who fetched

up in Damme by a circuitous route. The town has tried to reinvent itself as a book village modelled on Hay-on-Wye in Wales, but most visitors come for the restaurants, especially at weekends.

Lissewege ② is one of the best-preserved rural communities on the Flemish coastal plain; its pretty whitewashed houses have long been a draw for artists. A narrow canal, the Lisseweegs Vaartje, used to connect it with Bruges. The village is clustered around its early Gothic Onze-Lieve-Vrouwekerk (Church of Our Lady) (1225–50). Just outside the village used to stand the large Ter Doest abbey. Now only its vast tithe barn (1250) remains, attached to the manor farm, which is

Left: discovering Damme by paddle-steamer.

105-hectare (260-acre) country estate, the **Tillegembos**. In the eastern suburbs, in Assebroek, the **Zeven Torentjes** (Seven Towers) is a feudal manor farm that has been turned into a model farm, with animals and blacksmithing demonstrations.
SEE ALSO CHILDREN, P.44, 45; PARKS AND GARDENS, P.107

Ieper ③

A visit to Ieper (Ypres), southwest of Bruges near the border with France, requires a full day. Coach tours are available from Bruges, or you can travel by train (1hr 45 mins via Kortrijk), but you will need private transport to visit the cemeteries on the former battlefields.

One of the largest towns in Europe in the 13th century, with 40,000 inhabitants, Ieper was shelled to destruction during World War I, then reconstructed over the next 40 years. In the cloth hall on the Grote Markt, the powerful **In Flanders Fields Museum** uses historical documents, film footage, poetry, song and sounds to evoke the brutal experience of trench warfare in the Ypres Salient.

A short walk away is the **Menin Gate**, a memorial inscribed with the names of 55,000 of the 100,000 Commonwealth soldiers who died in battle but have no known grave. **Hill 62** remembers Canadian soldiers; at nearby **Sanctuary Wood Cemetery,** a few trenches are preserved; **Hill 60** commemorates the Australian dead. **Tyne Cot Military Cemetery** near Passendale has 12,000 graves. The German war-dead are remembered in **Langemark** and **Vladslo**.

Tales of Tijl Uilenspiegel's adventures first appeared around 1480, in German prose tales. Damme, his 'birthplace', acquired him as a freedom fighter in Charles de Coster's epic novel The Legend of the Glorious Adventures of Till Eulenspiegel (1867; English 1918), which achieved international renown. In this version, the hero symbolises Flanders in its struggle against Spanish occupation.

now a popular country inn, the Hof ter Doest.

Parks and Castles

There are many good options within 10km (6 mile) of Bruges to have a bracing walk and allow the kids to let off steam. The two large country estates of Beisbroek and Tudor City Park are next to each other alongside the Brussels–Ostend motorway. **Beisbroek** covers 80 hectares (200 acres), and has a nature centre, planetarium and observatory; **Tudor City Park** covers 40 hectares (100 acres) and has a botanical garden, beehives and a castle (now a conference centre). The **Boudewijnpark** is a theme park with dolphinarium. South-west of Bruges, **Kasteel Tillegem** (Tillegem Castle) is a 14th-century moated castle surrounded by a

Below: remembering the dead of the Great War.

17

Ghent

The prosperous capital of the province of East Flanders, situated at the confluence of the Leie and Scheldt rivers, Ghent – Gent in Dutch – is a larger city than Bruges (population 248,000, of which 70,000 are students), with a younger vibe and a rich cultural life. It may not have such an unspoiled appearance, but its historic centre is well-preserved, with winding canals, cobbled streets and old buildings. Ghent was also seat of the Counts of Flanders and of their successors, the dukes of Burgundy, and flourished thanks to the cloth trade. Today, its port is the country's third largest, after Antwerp and Zeebrugge, connected to the sea by a canal.

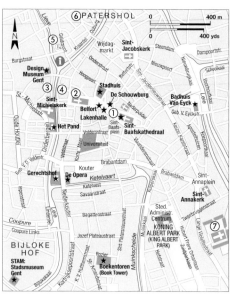

with a lift. Together with the Belfort, the adjacent **Laken-halle** (Cloth Hall) expresses Ghent's civic pride and wealth. The building, much restored, dates from 1441.

Across the road from the Lakenhalle in Botermarkt is the **Stadhuis** (Town Hall), built over several centuries starting in the early 16th.

Sint-Niklaaskerk

On the other side of the Belfort (Korenmarkt), **Sint-Niklaaskerk** ② (St Nicholas Church), built in the 13th-15th century, was the earliest of Ghent's three great towers

Below: Ghent has a younger vibe and lots of students.

Sint-Baafsplein ①

The largely Gothic brick and granite **Sint-Baafskathedraal** was built over several centuries: the chancel dates from the turn of the 14th century.

The innovative Tourist Information Centre of Visit Ghent is located at Sint-Veerleplein 5 in the Old Fish Market (Oude Vismijn), tel: 09 266 56 60, www.visitgent.be

The cathedral's (and possibly the nation's) greatest treasure is **The Adoration of the Mystic Lamb** (1432), a 20-panel polyptych altarpiece regarded as the crowning achievement of Jan van Eyck's Gothic style and worth the trip to Ghent on its own (under renovation until 2017 so only parts of the polyptych are open to public).

Opposite the cathedral, the **Belfort** (Belfry), completed in 1380, has a 91m (298ft) tower

18

Left: a horse-and-carriage ride is a fun way to see Ghent.

For 10 days in mid-July, the city is given over to the annual Gentse Feesten (Ghent Festivities), a vast street festival centred around Bij Sint-Jacobs, Vlasmarkt and Sint-Jacobskerk (St James's Church). Part of the proceedings re-enacts the Stroppendragers (Noose Bearers) Procession, recalling Emperor Charles V's humiliation of the rebellious citizenry in 1540. For information, see www.gentsefeesten.be.

(the others are the Belfort and Sint-Baafskathedraal).

Korenlei and Graslei

The two banks of the river Leie north of Sint-Michielsbrug are lined with medieval guild-houses. Korenlei ③, on the left, and Graslei ④, on the right, comprise Ghent's oldest harbour, the **Tussen Bruggen** (Between the Bridges), the commercial heart of the medieval city. At Korenlei 7 is the 1739 **Gildehuis van de Onvrije Schippers** (House of the Tied Boatmen), while at No. 9 is the 16th-century **De Zwane** (The Swan), a former brewery. Across on Graslei is the **Gildehuis van de Vrije Schippers** (House of the Free Boatmen), built 1531 in Brabant Gothic style. Next door, the Baroque **Gildehuis van de Graanmeters** (House of the Grain Weighers) dates from 1698.

There is a small **Tolhuisje** (Customs House), built in 1682, with the Romanesque-style **Het Spijker,** also known as Koornstapelhuis (a former grain warehouse dating from about 1200) next door. On the other side is the **Korenmetershuis** (Corn Measurer's house), followed by the Gothic-style **Gildehuis van de Metselaars** (House of the Masons), built 1912 according to plans of the original.

Gravensteen ⑤

This heavily renovated island fortress was once the Castle of the Counts. Work began on the structure in 1180, on the site of a 9th-century castle and modelled on the Crusader castles of the Holy Land. The battlements and keep can be visited; the latter includes the Great Hall where the Knights of the Golden Fleece were feted in 1445.

Patershol ⑥

A former working-class neighbourhood with nar-

row cobbled streets and quaint terraced houses, the Patershol district has been refurbished in recent years to become a lively restaurant quarter, buzzing with life by night. The nearby **Huis van Alijn** folklore museum offers a fantastic snapshot of daily life in Ghent over the centuries.

Vrijdagmarkt

The people of Ghent – Gentenaars – have risen up more than most in Flanders. They mainly gathered on Vrijdagmarkt, the city's main square, bordered by guild-houses and mansions, now cafés. A Friday market has been held here since the 13th century.

Small Begijnhof

Along Lange Violettenstraat, near Koning Albertpark (King Albert Park) is the tranquil **Klein Begijnhof** ⑦ (Small Begijnhof) or Onze-Lieve-Vrouw Ter Hoye (Our Lady of Hoye). Today it looks like a miniature walled 17th-century town, and is one of the finest surviving examples in the Low Countries.

SEE ALSO BEGUINAGES, P.28

The Coast

Just 15km (9 miles) from Bruges is the North Sea coast and Belgium's short stretch of coastline, dotted with resorts and dunes. Access to the coast is easy with the coastal tram, which runs from the Dutch border to the French, often just metres behind the dunes. Its journey takes in ritzy Knokke-Heist; the seaport of Zeebrugge; the yacht harbour at Blankenberge; the beach and dunes of Wenduine; the Belle Epoque glory of De Haan; popular Ostend; the fishing harbour of Nieuwpoort; the seafood restaurants of Oostduinkerke; and the beaches of Koksijde and De Panne, where sand-yachts sail in the wind. Three resorts are described below.

Zeebrugge ①

The nearest coastal town to Bruges is Zeebrugge, literally 'Sea-Bruges', a port-town created by King Leopold II (1835–1909) in 1904, and joined to it by a 12km (7.5-mile) canal – the Boudewijnkanaal. The port was destroyed in both World Wars, but Zeebrugge rose again to become Belgium's largest fishing port, as well as a major container-ship and ferry port. The main attraction is a maritime theme park in the former fish market: **Seafront Zeebrugge**.
SEE ALSO CHILDREN, P.45

De Haan ②

Another King Leopold II project, designed as a bathing resort, De Haan has a genteel charm. Reached from Bruges by a train to Ostend and then the tram towards Knokke, the town is named after the first hotel that opened here, in 1888: **De Haan Hotel** (The Rooster Hotel). Shortly after,

the king instructed two architects to build a beach town. The result was a series of individual villas in Belle-Epoque style. Strict rules determined the planting of green areas and the height of buildings. The rules still apply and the district, known as the Concession, lends De Haan its character. The **tram shelter** dates from 1902 and is in art

nouveau style; it also houses the tourist office. Belgium's first golf course, the 18-hole **Royal Golf Club**, opened here in 1903, and Albert Einstein lived here for six months in 1933. Two typical hotels are the **Grand-Hôtel Belle-Vue**, which opened in the 1920s, and the **Hôtel des Brasseurs**, which dates from 1900. The country-style villas at

Below: De Haan's tourist office is in this former tram shelter.

20

Left: fishing and walking the dogs on the beach.

The British frequented Ostend en masse during its 19th-century heyday, arriving in ferries from Dover to play lawn tennis, golf and beach croquet. In the 1860s, there were 2,000 British residents out of the town's population of 16,000.

(Kunstmuseum aan Zee, Art Museum by the Sea), where the collection also includes works by René Magritte, Constant Permeke, Leon Spilliaert, Pierre Alechinsky and Panamarenko, shown on rotation. It also hosts temporary shows by contemporary artists.

Visserskaai is lined with fish stalls and restaurants serving whelk soup, Ostend sole, oysters and mussels. Fishing boats draw up here and sell their catch to restaurateurs. Set into the quay, the Amandine is a former Icelandic trawler that makes for a good visit. The highlight of the marina round the corner is the three-masted former Belgian Navy training yacht, the **Mercator**.

SEE ALSO PAINTING AND SCULPTURE, P.96

Soul legend Marvin Gaye lived in Ostend for two years, and wrote his 1982 hit Sexual Healing there, in self-imposed exile from a life of drug and alcohol abuse. Shortly afterwards, he returned to Los Angeles where, aged 44, he was shot dead by his father.

Rembrandtlaan 10–19 date from 1925–7. De Haan has an active sailing and windsurfing club, **Watersportclub De Windhaan**, which rents out catamarans and teaches kite-surfing. Behind the long sandy beach are several nature reserves, including **Natuurreservaat De Kijkuit**, with sand-fixing vegetation to prevent coastal erosion.

Ostend ③

There are three trains an hour from Bruges to Belgium's largest seaside resort, which in the 19th century tried to rival the grand French resorts

of Deauville and Biarritz. The Belgian royal family kept a villa here until 2005, and wealthy foreigners stayed here including Russian tsars and Britain's Queen Victoria, who attended the **English church**. The **Casino Kursaal** was rebuilt in 1953, and recently reopened as a convention and concert venue, with a fish restaurant on the top floor. At the other end of the promenade is the **Thermae Palace Hotel**, a 1930s former spa, now a hotel. It stands above the 400m (1,300ft) of **royal arcades**, a colonnaded walkway built in 1905 to link the royal villa to the racecourse. Painter James Ensor (1860–1949), whose work opened the way for Surrealism and Expressionism, lived and worked in Ostend: his former house, the **James Ensorhuis** (part of MuZee) is now a museum including his studio. Original artworks by Ensor can be seen at the decent **MuZee**

Below: colourful boats at Ostend marina.

21

A–Z

In the following section Bruges's attractions and services are organized by theme, under alphabetical headings. Items that link to another theme are cross-referenced. All sights that are plotted on the atlas section at the end of the book are given a page number and grid reference.

Architecture

Long agreed to be one of the most beautiful cities in Europe, Bruges' architectural wealth gained official recognition when Unesco designated the historic centre a World Heritage site in 2000. The city was instrumental in developing the brick Gothic style from the 13th century, but after the neo-Gothic restoration of the old centre in the 19th century, there was scant enthusiasm for subsequent movements. The recent economic revival in Flanders, however, has kick-started enthusiasm for new, bolder projects. This section highlights buildings that have made significant architectural contributions to Bruges.

Concertgebouw

't Zand 34; tel: 050 47 69 99; www.concertgebouw.be; guided visits by arrangement only; bus: 1; map p.134 B3

A striking example of contemporary architecture in a city that thrives on the past, the vast concert hall designed by Paul Robberecht and Hilde Daem to mark the city's year as European Capital of Culture in 2002, is clad in 68,000 terracotta tiles, a nod to the red-brick of medieval Bruges. The taller part of the structure, known as the 'lantern tower', twinkles at night through dozens of tiny windows overlooking the square. Inside, the space is minimalist, with bare concrete walls and columns. The Kamermuziekzaal (chamber music hall) is highly original: the audience sits in single rows in bays arranged vertically around the stage.
See also Music, p.92

Heilig Bloedbasiliek

Burg 15; tel: 050 33 67 92; www.holyblood.com; Apr–mid-Nov daily 9.30am–noon, 2–5pm, mid-Nov–Mar Thu–Tue 9.30am–noon, 2–5pm, Wed 9.30am–noon; Basilica free, treasury/museum charge; bus: 1; map p.134 C4

Behind the intricate Renaissance facade of the Basilica of the Holy Blood is the Romanesque lower chapel (1139), one of the few local examples of the style said to copy that used during Roman times. The heavy cylindrical columns, semicircular arches, small

---

Below: the decorative facade of Oude Griffie.

windows and thick stone walls are characteristic of the style. The late 15th-century upper chapel was remodelled in the late 18th century: the pulpit dates from 1728; the stained glass windows from 1845.
See also Churches, p.46; Museums and Galleries, p.82

Onze-Lieve-Vrouwekerk

Mariastraat; tel: 050 44 87 11; www.brugge.be/musea; Mon–

Many of the domestic buildings in Bruges have step gables, which also feature in many cityscapes by the Flemish Primitives. The step form offered a type of fire protection for urban houses: the gable extension would slow the spread of sparks from one roof to another. The steps also provided convenient access to the roof for chimney sweeps and roofers in times when cranes were non-existent and tall ladders uncommon. Fine examples are at Jan Van Eyckplein and, in more modest form, in the old tradesmen's houses facing the Belfry on the Markt.

Left: orange tiles and stepped gables on Bruges rooftops.

Built 1534–7, the ornate Oude Griffie (Old Recorder's House), or Civic Registry, is an example of Flemish Renaissance, adapted from the Italian style to suit the practical needs and stylistic sensibilities of the Low Countries, and recently renovated with a colourful, authentic, polychrome facade. The bas-relief depicts the ancient Persian legend of a king having a corrupt judge skinned alive (see Gerard David's 1498 painting on the same gruesome theme in the Groeningemuseum, *p.85*), a popular cautionary tale for lawmakers in medieval times. Today the building is occupied by the law courts and is not open to the public.

Sat 9.30am–5pm, Sun 1.30–5pm; free; bus: 1; map p.134 C3
The dominant spire of the Church of Our Lady is characteristic of the austere, Scaldian (river Scheldt) Gothic style, which developed in the early 13th century. The movement was characterised by its solid aspect, and double or triple lancet windows.

Built out of brick, the 122m (400ft) spire is the city's tallest landmark. The church is currently undergoing a major renovation so it's only partially accessible to the public.
SEE ALSO CHURCHES, P.47

Oude Griffie

Burg 11a; closed to public; bus: 1; map p.135 C4

Paleis van het Brugse Vrije

Burg 11a; tel: 050 44 87 43; www.brugge.be/musea; daily 9.30am–12.30pm, 1.30–5pm; bus: 1; map 135 C4

Below: the Concertgebouw is a rare example of contemporary architecture in Bruges.

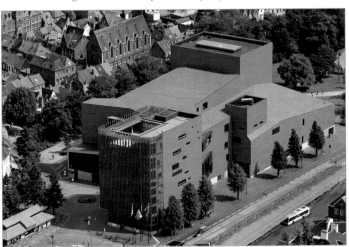

Although at its heart is a much older building, the visible face of the Brugse Vrije is typical of the neoclassical architectural fashion of the 18th century, adopting a more restrained form of classical architecture than the preceding Baroque period. It was not widely adopted in Flanders, where many Catholics rejected what they saw as an aping of styles developed by ancient pagan cultures. They were happy to embrace the neo-Gothic revival which followed soon after. The buildings around the courtyard are mainly city council offices, but they also give access to the fine Renaissancezaal.
SEE ALSO MUSEUMS AND GALLERIES, P.82

't Pandreitje
Pand 7; bus: 1, 11; map p.134 C3
A modern housing complex begun in 2000 on the site of a former prison alongside Koningin Astridpark. The small 'garden city' was the result of a competition held to provide family homes close to the city centre. The car-free estate is composed of 75 urban dwellings with underground parking, made of brick and with small walled gardens or terraces sympathetic to the city's medieval housing style. The complex was completed in 2002.

Paviljoen Toyo Ito
Burg; bus: 1; map p.135 C4
The honeycomb steel-and-glass pavilion on the Burg was commissioned from leading Japanese architect Toyo Ito, like the Concertgebouw, for Bruges' year as European Capital of Culture in 2002. Originally intended as a temporary structure, the walkway was designed to symbolise the connection between the Bruges of yesterday and today: the circle of gravel (which has replaced the original watery surround) marks the site of the altar of the city's former cathedral, St Donatian's, whose footings and ruins can be seen in the basement of the Crowne Plaza hotel. Locally, the pavilion is known as the 'Governor's Carwash' (the provincial governor's palace lies next door, to the west).

Provinciaal Hof
Markt 3; not open to public; bus: 1; map p.134 C4
The former provincial government building, built 1881–1921, is a proud example of the neo-Gothic style, which found such favour in Bruges. Bruges-born architect Louis Delacenserie (1838–1909) designed the palatial structure, and was behind the restoration of many other medieval buildings in the city. The red-brick building to the right is the main post office, on the site of the old medieval cloth hall, which spanned the canal that passed under the building. Delacenserie also designed Antwerp's grandiose Centraal Station.

Sint-Walburgakerk
St Maartensplein; daily 10am–1pm, 2–6pm; free; bus: 6, 16; map p.133 C1

Below: the stately facade of the Provinciaal Hof.

Art nouveau, the 'new art' style adopted by architects across Europe in the 19th century in a bid to break free of derivative forms such as neo-Gothic, made an enormous impact in Brussels but largely passed by Bruges. Just three examples can be seen in the city: the shopfront of De Medici Sorbetière at 9 Geldmuntstraat; a pair of house facades behind the Onze-Lieve-Vrouwekerk (Onze-Lieve-Vrouwekerk-Zuid 6–8), built in 1904, with murals depicting Day and Night painted over the doorways; and the facade of Pietje Pek bistro at 13 Sint-Jakobsstraat.

This elegant church is a rare example in Bruges of pure Baroque architecture, designed by Jesuit priest Pieter Huyssens and built 1619–41. Exemplifying the renewed confidence of Catholicism and the Counter-Reformation after the religious strife of the 16th century, it has all the rich embellishment for which the style is known: garlands, swirls, barley-sugar twists, broken pediments, oval windows and cherubs. The light interior features black-and-white marble floor tiles and white columns. Baroque features can also be observed inside many other Bruges churches (Sint-Anna, for example), although their external structures mainly date from earlier periods. Exuberant carved pulpits by the likes of Artus Quellinus the Younger and Hendrik Verbruggen are typical of the style.

SEE ALSO CHURCHES, P.50

Stadhuis

Burg 12; tel: 050 44 87 43; www.brugge.be/musea; daily 9.30am–5pm; bus: 1; map p.135 C4

The late 14th century saw the emergence of Flamboyant Gothic, adopted for secular use such as for this, the oldest town hall in the Low Countries, built 1376–1421. The style can be recognised for its delicate window tracery, spires, finials and sculpture. The building became the model for several city halls in Belgium, most notably those in Leuven, Brussels and Oudenaarde. The facade would originally have been brightly painted.

Beneath the windows are the coats of arms of towns that came under the jurisdiction of Bruges until 1795; they are not all correct because their design was based on an inaccurate document. The 34 figures of saints, prophets and noblemen and women that decorate the niches are copies of the originals, which were removed by the Jacobins and their Flemish sympathisers, then destroyed on the Markt. They represent 34 important figures in the history of Flanders.

On the top of the twisted chimney stacks sit gold crowns, a gift from the king of France, who so admired the wise aldermen of Bruges that he wanted to crown their breath as it left the chamber.

The fantastic Gothic Hall on the first floor is the only area open to the public.

SEE ALSO MONUMENTS, P.81

Below: the light and cool interior of Sint-Walburgakerk.

Beguinages

Flanders is famous for the number of its surviving enclosed residences for Beguines, unmarried or widowed women who adopted a life of religious devotion but without taking the full vows of a nun. The Beguinage of Bruges is a well-preserved example of this form of residence, and is one of the best loved and most photographed sights in the city. A wander through its walled garden-courtyard, with swishing poplars and cooing doves, is like a trip back in time to another age. This chapter explains the origin and the life of these unique, fascinating communities.

Origin

Beguines were initially solitary women who worked helping the poor and preaching. Progressively, and in the face of a growing suspicion on the part of male religious authorities, they grouped together to live in a walled residential community known as a Beguinage (French) or Begijnhof (Dutch). The first Beguinage in Belgium appeared in Mechelen in 1207.

Beguinages were formed across the southern Netherlands from the 12th century onwards. Of the 100 that existed in the 14th century, around 25 remain. In 1998, 13 surviving Flemish Beguinages were placed on the Unesco World Heritage list. They are located in the following towns: Hoogstraten, Lier, Mechelen, Turnhout, Sint-Truiden, Tongeren, Dendermonde, Ghent (2), Diest, Leuven, Bruges and Kortrijk. Most of their buildings date from the 17th century. In their original, medieval form, the houses would have been wooden constructions.

Above: the Begijnhof entrance can be seen from the water.

Beguines

Beguines lived in solitude in separate small houses. They divided their time between prayer, manual work (sewing or lace-making) and taking part in collective Beguinage events, such as religious services and processions. Some Beguinages selected their members on the basis of social status; others were open to all, and numbered their inhabitants in thousands.

Beguines have been described as the earliest women's movement in Christian history, a community of financially independent women who existed outside the church and the home, the only acceptable domains for women at the time.

The male counterparts of Beguines were known as Begharads, and were usually of humble origin. Similar to Beguines in that they were

Left: a nun crosses the Begijnhof courtyard.

French Revolution and they became extinct in the early 20th century.

Current Inhabitants

The Beguinage in Bruges is today occupied in part by a community of Benedictine nuns, who wear the traditional clothes of the Beguines and maintain some of their predecessors' customs. Other houses are occupied by lay people. The Beguinage in Leuven is inhabited by university students and lecturers. Elsewhere, they are occupied by retired people or cultural institutions.

The Bruges Beguinage
Prinselijk Begijnhof De Wijngaarde
Wijngaardplein; daily 6.30am–6.30pm; free; bus: 1; map p.134 B2

At their origin in the 12th century, Beguinages were usually built on the edge of a city, and became a tiny town within a town, situated near water that the residents could use for their textile work and vegetable plots. Later, with the wars of religion, the area surrounded by the city walls was extended, and encapsulated the Beguinage. Interest in preserving Beguinages grew from the mid-19th century, when artists started to depict the folkloric charm of these uniquely preserved, miniature towns.

became centres of mysticism, their members practising flagellation and other activities considered heretical. In 1311, Pope Clement V accused Beguines of spreading heresy; they were persecuted by the Church for many years, until rehabilitated in the 15th century. In Belgium, the Beguinages flourished under Spanish rule, especially from the 17th century on. However, most were quashed following the

The Prinselijk Begijnhof De Wijngaard was founded in 1245. At its height, in the 17th century, it numbered up to 300 houses, stretching as far as today's railway station, and was a self-governing community, with a hospice, farm and brewery, as well as a church. Carved bunches of grapes on the bridge handrail and over the doorway by the entrance (1776) recall its earlier surroundings: a vineyard where grapes were cultivated for vinegar-making, hence the name: Princely Beguinage of the Vineyard. The word 'sauvegarde' above the door attests to the royal protection granted by the Duke of Burgundy, assuring the Beguinage's independent status. The last Beguines left in 1927.

Below: a detail from the gate to the Begijnhof.

not bound by vows and did not follow a uniform rule of life, they differed in that they had no private property, lived together in a cloister and ate at the same table.

Decline

Over time, Beguinages grew to resemble monastic orders: Beguines had to follow strict rules and were not allowed to leave without permission from their superior. The enclosures also

SEE ALSO CHURCHES, P.47; MUSEUMS AND GALLERIES, P.84

29

Cafés and Bars

There are few greater pleasures in Bruges than reflecting on the historical treasures around you while sitting in a bar or café sipping a Belgian beer. You will be spoilt for choice: most bars stock at least 20 beer varieties; a few have more than 100. Or how about a coffee and *pannekoeken* (pancakes) for a spot of people-watching after a museum? Many bars and cafés stay open until the early hours of the morning, until the last customers leave. For a guide to Belgian beers, *see 'Food and Drink'*. For bars that have live music or DJ sets, see *'Nightlife'*. Many bars and cafés listed here will serve food, but *see also 'Restaurants'*.

Markt and Burg

Cambrinus
Philipstockstraat 19; tel: 050 33 23 28; www.cambrinus.eu; daily 11am–11pm, later at weekends; bus: 1; map p.134 C4
Under the same ownership as the nearby De Bier Tempel store and with rather a tourist focus, this newish bar-brasserie has similar expertise in the hallowed hop: 400 beers are on offer in a renovated pub-like decor with coloured glass lamps, a long bar and table service. Good portions of hearty food – including some recipes cooked with beer – complete the experience and ensure that if you spend enough time in here, you could end up looking like the rotund chap straddling a beer barrel in the establishment's logo. That will be Cambrinus, the 'king of beer'. You have been warned.

Charlie Rockets
Hoogstraat 19; tel: 050 33 06

Above: Cambrinus's rotund logo, a warning to all beer drinkers…

60; www.charlierockets.com; daily 8am–late; bus: 1, 6, 16; map p.135 C4
A young, alternative clientele comes to this American-style bar-diner that stays open late into the night (be warned anyone considering staying in the youth hostel upstairs). It is on two floors, located in a former cinema that is still intact. There are also five pool tables, darts and a resident DJ at weekends.

Craenenburg
Markt 16; tel: 050 33 34 02; www.craenenburg.be; daily

from 7am, Sun–Thu until 11pm, Fri–Sat until 1am; bus: 1; map p.134 C4
Probably the best-known café in Bruges, due to its location and history: it was here that Margaret of York stood to watch jousting tournaments in honour of her marriage to Charles the Bold in 1468. Twenty years later, Archduke Maximilian of Austria was held hostage here by locals furious at his attempt to impose taxes on them; his advisers were tortured here, too. A traditional Flemish

Smoking is banned in restaurants and bars in Belgium, except in bars that have a separated smoking area.

Left: enjoying the local Brugse Zot beer in Langestraat.

Staminée de Garre
De Garre 1; tel: 050 34 10 29; www.degarre.be; Mon–Thu and Sun noon–midnight, Fri noon–1am, Sat 11am–1am; bus: 1; map p.134 C4

A place of pilgrimage for beer-lovers, many of whom struggle to find the narrow alley De Garre – more a door in the wall off Breidelstraat – or cannot get a seat once in (and standing is not allowed). On two floors of an old house (though be warned the serving staff may forget you are up there), it is a friendly place where the 130 beers on offer come served with cheese. House brew Tripel de Garre (11.5 percent) is a must-try; it is limited to three glasses per person.

Wijnbar Est
Braambergstraat 7; tel: 050 33 38 39; www.wijnbarest.be; Fri–Mon 4pm–midnight; bus: 6, 16; map p.135 C4

Attractive, tiny wine bar on two floors run by a welcoming and knowledgeable family. Daily menu of wines by the glass, plus 90 more by

Hot drinks are usually served with a sweet biscuit, piece of chocolate or small cake; beers come with savoury nibbles. If you prefer a milky coffee, ask for a *'koffie verkeerd'*, which is made with more hot milk than coffee. This is not to be confused with cappuccino, which in Belgium is usually made with a dollop of whipped cream on a black coffee and not frothy milk, as you find in Italy (and most other places). Tea served in Belgium is generally disappointing, especially if you like a strong brew. It invariably comes served as a cup of hot (not boiling) water with a flavourless bag on the side.

café, it has been run by the same family since the 1960s. Good terrace for people-watching, and for breakfast, as the sunlight falls here in the morning. Varied brasserie fare.

Het Dagelijks Brood
Philipstockstraat 21; tel: 050 33 60 50; www.painquotidien.com; Mon–Sat 7am–7pm, Sun 8am–6pm; bus: 1; map p.134 C4

Local branch of hit Belgian bakery and café (known as Le Pain Quotidien in French-speaking parts), which has franchised its scrubbed-pine communal table philosophy to cities around the world. Wholesome bread, dangerously addictive chocolate spreads and tarts, and generous breakfasts, but the tasty open sandwiches are not for larger appetites.

Below: the historic Craenenburg café.

31

the bottle. Platters of cheese and charcuterie plus salads and pasta enhance the tasting experience, and there are live concerts of jazz, blues, boogie, folk or pop every Sunday from 8–10.30pm; free entry.

South
De Bühne
Sint-Salvatorskoorstraat 6; tel: 050 34 66 49; Wed–Sun noon–2.30pm, 6–9pm, also Oct–Mar Tue 6–9pm; bus: 1; map p.134 B3
Inviting tea room and lunch spot off Simon Stevinplein that does divine pastries, for a break away from the crowds and no risk of soggy pancakes.
Carpe Diem
Wijngaardstraat 8; tel: 050 33 54 47; www.tearoom-carpe diem.be; Wed–Mon 7am–6pm;

bus: 1; map p.134 C2
Wood-panelling, antiques and stained-glass doors make the perfect accompaniments to an 'olde-worlde' experience in the tearoom adjoining the Detavernier patisserie and bakery. Run by a dynamic couple, it is quiet and civilized without being over-smart. Mouthwatering cakes and biscuits.
L'Estaminet
Park 5; tel: 050 33 09 16; www.estaminet-brugge.be; Fri–Wed 11.30am–late, Thu 4pm–late; bus: 1, 11; map p.135 D3
Open since 1900, this family-friendly café gets packed with locals on a Sunday afternoon, after the obligatory stroll round the Astridpark just across the road. A jolly, laid-back establishment, which serves tasty spaghetti

Two beers are still brewed in Bruges: Straffe Hendrik and Brugse Zot, both made by the Halve Maan Brewery. Try them unfiltered exclusively in the brewery's bar. Halve Maan had transferred production of Straffe Hendrik to another brewery in 1988, but brought it back in-house in 2008, restoring to the city its only 'Tripel'. A number of other Belgian beers are named after Bruges: Brugge Blond, Brugge Tripel, Brugs, Brugs Tarwebier and Brugse Babbelaar.

Bolognese and other simple bar meals, plays the blues and sometimes hosts live music.
De Halve Maan
Walplein 26; tel: 050 44 42 22; www.halvemaan.be; daily 10am–6pm, Sat until 7pm; bus: 1; map p.134 C2
The sole working brewery in Bruges, run by one family since 1856, and a brewery museum as well as a bar. Records from 1564 also note the existence on Walplein of a brewery called Die Maene (The Moon). Its two house beers are Straffe Hendrik (Strong Henry) – recently repurchased after it was sold to another producer – and Brugse Zot (Bruges Fool), created in 2005. A vast range of other brews are served in the roomy and family-friendly tavern, as well as an affordable dish-of-the-day. The sunny courtyard gets busy in fine weather. Tours are on the hour (Sun–Fri 11am–4pm, Sat 11am–5pm)

West
De Belegde Boterham
Kleine Sint-Amandsstraat 5; tel: 050 34 91 31; Mon–Sat 11.30am–4pm; bus: 1; map p.134 B4

Below: the sign for De Halve Maan brewery.

Above: if you like beer, 't Brugs Beertje is the place for you…

A fresh and funky small sandwich bar and tea room on a little pedestrianised street near the Markt, serving tasty salads, sandwiches and light lunches.

't Brugs Beertje
Kemelstraat 5; tel: 050 33 96 16; www.brugsbeertje.be; Thu–Fri and Mon 4pm–midnight, Sat–Sun until 1am; bus: 1; map p.134 B3
The beer connoisseur's favourite bar in Bruges, as small inside as its reputation is large, this has become a beer-lovers mecca since it was established some 20 years ago. The friendly and knowledgeable landlord will

advise on all aspects of his 300 or so beers. Snacks and light meals are served, and there is a shop where you can buy the T-shirt.

Concertgebouwcafé
't Zand 34; tel: 050 47 69 99; www.concertgebouw.be/en/cafe; Wed–Sat 11am–late plus on performance days from 1hr before show; bus: 1; p.134 B3
The new concert hall café – located between the tourist office and the hall's main entrance – is as minimalist and stylish as the rest of the building. A light food menu and varied wine list is complemented by refined music on the sound system and a no-smoking policy.

De Medici Sorbetière
9 Geldmuntstraat; tel: 050 33 93 41; www.demedici.be; Mon 1am–6pm, Tue–Sat 9am–6pm; bus: 1; map p.134 B4
An ice-cream parlour and tea-room that upholds the Burgundian traditions of fine feasting in a pretty art deco interior on two floors with a

Below: …and it is a cosy spot to pause and catch up.

33

Cocktails

Mojito · Pina Colada · Tequila Sunrise
Mojito Royal · Nutty Colada · Tequila Steeler
Caipirinha · White Russian · Harvey Wallbanger
Caipiroska · Black Russian
Margarita · Long Island Iced tea · Singapore Sling
Daiquiri · Mai Tai · Bee's Knees

Above: the De Republiek café has an extensive cocktail menu.

terrace on the first floor to the rear. Also does some seriously wicked cakes.

North

't Opkikkertje
West-Gistelhof 13; tel: 0485 94 94 83; www.opkikkertje.be; Mon–Tue, Thu–Fri from 4.30pm, Wed from 6pm, Sat from 5pm; bus: 4, 14; map p.132 C2
Mingle with local workers and bohemians at this tucked away and very local

Below: try something fruity…

bar, which serves the cheapest beers in town during its daily happy hour (on Friday 8–9pm) and has live music every other week or so.

Patisserie Servaas van Mullem
Vlamingstraat 56; tel: 050 33 05 15; Wed–Sun 8am–6.45pm; bus: 1, 3, 13; map p.132 C1
Well-dressed professionals and academic types take their morning coffee over a paper at this upmarket bakery and pastry shop with a tempting spread of cakes and fruit tarts. There is a small terrace alongside the shop, facing the theatre.

Poatersgat
Vlamingstraat 82; daily 5pm–1am; bus: 3, 13; map p.132 C1
Atmospheric beer pub (120 brews on the menu) in a

Table service is standard in all bars and cafés but the most hip – a trend that we hope does not catch on. You are not expected to tip the staff, but they will appreciate it if you leave a few coins to round up the bill, especially if you are in a group.

stunning vaulted cellar, prettily candlelit and popular with a local, younger crowd late in the evening. The name means 'monk's hole' in the local dialect, a reference to the below-ground entrance from the street.

Prestige
Vlamingstraat 12–14; tel: 050 34 31 67; Tue–Sun 7.30am–6.30pm; bus: 1; map p.132 C1
Chintzy, luxurious tearoom alongside a good bakery

Below: or cool and refreshing.

Above: Vino Vino is a popular tapas and live music bar.

and pastry shop just off the Markt. A recent makeover has seen prices escalate, but the decor is delightful and service welcoming, whether for breakfast, lunch or tea.

De Republiek
Sint-Jakobsstraat 36; tel: 050 34 02 29; 11am–late; bus: 1, 3, 13; map p.134 B4
Café of the Cultuurhuis de Republiek that includes the Lumière art-house cinema. Popular with a local, alterna-

tive crowd, it also serves cocktails and exotic light meals (up to 11pm, after which there is only a limited choice). Large courtyard behind is a real suntrap.

Terrastje
Genthof 45; tel: 050 33 09 19; Fri–Mon noon–11pm; bus: 4, 14; map p.133 C1
Cosy brown café in a tiny building with a slightly larger terrace, right on a road junction overlooking the canal.

Run by a friendly English-Dutch couple and loved by locals and visitors alike, it is prized for its good beer selection, tasty brasserie fare (soup, snails, *waterzooi*, omelette, salads), wide selection of nibbles (ham and cheese platters) and desserts (ices and pancakes). Live jazz every first Mon of month from Apr–Sept.

Vino Vino
Grauwwerkersstraat 15; tel: 0486 69 66 58; Thu–Tue 6pm–

Below: sticky, sweet pancakes and waffles are a Belgian staple.

Above: nibbles are often served with your drinks order.

2am; bus: 3, 13; map p.132 B1
Jugs of sangria, portions of tapas, blues on the sound system and a friendly owner have earned this backstreet wine bar a faithful following.

East

Barsalon
Langestraat 15; tel: 050 33 41 13; www.rock-fort.be; Mon–Fri noon–2.30pm, 6.30–11pm; bus: 6, 16; map p.135 D4
Trendy lounge bar-brasserie merged in a sliver of a place with Rock Fort restaurant, whose dining area spills into the bar. Ideal for a tête-à-tête, the high tables have white leather-covered fixed stools.
SEE ALSO RESTAURANTS, P.119

Bauhaus
Langestraat 135–137; tel: 050 34 10 93; www.bauhaus.be; daily 10am–2am; bus: 6, 16; map p.133 E1
Laid-back café attached to the youth hostel and budget hotel; so populated by young people from all over the world, and plenty of locals, too. They come here for the cheap eats, large beer selection, monthly open mic night and the DJ on Fri and Sat. Spread across two rooms, with smoking permitted on the bar side.

Du Phare
Sasplein 2; tel: 050 34 35 90; www.duphare.be; daily 11.30am–midnight; bus: 4; map p.133 D4
Up near the Dampoort, this music bar-brasserie has a friendly atmosphere, varied menu (including Creole and Thai dishes, as well as steaks) and live blues and jazz bands. A large south-facing terrace beside the canal is a draw. Busiest at night, but a pleasant spot for lunch or drinks when you are in this neck of the woods.

Vlissinghe
Blekersstraat 2; tel: 050 34 37 37; www.cafevlissinghe.be;

Below: friendly bar service at backpacker haven, Bauhaus.

36

Above: De Dulle Griet's Kwak beer comes in a 1.5-litre glass.

Wed–Thu 11am–10pm, Fri–Sat 11am–midnight, Sun 11am–7pm; bus: 4, 14; map p.133 D1
Founded in 1515, this is the oldest café in Bruges, with wood-panelled walls, long oak tables and a good-sized garden. The beer list is not that impressive and the bar food is simple, but this is an institution: come to relive the Bruges of yore. Open later than advertised on Fri and Sat, as long as the punters keep drinking.

Ghent
Brooderie
Jan Breydelstraat 8; tel: 09 225 06 23; Wed–Sun 8.30am–6pm; tram: 1; map p.136 C4
Facing the Design Museum, this homely bakery store (with B&B rooms upstairs) serves breakfast, lunch and afternoon teas on scrubbed pine tables. Cakes are home-made and portions are generous: try the moist, dark spice cake.

De Dulle Griet
Vrijdagmarkt 50; tel: 09 224 24 55; www.dullegriet.be; Mon 4.30pm–1am, Tue–Sat noon–1am, Sun noon–7.30pm; tram: 1; map p.136 C4
There is no shortage of cafés on Vrijdagmarkt, but this is one of the highlights, an Old Flemish-style bar with 250 different beers, including the renowned Kwak – the 1.5-litre glasses are on proud display – and Ghent's own brews Stropken, Gentse Tripel and Augustijnerbier. Last orders half an hour before closing time.

't Dreupelkot
Groentenmarkt 12; tel: 09 224 21 20; www.dreupelkot.be; daily 4pm–no fixed time; tram: 1; map p.136 C4
Bruges no longer has a dedicated genever specialist but Ghent does, run by the same team as the Waterhuis aan de Bierkant. Step inside to sample this traditional Belgian tipple in all its varieties.

Kafee Vooruit
Sint-Pietersnieuwstraat 23; tel: 09 267 28 48; www.vooruit.be; Mon–Wed 10am–1am, Thu–Sat 10am–2am, Sun noon–1am; tram: 22; map p.137 C2
The restored Kunstcentrum Vooruit is a remarkable vision of a working-class culture palace dating from 1912. Its vast café is popular with students and bohemian types, and serves drinks, coffee as well as light veggie meals.

Het Waterhuis aan de Bierkant
Groentenmarkt 9; tel: 09 225 60 80; www.waterhuisaande bierkant.be; daily 11am–2am; closed two weeks in Jan; tram: 1; map p.136 C4
A justifiably popular bar in a great location right beside the Leie; try Ghent's own beers Stropken, Gentse Tripel and Augustijnerbier, among the 150 on offer.

Canals and Bridges

The canals – *reien* – of Bruges give the city its almost impossible prettiness. The red-brick architecture is duplicated in reflection to create picture-perfect views of a bygone age. But what delights us today once came with an ugly smell: sewage was dumped into the canals right up until 1980. A boat tour is an excellent way to view the city, but to best appreciate the canals, wander on foot or cycle around the following highlights, presented in alphabetical order by quayside, followed by bridges along that particular stretch of water.

Coupure

Bus: 6, 16; map p.135 D1–E3
The Coupure is a former industrial leg of canal, dug in 1752 to allow river traffic from Ghent a shorter route via the Sint-Annarei to the Langerei. It was an industrial neighbourhood until the start of World War II. Towards the southern end is a popular mooring spot for yachts and cabin cruisers, and for fishermen trying their luck from the quay. It feels quite rural compared to the rest of the city.

The open-topped canal boats operate Mar–mid-Nov daily 10am–6pm and at weekends and holiday periods through the winter, weather permitting. Boats depart from Rozenhoedkaai, Dijver and Mariastraat.

Conzett Brug

Bus: 6, 16; map p.135 E3
This modern footbridge was designed by architect Jürg Conzett to mark Bruges' year as European Capital of Culture in 2002. Great scrolls of rusted

steel span the canal above the walkway of weather-washed wood, which has proved very welcome to locals since it was built, providing the missing link in the ring canal park.

Dampoort

Bus: 4; map p.133 D4
The modern working canal, complete with lifting bridges, makes fun family viewing at Dampoort and the adjacent Handelskom Docks. These were dug in 1664–65 to take advantage of the new network of inland waterways passing through Bruges, and were once used by sea-going vessels. It is still busy with working barges as it is close to the start of the Boudewijnkanaal (Baudouin Canal) to Zeebrugge and the canal to Ostend which, from 1622 onwards, restored the city's link with the sea, lost after the route via Damme and the Zwin estuary inlet silted up.

Gouden-Handrei

Bus: 4, 14; map p.133 C1
The start of a tranquil stretch of canal branching off Langerei, providing welcome

Below: the Conzett Brug is one of the city's newest bridges.

Left: the Peerdenbrug *(see p.40).*

Swans have swum in Bruges' canals, so the story goes, since 1448, when Emperor Maximilian was imprisoned in the city and his councillor Pieter Lanchals was beheaded. Lanchals' coat of arms featured a swan (the family name is derived from '*lang hals*': long neck), and the emperor ordered that swans be kept on the canals of Bruges for evermore, as a reminder of the city's dreadful crime.

respite from the tour-boat microphones. The canal traces an arc from here to the 't Zand in the west of the city: wander or cycle along its route (although the road does depart from the bank at times) in the early morning or at dusk to glimpse a golden-hued and lesser-visited Bruges. It follows Spaanse Loskaai, the quay where Spanish ships used to unload their cargo,

including Castillian wool to replace the increasingly rare English product, for Flemish weavers to transform into the finest cloth in Europe.

Augustijnenbrug
Bus: 3, 13; map p.132 C1
Crossing from Spaanse Loskaai to Augustijnenrei is the triple-arched Augustijnenbrug (Augustinians' Bridge), the first stone bridge in Bruges, built 1294 by

monks from the former – you guessed it – Augustinian friary on the north side of the canal. A modern apartment block now occupies the site of the friary. Legend has it there was once a secret tunnel under the canal through which the monks would reach a convent on the opposite bank, for illicit trysts with nuns. The house on the corner of Spanjaardstraat by the bridge – Den Noodt Gods, built 1616 by Spanish merchant Francisco de

Below: the three arches of the Augustijnenbrug.

Peralta – has been known since the 19th century as the Spookhuis, inspired by stories of a monk who killed the object of his devotion in a fit of passion. Their two spirits allegedly haunt the building, which has changed hands repeatedly, and been abandoned on more than one occasion.

Vlamingbrug
Bus: 3, 13; map p.132 B1
Built in 1331 as a continuation of the busy thoroughfare leading to the artists' district to the north, this two-arched bridge leads to the pretty Pottenmakersstraat.

Groenerei
Bus: 6, 16; map p.135 D4
The stretch of canal along Groenerei is one of the most picturesque. Admire the back gardens of the lucky residents who live alongside it.

Meebrug and Peerdenbrug
Bus: 1, 6, 16; map p.135 C4–D4
The grey stone of these two bridges along Groenerei is softened by a covering of foliage. Their single arches

Near Ezelbrug (Donkey Bridge), along Grauwwerkersstraat, there remains a fine stretch of old city wall, including part of a defensive tower dating from 1127 in the back garden of one of the houses (best viewed from across the water in Pottenmakersstraat). These original city walls were thrown up around the inner canal circuit in the aftermath of Charles the Good's assassination. Their purpose was to defend what was then a much smaller city than that enclosed by the second line of circumvallation, whose outline dates from the 14th century and is preserved today by the ring canal and a park.

reflected in the canal frame a shimmering image of quayside houses. Do not miss the view from Peerdenbrug along to the tower of Sint-Salvatorskathedraal.

Jan van Eyckplein
Bus: 4, 14; map p.133 C1
Bruges has many former harbours, and this one – along

adjoining Spiegelrei – was the busiest of them all; the canal that terminates here once led as far as the Markt. Along here came boats laden with Castillian oranges and lemons, Oriental spices, Mediterranean velvet and brocade, Baltic fur and amber. This was also the commercial and diplomatic centre for medieval Bruges, with foreign consulates situated along the length of Spiegelrei.

Langerei
Bus: 4, 14; map p.133 D4–C1
In the Middle Ages, this would have been one of the city's busiest canal thoroughfares, between the Dampoort and the canal to Damme and the merchants' quarter along Spiegelrei. Right up until World War II, coal, wheat and wood were unloaded down here. Today, however, a relaxing canalside stroll up either side – along the street named Langerei or Potterierei opposite – offers a glimpse of 'ordinary' Bruges, and it is indicative of this city's great beauty that it lacks little, or

Below: the much-photographed Rozenhoedkaai.

Above: the attractive Duinenbrug is a wooden drawbridge.

nothing, of the splendour of better-advertised locations. The Potterierei (east) side is a slightly quieter road, and is sunny in the afternoon.

Carmersbrug
Bus: 4, 14; map p.133 C1
Look down from this bridge to the wall by the water where a modern stone statue of a Carmelite monk holds a staff to measure the water's depth.

Duinenbrug
Bus: 4, 14; map p.133 D3
This small wooden drawbridge, towards the top of the Potterierei near the Groot-Seminarie, is supported on two stone arches, and makes this part of the canal seem distinctly less urban.

Early tourists to Bruges would have arrived by luxury barge from Ghent, Nieuwpoort or Ostend and alighted at the Bargehuis (barge house), now a bar, near the Katelijnebrug swing bridge. Many of today's tourists also arrive in this neck of the woods, just down the Bargeweg in the main coach park.

Minnewater
Bus: 1; map p.134 C1
The Minnewater is not just a pretty lake with weeping willows; it also serves a practical purpose: water for the canals enters the city here, fed from the Ghent and perimeter canals. The pink brick lockhouse (Sashuis; 1519), which overlooks the long rectangular basin, regulates the level of the canals in the city centre.

The name Minnewater (often translated as 'Lake of Love') seems to be a mistranslation of an earlier name for this stretch of water, which once served as an interior port; the Binnenwater. As many as 150 seagoing ships and canal barges loaded and unloaded cargo here daily before the river silted up and they had to stop at Damme. Boats would dock here before sailing on into Flanders and to Ghent.
SEE ALSO PARKS AND GARDENS, P.105

Rozenhoedkaai
Bus: 1, 6, 16; map p.135 C4
The view over the canal from Rozenhoedkaai (Rosary

Quay) graces many a postcard. It follows the line of the River Dijver, the old waterside houses and the Belfort (Belfry). Winston Churchill is one of the many artists, amateur and professional, who have painted the scene from this spot. It is also where the maudlin protagonist of Georges Rodenbach's novel *Bruges-la-Morte* lived: 'He would spend the whole day in his room, a vast retreat on the first floor whose windows looked out onto the Quai du Rosaire, along which the facade of his house stretched, mirrored in the canal.' The location also inspired the 1906 poem *Quai du Rosaire* by Rainer Maria Rilke, a Rodenbach admirer.
SEE ALSO LITERATURE AND THEATRE, P.74

Bonifaciusbrugje
Bus: 1; map p.134 C3
This scenic footbridge across the canal behind the Arentshuis and Gruuthuse Museum is a majestic example of the Gothic revival in Bruges. It was built in 1910 but could have been here for centuries from the patina of its stone. It bridges a cool green stretch of canal flanked by vine-covered houses and a rare surviving timber facade.

Sint-Jan Nepomucenusbrug
Bus: 1, 6, 16; map p.135 C3
This busy bridge (also known as Eekhoutbrug) across the Dijver, a canalised offshoot of the Reie river, is crowned by the imposing statue of St John of Nepomuk (1767), which stands between two wrought-iron lamps. St John, patron saint and protector against flooding, was thrown in the Moldau in Prague in 1393 by King Wenceslas IV.

Children

Bruges may be best known for its churches and museums, but there is still plenty to keep children entertained, both in the city or at the many attractions in the surrounding countryside and nearby coast. The compact size of the place and relative absence of traffic make it a much less tiring destination for kids than many city trips, and the canals and bridges add to its appeal. As well as the selection of child-friendly museums, monuments, parks and theme-parks described in alphabetical order below, young ones are also sure to enjoy the pancakes, waffles, hot chocolate and chips that are local specialities.

Accommodation

Most hotels have family rooms or will provide a child's bed on request. It is always worth phoning ahead to check this sort of detailed information.

Coast

The coast near Bruges has wide and safe sandy beaches, dunes, and a gentle gradient into the sea. Most resorts have child-friendly markers along the beach – bright-coloured animals on posts – so that children can easily locate the spot where their family is sitting. De Haan has a mini-golf course and a small enclosure with goats and rabbits, and here and in other resorts there are many places that rent out pedal-powered buggies for driving along the promenade, as well as bikes. At Ostend there is a good museum aboard a former Icelandic trawler and a navy training ship, the *Mercator*, open to visitors in the attractive town-centre marina. A ride on the kusttram (coast tram) is also fun, although parents – and, indeed, anyone – should be extra careful

when crossing the coast road at any point, as the tram travels very fast down the central reservation, and accidents are not uncommon.
SEE ALSO THE COAST, P.20–1

Eating Out

Taking children to restaurants is standard practice in Belgium in all except the most upmarket places. Most brasseries, cafés and lower-priced establishments have children's menus, or will adapt their dishes to suit. Children will like the *croque-monsieur* (toasted ham and cheese sandwich; with an egg on top: *croque-madame*), omelettes, plates of ham and cheese chunks that most bars serve as snacks, and the tiny North Sea shrimps served stuffed in tomatoes or deep-fried in a white sauce *(garnalkroketten)*.

Festivals and Events
Meifoor
't Zand; late Apr–late May; bus: 1; map p.134 A3
A sprawling funfair sets up on the 't Zand square and Koning Albertpark every year,

with dozens of stalls and rides for all ages.
Snow and Ice Brugge
Stationsplein; www.ijssculptuur. be; late Nov–early Jan, check website for dates; daily 10am–6pm; bus: 1; map p.134 B1
Each winter over the Christmas period, a large ice sculpture festival takes place in tents in front of the station, with buildings, figures and animals crafted by dozens of professional ice artists who travel from northern climes. The theme changes each year and is always very child-friendly, although kids will need to be wrapped up warm. There is a heated drinks tent in which to thaw out at the end. An ice-skating rink takes up residence on the Markt square throughout the festive season from the last week of November until the first week of January; children will also like the Christmas market with fairground carousels on Simon Stevinplein.

Indoor Play Centres
BO BO's Land
Vissersstraat 97, 8340 Moerkerke – Damme; tel: 050

Left: ice sculpture at Snow and Ice Brugge.

Space-themed play centre with a climbing structure and chutes in a former industrial building just west of the city centre, with a large café area.

Monuments
Belfort
Markt 7; tel: 050 44 81 43; www.brugge.be/musea; daily 9.30am–5pm; bus: 1; map p.134 C4

Not for tiny children but for those who can manage 366 steps up a narrow, steep and often crowded spiral staircase. The experience is well worth it and a spectacular view awaits.
SEE ALSO MONUMENTS, P.78

Sint-Janshuismolen
Kruisvest; tel: 050 44 81 11; www.brugge.be/musea; June–Sept Tue–Sun 9.30am–12.30pm, 1.30–5pm; bus: 6, 16; map p.133 E2

The knowledgeable attendants demonstrate how an old grain mill works, and as long as there is a little wind you can watch it make flour. There is a rather steep climb up the steps to the windmill.
SEE ALSO MONUMENTS, P.80

Entrance to all city-owned museums (the 'Bruggemuseum', which include the Belfort, Groeninge, Volkskunde, etc.) is free to children under 13. For most other attractions, entry is free for children under 3.

50 01 27; www.bobosland.be; Tue, Thu–Sun from 11am, Wed from noon; bus: 43
Large indoor (and outdoor) play centre for children up to 12 years old, with a soft play area for under fives. A café serves crêpes, milkshakes and ice creams, while the bistro menu includes soups, salads and daily specials.

De Toverplaneet
Legeweg 88; tel: 0478 22 69 29; www.detoverplaneet.be; Wed 1–8pm, Fri 3.30–7pm, Sat–Sun 10.30am–7pm, school holidays daily 10.30am–7pm, closed on hot summer days; bus: 9

Museums and Galleries
The following are particularly suited to children:
Choco-Story
Wijnzakstraat 2; tel: 050 61 22 37; www.choco-story.be; daily 10am–5pm, except two weeks mid-Jan; bus: 1, 6, 16; map p.132 C1

Children aged 6–12 can play the Choclala sticker game provided at the entrance to this museum about the history and traditions of chocolate-making. There is a gift on the way out for all those who complete the game correctly.
SEE ALSO MUSEUMS AND GALLERIES, P.89

Below: parent-powered buggies on the coastal promenade.

Above: mother and babies in Minnewater park.

Groeningemuseum
Dijver 12; tel: 050 44 87 43;
www.brugge.be/musea; Tue–
Sun 9.30am–5pm; bus: 1; map
p.134 C3
The modern art in the collection may interest children, but
there is also a children's corner and play house designed
to keep them entertained
while their parents look at the
works of van Eyck, Bosch
and other Flemish Primitives.
SEE ALSO MUSEUMS AND GALLERIES,
P.85

**Bruggemuseum-
Volkskundemuseum**
Balstraat 43; tel: 050 44 87
43; www.brugge.be/musea;
Tue–Sun 9.30am–5pm; bus: 6,
16; map p.133 D1
The folklore museum gives
an idea of how people in
Bruges lived around 200
years ago and makes for
a fascinating visit, particularly for children. A row of
tiny almshouses contains
re-creations of the interiors
of old shops – including a
chemist, clogmaker and hat-
ter – as well as a schoolroom
and several family homes. In
fair weather, there are traditional toys to play with in the
garden and afternoon sweet-

making demonstrations are
held in the candy shop on
the first and third Thursday of
each month.
SEE ALSO MUSEUMS AND GALLERIES, P.90

Parks and Gardens
Beisbroek
Zeeweg, Sint-Andries;
www.beisbroek.be; park: daily,
dawn to dusk; nature centre:
Apr–Nov Mon–Fri 2–5pm, Sun
2–6pm; planetarium shows
(occasionally in English): Wed
and Sun 3pm and 4.30pm, Fri
8.30pm; park and nature centre
free; bus: 52, 53; map p.138 C3
Outdoor attractions at this
large country park include
a deer compound; indoors
there is a nature centre,
observatory and planetarium.
SEE ALSO PARKS AND GARDENS, P.107

Hof Sebrechts
entrances on Beenhouwers
straat and Oude Zak; bus: 9, 41,

For swimming, both the
**Provinciaal Zwembad
Olympiabad** (Doornstraat
110, Sint-Andries; tel: 050 39
02 00; map p.138 C3) and
**Intercommunaal Zwembad
Interbad** (Veltemweg 35; tel:
050 35 07 77) have slides.

42; map p.134 B4
Attractions for kids in this
tranquil park include a sandpit, playground and regular
sculpture exhibitions. The
park is behind the houses so
it is not bordered by roads.
SEE ALSO PARKS AND GARDENS, P.104

Koningin Astridpark
Minderbroederstraat; bus: 1,
11; map p.135 D3
As well as a children's play
area and a pond, this park
has lots of trees and space to
run around; it is not too large
and the church in the corner
of the park makes it easy
to get your bearings. The
Estaminet café alongside is
popular with families, too.
SEE ALSO PARKS AND GARDENS, P.105

Minnewater
Minnewater; bus: 1; map
p.134 C1
Kids will like the lake with all
its ducks, geese and swans,
and the magical-looking
Minnewater castle along the
banks of the lake. At the end
of the park, on Wijngaardplein, is the horse fountain,
a popular spot, where the
horses that pull the carriages
around town wait in line
to take a drink and munch
some hay.
SEE ALSO PARKS AND GARDENS, P.105

**Provinciaal Domein
Tillegembos**
Tillegemstraat 83, 8200 Sint-
Andries; tel: 050 40 35 43; bus:
25; map p.138 C3
An extensive park with
woodland, playgrounds and
a moated castle, just to the
south of Bruges.

De Zeven Torentjes
Canadaring 41, 8310 Asse-
broek; tel: 050 35 40 43;
daily 8am–dusk; free; bus: 2
Sint-Lucas/Assebroek; map
p.139 C3
This country estate on the
outskirts of Bruges has been
turned into a dedicated children's farm with pigs, hens,
horses, rabbits and more.

Sun Parks, a holiday village near De Haan, has a number of special child-friendly chalets among its choice of accommodation, and the whole complex is car-free. There is an indoor children's play area for under-13s, and a large leisure pool area – Aquafun – which is also open to non-residents. *See* www.sunparks.be; coast tram (stop Sun Parks).

There are also demonstrations by a blacksmith, some educational programmes and horse-and-cart rides.

Theme Parks
Boudewijn Sea Park
A. De Baeckestraat 12, 8200 Bruges; tel: 050 38 38 38; www.boudewijnseapark.be; opening hours vary, but at least Sat–Sun afternoons in summer, school holidays more often; free for children under 85cm (2.8ft) tall, reduced price for children under 12; bus: 7, 17
Sea park with dolphinarium in the southern suburbs of Bruges (2.5km/1.5 miles from rail station) that is a big favourite with children and adults. Plenty of rides and boats, as well as regular shows with performing dolphins.
Seafront Zeebrugge
Vismijnstraat 7; tel: 050 55 14 15; www.seafront.be; daily 10am–5pm, closed 2 weeks in Jan; children under 1m, free; train: Zeebrugge Kerk (then 100m/yd walk); map p.138 C4
A maritime theme park-cum-museum ideal for a half-day visit. There are interactive exhibits, videos, a pirates play-ship, a real lightship and the prize exhibit, a 100m (330ft) -long Soviet Foxtrot submarine, built 1960, in which visitors can experience a 4-min sound-and-light show simulating an attack. There is free parking.

Tours

BIKE TOURS
Quasimundo Bike Tours
Nieuwe Gentweg 5; tel: 050 33 07 75; www.quasimundo. com; tours run Mar–Oct daily 9.50am, starting in front of the City Hall on the Burg (reservation required); map p.134 C2
Quasimundo has a huge stock of bikes in all sizes, as well as safety helmets and child seats. Children under the age of eight go free. The guides are knowledgeable and entertaining.

BOAT TOURS
Katelijnestraat 4; tel: 050 33 27 71; www.nvstael.com; Mar–Nov 10am–6pm; bus: 1; map p.134 C2
Boat tours around the canals of Bruges are fun for children, as the small boats hug the water and skim under very low bridges. There are several starting points in the city – behind the Onze-Lieve-Vrouwekerk (the company listed above departs from here), along the Dijver, beside the Vismarkt and on the Rozenhoedkaai.

Below: cycling in Bruges is fun and safe for everyone.

HORSE-DRAWN CARRIAGES
Markt; tel: 050 34 54 01; www.hippo.be/koets; daily 9.30am–5.30pm; bus: 1 (Markt); map p.134 C4
There is room for up to five adults in one of the horse-drawn carriages that tour the streets of Bruges. Each tour lasts around 35 mins, including a drink-stop for the horse at the Begijnhof, where passengers can get off and visit. The carriages depart from the Markt daily except Wednesday – market day, when they decamp to the Burg.

PADDLE STEAMER TRIPS
Bruges-Damme
Damme tourist office; tel: 050 28 86 10; www.bootdamme-brugge.be; Apr–Sept four departures each way per day; bus: 4; map p.139 C3
The *Lamme Goedzak* stern-wheel paddle-steamer moors in Bruges at Noorweegse Kaai 31, just beyond Dampoort, and departs several times a day for Damme, 7km (4 miles) away, before making the return trip, half an hour each way.

Below: horse-powered carriages tour the town.

Churches

Ever since Flemish knight Dirk of Alsace returned to Bruges from the Second Crusade in 1150 with what was said to be a relic of the blood of Christ, the city has been a centre of pilgrimage and great piety: various religious communities flourished and churches grew rich with the gifts of foreign merchants and other wealthy benefactors. As a result, there are treasures aplenty behind the doors of most places of worship in the city; and seeking out these historic artworks and artefacts is to take a fascinating journey back in time to the golden age of medieval Bruges.

Markt and Burg

Heilig Bloedbasiliek (Basilica of the Holy Blood)

Burg; tel: 050 33 67 92; www.holyblood.com; mid-Mar–mid-Nov daily 9.30am–noon, 2–5pm, mid-Nov–mid-Mar Thu–Tue 9.30am–noon, 2–5pm; free; bus: 1; map p.134 C4

Named after the relic of Christ's blood that it was built to house, the Heilig Bloed-basiliek has been a place of pilgrimage for centuries. Its three-arched facade, completed in 1534, has ornate stone carvings and gilded statues of angels, knights and their ladies, below two towers of great delicacy. The interior is divided into two chapels, a 12th-century Romanesque lower chapel and a more recent Gothic upper chapel, providing a dramatic contrast in styles.

THE LOWER CHAPEL

The lower chapel is a study in shadows, with austere, unadorned lines, Romanesque pillars, and little decoration except for a relief carving over an interior doorway depict-ing the baptism of St Basil (an early Church Father). St Basil's relics were brought back from Palestine by Robert II, the Count of Flanders. The faded carving, which dates from around 1150, is naïve in style, and this is emphasised by the two mismatched columns supporting it. In the right nave, the wooden statue of a Virgin and Child has been venerated since the 14th century. The wooden trap door in the floor led to the tomb of 14th-century master stonemason Jan van Oudenaerde.

THE UPPER CHAPEL

Access to the upper chapel is through a beautiful Late Gothic doorway. Ascending by the broad, well-worn 16th-century spiral staircase, you can enter the upper chapel beneath the organ case. The lines of the chapel may have been spoiled somewhat by over-eager 19th-century decoration and murals, but the impression is of warmth and richness. The ceiling looks like an upturned boat and the room is flooded with a golden light. The bronze-coloured

On Ascension Day every year, the relic of the holy blood is carried through Bruges in the famous Heilig-Bloed Processie (Procession of the Holy Blood), the most important of West Flanders' festivals. The venerated phial is transported in a flamboyant gold and silver reliquary that is normally kept in the treasury of the chapel.

pulpit is a curious sight, bearing a remarkable resemblance to a cored and stuffed tomato.

In a small side chapel you will find the holy relic from which the church derives its name. Flemish knight Dirk of Alsace returned from the Second Crusade in the Holy Land in 1149 and is said to have brought with him a crystal phial believed to contain some drops of Christ's blood. Soon venerated all over medieval Europe, it is still brought out each Friday afternoon for the faithful. The dried blood turned to liquid at regular intervals for many years, an event declared to be a miracle by Pope Clement V. The phial is stored in a

Left: upper chapel of the Basilica of the Holy Blood.

different styles, but the interior is filled with treasures. Chief among them is the marble *Madonna and Child* (1504) by Michelangelo, originally intended for Siena Cathedral and the only one of the sculptor's works to have travelled outside Italy during his lifetime. It was brought to Bruges by a Flemish merchant, Jan van Moeskroen. The Madonna is a subdued, preoccupied figure, while the infant leans nonchalantly on her knee.

There are some fine paintings here by Pieter Pourbus (*Last Supper* and *Adoration of the Shepherds*) and Gerard David (*Transfiguration*), but it is the chancel area that holds most interest, after the Michelangelo. Here you can see the tombs of Charles the Bold and his daughter Mary of Burgundy, fine examples of, respectively, Renaissance and Late Gothic carving. Both sarcophagi are richly decorated with coats of arms linked with floral motifs in

richly ornate silver tabernacle presented by the archdukes of Spain in 1611. It is carried in a grand procession through the streets every year on Ascension Day.
SEE ALSO ARCHITECTURE, P.24; MUSEUMS AND GALLERIES, P.82

South
Begijnhofkerk
Begijnhof; tel: 050 33 00 11; open daily; free; bus: 1; map p.134 B2
The Begijnhofkerk (the church of the Begijnhof) is lesser known under its official name, Onze-Lieve-Vrouw van Troost van Spermalie (Our Lady of Consolation of Spermalie) and dates from 1245, although it was rebuilt in 1605 after a fire, then given a Baroque makeover around 1700. The only object saved from the fire is a wooden (now gilded) statue of the Madonna (1300) on the side altar; an original Romanesque door is also visible on the north facade. Services held by the convent nuns are open to the public and include Gregorian sung offices.
SEE ALSO BEGUINAGES, P.29; MUSEUMS AND GALLERIES, P.84

Onze-Lieve-Vrouwekerk
Mariastraat; Mon–Sat 9.30am–5pm, Sun 1.30–5pm; free (entrance charge to parts of the church); bus: 1; map p.134 C3
The vertiginous brick spire of Onze-Lieve-Vrouwekerk (Church of our Lady) makes this the city's tallest landmark, recognisable across the flat polders around Bruges. The exterior is a hotchpotch of

Below: towering spire of Onze-Lieve-Vrouwekerk.

47

Above: exquisite Madonna and Child by Michelangelo.

copper-gilt, gold, reds and blues; the figures themselves (with domestic details like the pet dogs at Mary's feet) are also in copper gilt. However, whether or not Charles and Mary are actually buried here is a matter of some dispute. Charles died in battle in Nancy in 1477 and it was difficult to identify the body. Mary, who died in a riding accident at the age of 25 (bringing to a close the 100-year reign of the House of Burgundy), may in fact be buried among a group of polychrome tombs in the choir that were discovered in 1979. You can see the frescoed tombs beneath your feet

> Michelangelo's *Madonna and Child* in the Onze-Lieve-Vrouwekerk is a rare work by the artist to have left Italy. It did so by accident, sold to a Flemish merchant after the Italian family who commissioned it for Siena Cathedral failed to pay the artist. Walpole tried, unsuccessfully, to buy it for England in the 18th century; the French whisked it away to Paris during the Revolution; and the Germans swiped it in World War II.

through windows in the floor and by means of mirrors in front of the sarcophagi.

Elsewhere in the church, you will find the funerary chapel of Pieter Lanchals – fated advisor to Maximilian of Austria, killed by the angry citizens of Bruges – containing frescoed tombs in maroon and black, as well as Van Dyck's starkly atmospheric painting of Christ on the Cross. The splendid wooden gallery overlooking the chancel belongs to the adjacent Gruuthuse mansion and dates from the 15th century.

The church is currently undergoing a major renovation and it's only partially accessible to the public; it is not possible to visit the tombs or see some of the artworks.
SEE ALSO ARCHITECTURE, P.24; MUSEUMS AND GALLERIES, P.86

West
Karmelietenkerk
Ezelstraat 28; tel: 050 44 38 89; daily 6.45–8am, 5–7pm; free; bus: 3; map p.132 B1
The 15th-century Karmelietenkerk (Carmelite Church) belonged to the big Carmelite Monastery that has occupied the former Hof van Uitkerke here since 1633. The Baroque interior dates from 1688–91 and is a peaceful place. The monastery is an unusual-looking building, perhaps because it was built by monks who were involved with the care of plague victims at the time. The Carmelites were expelled by the French in 1795 but returned in the 19th century, and the church is one of the few places in Bruges which is occupied by religious men and women and where you are likely to catch sight of any of them. Every Sunday at 10am there is a sung Gregorian Mass; the church is also regularly used for concerts.

> Foundations of the old cathedral of St Donatian's can be viewed in the basement of the Crowne Plaza hotel on the Burg. These were discovered and preserved during works on the hotel in the 1990s; access is free to visitors. The Toyo Ito Pavilion on the square occupies the site of the former church, which was destroyed after the French Revolution; it stands in a circle of gravel that demarcates the cathedral's central chapel.

Onze-Lieve-Vrouw-van-Blindekens
Kreupelenstraat, daily 9am–5pm; free; bus: 1 ('t Zand); map p.134 A3
Just outside the main city perimeter but worth a look if you are in the neighbourhood on a tour of all the city's alms-houses, Onze-Lieve-Vrouw-van-Blindekens (Our Lady of the Blind) is a bright and simple 17th-century church. Its founding honours a promise made at the battle of Mons-en-Pévèle in 1304, against the French. It has a carved pulpit from 1659 and, most notably, a gilded 14th-century statue of the Madonna and Child above a side altar. The chapel is the departure point for the annual Feast of the Assumption procession held on 15 August, wending its way to the church of Onze-Lieve-Vrouw-ter-Potterie (Our Lady of the Pottery).
Sint-Jakobskerk
Sint-Jakobsstraat; daily 10am–1pm, 2–5pm; free; bus: 1; map p.132 B1
Built 1220 over an earlier chapel, Sint-Jakobskerk (St James's Church) was quickly enlarged into a three-naved Gothic hall-church. It grew incredibly wealthy during the 15th century, thanks to generous endowments from parishioners, including wealthy

48

Above: colourful stained glass in Sint-Salvatorskathedraal.

Vrouwekerk and the Belfry, is a principal feature on the Bruges skyline.

The 15th-century wooden choir stalls flanking the altar bear a complete set of escutcheons of the Knights of the Golden Fleece, who held a chapter meeting here in 1478. Other notable features are the Baroque rood-screen surmounted by the sculpture *God the Father*, by Antwerp artist Artus Quellin, the elaborate pulpit and the 18th-century tapestries beside the altar.

SEE ALSO MUSEUMS AND GALLERIES, P.88

North

Sint-Gilliskerk

Sint-Gilliskerkhof; daily 10am–1pm, 2–6pm; free; bus: 4, 14; map p.133 C2

The parish church of Sint-Gilliskerk (St Giles' Church), a neo-Gothic church founded in 1241 and built in the early Gothic style, was drastically altered in the 15th century, leaving it with three aisles in place of the earlier cruciform shape. Now an edifice of agreeably stout proportions and with a brick tower similar to that of Sint-Salvators-kath-edraal, only the chunky stone pillars inside date from the original construction. Among the treasures to be seen within are a superb organ, a polyptych (1564) by Pieter Pourbus, and a cycle of paintings from 1774 by Bruges artist Jan Garemijn depicting the history of the Trinitarian Brothers, and their retrieval of white slaves from Algeria. The painter Hans Memling was buried here in 1494 in the no longer extant churchyard, and is remembered on a plaque beside the entrance.

Sint-Walburgakerk

Sint Maartensplein; daily 10am–1pm, 2–6pm; free; bus: 1, 6, 16; map p.133 C1

merchants and the residents of the Duke of Burgundy's Prinsenhof. The 18 altars around the church were each sponsored by a trade guild or corporation: note Lancelot Blondeel's 1523 altarpiece, made for the surgeons' and barbers' corporation.

A number of Flemish Primitive masterpieces were painted for this church, including works by Hans Memling, Hugo van der Goes and Roger van der Weyden. These have been removed, with one exception: the triptych of *The Legend of St Lucy* (1480). Painted by an anonymous contemporary of Memling known as the Master of the Legend of St Lucy, it is located in St Anthony's Chapel, and tells the story of a wealthy Sicilian virgin who, in gratitude for the recovery of her sick mother after her pilgrimage to St Agatha's tomb, gave all her worldly goods to the poor. This did not please the man to whom she was betrothed and he had her condemned to death. There are also two

triptychs by Pieter Pourbus, and the mausoleum of Ferry de Gros (1544), treasurer of the Order of the Golden Fleece, which is one of the finest examples of Flemish Renaissance sculpture.

Sint-Salvatorskathedraal

Zuidzandstraat; tel: 050 33 68 41; www.sintsalvator.be; Mon–Fri 10am–1pm, 2–5.30pm, Sat 10am–1pm, 2–3.30pm, Sun 11.30am–noon, 2–5pm; closed to casual visitors during services; museum: Sun–Fri 2–5pm; free except museum; bus: 1; map p.134 B3

Bruges' original parish church, dating from the 9th century, Sint-Salvatorskathedraal (Holy Saviour's Cathedral) only became the cathedral in 1834, replacing the Burg square's St Donatian's, which had been destroyed by the French in the late 18th century. The structure is mainly Gothic in style (13th–16th century), having succumbed to several fires, but it retains some Romanesque elements. Its brick belfry rises 100m, and, with the spire of Onze Lieve

49

Above: Sint-Jakobskerk's interior is filled with treasures *(see p.48)*.

This oratory was built in 1619–42 by the Jesuits, who had moved into Bruges in force after the Spanish authorities crushed the Calvinists in 1584. They set up base around here, building a monastery, a college and this church, which is all that survived their suppression in 1774. There is not much space in front of the building to stand back and admire its orderly dimensions, but there are treasures aplenty in the cool interior, flooded with silvery light by two decks of pale grey stained-glass windows reflected in the black-and-white marble floor tiles. Probably the most remarkable is the carved Carrara marble communion rail that stretches across the width of the three marble altars. There is also a fabulously over-the-top oak pulpit (1669) by Artus Quellin the Younger, which has twin stairways with a scalloped canopy uplifted by trumpeting angels. Anything but discreet, this nevertheless survived the French Revolution, when the church was transformed into a temple of law. The triptych on the right-hand wall, *Our Lady of the Dry Tree* (1620), portrays the apparition of the Virgin to Philip the Good as he prayed before his victory against the French. It is the work of Pieter Claeissens the Younger.

Today the church is the venue for concerts of classical and church music during the Festival of Flanders.
SEE ALSO ARCHITECTURE, P.26

East
Engels Klooster
Carmersstraat 85; tel: 050 33 24 24; www.the-english-convent.be; Mon–Thu and Sat 2–3.30pm, 4.15–5.30pm; free; bus: 4, 14; map p.133 D2
The Engels Klooster (English convent) houses a community of Augustinian sisters and was established in the wake of England's Dissolution of the Monasteries under King Henry VIII. Its imposing dome dates from the first half of the 18th century. Anne Mary Edmonstone was sent here to complete her education and to convert to Catholicism in order to marry pioneering naturalist Charles Waterton (1782–1865), founder of the world's first nature reserve. The convent has an historically important library of English books and runs a guesthouse.

Jeruzalemkerk
Peperstraat 3A; tel: 050 33 88 83; www.adornes.org; Mon–Sat 10am–5pm; bus: 6, 16; map p.133 D1
The striking Jeruzalemkerk was built between 1428 and 1465 and is a curious combination of Byzantine and Gothic styles. It was built by the Adornes family, originally merchants from Genoa, who had travelled on a pilgrimage to Jerusalem and were so impressed by the Church of the Holy Sepulchre that they built a copy of it in Bruges. There is even a copy of Christ's memorial tomb in the crypt. Spared pillage or destruction throughout the centuries thanks to its private chapel status it is remarkably well preserved. The church is still owned by the family's descendants and is part of the Adornesdomein (Adornes estate), which also includes the old family mansion (the Gothic facade is the only surviving original feature), the former Jerusalem almshouses founded by the family in the 15th century and a small museum (combined ticket with Jeruzalemkerk).

The lofty interior is sombre

and laden with symbols of mourning and penitence, and with very good examples of 15th- and 16th-century stained glass, some of which depicts members of the Adornes family. The space is dominated by the mausoleum of Anselm Adornes, and his wife, Marguerite van der Banck. Other family members are buried beneath the church, and their shields adorn the mausoleum. Anselm (b.1424) was burgomaster of Bruges, but was murdered in Scotland in 1483 while on a consular mission. Although buried in Linlithgow, his heart was brought back to Bruges in a lead box to be laid to rest beside his wife.

The altar is carved in a rather macabre fashion, with skulls and bones, and the cave-like atmosphere of the church is emphasised by the space behind the altar and above the crypt, which rises almost to the full height of the tower to create a rather eerie cavern.

Atop the tower outside sit the Jerusalem cross, and the wheel and palm leaf of St Catherine, to commemorate the journey of Anselm and his son to Jerusalem and Mt Sinai in 1470.

Onze-Lieve-Vrouw-ter-Potterie

Potterierei 79; Tue–Sun 9.30am–12.30pm, 1.30–5pm; free except adjoining museum; bus: 4; map p.133 D3

The 14th-century Onze-Lieve-Vrouw-ter-Potterie (Our Lady of the Pottery) used to be the chapel of the Potters' Guild, and is a little gem. It started life as part of a hospice, founded in 1276 by Augustinian nuns and became a retirement home in the 15th century (a large part of the complex retains this role today). A

Ignatius de Loyola, the Spanish priest who founded the Jesuit Order in Paris in 1534 (it was formally approved by the Pope in 1540), was a frequent guest of Spanish merchant Gonzalez d'Aguilera between 1528 and 1530, in his house at No. 9 Spanjaardstraat. Loyola was also in regular contact in Bruges with the Spanish-born humanist philosopher Juan Luis Vivés (1492–1540), a statue of whom stands behind the Onze-Lieve-Vrouwekerk beside the Bonifaciusbrugje.

former ward of the hospice and the cloisters are now the Potterie-museum.

The oldest part of the church is the left-hand nave, dating from 1359. Its two side altars are adorned with embroidered hangings made of gold and silver thread (c.1565). The choir altarpiece is an *Adoration of the Shepherds* by 17th-century local artist Jacob van Oost the Elder. In the right nave stands what is said to be the oldest Netherlandish miracle statue, Our Lady of Mons-en-Pévèle,

crafted in wood in the early 14th century and named after the 1305 battle of the same name. The 16th-century tapestries flanking the left side of the right nave depict miracles associated with the Virgin Mary reproduced in a lively style reminiscent of 16th-century daily life.
SEE ALSO MUSEUMS AND GALLERIES, P.91

Sint-Annakerk

Sint-Annaplein; daily 10am–1pm, 2–6pm; free; bus: 6, 16; map p.133 D1

Enclosed by an elegant square, Sint-Annakerk (Church of St Anne) is a 1624 Baroque replacement for the Gothic church destroyed by fire in 1561. Inside, the carving of the rood screen, confessionals and pulpit, as well as the rich panelling, are all well worth viewing. The mural depicting the *Last Judgement* (1685) is by Henri Herregoudts. The counter on the left as you enter used to be where the poor of the parish would sign (or make a mark) each time they attended Mass, so they could receive tokens to exchange for food and clothing on feast days.

Below: high brick walls hung with escutcheons in Jeruzalemkerk.

Environment

Bruges has little to complain about when it comes to the environment. Refreshed by North Sea winds; encircled by grassy fields reclaimed from the sea centuries ago for farming, and the icon of affluent Flanders, it has become a model of sustainable town planning, served by excellent public transport and flat enough to encourage anyone to hop on a bike. The only serious threats to the environment are found on the outskirts of the city and around Zeebrugge port, where pressure to pave over swathes of countryside has provoked fierce local protest and the creation of a militant 'green belt' movement.

Clean Water

Everyone loves the canals in Bruges. What few people know is that, until 1980, much of the city's waste water was dumped directly into them. A lot has changed since then: the waters are so clean now that even the fish have returned.

No private boats besides the tourist boats are allowed on the inner canals, and locks at the city borders are kept closed to prevent dirtier water from the Ghent and Ostend canals entering the inner canal system. To help the water stay clean, a water aeration system is used at the Coupure lock and the Ezelpoort fountain.

Properties that border the canals do not suffer the same level of degradation as canalside houses in areas of tidal, sea water (such as Venice), but to allow residents to maintain their properties below the waterline, the city regularly lowers the water level by up to 1m (3ft), on request. This is done during the winter months when the tourist boats stop operating.

Above: cycling is the greenest way to get around the city.

Energy

The brisk winds off the North Sea make the flat polders around Bruges ideal for harnessing wind energy; the turbines visible from the Belfort are along the canal to Zeebrugge. Other renewable energy projects in the region include a thriving business by local food and farming producers to transform their waste into biogas, which they then sell to the national electricity grid. Homeowners, meanwhile, can get subsidies

to install double glazing, solar thermal panels and energy-efficient boilers.

Green Belt

Recent years have seen the growth of a 'green belt' movement in an effort to stem development on greenfield sites around the edge of the city. The movement grew out of fierce opposition, five years ago, to a plan to build offices and a road through the Lappersfortbos, on the edge of Bruges. This woodland area was occupied by environmentalists for over a year, climaxing with violent clashes with police and the city authorities. Some of the woodland was saved, but the struggle became a symbol for the movement. Today much debate surrounds plans to build a larger stadium for Club Brugge football team in fields outside Bruges, and with it a new shopping centre and business park. Campaigners say that the few remaining wooded areas in Flanders are being eroded at a rate of 1 hectare (2.5

Left: the port of Zeebrugge is undergoing major development.

(and sell) chickens to residents to use as living, eating waste disposal units.

Transport

Bruges is a place of pedestrians and cyclists: there are more bikes than cars in the city, and the proportion of bikes is on the rise. Tourist coaches are not allowed to enter Bruges except to drop off luggage at hotels, and motorists are dissuaded from entering the city by tortuous one-way systems, free bus shuttles from car parks to the centre and 'park and bike' schemes. Unlike bike-mad Amsterdam, however, Bruges is not a student town with seemingly kamikaze cyclists bearing down on you from every direction: the population is older and rather more sedate in the saddle.

The push to support sustainable transport is happening right across Flanders. All public sector employees are eligible for a free season ticket for public transport if they agree not to commute by car and, in 2015, several electric buses began running on the city's bus network. Those who cycle or walk to work are eligible for tax deductions relative to the distance they travel each day.

There are also, in West Flanders, initiatives to encourage people to go shopping by bike: you collect points for cycling at shops and enter a prize draw. For school pupils, there are growing stretches of safe cycle track separate from the road in streets around schools, which also organise 'bike pools' for children to ride to school in a chaperoned group.

'I've planted many trees in my life. I believe now that planting and re-planting forests is the most productive cultural activity that one can do.' (Amedée Visart de Bocarmé, burgomaster of Bruges 1876–1924) Count Visart de Bocarmé was a pioneer in the creation of parks and green spaces around Bruges. He transformed the city ramparts into the ring canal park; the Visartpark outside the ring is named in his honour.

acres/two football pitches) every 36 days.

Towards the coast, the development of Zeebrugge into a major port has led to factories, warehouses and roads encroaching on the historic villages of Lissewege and Dudzele. However, development around the port is restricted, in an official bird protection zone, which has been recognised as an internationally important breeding area for species including the Little Tern, Common Tern and Sandwich Tern.

Recycling

Lots of tourists mean heaps of restaurant waste, so in Bruges, all restaurants have to separate food waste for composting. Flanders claims to be the world champion for separating and recycling waste. Over 70 percent of domestic waste collected is separated, and of the 560kg of waste that each inhabitant produces per year, just 150kg is not recycled, and must be incinerated (there is no landfill in Flanders). A strong carrot-and-stick policy has led to this: the requisite bin-bags for roadside collection of non-recyclable waste cost €1–1.50 each, to cover the cost of incineration – bags for recyclable tins, cans, plastic bottles and cartons are very cheap, and paper and cardboard can be bundled with string and left in a cardboard box for collection.

One-third of Flemish families also do home-composting (garden waste is collected). The province of West Flanders, of which Bruges is the capital, was the first in Belgium to promote

Essentials

Bruges is small, compact and among the easiest of European cities to negotiate. The locals are open, helpful and friendly, and most speak very good English. This section contains all the practical information that you may need during your trip or before departing. It describes how to understand postcodes, use the phone, where to go to check your e-mail and what to do in an emergency or if you fall ill. It gives approximate currency conversions to use as a guide and tourist office information. It also lists the public holidays in Belgium, when museums, shops and many restaurants will be closed.

Embassies/Consulates

Australia
Avenue des Arts 56, 1000 Brussels; tel: 02 286 05 00

Canada
Avenue de Tervueren 2, 1040 Brussels; tel: 02 741 06 11

New Zealand
Avenue des Nerviens 9-31, 1040 Brussels; tel: 02 512 10 40

Republic of Ireland
Chaussée d'Etterbeek 180, 1040 Brussels; tel: 02 282 34 00

South Africa
Rue Montoyer 17–19, 1000 Brussels; tel: 02 285 44 00

UK
Avenue d'Auderghem 10, 1040 Brussels; tel: 02 287 62 11

US
Boulevard du Régent 27, 1000 Brussels; tel: 02 811 40 00

Emergencies

Ambulance, Fire: 100
Police: 101
Pan-European emergency number: 112
You can also visit the Bruges police station at Lodewijk Coiseaukaai 3, just outside the perimeter canal in the north (or ring 050 44 88 44).

Health

EU NATIONALS
EU nationals who fall ill in Belgium are eligible to receive emergency treatment. You will have to pay part of the costs of hospital treatment, but are entitled to claim back 75 percent of the cost of seeing a doctor or dentist and of prescription drugs. Ambulance travel is not covered.

To receive a refund you need a European Health Insurance Card (EHIC). For UK citizens, these are available online at www.dh.gov.uk, by picking up a form in a post office or by phoning: 0845 606 2030. Reimbursements are handled in Belgium by Sickness Funds Offices (Mutualité/Ziekenfonds).

NORTH AMERICANS
International Association for Medical Assistance to Travellers (IAMAT), 2162 Gordon Street, Guelph, Ontario N1L 1G6, Canada; tel: 416 652 0137; www.iamat.org
This non-profit group offers members fixed rates for medical treatment. Members receive a medical record com-

Metric to Imperial Conversions		
Metres-Feet 1 = 3.28		
Kilometres-Miles 1 = 0.62		
Hectares-Acres 1 = 2.47		
Kilos-Pounds 1 = 2.2		

pleted by their doctor and a directory of English-speaking IAMAT doctors on call 24 hours. Membership is free but donations are appreciated.

HOSPITALS
AZ Sint-Jan
Ruddershove 10; tel: 050 45 21 11; www.azbrugge.be; bus: 13

PHARMACIES
For details of duty pharmacies *(apotheeke)* open at night, check notices in any pharmacy window or call 0900 10 500. Pharmacies are identifiable by a green neon cross sign.

Internet

Many hotels offer e-mail facilities, and the city authorities plan to provide free wifi access throughout the city centre – along with the public wifi already available at t'Zand, the Markt and the Burg (note

Left: a pharmacy.

Telephones

Fixed-line telephone numbers in Bruges start 050. You need to use the area code. The code for Belgium is +32. For English-speaking directory enquiries, tel: 1405 (international: 1304). For online information: www.infobel.be.

Time

Belgium is GMT+1 hour (+2 Apr–end Oct).

Tourist information

IN BRUGES
In&Uit
Concertgebouw building; 't Zand 34; tel: 050 44 46 46; www.bruges.be/toerisme; Mon–Sat 10am–5pm, Sun 10am–2pm; bus: 1; map p.134 B3

UK
Tourism Flanders-Brussels
Flanders House, 1a Cavendish Square, London W1G 0LD; tel: 0207 307 7738; www.visit flanders.co.uk
Belgian Tourist Office Brussels and Wallonia
217 Marsh Wall, London E14 9FJ; tel: 0207 537 1132; www.belgiumtheplaceto.be

US
Belgian Tourist Office
300 East 42nd Street, 14th floor, New York, NY 10017; tel: 212 758 8130; www.visit belgium.com

Visas

EU nationals require a valid identity card or passport to visit Belgium. Other visitors require a valid passport. No visa is required by visitors from the EU, US, Canada, Australia, New Zealand or Japan. Nationals of other countries may need a visa. For more information, visit www.diplomatie.belgium.be.

that the connection is unreliable). Internet cafés include:
Bauhaus
Langestraat 135; tel: 050 34 10 93; www.bauhaus.be; bus: 6, 16; map p.133 E1
The Cosy Bistro
Genthof 5; tel: 050 70 35 72; bus: 4, 14; map p.132 C1
Snuffel Backpackers Hostel
Ezelstraat 42; tel: 050 33 31 33; www.snuffel.be; bus: 3, 13; map p.132 B1

Money

Belgium uses euros (€), divided into 100 cents. The exchange rate is approximately £1 to €1.35 and US$1 to €0.9. There are plenty of ATMs scattered throughout the city. Most shops, restaurants and hotels accept credit cards, but few cafés or bars do.

Post

Bruges Central Post Office
Markt 5; tel: 022 01 23 45; www.post.be; Mon–Fri 9am–6pm, Sat 9am–3pm; map p.134 C4; see website for other branches. Mail boxes are red. Buy

stamps from post offices and shops selling postcards.

Public holidays

1 January New Year's Day
1 May Labour Day
21 July National Day
15 August Assumption
1 November All Saints' Day
11 November Armistice Day
25 December Christmas Day
Moveable holidays include Easter Monday, Ascension Day and Whit Monday. Holidays falling on a weekend are taken the following Monday.

Below: a Bruges postbox.

55

Food and Drink

Belgians know how to get the best out of their land (and sea) and onto their plates, from the game-based dishes of the Ardennes and white asparagus around Mechelen, to the eels, shrimps and Ostend sole of the North Sea coast, behind the dunes of which graze herds of 'Belgian blue' beef cows. The locals are proud of producing the world's best beer, chocolate, and chips, but not ashamed that their 'national dish', mussels, comes mainly from the sea off the Netherlands. Bruges has an enormous variety of restaurants, although a large number are geared towards tourists. That said, it is hard to eat badly in Belgium.

Belgian Cuisine

Not a lot has changed in Belgian attitudes towards eating and drinking since the days of medieval banquets and Brueghelian feasts: the local cuisine may not be widely known, but Belgians have a hearty taste for good food, enjoyed with cheery company in comfortable surroundings, and washed down

Below: prawns washed down with a Belgian beer.

with a few glasses of beer or (usually French) wine.

There are two main regional cuisines: Flemish and Walloon. The former features plenty of fish, eels, chicken and vegetables, the latter is rich in game and mushrooms. Brussels is famous for its *stoemp* (mash with different vegetables, served with sausage), meatballs in tomato sauce and Brussels sprouts.

It is often reported that Belgium has more Michelin-starred restaurants per capita than France, and there is a trend in pricier restaurants for 'tasting menus' – lots of courses, small portions and showy presentation of unidentifiable ingredients – but most restaurants prefer to remain informal and family-friendly. Typical dishes include:

Waterzooï – a Ghent stew of fish, potatoes, carrots, onions and more in a thin, creamy soup-like sauce. More commonly made with chicken these days, which is cheaper.

Mosselen-frieten (moules-frites) – the classic

dish of mussels and chips: mussels (bred in Zeeland, the Netherlands) are served in a large black casserole dish in a thin stock of celery and onion (plus possibly white wine, garlic, or other variation on the theme). Chips are served on the side, with mayonnaise. The price of a kilo of mussels is always of keen interest at the start of the season, in August. In a good year, they will be plump and plentiful. Some restaurants will only serve mussels during the season (a month with an 'r' in its name); others buy in from Spain or elsewhere, although these are generally viewed as an inferior product.

Frietjes (frites) – chips, fried twice for the unique Belgian consistency. Sold out of a roadside van (*frietkot*) and accompanied with a wide choice of sauces, most with a mayonnaise base.

Gegratineerd witloof – baked Belgian endive wrapped in a slice of ham and baked in the oven in a white sauce topped with cheese.

Garnaalkroketten – shrimp croquettes: a restau-

Left: mussels cooked with celery and onion.

Leuven is the beer capital of Belgium, home to the world's largest brewer, Inbev (which makes Stella Artois, Hoegaarden, Leffe and Jupiler).

Lambic beers are wild beers, so called because their fermentation involves exposure to wild yeast. Many have a sour, apple-like taste, but fruit may have been added to these to impart a distinctive flavour. Kriek, a lambic beer flavoured with cherries, comes in a round glass, while Frambozen is a pale pink raspberry brew served in a tall stemmed glass.

Gueuze is a type of lambic made by blending very young lambics which are fermented for a second time in a corked bottle (hence its nickname: Brussels Champagne). Gueuze beers have an almost cidery flavour. Boon, Cantillon and the award-winning Oud Beersel breweries produce gueuze varieties.

White beer *(witbier)* is a wheat beer flavoured with coriander and orange peel. Cloudy and generally light

Even though tap water is perfectly drinkable, regrettably few restaurants in Belgium are happy to serve it with a meal. Belgium's own mineral waters are Spa (the blue label is flat, the red sparkling) and Bru (sparkling).

rant's reputation can stand or fall depending on how they prepare this popular starter. The more of the tiny North Sea shrimps that are combined with bechamel sauce and then deep-fried in breadcrumbs, the better. Served with deep-fried parsley on the side.

Vlaamse stoofkarbonaden (carbonnades flamandes) – thick, rich beef stew, where chunks of meat are cooked for hours in beer.

Maatjes – raw herring, sold on seafood stalls and fishmongers and eaten as they come with chopped raw onions: the Belgian sushi.

Paling in 't groen – eel in green sauce: a subtle dish where the eel is cooked in a mixture of chervil, spinach, parsley, sorrel, tarragon and lemon balm; every chef has his own recipe.

Beer

Beer is to the Belgians what wine is to the French and, indeed, many Belgian beers complete the last stage of their fermentation in corked bottles. Several hundred types are produced, all of which have their distinctive character – and are served in their own, distinctive glass.

Below: in Belgium chips are served with mayonnaise.

57

and youthful in flavour, it often comes with a slice of lemon.

Trappist is a term for beers brewed in an abbey or under the control of Trappist monks. Only six breweries in Belgium (plus one in the Netherlands) bear the authentic Trappist label: Chimay, Orval, Rochefort, Westmalle, Westvleteren, Achelse Kluis. Among their beers, Tripel denotes a very strong beer that was served to the abbot and other important personages; the monks drank the Dubbel, while the peasants (i.e. everyone else) had only a watery version.

Kwak (a strong, light-coloured beer) is served in a glass with a spherical base that sits in a wooden stand in order to remain upright. The 1.5-litre glass and its stand are so valuable that customers must often give up a shoe to ensure they do not run off with the merchandise.

One highly acclaimed strong beer (8.5 percent) is **Delirium Tremens**, which can take you by surprise if you are not used to it – though if you see pink elephants, they are on the label and not in your head. Another powerful but delicious beer is **Corsendonck Agnus Dei**.

Bruges has one brewery, the **De Halve Maan**, which produces two beers: the Tripel ale Straffe Hendrik (9 percent) and the gentler Brugse Zot (6 percent), a blond.
SEE ALSO CAFÉS AND BARS, P.30

Genever

The Belgian gin, genever was invented in the Low Countries around 1580, and the juniper-flavoured spirit was discovered by British troops fighting against the Spanish in the Dutch War of Independence. They knocked it back gratefully to give them what became known as 'Dutch courage'. At the beginning of the 19th century, there was a genever brewery and distillery in every town. Today, only a handful remain. Bruges' one specialist genever bar closed a few years ago, although there is still one in Ghent.

The spirit is made by distilling an unfiltered and fermented mash of malted grains – mainly barley – and flavouring it with aromatics such as juniper berries, caraway seeds or fennel. The barley malt gives traditional genever more body and grain flavour than English-style gin, which uses neutral spirits and was developed after 17th-

Belgium is home to the world's largest brewery, AB InBev. The Leuven-based brewer makes Stella Artois, Hoegaarden, Leffe and Jupiler, amongst other well-known brands, and has roots that can be traced back to 1366.

century Flemish distillers began trading in London.

There are three types of genever: Oude, the old, straw-coloured, pungently sweet style; Jonge, a newer style which tastes cleaner and more delicate; and Korenwijn, which is cask-aged with a high percentage of malted spirit.

Chocolates

Belgium makes some of the best chocolate in the world, and is most famous for its pralines – sculpted shells containing soft fillings, of which a dizzying variety exist. The industry took off in the 1880s, helped by the acquisition of the Congo, which opened up access to Africa's cocoa fields. Every Belgian has their own opinion on who makes the best chocolate and which shop they prefer. On Saturday afternoons, people line up outside chocolatiers' win-

Below: rows of flavoured genever, the Belgian gin.

Above: Belgium is famous for its high-quality chocolate.

dows to purchase a box of mixed pralines (a common gift to a hostess when you are invited to dinner). Sample a variety and then take your own pick.

Food Shops

CHOCOLATE
Van Oost
Wollestraat 11, tel: 050 33 14 54; www.chocolatiervanoost. net; Wed–Mon 10am–6pm; bus: 1; map p.134 C4
Arguably the best choc shop in town. The service can be a little frosty but their walnuts coated in chocolate – produced during autumn – are to die for.
Sweertvaegher
Philipstockstraat 29; tel: 050 33 83 67; www.sweertvaegher.be; Tue–Sat 10am–6.30pm; bus: 1; map p.134 C4
Tiny little shop that does excellent chocs, including wooden-boxed flocks of Brugsche Swaentjes (Bruges Swans).

Otherwise, the following chains (Leonidas being the cheapest) do a wide selection and are reliable and good:
Galler
Steenstraat 5; tel: 050 61 20 62; www.galler.com, Mon–Sat

10am–7pm, Sun 11am–5pm; bus: 1; map p.134 C4
Leonidas
at Confiserie Dalipan, Steenstraat 4; tel: 050 33 40 60; www.leonidas.be; Mon–Sat 9.30am–6.30pm, Sun 10am–6.30pm; bus: 1; map p.134 C4
Neuhaus
Streenstraat 66; tel: 050 33 15 30; www.neuhaus.be; daily 10am–6pm; bus: 1; map p.134 B4

Drinks
2be – Foodshopping
Wollestraat 53; tel: 050 61 12 22; www.2-be.biz; daily 10am–7pm; bus: 1; map p.134 C4
Emporium of Belgian food and drink – from beer to sweets to herbal teas – in a medieval mansion and with a superb view from the bar terrace.
Bacchus Cornelius
Academiestraat 17; tel: 050 34 53 38; www.bacchuscornelius. com; Wed–Mon 2–6pm; bus: 1, 4, 14; map p.132 C1
A good beer selection, including some rarities, and an open fire in winter. They make their own genever too.
De Bier Tempel
Philipstockstraat 7; tel: 050 34 37 30; daily 9.30am–6.30pm; bus: 1; map p.134 C4

Centrally located but not large; under same ownership as nearby beer-brasserie Cambrinus, and with lots of suitable gift items – T-shirts, glasses, greeting cards – for the beer-lover in your life.
The Bottle Shop
Wollestraat 13; tel: 050 34 99 80; www.thebottleshop.be; daily 10am–6.30pm; bus: 1; map p.134 C4
Around 450 ales on offer, including Trappist beers and gift-friendly packs. It also sells Belgian genever in stoneware jars and a wide selection of bottled water.

Further Reading
Everybody Eats Well in Belgium Cookbook by Ruth Van Waerebeek-Gonzalez and Maria Robbins, illustrated by Melissa Sweet, Workman Publishing. A lovingly detailed cookbook.

Michael Jackson's Great Beers of Belgium, 6th edition, Brewers Publications. The late beer expert drank his way devotedly through the beer rosters of many a land. He came away from Belgium convinced that it has one of the world's greatest beer-brewing traditions.

59

History

c.1000–800 BC
Celtic tribes settle in what is now Flanders.

1ST CENTURY BC
Celtic farmers are established on the coastal plain around what is now Bruges.

57 BC
Julius Caesar's invading Roman legions defeat the Belgae, a conglomeration of Celtic tribes, in the northern part of Gaul (today's France).

1ST CENTURY AD
A Gallo-Roman settlement is founded beside the Rivers Reie and Dijver, on the site of present-day Bruges, and maintains trading links with Britain and Gaul.

4TH–6TH CENTURY
The Franks, a Germanic people, cross the Rhine and settle between the rivers Meuse and Schelde.

498
Conversion to Christianity of Frankish King Clovis.

8TH CENTURY
Foundation of Ghent abbeys; St Eloy writes of the municipium Flandrense, an important town in the Flemish coastal plain, which seems likely to have been Bruges.

768
Charlemagne's unified kingdom is established.

800
Charlemagne, King of the Franks, is crowned Emperor of the West.

814
Death of Charlemagne and division of empire.

843
The Frankish Empire splits into three. Flanders west of the Schelde joins West Francia; the territory east of the Schelde becomes part of the Middle Kingdom, then, in 855, of Lotharingia (Lorraine).

c.850
A fort is built in the town for defence against attacks by Viking raiders.

861
Baldwin Iron Arm elopes with the daughter of Carolingian King Charles the Bald.

863
Baldwin becomes first Count of Flanders and occupies the Burg castle in Bruges.

864
The first record of the name 'Bruggia – a melding of the Old Norse bryggja (jetty) and Rugja, the original name of the River Reie – appears on coins of Charles the Bald.

c.940
Count Arnulf I develops the Burg, building his castle and the Church of St Donatian there.

c.1040
An English text calls Bruges an important maritime trading centre, but by the end of the century access to the sea is closed by silting.

1127
Count Charles the Good is murdered in St Donatian's. Thierry of Alsace becomes Count of Flanders. Bruges is granted its first charter and building of the city wall begins.

1134
Flooding creates a channel, the Zwin, from the sea to Damme. Bruges builds a canal to Damme, reopening a maritime trading route.

1150
Count Thierry of Alsace is said to bring back from the Second Crusade a relic of the Blood of Christ.

1177
Bruges is granted a revised charter by Count Philip of Alsace.

13TH CENTURY
Some of Bruges' most prominent buildings, including the Belfort, Hallen, Begijnhof and Sint-Jans hospitaal are begun.

1250
With a population of 40–50,000, Bruges is among the biggest and richest cities in north-west Europe, through trade and textiles manufacture.

1297
King Philip IV of France annexes Flanders. New fortifications are begun.

1302
Weaver Pieter de Coninck and butcher Jan Breidel foment rebellion against France. French citizens and sympathisers are massacred in the 'Bruges Matins', and an army of Flemish peasants and craftsmen slaughters the French knights at the Battle of the Golden Spurs at Kortrijk.

1305
War with France ends in a treaty unfavourable to Flanders. Bruges' defences are dismantled.

1316
Famine strikes the city, killing thousands; 33 years later thousands more lives are lost in a plague.

1376
Building of the Town Hall begins, at a time of great prosperity from international trade.

1384
Count Louis is succeeded by his daughter Margaret, wife of Philip the Bold, Duke of Burgundy. Flanders becomes part of Burgundian kingdom. The dazzling Burgundian century begins.

15TH CENTURY
Cloth-making declines, but prosperity continues from trade and banking.

1419
Philip the Good of Burgundy made Duke of Flanders.

1430
Duke Philip the Good founds the Order of the Golden Fleece in Bruges.

1436
Jan van Eyck paints the Virgin and Child.

1436–8
Philip the Good cruelly crushes a rebellion against him in Bruges.

1474–9
Hans Memling paints the Triptych of St John.

1477
Death of Duke Charles the Bold sparks another rebellion. His successor is Mary of Burgundy, wife of Habsburg Crown Prince Maximilian of Austria. She grants the city a new charter.

1482
After Mary's death in a riding accident, the Habsburg reign begins, with Maximilian of Austria. Bruges rebels against its new rulers, imprisoning Maximilian in the Craenenburg mansion. When freed, he moves the ducal residence to Ghent.

1520
Silting of the Zwin closes Bruges' access to the sea. Economic decline begins.

1527
Bruges' first Protestant martyr is burned at the stake in the Burg.

1541
Mercator draws first map of Flanders.

1555
Charles V abdicates in favour of his son, King Philip II of Spain.

1559
The Bishopric of Bruges is established.

1566
Protestant 'Iconoclasts' sack churches across the Low Countries.

61

1567–79
Religious wars in the southern Low Countries.

1577
Bruges hesitantly joins the Low Countries' rebellion against Spanish rule.

1580
The city signs the Treaty of Utrecht against Spain; Protestantism becomes the only permitted religion.

1584
Spain re-establishes control. Many Protestant merchants, artists and craftsmen flee to Holland. The following year the Scheldt estuary is blockaded and Bruges goes into steep decline.

1622
Opening of a canal to Ostend gives Bruges an outlet to the sea again.

1701–14
War of the Spanish Succession.

1715
By the Treaty of Utrecht, Belgium passes under the authority of the Austrian Holy Roman Emperor Charles VI.

1744–8
Bruges is occupied by the French.

1753
The Coupure Canal opened, allowing sea-going vessels into the city centre.

1780
Maria Theresa dies; Joseph II accedes.

1789–90
Pro-French revolutionaries proclaim the short-lived 'United States of Belgium'; the Austrian Army regains control.

1794–5
Revolutionary France invades and occupies the city. Many churches and monasteries are destroyed. French occupy the country for 20 years.

1815
Napoleon defeated at Waterloo. Bruges becomes part of the Kingdom of the Netherlands under William I of Orange.

1830
Bruges joins the Southern Netherlands' revolt against Dutch rule, resulting in the formation of the Kingdom of Belgium, under King Leopold I.

1838
Railway connecting Brussels, Ghent, Bruges and Ostend opens.

1847
Hunger riots erupt in Bruges, the poorest city in Belgium.

1892
Georges Rodenbach's novel *Bruges-la-Morte* is published.

1892
The Flemish poet Guido Gezelle dies in the city.

1904
Work on the new Bruges sea harbour, Zeebrugge, is completed.

1914–18
World War I. Germans invade neutral Belgium and occupy Bruges for four years, destroying Zeebrugge harbour as they retreat. Battles around Ieper (Ypres) and along River Ijzer are among the war's bloodiest.

1940–44
World War II. Germans occupy Bruges for 4 years, again destroying Zeebrugge harbour as they retreat. The government is in exile in London.

1948
Customs union between Belgium, the Netherlands and Luxembourg (Benelux).

1949
Belgium joins NATO.

1950
Modern tourist boom begins.

1951
King Baudouin I ascends the throne after the abdication of Leopold III.

1957
Belgium is a founder member of the European Economic Community, the forerunner of today's EU.

1971
Bruges merges with surrounding municipalities, making it Flanders' third biggest city. Flemish and Walloon communities are given greater autonomy.

1977
Prime minister Leo Tindemans establishes three federal regions in Belgium: Flanders, Wallonia and Brussels. Bruges city centre is made virtually car-free.

1984
Flanders bilingual Brussels as its regional capital.

1993
King Baudouin I dies and is succeeded by his brother Albert II.

1990
Regional governments created.

1994
A new constitution completes Belgium's transition to a federal state, with considerable powers devolved to regions.

2002
Euro becomes Belgium's currency.

2008
Flemish Christian Democrat Herman Van Rompuy becomes prime minister after predecessor Yves Leterme resigns over a banking scandal.

2013
Renaat Landuyt of the Socialist Party Differently becomes Bruges' mayor.

2013
King Albert II abdicates for health reasons and his son Philippe ascends to the Belgian throne.

2014
Charles Michel of the Reformist Movement, at 39, becomes the youngest Prime Minister since 1845.

2015
Two suspected Islamic militants are shot dead by police in an anti-terrorist operation in Verviers.

63

Hotels

A small city with few corporate travellers, Bruges has been spared the plague of dreary chain hotels that blights many a destination. At the same time, there are few large, grand hotels. Most occupy historic properties in the city centre, with rooms decorated in romantic, English country house style or, increasingly, a more contemporary Flemish aesthetic. Be warned that room sizes and features can vary considerably within the same establishment, and expect to pay more for a canal view. There are also a growing number of bed and breakfast places in tastefully renovated homes in the heart of Bruges.

Markt and Burg
Crowne Plaza Brugge
Burg 10; tel: 050 44 68 44; www.crowneplaza.com/brugge bel; €–€€€; bus: 1; map p.134 C4
This modern block is an eyesore on the historic Burg square. Inside, however, you get the fabulous view out, capacious beds and the details and service you would expect from a top-flight hotel. The basement contains the ruins of St Donatian's, the former cathedral, which make for a bizarre feature in a con- ference suite. Low-season room rates can be excellent.
Hotel de Orangerie
Karthuizerinnenstraat 10; tel: 050 34 16 49; www.hotelorangerie. be; €€€; bus: 1; map p.134 C3

Price ranges, which are given as a guide only, are for a standard double room with bathroom, including service, tax and usually breakfast (pricier establishments will charge an extra €15–30):
€ = under €85
€€ = €85–125
€€€ = €125–180
€€€€ = over €180

A firm favourite with visiting celebrities, the Orangerie occupies a charming 15th-century convent with water lapping the walls. Located in a narrow street close to the belfry, it could not be more central. A recent stylish makeover has transformed it into a chic boutique hotel

furnished with fine antiques. There is a lakeside terrace and a romantic orangerie. Try to avoid ground-floor rooms facing the street.
The Pand
Pandreitje 16; tel: 050 34 06 66; www.pandhotel. com; €€€€; bus: 6, 16; map p.135 C3

Below: a superior 'pergola' room at De Swaene hotel.

64

Left: Martin's Orangerie is right by the water.

For longer stays, you might consider booking a self-catering flat or house. This is often much cheaper than a hotel, especially as you can eat at home. The minimum stay is usually two days. The tourist office recommends 26 owners of rental properties on its website https://bezoekers.brugge.be. Most properties can be booked online through their own websites.

Die Swaene
Steenhouwersdijk 1; tel: 050 34 27 98; www.dieswaene.com; €€€; bus: 6, 16; map p.135 C4
Most people fall in love with this lovely brick hotel by a quiet, tree-lined canal. The main building, a former tailors' guildhouse, has old wooden staircases and heavy oak furniture; the 'Pergola' extension, a historic former warehouse across the canal, is decorated in luxurious modern style. The 30 rooms come in different sizes and styles, some of them with elegant four-poster beds, some

A boutique hotel with 26 rooms in a converted 18th-century carriage house close to the picturesque Rozenhoedkaai. Owned by antique dealers, it is brimming with cachet and the bedrooms are all individually styled.
Relais Bourgondisch Cruyce
Wollestraat 41–47; tel: 050 33 79 26; www.relaisbourgondischcruyce.be; €€€€; bus: 1, 6, 16; map p.135 C4

A gorgeous small hotel in two gabled houses with timbered facades backing onto a canal and facing a pretty, off-street courtyard. Decorated in sumptuous 17th-century Flemish style with carved furniture, stone floors and large fireplaces, it featured in hit film *In Bruges*. The 16 bedrooms are individually designed, combining traditional decor with a hint of modern design. Get a room with a canal view if you can.

Below: the clean and cosy breakfast room at The Pand.

65

The local phone numbers given in this guide include the Bruges area code '050'. When dialling from abroad, omit the first 0 of the code.

– the downstairs rooms – rather dark and pokey. There is a pool and sauna and a Romeo and Juliet package aimed at honeymooners.

South
Boat-Hotel De Barge
Bargeweg 15; tel: 050 38 51 50; www.hoteldebarge.be; €€€; bus: 2, 12

Wake up to the sound of ducks outside the window in this unusual hotel located in a converted Flemish canal barge. The rooms may be small, but they have an

appealing nautical flavour, with white wood, blue paint and bright red lifejackets laid out on the beds. The hotel has a bar, terrace, restaurant and car park. Located just outside the old town, a brisk 10-min walk from the centre.

Botaniek
Waalsestraat 23; tel: 050 34 14 24; www.botaniek.be; €€; bus: 6, 16; map p.135 D4

A simple, friendly hotel located in a quiet street close to the Astridpark. The nine-room establishment occupies an 18th-century town house furnished in traditional, Louis XV style. Top-floor rooms have wonderful views of gabled houses and ancient spires.

Egmond
Minnewater 15; tel: 050 34 14 45; www.egmond.be; €€; bus:

The Bruges tourist office offers a free booking service which is extremely useful for last-minute reservations. Check out availability or make a booking via its website, https://bezoekers.brugge.be. The Hotels Brugge website (www.discoverbruges.com) also provides an instant online booking service and is more user-friendly.

2, 20, 21; map p.134 C1

This attractive, small hotel is located in a gabled Flemish mansion next to the romantic Minnewater lake. The interior is furnished in an appealing Flemish traditional style, complete with tiled floors, oak chests and 18th-century fireplaces. The eight bedrooms look out on a rambling garden, making for peaceful nights. There is a car park for guests, and the station is just a 10-minute walk away.

Ibis Hotel
Marie Popelinplantsoen 4; tel: 050 40 51 20; www.accorhotels.com; €; bus: 1, 3–9, 11, 13–17; map p.134 B1

This new Ibis budget hotel is adjacent to the station. The rooms are basic but clean, with television and paid-for internet access. Late arrivals can rest assured that reception is open 24/7 and that there is parking nearby. It may not be Bruges' most romantic hotel, however the location should not be underestimated – with visitors arriving by train able to immediately drop their bags off before a quick 10-minute walk to the centre. A good-value, practical option.

Jan Brito
Freren Fonteinstraat 1; tel: 050 33 06 01; www.janbrito.eu; €€€; bus: 6, 16; map p.135 D4

A real gem in the heart of Bruges but away from the

Below: De Tuilerieen's beautifully designed interior.

Above: the grandly styled breakfast room at the Jan Brito hotel.

bustle, this 37-room hotel occupies a 16th-century merchant's house and 18th-century rear building with a secluded Renaissance garden. Tastefully decorated, with marble fireplaces, thick carpets and an oak staircase.

't Keizershof
Oostmeers 126; tel: 050 33 87 28; www.hotelkeizershof.be; €; bus: 1; map p.134 B1
The perfect place for anyone travelling on a tight budget, this compact, seven-room establishment is located in a pretty street close to the railway station. The rooms are as cheap as they come, yet they are clean and comfortable; each has a sink, while WC and shower are shared. A notice at the entrance sums up the owner's outlook: 'When you are sleeping, we look just like one of those big fancy hotels.' Free parking.

Montanus
Nieuwe Gentweg 78; tel: 050 33 11 76; www.montanus.be; €€; bus: 1, 11; map p.135 C3
Tasteful, restrained elegance in a historic house, once the

home of one of Belgium's most famous statesmen. In addition to the main house, there are colonial-style pavilion rooms in the serene private garden, and these are cheaper. Of the 20 rooms, one is suitable for disabled guests.

De Tuilerieen
Dijver 7; tel: 050 34 36 91; www.hoteltuilerieen.com; €€€€; bus: 1; map p.134 C3
The most luxurious hotel in town: a 45-room buff colour mansion facing the main canal. With courteous staff and antique-stuffed rooms, this recently renovated hotel is hard to resist. Some rooms have views of the canal, while others face the garden. There is also a bright swimming pool, sauna and steam room. Breakfast is expensive; you may prefer to order coffee and croissants in a nearby patisserie.

West
Hotel Dukes' Palace
Prinsenhof 8; tel: 050 44 78 88; www.hoteldukespalace.com;

€€€€; bus: 1; map p.134 B4
An exclusive choice located in the neo-Gothic Prinsenhof, a 19th-century rebuild of the Medieval Princes' Court created by Burgundian Duke Philip the Good in 1429. The 93 rooms, pool, banqueting suite and spa ensure 21st-century standards of luxury, while the listed chapel and other details uphold the building's rich history.

Ensor
Speelmansrei 10; tel: 050 34 25 89; www.ensorhotel.be; €; bus: 1; map p.134 A4
This friendly 12-room hotel occupies a brick building on a quiet canal near the

Price ranges, which are given as a guide only, are for a standard double room with bathroom, including service, tax and usually breakfast (pricier establishments will charge an extra €15–30):
€ = under €85
€€ = €85–125
€€€ = €125–180
€€€€ = over €180

67

There are a growing number of bed and breakfasts (gasthuizen) in and around Bruges. These are located in private homes – including an improbably grand neo-Gothic castle just outside the city – and offer an inexpensive alternative to hotels. Many are owned by local artists, architects and designers, and some have stunning interiors and gardens. The owners are nearly always ready to provide you with insider advice on the best restaurants and cafés in the area. To locate a B&B, visit the Bruges Guild of Guest Houses website, which lists 62 approved addresses (www.brugge-bedandbreakfast.com), or the city tourist office, https://bezoekers.brugge.be. Bookings can normally be made online. Be aware that most owners do not accept credit cards.

Above: not all hotels offer breakfast, so check before booking.

't Zand. The rooms are plainly furnished, but well-maintained, and all have en-suite bathrooms, making this one of the best budget hotels in the city.

Karel De Stoute
Moerstraat 23; tel: 050 34 33 17; www.hotelkareldestoute.be; €–€€; bus: 1, 12; map p.134 B4
Named after 15th-century Duke of Burgundy Charles the Bold, this charming hotel occupies a building that once formed part of the Prinsenhof ducal residence. Run by a friendly couple, the nine-room hotel offers a relaxed atmosphere in the heart of the old town. The rooms are tastefully furnished, and priced according to size. Some have oak beams, while two have bathrooms located in a 15th century circular staircase tower. The bar is in an ancient cellar with a vaulted brick ceiling. There is also free internet access.

Parkhotel Brugge
Vrijdagmarkt 5; tel: 050 33 33 64; www.parkhotelbrugge.be; €€€€; bus: 1; map p.134 A3
This modern 86-room luxurious hotel, located on the 't Zand square in the centre of medieval Bruges, has an atmospheric lobby and bar.

Prinsenhof
Ontvangersstraat 9; tel: 050 34 26 90; www.prinsenhof.be; €€€; bus: 1; map p.134 B4
This elegant small hotel around the corner from the former Prinsenhof building (now Hotel Dukes' Palace) is traditionally furnished, with wood panelling, chandeliers, and other antiques; it also has excellent bathrooms. There is a warm atmosphere, and the staff are very friendly. 24 rooms.

North

Aragon
Naaldenstraat 22; tel: 050 33 35 33; www.aragon.be; €€€;

bus: 1; map p.132 B1
This well-run hotel is located in the heart of the old merchant's quarter, opposite a palace once owned by the Italian Medici family. The 42 rooms were recently renovated in a comfortable English country-house style.

Asiris
Lange Raamstraat 9; tel: 050 34 17 24; www.hotelasiris.be; €; bus: 4, 14; map p.132 C2
A small, family-run hotel in a quiet quarter close to the lovely Sint-Gilliskerk. The 13 bedrooms are furnished in a plain, modern style aimed at travellers on a budget and families. The rooms under the eaves are a tight squeeze and are cheapest. Breakfast is included in the price, making this one of the best inexpensive hotels in town.

Bryghia
Oosterlingenplein 4; tel: 050 33 80 59; www.bryghiahotel.be; €€; bus: 4, 14; map p.132 C1

This friendly, family-run hotel is situated in one of Bruges' most peaceful neighbourhoods, rarely visited by tourists. Part of the 18-room hotel occupies a 15th-century building that once belonged to Hanseatic merchants. The interior is quite cosy and tastefully furnished with comfortable sofas and exposed wood beams. Some rooms enjoy a view of a sleepy canal.

Cavalier
Kuipersstraat 25; tel: 050 33 02 07; www.hotelcavalier.be; €; bus: 1; map p.132 B1

In spite of its slightly ramshackle external appearance, this small hotel behind the city theatre is friendly and ordered and provides good value for the cheaper range of hotels. 8 rooms.

Martin's RelaisOud-Huis Amsterdam
Genthof 4a; tel: 050 34 18 10; www.martins-hotels.com; €€; bus: 4, 14; map p.133 C1

Overlooking a quiet canal in the heart of the old merchants' quarter and near the Markt, this romantic 44-room hotel, set in a 17th-century trading house, has a wooden staircase, chandeliers, beams

and antique furniture. There is also a pretty interior courtyard. Skip the hotel breakfast, which costs extra, and walk 5 mins to Het Dagelijks Brood (Philipstockstraat 21) to enjoy coffee and delicious croissants in a typical French farmhouse interior.

Snuffel Backpacker Hostel
Ezelstraat 42; tel: 050 33 31 33; www.snuffel.be; €; bus: 3, 13; map p.132 B1

A simple youth hostel with pine bunks in rooms sleeping 4 to 12 people (the small rooms can also be booked as private rooms for two people). Located in a traditional gabled house, it has a ground-floor bar with English newspapers, internet access, its own 'Snuffel' beer and free live gigs every first and third Saturday of the month, except July and August.

Ter Brughe
Oost-Gistelhof 2; tel: 050 34 03 24; www.hotelterbrughe.com; €€; bus: 4, 14; map p.132 C1

Attractive hotel in the elegant St Giles quarter, 5 mins' walk from the centre of Bruges. Breakfast is served in the 14th-century beamed and vaulted cellar, which was

Price ranges, which are given as a guide only, are for a standard double room with bathroom, including service, tax and usually breakfast (pricier establishments will charge an extra €15–30):
€ = under €85
€€ = €85–125
€€€ = €125–180
€€€€ = over €180

once a warehouse for goods brought along the canal. The 46 rooms are comfortable, if rather faded.

Ter Duinen
Langerei 52; tel: 050 33 04 37; www.hotelterduinen. eu; €€–€€€; bus: 4, 14; map p.132 D3

A little out of centre, 'The Dunes' takes its name from the former abbey across the canal. The conservatory and formal garden are stylish; the rooms are neutrally decorated and pleasant. The cobbled Langerei is quiet at night and windows are super-insulated. Air-conditioning in all rooms.

Ter Reien
Langestraat 1; tel: 050 34 91 00; www.hotelterreien.be; €€; bus: 6, 16; map p.135 D4

As its name suggests, the 'hotel on the canal' is located along one of the many beautiful canals in the city. Notably, it occupies the house where the Symbolist painter Fernand Khnopff spent his childhood. The 26 rooms are bright and comfortable. There is a breakfast courtyard.

East

Adornes
St Annarei 26; tel: 050 34 13 36; www.adornes.be; €€€; bus: 4, 14; map p.133 D1

This pretty little 20-room hotel occupies a row of traditional brick houses beside a peaceful canal in the charm-

Below: the Walburg's gleaming white restaurant.

69

Above: the traditional Adornes hotel, as seen from the outside and in.

ing St Anna quarter. The rooms are comfortable and bright, some with oak beams. Breakfast is included in the price of the room. There are free bikes for guests' use as well as a limited number of free parking spaces. All Adornes guests receive an advantage card to enjoy special entrance prices to museums and boat trips.

Bauhaus
Langestraat 133–137; tel: 050 34 10 93; www.bauhaus.be; €; bus: 6, 16; map p.133 E1
Large budget hotel and youth hostel offering a variety of cheap accommodation: en-suite rooms with shower and toilet,

Price ranges, which are given as a guide only, are for a standard double room with bathroom, including service, tax and usually breakfast (pricier establishments will charge an extra €15–30):
€ = under €85
€€ = €85–125
€€€ = €125–180
€€€€ = over €180

well-appointed flats for 2–12 people, and dorms with up to eight beds. There is bike rental, a cybercafé and a bar, which, given the meagre nightlife offerings in Bruges, is lively and sociable.

Rosenburg
Coupure 30; tel: 050 34 01 94; www.rosenburg.be; €€; bus: 6, 16; map p.135 D3
A quiet hotel situated on the banks of a canal approximately a 10-min walk from the centre of Bruges. The atmosphere in this modern brick building is relaxed and friendly, staff are particularly helpful, and there are good business facilities. The 27 rooms are larger than average for the city.

Around

DAMME
Hoeve De Steenoven
Damse vaart zuid 2; tel: 050 50 13 62; www.hoevede steenoven.be; €; boat or bike to Damme; map p.139 C3
Small six-room simple but lovely country hotel in an old building with modern rooms,

beside the canal to Bruges.
Leonardo
Chartreuseweg 20; tel: 050 40 21 40; www.leonardo-hotels. com; €€; bus: 7, 74; map p.139 C3
Out-of-town option between the motorway and the centre with good amenities, an outdoor pool with children's play area, and easy parking.

GHENT
Boatel
Voorhoutkaai 44; tel: 09 267 10 30; www.theboatel.com; €€; train to Gent-Dampoort; map p.137 D3
Ghent's first floating hotel caused a stir when it opened a few years ago. Located in the Portus Ganda, a new city marina, this former 1951 canal barge has been converted into an unusual hotel. It has five small rooms with porthole windows located in the former cargo hold and two more roomy suites on the upper deck. A 10-min walk to town.
Chambre Plus
Hoogpoort 31; tel: 09 225 37 75; www.chambreplus.be; €€;

tram 1 (Sint-Niklaasstraat); map p.137 E2

Homeowner Mia Ackaert has created three sublime Bed and Breakfast rooms in the rear of her family's 18th-century mansion. Ask for the Sultan Room for a wildly romantic decor inspired by the Middle East, or pick the Congo Room for jungle-print fabrics. The best (and priciest) choice is the Côté Sud, a separate apartment decorated in Mediterranean style, with a lounge, an open fire and a Jacuzzi where you can take a bath under the night sky. A delicious breakfast is included in the price.

Ghent River Hotel
Waaistraat 5; tel: 09 266 10 10; www.ghent-river-hotel.be; €€€€; tram 1 (Gravensteen); map p.136 C4

This waterfront hotel near the Vrijdagmarkt evokes the trading history of Ghent. Some rooms occupy a restored 19th-century sugar factory, while others are in a 16th-century town house; the square was the site of a yarn market in the Middle Ages and the 19th century. When booking, ask for one of the rooms in the former factory, as these have oak beams, brick walls and odd industrial implements used for decoration. The rooms in the modern extension are plainer. The hotel has a rooftop breakfast room with striking views of the old city, a jetty and a fitness room.

Gravensteen
Jan Breydelstraat 35; tel: 09 225 11 50; www.gravensteen. be; €€€; tram 1 (Gravensteen); map p.137 B4

This 19th-century mansion, once the home of an industrial magnate, has been turned into one of the city's most elegant hotels. It is situated across the water from Gravensteen Castle, of which

rooms at the front have a fine view, and it has been tastefully renovated and extended. Fitness room and sauna. Disabled access. 49 rooms.

Marriott Ghent Hotel
Drabstraat; tel: 09 233 93 93; www.marriott.com; €€€; tram: 1 (Korenmarkt); map p.137 B4

An enviable location near all the sights and the upmarket chain's high standards have firmly established this newcomer. Part of the hotel fronts on Korenlei, facing the lovely Graslei and looking down to St Nicholas Bridge. Rooms are very comfortable though few have canal views. There is parking beneath the hotel.

The Coast

DE HAAN
Auberge des Rois
Zeedijk 1; tel: 059 23 30 18; www.beachhotel.be; €€; coast tram (De Haan aan Zee); map p.138 B4

Fine modern hotel on the beach, built in De Haan's Belle-Epoque-villa style.

Grand Hôtel Belle Vue
Koninklijk Plein 5; tel: 059 23 34 39; www.hotelbellevue.be; €€; coast tram (De Haan aan Zee); map p.138 B4

A more traditional old villa, this superb and rather

Check for special deals and extras: many hotels offer a complimentary beer, free guided tour or museum entry for guests, while the tourist office website features promotions such as 'three nights for the price of two' during winter.

fanciful-looking domed hotel is close to the stop for the Coast Tram.

Heritage
Leopoldlaan 5; tel: 059 70 77 20; www.heritagehotel; €€€; coast tram (De Haan aan Zee); map p.138 B4

A grand old villa given a modern makeover, and converted into a notable hotel with modern facilities, and close to the beach.

OSTEND
Hotel du Parc
Marie-Joseplein 3; tel: 059 70 16 80; www.hotelduparc. be; €€; bus: 5 from station to Marie-Joséplein; map p.138 B3

A rare surviving pre-war building in Ostend, this Art Deco hotel behind the casino and the promenade has a wealth of stylish, original fittings in the bar-brasserie on the street. Get a room at the front; those at the rear can be pokey.

Below: the Hôtel Belle Vue has seen many prestigious guests.

Language

The people of Flanders speak Dutch. Behind this simple statement lies a thicket of complication. There is no such language – the word reflects the historical English inability to distinguish between the languages of Germany (Deutsch) and the Low Countries (Nederlands), and their lumping of them together and corrupting it to Dutch. The language academy of Flanders calls its language 'Netherlandic', but is willing to live with Dutch as an internationally accepted substitute. If this is far too complicated, most people in Bruges are happy to speak English or German (but not necessarily French).

General

Yes *Ja*
No *Nee*
Please *Alstublieft*
Thank you (very much) *Dank u (wel)*
Excuse me *Excuseer/pardon*
Hello *Dag/Hallo*
Goodbye *Dag/tot ziens*
Good morning *Goedemorgen*
Good afternoon *Goedemiddag*
Good evening *Goedenavond*
Do you speak English? *Spreekt u Engels?*
I don't understand *Ik begrijp het niet*
I am sorry *Het spijt me/Sorry*
No problem *Geen probleem*
Can you help me? *Kunt u mij helpen?*
What is your name? *Wat is uw naam?/Hoe heet u?*
My name is… *Ik heet…*
I am English/American *Ik ben Engelsman/Engelse/Amerikaan*
When? *Wanneer?*
At what time? *Hoe laat?*
What time is it? *Hoe laat is het?*
today *vandaag*
yesterday/tomorrow *gisteren/morgen*

now/later *nu/later*
this morning *vanmorgen*
this afternoon *deze namiddag/vanmiddag*
this evening *vanavond*
day/week *dag/week*
month/year *maand/jaar*
here/there *hier/daar*
left/right *links/rechts*

On Arrival

How do I get to... from here? *Hoe kom ik van hier naar…?*
Is there a bus to…? *Is/Gaat/Rijdt er een bus naar…?*
railway station *station*
I want a ticket to… *Ik wil graag een kaartje naar...*
single (one way) *enkele reis*
return (round-trip) *retour/heen en terug*
first/second class *eerste/tweede klas*
Do you have any vacancies? *Hebt u een kamer vrij?*
a single room *een eenpersoonskamer*
a double room *een tweepersoonskamer*
What is the charge per night? *Hoeveel is het per nacht?*
May I see the room? *Kan ik de kamer bekijken?*

Emergencies

Help/Stop! *Help/Stop!*
Call a doctor/an ambulance *Bel een dokter/een ziekenwagen*
Call the police/fire brigade *Bel de politie/brandweer*
Where is the nearest telephone/hospital? *Waar is de dichtstbijzijnde telefoon/het dichtstbijzijnde ziekenhuis?*
I do not feel well *Ik voel me niet goed/lekker*
I have lost my passport/money/handbag *Ik heb mijn paspoort/geld/handtas verloren*

Shopping

How much is it? *Hoeveel is/kost het?*
Where can I buy…? *Waar kan ik… kopen?*
Have you got…? *Hebt u…?*
Can I have…? *Mag ik … hebben?*
What size is it? *Welke maat is het?*
too much *te veel*
each *per stuk*
cheap/expensive *goedkoop/duur*
I will take it *Ik neem/koop het*
Do you take credit cards? *Aanvaardt u kredietkaarten?*

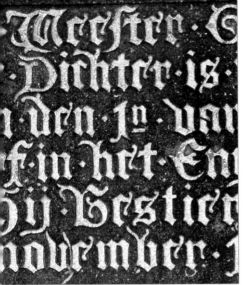

the bill *de rekening*
I am a vegetarian *Ik ben vegetariër*
What do you recommend *Wat beveelt u aan?*
I'd like... *Ik wil/zou graag...*
I'd like to order *Ik wil bestellen/zou graag bestellen*
That is not what I ordered *Dit is niet wat ik besteld heb*
Is smoking permitted? *Is roken toegestaan?/Mag er gerookt worden?*

Days of the Week

Sunday *Zondag*
Monday *Maandag*
Tuesday *Dinsdag*
Wednesday *Woensdag*
Thursday *Donderdag*
Friday *Vrijdag*
Saturday *Zaterdag*

Numbers

0 *nul*
1 *een*
2 *twee*
3 *drie*
4 *vier*
5 *vijf*
6 *zes*
7 *zeven*
8 *acht*
9 *negen*
10 *tien*
11 *el*
12 *twaalf*
13 *dertien*
14 *veertien*
15 *vijftien*
16 *zestien*
17 *zeventien*
18 *achttien*
19 *negentien*
20 *twintig*
21 *een en twintig*
30 *dertig*
40 *veertig*
50 *vijftig*
60 *zestig*
70 *zeventig*
80 *tachtig*
90 *negentig*
100 *honderd*
200 *tweehonderd*
1,000 *duizend*

As a rule, the 'hard consonants' such as t, k, s and p are pronounced almost the same as in English, but sometimes softer. Other pronunciations differ as follows: $j = y$; $v = f$; $je = yer$, $tje = ch$; $ee = ay$, $oo = o$; $ij = eay$; $a = u$.

Is there a bank near here? *Is er hier een bank in de buurt?*
I want to change some pounds/dollars *Ik zou graag ponden/dollars wisselen*
chemist *de apotheek*
department store *het warenhuis*
market *de markt*
supermarket *de supermarkt*
receipt *de kassabon*
postcard *de briefkaart*
stamp *de postzegel*

Sightseeing

I am looking for... *Ik zoek... naar*
Where is...? *Waar is hier...?*
tourist information office *de toeristische dienst*
museum *het museum*
church *de kerk*
exhibition *de tentoonstelling*
When does the museum
open/close? *Wanneer is het museum open/gesloten?*
free *gratis*

Dining Out

breakfast *het ontbijt*
lunch *de lunch/het middageten*
dinner *het diner/avondeten*
meal *de maaltijd*
menu *de (spijs) kaart/het menu*
Can we see the menu? *Kunnen we de (spijs) kaart bekijken?*
first course *het voorgerecht*
main course *het hoofdgerecht*

Below: tourist areas will have menus in English.

Literature and Theatre

The city of Bruges has long provided a rich backdrop for literary works of religious inspiration, political intrigue and romance. This section introduces writers and dramatists for whom Bruges has provided creative stimulation, as well as a selection of contemporary Flemish writers who have made their mark on the Dutch-language scene. Pageant and performance also have a long tradition in Bruges and are continued today in annual festivals, while the scattering of theatres put on an excellent programme of contemporary fare.

Writers and Dramatists

Bruges had its first literary boom in medieval times. The then Cathedral of St Donatian's on the Burg had a great library, a music school and a scriptorium, where illuminated manuscripts were produced. Bookshops were clustered around the cathedral and attracted pioneers of the trade: William Caxton produced the first printed book in the English language in Bruges in 1474, a *Recuyell of the Histories of Troy*, ordered by Margaret of York, Duchess of Burgundy, before he left to introduce printing in England.

Pre-20th Century

To learn more about the Bruges-inspired revolt against the French in 1302, read **Hendrik Conscience**'s novel *De Leeuw van Vlaanderen* (The Lion of Flanders, 1838). In nearby Damme, the poet **Jacob van Maerlant** (1235–1300) was the greatest Flemish poet of the Middle Ages, and remained the most popular for centuries after his death. He wrote long didactic poems. **Charles de Coster**'s

Above: an illustration of poet Jacob van Maerlant.

The Glorious Adventures of Tijl Uilenspiegel (1867, *see p.17*), inspired by a medieval character, gave the same village its legendary hero.

The Catholic priest and teacher **Guido Gezelle** (1830–

99) was a one-man literary movement, who gave Flemish poetry a new lease of life with his volume *Kerkhofblommen* (Graveyard Flowers, 1858), a mixture of literary Dutch and the dialect of West Flan-

Left: Hugo Claus (centre), pictured in Paris in 1955.

popular TV series (2004–2014). All based in Bruges, his stories centre on murder investigations carried out by two police officers.

Hugo Claus (1929–2008) was the most important Flemish writer of the post-World War II period. He received more awards than any other Dutch-language writer, and his work has been translated into 20 languages. His *Het verdriet van België* (1983; The Sorrow of Belgium) – an epic story of collaboration during the Nazi era – is essential reading for anyone who wants to understand modern Belgium. Claus was born in Bruges.

Bart Moeyaert (b.1964) was born and grew up in Bruges, but now lives in Antwerp. A prize-winning author, he has also had several books translated into English, including novels for young adults which deal with family problems, and *Brothers*, a collection of stories that describe his life growing up as the youngest of seven brothers (www.bart moeyaert.com).

Peter Verhelst (b.1962), another Bruges-born writer who moved away, this time to Ghent, writes poems, novels and poetic texts for dance and theatre productions. His poem for Brugge 2002, the city's year as European Capital of Culture, is engraved into the seat-backs of the Concertgebouw.

Paul De Wispelaere (b.1928), also born in Bruges, is a literary critic and novelist, essayist and lecturer in Dutch-language literature. Editor for years of literary journals, his works are avant-garde and examine the quest for identity and the relationship between literature and life.

Texas-born calligrapher Brody Neuenschwander – who worked with Peter Greenaway on the films *Prospero's Books* (1991) and *The Pillow Book* (1996) – lives in Bruges. His work frequently features in exhibitions and performance pieces.

ders. His ideas and beliefs brought him into conflict with the church and educational authorities, and he abandoned poetry in the 1870s in favour of writing essays and doing translations. Gezelle returned to his first love in *Tijdkrans* (Time's Garland, 1893) and *Rijmsnoer* (String of Rhymes, 1897), poems dealing with nature, religion and Flemish nationalism that show an original use of rhyme, metaphor and sound.

Georges Rodenbach (1855–98) never lived in Bruges but immortalised the city in his 1892 novel *Bruges-la-Morte*. It tells the story of a widower who has retreated to Bruges to grieve for his young wife in a city chosen for its silence, monotony and melancholy.

The novel provoked a 'cult of Bruges' among Symbolist artists and poets – Mallarmé, Rodin and Proust were fans – and inspired Thomas Mann (*Death in Venice*), Korngold's opera *Die tote Stadt* (1920) and, it has been claimed, Hitchcock's *Vertigo*.

20th Century and Beyond

Pieter Aspe (b.1953) writes crime fiction best-sellers which were made into a

Below: the novelist Georges Rodenbach.

Above: the elegant Stadsschouwburg theatre.

Bookshops

Boekhandel Raaklijn
Kuipersstraat 1; tel: 050 33 67 20; www.boekhandelraaklijn. be; Mon–Sat 9am–6pm; bus: 1; map.134 B4
Delightful bookshop just off the Markt, a local favourite, which stocks a wide selection of fiction and non-fiction in Dutch, French and English.

Brugse Boekhandel
Dijver 2; tel: 050 33 29 52; www.brugseboekhandel. be; Mon–Sat 9am–12.30pm, 1.30–6.30pm; bus: 1; map p.134 C3
Canalside bookshop selling a broad range of books, newspapers and maps, including many in English.

FNAC
Markt 18–19; tel: 050 47 62 62; www.fnac.be; Mon–Sat 10am–6.30pm, Fri until 7pm; bus: 1; map.132 C4

This French chainstore is an emporium of music, books, DVDs, games and multimedia, plus audiovisual goods.

De Reyghere
Markt 12–13; tel: 050 33 34 03; www.dereyghere.be; Mon–Sat 8.30am–6.15pm; bus: 1; map p.134 C4
Founded in 1888, this shop sells literature in several languages, as well as international newspapers and magazines. The travel bookshop next door (Mon 12.30–6pm, Tue–Sat 9.30am–12.30pm, 1.30–6pm) sells international guide books and maps.

Theatre

Cultuurcentrum Brugge/ Stadsschouwburg
Vlamingstraat 29 (Stadsschouwburg); tel: 050 44 30 40/60; www.cultuurcentrumbrugge. be; bus: all city lines except for 10 and 23; map p.132 C1
The Bruges cultural centre is a centralised arts organisation for seven performance venues in the city centre and the nearby suburbs. The most prominent venue is the Stadsschouwburg, the elegant city theatre, on Vlamingstraat 29, while the programme

Below: the well-stocked De Reyghere bookshop.

Above: a scene from cult film *Malpertuis*.

encompasses everything from classical and contemporary drama to music and dance.

De Werf

Werfstraat 108; tel: 050 33 05 29; www.dewerf.be; bus: 3, 13; map p.132 B3

Contemporary drama plays at this popular jazz club.

SEE ALSO MUSIC AND DANCE, P.93

A vast medieval pageant takes place in Bruges every five years in August. The **Praalstoet van de Gouden Boom** (Pageant of the Golden Tree) was conceived in 1958 and recalls the sumptuous marriage in Damme of the Duke of Burgundy, Charles the Bold, to English Princess Margaret of York, in 1468. A great procession and tournament (the 'Tournament of the Golden Tree') was held in the Markt to celebrate the occasion, and it is this that the pageant celebrates, with 2,000 participants. The last two events have made an attempt to incorporate the history of Flanders into the festivities, and the struggle of the lower and merchant classes against their rulers (who were of course French-speaking). The next pageant takes place in 2017.

Film in Bruges

The Nun's Story (1959). Audrey Hepburn portrays a young woman in turmoil as she seeks her true path in life. Fred Zinnemann's picture was based on a fictionalised account of a Belgian nun's true story, and was shot on location in Bruges.

Malpertuis (1971). Cultish horror film directed by Belgian Harry Kümel. Orson Welles stars as a dying patriarch who leaves his mansion to a group of heirs on the condition that they must live there for the rest of their lives. Behind its closed doors are a nightmarish assortment of creatures and characters from mythology.

In Bruges (2008). Colin Farrell and Brendan Gleeson star in this comedy-drama as hit men lying low in Bruges after a job gone wrong. To tourism bosses' delight, Martin McDonagh's slick-talking film lent the city a darker vibe, reaching a market that may once have been put off by its traditional, twee reputation.

The Monuments Men (2014). George Clooney, Bill Murray and Matt Damon search for masterpieces stolen by the Nazis during World War II, including Michelangelo's *Madonna and Child* statue (on display at the Church of Our Lady in Bruges since the 15th century, stolen during the war and recovered in 1945).

Below: *In Bruges* has given the city an edgier reputation.

77

Monuments

One monument stands head and shoulders above the competition: the Belfort (Belfry) on the Markt square, one of Bruges' most popular attractions, whose clocktower and carillon make it a handy landmark when you are finding your way around. This chapter also highlights smaller – and quieter – places that, besides the city's churches and museums *(see pages 46–51 and 82–91)*, help tell the story of Bruges, from a string of windmills and fortified gates around the former city walls, to elite archery and crossbow clubs founded at the time of the crusades.

Belfort

Markt 7; tel: 050 44 81 43; www.brugge.be/musea; daily 9.30am–5pm; bus: 1; map p.134 C4

Dominating the Markt, the skyline, and the earshot of anyone nearby, the Belfort (Belfry) dates from the 13th century. The final storey (with the clock) was built in the 15th century. A wooden spire once crowned the tower, but was destroyed, first by lightning in 1493, and then by fire in 1741, leaving it with its current truncated look. Look closely and you may observe that the 83m (272ft) tower leans very slightly to the south-east, by 1.2m (4ft) at its summit.

The climb to the top is 366 steps, and rewards with a 360-degree view (the best time to visit is early morning

Twenty-six of the 47 bells in the Belfort carillon are originals, cast by Joris Dumery in the 18th century. His bell-foundry is honoured in Boeveriestraat, near where it was sited, with a large bell that used to hang in the Belfort: the *Dumeryklok*.

or late afternoon). The second-floor treasury is where the town seal and charters used to be locked behind the intricate Romanesque grilles (built 1292), each requiring nine separate keys to open them: the burgomaster (mayor) and the eight trade guilds' leaders held one key each, so the doors could only be opened with the agree-

Below: the Belfort towers over Bruges' centre.

City walls were thrown up around the inner canal circuit in the aftermath of Charles the Good's assassination in 1127. A second line of walls, punctuated by nine city gates, whose outline is preserved in the ring canal and its park, was built during the 14th century. These were dismantled between 1782–4 by order of the Austrian emperor.

ment of them all.

Further up is the 6-tonne great bell, and at the top the 47-piece carillon, which plays a different peal every quarter-hour. The bells are controlled either manually by the city bell-ringer, who sits in a room just below and gives regular concerts; or, more commonly, by a rotating metal drum.

Gentpoort

Gentpoortstraat; tel: 050 44 81 11; www.brugge.be/musea; Sat–Sun 9.30am–12.30pm, 1.30–5pm; bus: 1, 11; map p.135 D2

One of four remaining medieval city gates, recently renovated. The other three are

Left: a coat-of-arms on the Oud Tolhuis.

The coat of arms on the facade (1477) of the Oud Tolhuis belongs to the Dukes of Luxembourg. Pierre of Luxembourg, Knight of the Golden Fleece, had the concession to levy import taxes on goods entering the ports of Bruges.

Kruispoort (Holy Cross Gate), Smedenpoort and Ezelpoort (Donkey Gate) in the north-west. Note the different architectural styles of the gates when viewed from outside the city limits (fierce and fortified) or within (elegant and turreted).

Groot Seminarie – Ter Duinen Abdij

Potterierei 72; tel: 050 33 03 62; www.grootseminariebrugge.be; open to public by arrangement only; bus: 4, 14; map p.133 D3
The Duinen Abdij (Abbey of the Dunes) moved here in the 17th century from Koksijde on the coast – hence its name. Since 1833 it has been the Episcopal Seminary, and occasionally hosts exhibitions. You can visit its 18th-century church, gardens, greenhouse – and large meadow – with permission, obtainable (perhaps) at the main entrance.

Hallen

Markt 7; free; bus: 1; map p.134 C4
Below the Belfort are the heftily-proportioned Hallen (Market Halls) and courtyard (13th–15th-century), built to replace an earlier wooden structure on the same site, and with later additions made due to fire. For three centuries this was the pride of the city, and the focal point of its commercial life. It would have been crammed with traders, the air heavy with the scent of spices brought by Venetian merchants. City statutes and proclamations were announced from the balcony over the market entrance. It has recently come back into use as a commercial and exhibition centre. In front of the Hallen is a bronze replica of the Belfort and Hallen, with Braille inscriptions.

Oud Tolhuis

Jan van Eyckplein 2; not open to public; bus: 4, 14; map p.132 C1

Below: the Gentpoort guards the eastern entrance to the city.

79

Above: the Poertoren.

Behind the pointed gable of the Gothic Oud Tolhuis (Old Customs House) is a 13th-century merchant's house, with spacious rooms on lower floors for storing goods and living quarters upstairs. Boats entering the city had to visit this house to pay taxes on goods brought in from the outer ports of Damme and Sluis. The adjoining sliver of a house (15th-century) was occupied by *pijnders* (porters), who are represented in stone carvings at the base of a pillar. Next door used to be the public weighing house. The combined buildings are now the seat of the provincial library, which holds 600 religious manuscripts and early printed books.

Poertoren
Begijnenvest; not open to public; bus: 1; map p.134 B1
The Poertoren (Powder Tower) at the southern end of the Minnewater lake was built in 1398 and is the only one of the city walls' defensive towers to have survived. It is named after the gunpowder and munitions that it stored.

Poortersloge
Academiestraat 14; not open to public; bus: 4, 14; map p.132 C1
Overlooking Jan van Eyckplein, the tower of the Poortersloge (Burghers' Lodge) was the meeting place for the wealthiest bankers and merchants of Bruges. It dates from the 14th century; on its facade there is a statue of the bear that features in the city's coat of arms. It was also the emblem of a jousting club that held events in the marketplace outside. Used as the city's fine arts academy until 1890, it now houses the city archives.

Provinciaal Hof
Markt 2; not open to the public; bus: all city lines except for 10 and 23; map p.134 C4
On the east side of the Markt stands the Provinciaal Hof (Provincial House), built 1887–92 as the seat for the West Flanders provincial government and governor, who represents the royal court and federal government in the province.

Schuttersgilde Sint-Joris
Stijn Streuvelsstraat 59; sintjorisgilde.be; tel: 050 44 87 11; open by arrangement only; bus: 6, 16; map p.133 E1
Unlike at St Sebastian's, the boys of the Schuttersgilde Sint-Joris (St George's Archers' Guild) were crossbowmen. Their ornate guildhouse contains a collection of crossbows, as well as the guild's archives. The parksized garden has a vertical target-mast and sheltered walkways to protect against falling arrows.

Schuttersgilde Sint-Sebastiaan
Carmersstraat 174; tel: 050 33 16 26; www.sebastiaansgilde.be; May–Sept Tue–Thu 10am–noon, Sat 2–5pm, Oct–Apr Tue–Thu and Sat 2–5pm; bus: 6, 16; map p133 E2
The Schuttersgilde Sint-Sebastiaan (St Sebastian's Archers' Guild) is an ancient and prestigious longbow club, whose reputation grew from the time of the crusades. Inside is a fine collection of arms, furnishings, gold and silver plate, and other works of art.

Sint-Janshuismolen and Other Windmills
Kruisvest; tel: 050 44 81 11; www.brugge.be/musea; June–Sept Tue–Sun 9.30am–12.30pm, 1.30–5pm; bus: 6, 16; map p.133 E2
Dotted around the north-east perimeter of the city are four windmills, the only remaining examples from the 29 that stood along the city walls during the 19th century. Two are open to the public and still mill grain. The first, starting from the south, **Bonne Chièremolen**, is no longer in use. Standing on wooden stilt

Below: the Bonne Chieremolen windmill.

Above: the Stadhuis is situated on the Burg.

supports, it was built in 1888 at Olsene in East Flanders, and moved to its present location in 1911.

Sint-Janshuismolen (St John's House Mill) is operated throughout the summer as a museum piece, with a miller to show visitors around. This venerable structure, accessed via a vertiginous staircase, earned a living by twirling its blades here from 1770 to 1914. It was restored in 1964.

Next is **Nieuwe Papegaaimolen**, which was used as an oil-mill at Beveren-IJzer in West Flanders and rebuilt here in 1970. It is no longer in use.

The final mill of the quartet is the **Koeleweimolen** (Cool Meadow Mill; Kruisvest; July–Aug Tue–Sun 9.30am–12.30pm, 1.30–5pm), dating from 1765 and employed at Meulebeke in West Flanders until it was rebuilt here in 1996.

Stadhuis

Burg 12; tel: 050 44 87 43; www.brugge.be/musea; daily 9.30am–5pm; bus: all city lines except for 10 and 23; map p.135 C4

The town hall's magnificent first-floor is the only part of the building open to visitors. Its majestic Gothic Hall incorporates a rib-vaulted ceiling and polychrome decoration, renovated in the late 19th century. The ceiling is decorated with keystones depicting biblical scenes and its vaults rest on original stone consoles portraying the months of the year in scenes of rural life, and the four elements, a common Renaissance theme.

In the adjoining Maritime Chamber, an exhibition tells the story of the city's government through historic manuscripts, maps, engravings and paintings. Take time to study Marcus Gerards' 1562 engraving of the city and imagine how he must have climbed all the city's towers to get such a unique bird's eye view.

SEE ALSO ARCHITECTURE, P.27

Below: the grand interior of the Stadhuis.

Illustrious past members of St Sebastian's Archers' Guild include England's King Charles II, who paid for the banqueting hall, and his brother Henry, who were both in Bruges in exile from Oliver Cromwell. Charles formed a royal regiment of guards here in 1656, which accompanied him back to London when the monarchy was restored in 1660. All British monarchs since have been honorary members of the guild.

81

Museums and Galleries

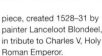

Even if you have wall-to-wall sunshine during your trip to Bruges, make time to step inside at least one of the city's museums. None require even a half-day's attention, yet each provides a fascinating insight into some aspect of the town's chequered history. Take your pick from priceless paintings commissioned by the wealthiest individuals in medieval Europe, glittering church artefacts, early medical instruments, implements of torture or the everyday household set-up of the poor, who eked out a living making lace.

Markt and Burg

Heilig Bloedbasiliek museum
Burg 15; tel: 050 33 67 92; www.holyblood.com; Apr–mid-Nov daily 9.30am–noon, 2–5pm, mid-Nov–Mar Thu–Tue 9.30am–noon, 2–5pm, Wed 9.30am–noon; bus: all city lines except for 10 and 23; map p.134 C4

On the right just before you enter the upper chapel, the one-room basilica museum contains items relating to the relic of holy blood and the basilica: precious and elaborate reliquaries, a Pieter Pourbus painting (1556) showing the 31 members of the Noble Brotherhood of the Holy Blood, and a curious 15th-century manuscript showing the robes worn by the brotherhood, which still provides inspiration to participants in the annual procession (see p.46). A tiny gold crown with precious stones belonging to Mary of Burgundy looks surprisingly crude in manufacture; and there is a ripped-open lead box that concealed the relic, first, for six years from 1578, when Bruges became a Protestant city and the basilica a public library, and again during the French Revolution (1797).

SEE ALSO ARCHITECTURE, P.24; CHURCHES, P.46

Bruges Beer Museum
Breidelstraat 3; tel: 0479 35 95 67; www.brugesbeermuseum.com; daily 10am–5pm; bus: all city lines except for 10 and 23: 1; map p.134 C4

Located on the upper floor of the old post office in the Market Square, this museum tells the story of beer in a fun and innovative way. An interactive iPad tour helps visitors navigate their way around. There is a special tour adapted for children aged 5–15, and a beer tasting area.

Bruggemuseum-Brugse Vrije
Burg 11a; tel: 050 44 87 43; www.brugge.be/musea; daily 9.30am–12.30pm, 1.30–5pm; bus: 1; map p.135 C4

The Paleis van het Brugse Vrije (Liberty of Bruges Palace) has one room that can be visited: the Renaissance Hall, containing a great black marble and oak chimneypiece, created 1528–31 by painter Lanceloot Blondeel, in tribute to Charles V, Holy Roman Emperor.

The Liberty of Bruges was a geographical concept, referring to the district around the city. The four burgomasters and 28 aldermen of the Liberty met in this room, which has been restored to its original condition, complete with aldermen's benches and big brass inkwells. Pride of place goes to the wall containing the black Dinant marble fireplace with an alabaster frieze and carved oak chimneypiece. This is one of the most memorable artworks in Bruges: the carving is on a

> The Bruggemuseum-Brugse Vrije is situated inside the Landhuis van het Brugse Vrije (Liberty of Bruges Palace), an early 18th-century neo-Classical building on the site of an older structure that formerly housed the law courts – a 16th-century facade can be seen from the canal-side of the building.

Left: *The Last Judgment* triptych by Hieronymus Bosch at the Groeningemuseum.

ess Mary of Burgundy, King Ferdinand II of Aragon and Queen Isabella I of Castile.

The alabaster friezes depict the biblical tale of Susanna and the Elders, by whom she is falsely accused and who get stoned to death.

The craftsmanship of the ensemble is quite overwhelming, but the brass handholds for the rural noblemen to use while drying their boots are the sort of domestic touch that everyone remembers.

Historium

Markt 1; tel: 050 27 03 11; www.historium.be; daily 10am–6pm (last entry 5pm); bus: 1; map p.134 C4

This new museum is dedicated to Bruges' Golden Age in the Middle Ages, evoking the period through a variety of films, performances,

monumental scale, covering an entire wall.

The fireplace celebrates the imperial army's victory at Pavia over Francis I of France in 1525. The Treaty of Madrid, which was signed the following year, broke Belgium free from French

domination. Charles, with raised sceptre and the orb of empire in his hands, stands in the centre beneath the double-headed eagle emblem of the Habsburg Empire. He is flanked by his grandparents: Emperor Maximilian of Austria, Duch-

Below: a selection of pottery in the Archeologisch Museum.

83

Above: *L'attentat* by René Magritte, from the Surrealist collection at the Groeningemuseum.

sounds, smells, decor and special effects.

South

Bruggemuseum-Archeologiemuseum

Mariastraat 36a; tel: 050 44 87 43; www.brugge.be/musea; Tue–Sun 9.30am–12.30pm, 1.30–5pm; bus: 1; map p.134 C3

The city's archaeological museum contains a small but interesting collection of pottery, glass, leather, wood, stone figurines and tomb paintings, including vestiges of the former St Donatian's Cathedral. The collection is presented in a lively, educational way, drawing parallels and contrasts between daily life in the Stone Age, the Middle Ages and the present.

Arentshuis

Dijver 16; tel: 050 44 87 43; www.brugge.be/musea; Tue–Sun 9.30am–5pm; bus: 1; map p.134 C3

This Arents House is divided between the ground floor, used for temporary exhibitions of the Groeningemuseum, and upstairs, which is devoted to the extensive collection of Welsh artist Frank Brangwyn (1867–1956). A disciple of the Arts and Crafts Movement and apprentice to its greatest exponent, William Morris, Brangwyn was born in Bruges and returned to paint here, donating most of his work to the city in 1936. His realistic paintings depict industrial life in the docks and factories, and there are items of furniture, prints and rugs which he designed.

The modern sculpture in the garden is Rik Poot's *Four Horsemen of the Apocalypse*,

Below: detail from Rik Poot's *Four Horsemen of the Apocalypse.*

Below: an ornamental fountain outside the Groeningemuseum.

representing the horrors of war, death, famine and revolution.

Begijnhuisje museum

Begijnhof 30; tel: 050 33 00 11; Mon–Sat 10am–5pm, Sun 2–5pm; bus: 1; map p.134 B2

This small house *(huisje)* in the corner of the Begijnhof's courtyard gives a glimpse into the life of a *begijn* – a religious woman similar to a nun but who took no vows, lived alone and supported herself by private means or by teaching, caring for the sick or making lace. Staffed by Benedictine nuns who now occupy the Begijnhof, and in a whitewashed cottage, it resembles a typical Beguine's house, still, essentially, in its 17th-century condition, with red-tiled floor, traditional furniture and a small cloister garden with a well.

SEE ALSO BEGUINAGES, P.29

Diamantmuseum

Katelijnestraat 43; tel: 050 34 20 56; www.diamondhouse. net; daily 10.30am–5.30pm, closed two weeks mid-Jan; bus 1; map p.134 C2

This museum documents the history of diamond polishing – a technique thought to have been invented by Bruges goldsmith Lodewijk van Berquem in the mid-15th century. On display you will find a reconstruction of van Berquem's workshop, examples of tools and machinery used in diamond polishing, plus models, paintings and rare rock samples. Daily demonstrations (at 12.15pm) further illustrate the technique.

Groeningemuseum

Dijver 12; tel: 050 44 87 43; www.brugge.be/musea; Tue–Sun 9.30am–5pm; bus: 1, 11; map p.134 C3

A pathway leads from the Dijver to the Municipal Fine

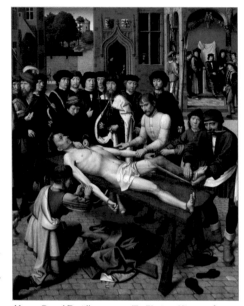

Above: Gerard David's gruesome *The Flaying of Sisamnes* from his two-panel *Judgement of Cambyses* at the Groeningemuseum.

Arts Museum (Stedelijk Museum voor Schone Kunsten), more commonly known as the Groeningemuseum. The gallery is relatively small, yet in terms of quality, it deserves to be ranked among the world's great museums. Visitors who are limited for time could restrict their visit to the first four rooms, which are arranged chronologically.

> Artist Jan Van Eyck, whose works can be seen in the Groeningemuseum, is said to have perfected – although not invented – the technique of oil painting: he mixed powder colours, egg white, water and resin in a new paint formula that allowed for greater variety of colour and thinner application; the recipe was a fiercely guarded secret among Netherlandish artists.

The informative audio guide is included in the ticket price.

The collection spans the artistic development of the Low Countries over six centuries and includes works by the so-called 'Flemish Primitives' of the 15th century. Far from being primitive, these painters were responsible for a revolutionary step forward in art, moving away from rigidly religious medieval themes towards portraying real people.

Their realism can be observed in such masterpieces as Jan van Eyck's *Madonna and Child with Canon Joris van der Paele, St Donatian and St John*, and the same artist's *Portrait of Margareta van Eyck* (his wife); Hans Memling's *Moreel Triptych*; Hugo van der Goes' *Death of the Virgin*; the fascinating

85

A fantastic Burgundian Gothic tracery of rose-coloured stone with high towers and arched windows (much of it 19th-century reconstruction), the Palace of the Lords of Gruuthuse was a refuge for the exiled English kings Edward IV in 1470–71 and Charles II in 1656.

Martyrdom of St Hippolytus (*c.*1468), a triptych by Dirk Bouts with a side panel by Hugo van der Goes, and works by Rogier van der Weyden, Pieter Pourbus and Gerard David.

A nonchalantly gruesome work is the *Judgement of Cambyses* (1498) by Gerard David, showing a corrupt Persian judge being flayed alive by torturers. Another wonderful painting is *The Last Judgement* by Hieronymous Bosch, a grim but complicated account of the trials that await sinners in the afterlife. Do not ignore less advertised paintings such as *The Town Docks at Bruges*

Above: exterior of the Gruuthuse Museum.

(1653) by Hendrik van Minderhout, which gives an idea of the size of the merchant ships that routinely called at Bruges. In later rooms, there are works by Belgian Symbolists including Fernand Khnopff, Flemish Expressionists Constant Permeke, Gustave De Smet, Jan Brusselmans and Gustave van

de Woestyne, and Surrealists René Magritte and Paul Delvaux.

Bruggemuseum-Gruuthuse
Dijver 17; tel: 050 44 87 43; www.brugge.be/musea; closed for renovation until late 2017; bus: 1; map p.134 C3
This former palace, which belonged to the Lords of Gruuthuse, is part of the city's historical museum (Bruggemuseum) network and contains a wealth of decorative arts, recalling life as lived – mainly by the high and mighty – in Bruges from the 13th–19th century. Highlights include Lodewijk van Gruuthuse's oak-panelled Gothic oratory, a 1520 bust of the young Charles V and a guillotine (which was used).

Onze-Lieve-Vrouwekerk
Mariastraat; tel: 050 44 87 43; www.brugge.be/musea; Mon–Sat 9.30am–5pm, Sun 1.30–5pm; bus: 1; map p.134 C3
The most valuable artwork in the Onthaalkerk Onze-Lieve-Vrouw (Church of

Below: detail of *The Last Supper* by Pieter Pourbus at the Onze Lieve Vrouwekerk.

Above: the church of Onze-Lieve-Vrouwekerk is rich with important artworks.

Our Lady), Michelangelo's *Madonna and Child* statue, can be viewed by all visitors, but you need to buy a ticket to see the church's other treasures, which are located in the side aisles, ambulatory and choir. Here you can see the magnificent side-by-side tombs of Charles the Bold and his daughter Mary of Burgundy. Charles was killed in 1477 at the Battle of Nancy (after his band of Italian mercenaries defected to the other side), while Mary died in a riding accident in 1482. Her sarcophagus, made from black marble surmounted by a graceful, reclining image of her in bronze, dates from 1502 and is a superb work of late Gothic art. Her father's, also furnished with a recumbent image of the deceased in bronze, was not completed until the mid-16th century. By that time the Renaissance style was

in vogue, and it is interesting to compare the differences between the two today.

Beneath the tombs are vaults with medieval frescoes uncovered in recent digs, while notable paintings include a *Last Supper* and *Adoration of the Shepherds* by Pieter Pourbus, Gerard David's *Transfiguration*, a painting of the Crucifixion by Anthony van Dyck, as well as works by Dirk Bouts and Hugo van der Goes.

The church is currently undergoing a major renovation so it's only partially accessible to the public; it is not possible to visit the tombs or see some of the artworks.
SEE ALSO ARCHITECTURE, P.24; CHURCHES, P.47

Memling in Sint-Jan
Mariastraat 38; tel: 050 44 87 43; www.brugge.be/musea; Tue–Sun 9.30am–5pm; bus: 1; map p.134 B3
A small but priceless collec-

tion of paintings by German-born painter Hans Memling (*c*.1440–94) are displayed in the 15th-century chapel of the Sint-Janshospitaal (St John's hospital), the main draw of this museum. Memling lived in Bruges from 1465 until his death, and four of the six works here were commissioned especially for this chapel. Each work testifies to his captivating

---

The In&Uit tourist bureau on 't Zand *(see p.55)* sells combined entry tickets to museums that represent significant savings: the Brugge City Card, €46 for 48 hours or €49 for 72 hours, gives access to 27 museums, a boat ride or bus tour plus further discounts on car parks, bike hire, cultural events and shopping – see www.bruggecitycard. be. Alternatively, a three-day ticket valid for entry to all the 16 municipal museums is €20.

87

Above: Hans Memling's wooden *Shrine of St Ursula*.

attention to detail and mastery of realism. They include the *Mystic Triptych of St John*, part of an altarpiece that has side-panel images of John the Baptist and John the Evangelist; the *Adoration of the Magi*, notable for its serene image of the Virgin Mary; and the exquisite *Shrine of St Ursula* (c.1489),

Construction of Sint-Janshospitaal (St John's Hospital) began in the 12th century and continued over the centuries; parts of the complex continued to function as a working hospital right up until 1976. You can see the later buildings if you wander around the courtyard at the back of the museum, where the former hospital is now used as a conference centre, shops and cafés.

a wooden reliquary in the shape of a Gothic church, on whose panels Memling painted several scenes from the life of St Ursula, including her martyrdom by the Huns at Cologne (along with a reputed 11,000 virgins who had set out with her on a pilgrimage to Rome). One of the greatest art treasures in the country, the shrine was commissioned by two sisters who worked in the church.

The rest of the former hospital, which was founded in the 12th century and is one of the oldest surviving in Europe, contains objects telling the story of medical care in medieval times. In what were once the wards, there is an exhibition of historical documents and rather alarming surgical instruments. The 17th-century pharmacy (closed 11.45am–2pm) has

a carved relief showing patients sleeping two to a bed. There is a strong sense of tradition in the place, enhanced by the informative visitor centre.

West
Sound Factory
't Zand 34; tel: 050 47 69 949; www.brugge.be/musea; group visits only (until Sept 2016); bus: 1; map p.134 B3
This museum offers visitors the chance to experiment with different sound installations, including the old bells from the Belfry Tower, whilst admiring one of the best views of the city.
Sint-Salvatorskathedraal
Zuidzandstraat; tel: 050 33 68 41; www.sintsalvator.be; Sun–Fri 2–5pm; bus: all city lines except for 10 and 23; map p.134 B3
The treasury of Sint-Salva-

torskathedraal (St Saviour's Cathedral), in the right transept, is home to paintings by Dirk Bouts, Adriaen Ysenbrandt, Lancelot Blondeel and Pieter Pourbus, and other ecclesiastical riches, including brass tomb plates, reliquaries and vestments, and a piece of a tunic which allegedly belonged to St Bridget of Ireland (d.523).
SEE ALSO CHURCHES, P.49

North
Choco-Story
Wijnzakstraat 2; tel: 050 61 22 37; www.choco-story.be; daily 10am–5pm except two weeks mid-Jan; bus: 1, 6, 16; map p.132 C1
No visit to Bruges is complete without sampling a praline – or three – of finest Belgian chocolate. This museum caters to visitors in need of a bit of culture to accompany their daily fix of something chocolately because it details the history of chocolate but without overlooking the importance

Above: statue at the Potteriemuseum.

of tasting. A privately-owned museum (owned by a Belgian food industry magnate who also owns the Fries Museum, below), it occupies a historic building on the corner of Sint-Jansplein.
SEE ALSO CHILDREN, P.43
Friet Museum
Vlamingstraat 33; tel: 050 34 01 50; www.frietmuseum.be;

daily 10am–5pm except two weeks mid-Jan; bus: 1, 3, 13; map p.132 C1
The Fries Museum occupies the historic Genuese Loge merchants house, and is devoted to the history of potatoes and chips, told through artefacts and lengthy wall texts (so not ideal for young children who cannot read). An important part of the history entails restoring to Belgium ownership of a food known worldwide as 'French fries', allegedly the result of confusion on the part of American soldiers after World War I. Little of the historic interior survives, except for the vaulted cellar, which is now the museum café and serves tasty *Belgian* fries.

East
Kantcentrum
Balstraat 16; tel: 050 33 00 72; www.kantcentrum.eu; daily 9.30am–5pm; bus: 6, 16; map p.133 D1
You may by this stage of your wanders in Bruges have

Below: *Martyrdom of Saint Hippolytus* by Dieric Bouts the Elder, at Sint-Salvatorskathedraal.

seen enough lace shops and people making lace to last a lifetime. But the Kantcentrum (Lace Centre) is appealing, as it is the place where the various strands come together. Housed in the renovated old lace school of the Sisters of the Immaculate Conception, it tells the story of the lace industry in Bruges and the teaching of the craft. There are antique lace specimens on display, and interactive screens explain different lacemaking techniques. Demonstrations of bobbin lacemaking (included in the ticket price) are held Mon–Sat 2–5pm. Round the corner is a shop where you can buy all of the materials you need to have a go at the painstaking art yourself.

SEE ALSO SHOPPING, P.125

Bruggemuseum-Gezellemuseum

Rolweg 64; tel: 050 44 87 43; www.brugge.be/musea; Tue–Sun 9.30am–12.30pm, 1.30–5pm; bus: 6, 16; map p.133 E2

This museum celebrates the work of Flemish poet-priest Guido Gezelle (1830–99) in the house where he

was born. The residence and large walled garden is devoted to the story of his life and work, from his childhood and teaching at a seminary to his political writings and poetry. Gezelle, whose poetry has been translated into 17 languages, became heavily involved in the Flemish Movement: he endeavoured to develop an language distinct from

Dutch, including elements of the West Flanders dialect, in which he wrote his poems. A brief hour spent in the house and garden here can be surprisingly rewarding and relaxing, even if you do not know Gezelle's poetry or read Dutch (there is a handout in English).

SEE ALSO LITERATURE AND THEATRE, P.74

Bruggemuseum-Volkskundemuseum

Balstraat 43; tel: 050 44 87 43; www.brugge.be/musea; Tue–Sun 9.30am–5pm; bus: 6, 16; map p.133 D1

Just up the road from the Jeruzalemkerk and Kantcentrum (Lace Centre), in a row of whitewashed cottages of the former Shoemakers' Guild almshouse, is the Volk-

Below: traditional bobbins, used for the manufacture of lace, at the Kantcentrum.

At its height, in 1840, lace-making in Bruges employed 10,000 women and girls out of a total population of 45,000. Although the Industrial Revolution was well under way by this time, this was still a cottage industry.

Left: artefacts from the life of poet Guido Gezelle, on display at the Guido Gezellemuseum.

lamp and tracing 400,000 years of history to the LED. More than 6,000 lamps, collected by an enthusiast, are on display.

Potterie-museum

Potterierei 79; tel: 050 44 87 43; www.brugge.be/musea; Tue–Sun 9.30am–12.30, 1.30–5pm; bus: 4, 14; map p.133 D3

A former hospice founded in 1276, the Potterie-museum adjoins Onze-Lieve-Vrouwter-Potterie (Our Lady of the Pottery) church and contains curious articles related to medical care, including a rare collection of lepers' rattles from the 16th century,

The curious assembly of artefacts in the Folklore Museum includes the extensive pipe collection of Belgium's first prime minister, Achille van Acker, who was born in Bruges.

and a wealth of furniture dating from the 15th–17th centuries. There are a number of devotional panels, tapestries and medieval sculptures, a triptych by Flemish Primitive Pieter Pourbus and a display of Delftware. Proceed to the church's treasury and feast your eyes on the glittering silverware, several 15th–16th-century Books of Hours and a rare 16th-century Book of Miracles.
SEE ALSO CHURCHES, P.51

skunde (folklore) museum. Modest yet appealing, it offers a peek into what people did in Bruges before they all started working in tourism. The rooms show reconstructed interiors of times past: a primary school class led by a young priest, a living room and clogmaker's, milliner's and cooper's workshops, a pipe room, a pharmacist's and a confectioner's (sweet-making demonstrations are held on Thursday afternoons). In summer, children and adults can play traditional games in the museum garden; and the visit ends in the museum's historic ale house, De Zwarte Kat (The Black Cat).
SEE ALSO CHILDREN, P.44

Lumina Domestica

Wijnzakstraat 2; tel: 050 61 22 37; www.luminadomestica.be; daily 10am–5pm, closed two weeks mid-Jan; bus: 6, 16; map p.132 C1

Adjoining the Choco-Story museum *(see p.89)*, this establishment tells the story of domestic lighting, starting with the torch and the oil

Below: iconic poster advertising the Stedelijk Museum voor Volkskunde's traditional ale house, the Black Cat.

91

M

Music and Dance

The musical reputation of Bruges has taken off since the new concert hall opened in 2002. True to tradition, it is best known for programming early and sacred music; the vast Festival of Flanders classical music bonanza starts in Bruges each summer. There is also a flourishing network of cultural venues coordinated from the Stadsschouwburg, the municipal theatre, which programmes world music, rock and contemporary dance, in addition to theatre. The Flemish dance scene has an international reputation, bolstered by energetic and cutting-edge troupes who attract companies from around the world to Bruges.

Classical Music
Bruges does not have a great music tradition, but, just as in the visual arts, was a hotbed of creativity during the 15th century, when St Donatian's cathedral was an important musical centre. The most prominent of Bruges composers is possibly **Jacob Obrecht** (1457/8–1505), who wrote at least 30 Mass cycles in the late 15th century. **Gilles Joye** (c.1424–83), in contrast, is known mainly for his secular songs, while **Adrien Basin** (c.1457–98) was one of Charles the Bold's personal singers at the Burgundian court. **Lupus Hellinck** (c.1494–1541) was choirmaster at Onze-Lieve-Vrouwekerk 1521–3, and then at St Donatian's from 1523 until his death, during which time he wrote Masses, motets, German chorales, French *chansons*, and songs in Flemish. **Clemens non Papa** was priest and choirmaster at St Donatian's from 1544. Known for his polyphonic settings of psalms, he also composed secular motets for Charles V.

The early music tradition of Bruges is celebrated each year in the vast **Festival van Vlaanderen**, a classical music festival that moves across Flanders, starting in Bruges with the pre-Renaissance period, then moving to other Flemish towns, where other traditions are emphasised. See www.festival.be.

One of Belgium's leading orchestras, the 60-piece freelance **Symfonieorkest Vlaanderen** (Flanders Symphony Orchestra), is based in Bruges but not in a performance venue, although it performs frequently at the Concertgebouw, *see right*, as well as in other Flemish cities. See www.symfonieorkest.be.

Main Venues
Cactus Musiekcentrum
MaZ, Magdalenastraat 27, 8200 Bruges Sint-Andries; tel: 050 44 30 60; www.cactusmusic. be; bus: 25; map p.138 C3
The main rock, world and alternative concert organiser in Bruges, whose principal venue is the MaZ (Magdalenazaal). It puts on an eclectic concert schedule featuring major inter-

national names in rock, pop, country, funk, electronica and experimental, to local young bands. In early July, it holds the three-day Cactus Festival in the Minnewater Park.
Concertgebouw
't Zand 34; tel: 050 47 69 99; box office: 070 22 33 02; www.concertgebouw.be; bus: 1; map p.134 B3
The terracotta-tiled Concertgebouw (concert hall) is known for the purity of its artistic programming: there is a strong emphasis on classical music performed as the composer would have intended, spanning the whole repertoire up to contemporary classical and electronica. Period instrument ensemble **Anima Eterna**, led by Jos van Immerseel, has been the orchestra in residence since the building opened in 2002.

Carillon concerts take place in the Belfort Wed, Sat and Sun at 11am and mid-June– mid-Sept also Mon and Wed 9pm. Seating is provided in the Hallen courtyard. See www.carillon-brugge.be.

92

Left: Bruges has its own annual jazz festival.

Brugge festival, held every two years over one week, focussing on current trends in European jazz (on alternate years, it puts on the smaller Flemish jazz festival). It also hosts contemporary and young people's theatre productions and other types of live music.

Music Shops
FNAC
Markt 18–19; tel: 050 47 62 62; www.fnac.be; Mon–Sat 10am–6.30pm, Fri until 7pm; bus: 1; map.132 C4

The Bruges branch of this French music, book and multimedia chainstore opened in 2008. It also sells concert tickets.

Rombaux
Mallebergplaats 13; tel: 050 33 25 75; www.rombaux. be; Mon 2–6.30pm, Tue–Fri 10am–12.30pm, 2–6.30pm, Sat 10am–6pm, plus Sun afternoons towards Christmas; bus: 1; map p.135 C4

The sort of place that makes you determine never to shop on the internet again, Rombaux is crammed with everything from classical music to new-wave Flemish folk; staff can track down almost any performer you can name, or sell you a piano, guitar or harp.

Look out for concerts in churches, too. The Sint-Walburgakerk is a regular venue for sacred music concerts during the annual Festival of Flanders, and provides a highly atmospheric setting. Organ recitals are often performed at the intimate Onze-Lieve-Vrouw-van-Blindekens (Our Lady of the Blind); the Karmelietenkerk hosts concerts of plainsong, among other things.

Touring ballet, dance and opera productions also play at the Concertgebouw, which holds an annual contemporary dance festival in December and co-produces the biennial Jazz Brugge festival with De Werf *(see below)*.

SEE ALSO ARCHITECTURE, P.24

Stadsschouwburg
Vlamingstraat 29; tel: 050 44 30 40; box office: 050 44 30 60; www.ccbrugge.be; bus: 3, 13; map p.132 C1

The neoclassical Stadsschouwburg (city theatre) is now the core of Cultuurcentrum Brugge, a network of cultural venues across the city, which is anything but classical in

its programming. Dance, live music (rock, world, folk) and theatre form the mainstay, but there visual art exhibitions too. The other venues include a 17th-century former chapel, the Hallen complex beneath the Belfort, and the MaZ, used by the Cactus Club.

De Werf
Werfstraat 108; tel: 050 33 05 29; www.dewerf.be; bus: 13; map p.132 B3

This jazz and blues venue has its own record label. It works in close association with renowned Bruges-born jazz pianist and composer Kris Defoort (b.1959), and is the motor behind the **Jazz**

Below: a classical recital at Concertgebouw.

Nightlife

Die-hard clubbers will travel from Bruges to the student centres of Ghent, Antwerp or Kortrijk for a night out, but several bars in the city have dance-floors, and because they are not nightclubs proper, do not charge for entrance, except on special nights. This section details the bars and cafés – mostly quite small places – that come alive after dark; as well as the city's two cinemas, and information for gay visitors to Bruges. Live music and theatre venues are listed elsewhere in this book *(see Music and Dance)*, as are bars and cafés best-suited for chilling out over a beer *(see Cafés and Bars)*.

After Dark

B-In
Zonnekemeers – Oud Sint Jan; tel: 050 31 13 00; www.b-in. be; Tue–Sat 11am–late; bus: 1; map p.134 B2
Trendy lounge bar in the pedestrianised area behind Memling in Sint-Jan museum, where staff and security drip attitude and customers include Club Brugge football team players, so dress to impress. Live DJ sets every Fri and Sat night.

Café De Vuurmolen
Kraanplein 5; tel: 050 33 00 79; 10pm–late; bus: 1; map p.132 C1
Fun and up-for-it party-bar, open all day as a regular café with terrace and way after many other places have shut up shop.

De Coulissen
Jacob van Ooststraat 4; Colt Vlamingstraat; 0486 10 51 41; Thu–Sat 10pm–6am; free; bus: 1; map p.134 C4
This dimly lit, dance and lounge venue plays R&B, techno and lounge sounds for all ages, but dress up if you want impress the door staff. Entrance charge on occasional special nights.

Entre Nous
Langestraat 145; tel: 050 34 10 93; www.bauhauszaal.be; parties most Fri and some Sat 10pm–6am; bus: 6, 16; map p.133 E1
New club venue – the first in the city centre – which is part of the ever-expanding Bauhaus youth hostel-hotel-café empire. Check flyers for party details. There are events most weekends, some free, some not.

La Fuente
Vrijdagmarkt 15; tel: 0478 20 33 07; Thu–Mon 4pm–late; bus: 1; map p.134 A3
Attractive and friendly bar on the 't Zand square run by a young couple, and popular with a slightly older crowd who just want to let loose to upbeat pop, disco and Latin sounds.

Het Entrepot
Binnenweg 4; tel: 050 47 07 80; www.hetentrepot.be; occasional weekends 9pm–4am; bus: 14
An old customs building just outside the ring canal, north of the city, which hosts anything from dance classes and jam sessions to organised club nights some weekends, fre-

Many venues in Bruges are gay-friendly. The website www.gaybruges.be details addresses of restaurants, bars, hotels and hair salons where gays, lesbians and bisexuals are welcome, as well as all the contacts required to organise a gay wedding, which is legal in Belgium. It also organises regular film nights and social gatherings.

quented by a youthful crowd. Check website or flyers and posters around town and be sure to have a means of getting back to the city later.

Joey's Café
Zilverpand; tel: 050 34 12 64; Mon–Sat 11.30am–late; bus: 1; map p.134 B3
Jazzy sounds play late into the night at this small café (with a large outdoor terrace) in the Zilverpand shopping centre, where no one will complain about the noise. Run by a friendly local musician, this is a relaxed place to enjoy good music long after most of Bruges has gone to bed.

Kaffee L'aMaRaL
Kuipersstraat 10; tel: 0497 39 19 29; 9pm–late; free; bus: 1;

Left: B-In, before the well-dressed masses descend.

Sat of the month, except July and Aug, starting 9pm.
Groot Vlaenderen
Vlamingstraat 94; tel: 050 68 43 56; www.grootvlaenderen. be; Wed–Sat 5pm–2am, Sun 5pm–midnight; bus: 3; map p.132 C1
Elegant bar ideal for late-night drinks, serving classic cocktails and a wide range of spirits.
SEE ALSO CAFÉS AND BARS, P.35

Gay
Studs Club
Hoogste van Brugge 1; www.gaybruges.eu; Thu–Sat 10pm–late, Sun 8pm–late; bus: 1; map p.134 B3
Men-only gay nightclub.

Cinema
Kinepolis
Koning Albert 1-laan 200; tel: 050 30 50 00; www.kinepolis. com; bus: 27; map p.134 A2
An eight-screen multiplex on the edge of town.
Lumière
Sint-Jacobsstraat 36; tel: 050 34 34 65; www.lumiere.be; bus: 1, 3, 13; map p.134 B4
Popular art-house cinema in the centre with three screens. It is attached to the De Republiek café.

map p.134 B4
DJ slots in this small venue off the Eiermarkt bar circuit are eclectic enough to satisfy all tastes in dance music and draw a friendly crowd of unpretentious young things.
De Lokkedize
Korte Vulderstraat 33; tel: 050 33 44 50; www.lokkedize.be; Wed–Sun from 6pm; bus: 1; map p.134 B3
A convivial café attached to a youth hostel that hosts bands playing R&B, as well as jazz, folk and rock. The young crowd show up into the early hours for home-cooked food.
Ma Rica Rokk
't Zand 7–8; tel: 050 33 24 34; www.maricarokk.be; Mon–Thu 7.30pm–3am, Fri–Sat 7.30pm–5am, Sun 11pm–3am; free; bus: 1; map p.134 A3
Pinball machines, bright-coloured chairs and graffiti murals: the teens' preferred café on 't Zand for a coke and sandwich between classes, and later for partying through the night. The café and terrace are open daily from 7.30am.
De Republiek
Sint-Jacobsstraat 36; tel: 050

34 02 29; daily 11am–late; bus: 1, 3, 13; map p.134 B4
A more arty crowd comes here to discuss politics, culture and the film they have just seen at the adjacent cinema. A good place to pick up flyers.
Snuffel Bar
Ezelstraat 42; tel: 050 33 31 33; www.snuffel.be; daily noon–midnight; free; bus: 3, 13; map p.132 B1
A youth hostel bar that attracts locals too, and everyone joins in and enjoys the party at its twice-monthly free live gigs, on the first and third

Below: some drinks are more potent than others.

95

Painting and Sculpture

The development of oil painting in the early 15th century coincided with the apex of economic prosperity in Bruges. Merchants and nobles who were in the city for business commissioned works by artists and the results were shipped around Europe in a trade that would influence the course of Western art. Over five centuries later, Flanders is rising again as a new force in contemporary art. This section describes the historical movements and artists associated with Bruges, as well as the artists working in Flanders today.

Early Flemish Art

Ever since Charlemagne established his court at Aachen in the 8th century, the artists of the Low Countries had been honing their skills to produce illuminated manuscripts; the culmination was the *Très Riches Heures du Duc de Berry* or Book of Hours (*c.*1411), by friars from the Flemish province of Limburg. In the early 15th century, these skills were transferred to a larger scale through the use of a new medium: oil paint.

Flemish Primitives

One of the earliest artists to adopt oil painting was **Jan van Eyck** (1390–1441), the first of the so-called Flemish Primitives, who moved to

Bruges in 1425 to cater to the cosmopolitan Dukes of Burgundy. No artist before him had observed nature so minutely, or was capable of rendering observations so precisely – you can visit his *Madonna with Canon George Van der Paele*, in Bruges' Groeningemuseum *(see p.85)*, and the Ghent Altarpiece in Sint-Baafskathedraal *(see p.18)*. Other masters of the time included **Rogier van der Weyden**, **Dirk Bouts** and **Hans Memling**, possibly the only true rival to Van Eyck, whose works for the Sint-Janshospitaal (Memling in Sint-Jan museum; *see p.87*) still hang there today. **Gerard David** is considered to be the last of the Flemish Primitives.

Where once the church had been the main patron of artists, the 15th century saw a rise in secular demand; oil paintings, unlike murals, were portable and marketable. Italian bankers and merchants in Bruges bought Flemish paintings and took them home, where they were greatly admired. Van Eyck painted the *Arnolfini Marriage* (1434) for Giovanni Arnolfini, a merchant from Lucca; the *Portinari Triptych* (1476–78) by Hugo van der Goes was painted for Tommaso Portinari, the Medici family's agent in Bruges. Flemish painters travelled to Italy, and Italian artists adopted oils, shifting away from more labour-intensive mediums.

Below: Knhoff's *Carresses/Art/The Sphinx* (1896) is a classic work of Symbolism.

96

Left: Memling's Madonna and Child with two Angels.

the French movements of Realism, Impressionism and Post-Impression. **Emiel Claus** (1849–1924) created Luminism, based on an Impressionist style.

By the mid-1880s, artists were seeking to express the inner workings of the mind – imagination, emotion, myth and dreams. The term given to this movement was **Symbolism**. North Belgian artists who took up the Symbolist theme included **Leon Spilliaert** (1881–1946) and **Fernand Khnopff** (1858–1921), whose work varies from the realistic to the dreamlike, such as the cheetah with a human head in *Caresses/Art/ The Sphinx* (1896; *see* left).

Ostend-born **James Ensor**'s work developed from realism to paintings peopled with skeletons, masks and grotesque cartoon figures. His style anticipated Expressionism by about two decades, and would give rise to the Surrealism of René Magritte (1898–1971) and Paul Delvaux (1897–1994).

Brueghel

Pieter Brueghel the Elder (*c.*1525–69) travelled to Italy, but his images of Flemish village life – exuberant marriage celebrations in snow-bound winter scenes – are resolutely North European in tone. The charm of Brueghel's work, and that of his son **Brueghel the Younger** (1564–1638), lies in its almost naive directness. Meanwhile, other Flemish painters were acquiring considerable technical skills. **Joachim Beuckelaer** (1533–74), for instance, produced market scenes of astonishing complexity.

Renaissance

After a period of decline in the 16th century, the economic centre of gravity moved to Antwerp – home to **Pieter Paul Rubens** (1577–1640), who restored Flemish art as an international commodity, and his pupil Van Dyck – as well as to the Netherlands, where the first sophisticated market for genre paintings developed. Artists who stayed in Bruges included **Pieter Pourbus** (*c.*1523–84) from Gouda in

> The term 'Flemish Primitives' sounds derogatory, but it relates rather to the original meaning of 'primitive': belonging to the first stage of a new development. The new development in this case was the Renaissance, to which the Primitives were precursors.

Holland, whose style harked back to the Flemish Primitives.

One of the great sculptures of the Renaissance can also be seen in Bruges: the *Madonna and Child* (1506) by **Michelangelo**, which stands in the Onze-Lieve-Vrouwekerk *(see p.47)*.

Independence to Fin-de-siècle

After two centuries of relative anonymity, Belgium greeted independence in 1830 with a renewed search for national and artistic identity. A trend for public statues of historical figures can be seen in **Paul de Vigne**'s (1843–1901) statue of medieval heroes Pieter de Coninck and Jan Breydel on Bruges' Markt *(see p.61)*. Meanwhile, painters echoed

Contemporary

In the 1960s, Flemish artists again began to win international recognition. **Marcel Broodthaers** (1924–76) became famous for his iconic mixed-media sculpture *Casserole and Closed Mussels* (1964–65), an amusing take on Pop Art. Installation artist **Panamarenko** (b.1940) produces huge flying machines of PVC, paper, wood and metal; the flat-colour figurative painting of **Luc Tuymans** (b.1958) is widely acclaimed, as is conceptual artist **Wim Delvoye** (b.1965), for his installation *Cloaca* (2000), which imitates the process of food digestion.

97

Palaces and Houses

Half of the 10,000 buildings in central Bruges are judged to be of historical value, yet most are not open to the public. This section highlights notable city houses, some built by patricians for their private residence; others – the almshouses dotted around the city – built by the wealthy for the needy and for their own future salvation. Several almshouse gardens and chapels may be entered. Also covered here are a number of abbeys and castles a short distance outside the city and not mentioned elsewhere in this guide.

Abbeys and Castles

Abdij Ter Doest
Ter Doeststraat 4, 8380 Lissewege; tel: 050 54 40 82; www.terdoest.be; daily 10am–7pm; free; bus: 47 or train to Lissewege; map p.139 C4
All that remains of this former Cistercian abbey, destroyed by Dutch rebels in the 16th century, is a remarkable Gothic barn dating from 1250, part of the old farm with pigeon-house (1651) and a monumental entrance gate (1662). The manor farm is now a popular restaurant, Hof Ter Doest. Artefacts from the abbey that survived its destruction can be seen in the Lissewege village museum.
SEE ALSO RESTAURANTS, P.120

Fort Beieren
Gemene Wedestraat, Koolkerke; café; tel: 050 67 95 86; www.hippo.be/fort; bus: 4 to Koolkerke Fort Van Beiren; map p.139 D4
Between the village of Koolkerke and the Damme Canal, 4km (2.5 miles) north-east of Bruges, this 1702 earthworks fort, and the vestiges of a demolished

19th-century château, are set in what is now a small country park of 26 hectares (64 acres). There is also a car park and café (Wed–Sun 11am–dusk).

Sint-Andriesabdij Zevenkerken
Zevenkerken 4, 8200 Bruges Sint-Andries; tel: 050 40 61 80; www.sint-andriesabdij.org; church: daily, all day except noon–2pm; free; bistro: Sept–June Mon noon–6pm, Tue–Sat 11am–6pm, Sun 10am–7pm, July–Aug daily Mon noon–7pm, Tue–Sun 11am–7pm; bus: 72 (stop: Heidelberg; then 1.5km (1 mile) walk along Torhoutsesteenweg back in the direction of Bruges); map p.138 C3

Above the shop-fronts on Steenstraat are some interesting old guildhouses, where details on the facades hint at their former function: at No. 40 is the shoemakers' guildhouse; at No. 38 the joiners' guildhouse; the stonemasons had their headquarters at No. 25; and the bakers at No. 19.

A large Benedictine abbey at Zevenkerken south-west of Bruges on Torhoutsesteenweg, founded around 1100 and rebuilt in the 19th century after being destroyed by the Revolutionary French. The abbey is situated amid forests, and the monks run a school and produce fine pottery as well as icons. Only the church is open for day visitors, but there is a bistro, Bistro Zevenkerken, serving cheap and cheerful food, and where you can buy the monks' handiwork.

Sint-Trudoabdij Male
Pelderijnstraat 14, 8310 Bruges Sint-Kruis; closed to public; bus: 58; map p.139 C3
A significant site in the history of Bruges, the St Trudo Abbey of the Sisters of the Holy Sepulchre, situated about 2km (1 mile) east of the Kruispoort city gate, was at one time the Castle of the Counts of Flanders. The 1369 marriage of Margaret, daughter and heir to Lodewijk of Male, to French duke Philip the Bold heralded the start of the Burgundian era in Flanders.

Left: castle-turned-abbey, Sint-Trudoabdij Male.

jousting tournaments and processions that took place on the Markt. It was in this house that angry Bruges traders held Maximilian of Austria prisoner for 100 days in 1488, after the Hapsburg authorities imposed new taxes. Held behind a barred window in an upper room, he was forced to listen to the torture of his advisers, including Pieter Lanchals, his right-hand man and treasurer. Lanchals had tried to mediate with the insurgents and was executed on the square below Maximilian's window. The hostage-taking of the Crown Prince of the House of Hapsburg, later Emperor Maximilian I, caused a stir across Europe. His father, Emperor Frederick III, dispatched warships and Maximilian was freed, but not before he had been forced to pledge respect for the rights of the burghers of Bruges. He never forgave the city for this episode; freed, he went back on his word and shifted his court

The original 12th-century castle has been rebuilt and destroyed again by military action or accidental fire throughout the centuries. The vast moated castle-turned-abbey gives a good indication of the power and wealth of the former rulers of Flanders. The Sisters of the Holy Sepulchre, unable to maintain such a huge property, sold the castle to a private buyer in 2011.

Houses and Palaces
Craenenburg
Markt 16; tel: 050 33 34 02; www.craenenburg.be; daily from 7am, Sun–Thu until 11pm, Sat–Sun from 1am; bus: 1; map p.134 C4

The turreted and crenallated facade of the busy café is all that recalls its past. Once a residence for the Count of Flanders' knights and their lady-folk, its upper floors afforded good views of the

Below: little remains of the original Abdij Ter Doest.

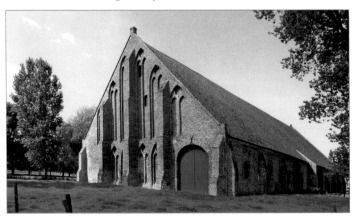

to Ghent and the commercial privileges to Antwerp, thus undermining Bruges' importance.

SEE ALSO CAFÉS AND BARS, P.30

Hof Bladelin

Naaldenstraat 19; tel: 050 33 64 34; www.brugge.be/musea; Mon–Fri 10am–noon, 2–5pm; bus: 1; 3, 13; map p.132 B1

The house was built by Pieter Bladelin (1410–72), who was treasurer to Philip the Good, Duke of Burgundy (the neo-Gothic niche – 1892 – on the outer facade shows Bladelin kneeling before a crowned Madonna and Child). He made a good living: as well as the house, he dabbled in polder reclamation, founded the village of Middelburg, 20km (12 miles) east of Bruges, and was a patron of artists, including Rogier van der Weyden (1399–1464).

The Medici Bank of Florence took over the house in 1466, and it is this con-

> Although many are still in use, it is possible to enter the almshouses by pressing the buzzer; you do not need to know the inhabitants.

nection that has given it an Italianate look, including the Renaissance courtyard and ornamental garden, which is thought to be the earliest example of the Renaissance style in the Low Countries. On the courtyard facade are two medallions dating from 1469, depicting Lorenzo de' Medici (Lorenzo the Magnificent) and his wife Clarisse Orsini.

Nearby, at Naaldenstraat 7, is another mansion, **Gistel House**, dating from the end of the 13th century but largely rebuilt in the 16th, by Antoine de Bourbon, Duke of Vendôme. It is now part of the city music conservatory.

Huis Bouchoute

Markt 15; not open to public; bus: 1; map p.134 C4

On the opposite corner of Sint-Amandstraat from the Craenenburg café stands this mansion, the Bouchoute House, where the exiled English King Charles II stayed in 1656–57. Dating from 1480, it was restored in 1995 to its original brick Gothic condition. The octagonal compass and weathervane (1682) on the roof allowed merchants to judge their ships' chances of entering or leaving port.

Hof van Watervliet

Oude Burg 27; tel: 050 44 03 77; www.hofvanwatervliet.be; not open to public; bus: 1; map p.134 C3

The restored 16th-century residence of humanist Marcus Laurinus, Lord of Watervliet (1530–81). He had many illustrious guests, including Spain's Juan Luis Vives and Erasmus of Rotterdam, who visited frequently between 1517 and 1521, and was so enthralled by the erudite company he met in Bruges that he called the

Below: a typical Bruges godshuis, or almshouse.

city the 'Athens of the Low Countries'. English statesman Sir Thomas More, who started writing his political treatise *Utopia* (1515) while in Bruges on official business, was another frequent caller. Together with the house next door – Hof Lanchals (No. 23), once home to Pieter Lanchals, the unlucky advisor to Maximilian of Austria *(see p.99)* – it is now used as offices and a meeting centre for health-related non-profit organisations.

Godshuizen

Godshuizen are typical Flemish almshouses, built from the 14th century onwards by wealthy families for the poor, sick or elderly, and by workers' guilds for retired members or their widows. Frequently named after their benefactor, they are of two types: built in a row along a street or clustered around a central garden, with a chapel (where the residents had to pray twice a day for their benefactor's soul) and shared privy, and where each resident was allotted a patch of garden to cultivate. Bruges retains 46 *godshuizen*, containing more than 500 houses, most still used for their original purpose, and allocated to the elderly by the town's social services department. The following list is a pick of the best.

Bouveriestraat
bus: 1; map p.134 A2

This street has more almshouses than any other street, several of which have been renovated very recently.

At the ramparts end of the street is the **Godshuis De Moor** (Nos 52–76), founded 1480 for retired stonemasons, carpenters and coopers by city magistrate Donaas De Moor, who died

Above: pelican engraving, Godshuis De Pelikaan.

in 1483. Next door, at No. 50, **Godshuis Van Volden** occupies the site of a medieval hospital for mentally ill children and foundlings. Near the Zand end of the street are the tiny **Godshuizen Sucx-Van Campen** (1436) and the 17th-century **Godshuis Van Peenen-Gloribus**, which look too small to be inhabited by anyone but a hobbit.

Other former *godshuizen* that have undergone a change in function but which are accessible to the public are the row of cobblers' almshouses that now form the **Bruggemuseum-Volkskunde** (Folklore Museum) at Balstraat 43, and the Adornes family almshouses at Peperstraat 3A. SEE ALSO MUSEUMS AND GALLERIES, P.89

Godshuis De Pelikaan
Groenerei 8; bus: 1; map p.135 D4

A small almshouse built

1714 along the now-elegant Groenerei with a beautiful house chapel; see the pelican engraved in the facade.

Godshuizen St Jozef and De Meulenaere
Nieuwe Gentweg 8-22; bus: 1; map p.135 C2

Two of the most accessible: built in the 17th century around a shared courtyard garden planted with cottage-style flowering beds, and with a tiny chapel and water pump.

Godshuis De Vos
Noordstraat 6–14; bus: 1; map p.134 C2

Eight houses, now converted to six, built 1713 and recently restored, with a smart formal garden and a chapel.

Rooms Convent
Katelijnestraat 9–15; bus: 1; map p.134 C2

The oldest surviving almshouse, built 1330 for women of standing who had chosen to adopt a life of poverty and religious teaching.

101

Pampering

Where better to come for a fashionable chocolate massage than the home of the best chocs in the world? The chocolate used in body treatments is not of the edible variety, however, so licking when the therapist leaves the room is not advised. The Flemings have a complex-free approach to beauty and body care and get themselves groomed and buffed in a no-nonsense manner. The following selection of cosmetic shops, spas and beauty salons is not exhaustive, but reflects the rather modest offering of this mid-sized town; many of the pricier hotels also provide pampering services.

Beauty Institutes
Ann Vandamme
Ezelstraat 55; tel: 050 33 74 07; www.annvandamme.be; Tue–Sat 9am–6.30pm; bus: 3, 13; map p.132 A2
Small beauty institute in town recommended for its use of visibly successful anti-cellulite treatment Endermologie, which conducts deep tissue massage and stimulates circulation through suction. The salon specialises in facials, and, for men, Tibetan massage, using warm herbs and hands. There is a small private sauna, too.
Esthetiek Elle
Ezelstraat 147; tel: 050 33 92 59; www.esthetiek-elle. be; Tue–Fri 9am–noon, 1.30–6.30pm, Sat 9am–noon, 1.30–6pm; bus: 3, 13; map p.132 A2
Stylish salon offering seasonal beauty treatment packages (see website for details), as well as chromatherapy (coloured light) sessions, non-surgical lifting treatment and epilation using IPL (Intense Pulsed Light) technology.

Mixed nudity is the norm in spas (except those in hotels), although swimsuits are sometimes allowed at designated times. Families are welcome.

Cosmetics and Skincare
Ici Paris XL
Noordzandstraat 10; tel: 050 33 73 78; www.iciparisxl.be; Mon–Sat 10am–6pm; bus: 1; map p.134 B4
Bruges branch of the largest Belgian cosmetics and perfumery chain, where top scents are traditionally sold at least 20 percent below recommended prices. Helpful, friendly service is its hallmark.
Parfumerie Liberty's
Smedenstraat 23–25; tel: 050 34 36 35; www.parfumerie libertys.com; Mon–Sat 9.30am–6pm; bus: 1; map p.134 A3
Chic perfume and cosmetics store on this smart shopping street, located on the opposite side of 't Zand from the centre, and rarely visited by tourists.

Spas
Het Hemelhuis
Groenerei 16; tel: 050 67 96 93; www.hemelhuis.be; Thu–Fri 1.30–10.30pm, Sat 12.30–6pm; bus: 1; map p.135 D4
The only city-centre bath house, the 'Heaven House' is a stylish sauna and hammam that blends Moorish decor with post-industrial design. As is typical for saunas in Belgium, mixed nudity is the rule, although there is a women-only slot on Tuesdays. A package comprising entry and choice of massage is a treat.
Hotel Dukes' Palace Spa
Prinsenhof 8; tel: 050 44 78 88; www.hoteldukespalace.com; daily 8am–9pm; bus: 1; map p.134 B4
The spa includes a gym, sauna, steam room, salt wall and infrared and UV cabins. It's complimentary for hotel guests and available to other clients for an extra charge.
Mozaiek
Dorpsstraat 6, 8200 Sint-Michiels; tel: 050 67 58 07; www.saunabrugge.be; daily 9am–0.30am; bus: 17; map

Left: the Sunparks 'Thermae' baths complex.

Private spa 3km (2 miles) south-west of Bruges, with fluffy white bathrobes and towels. As well as a pool, Finnish sauna and hamman with eucalyptus, there is a selection of 2, 2.5 and 3-hour spa packages. Massage by a therapist and breakfast or lunch/dinner on request. Five complimentary Rituals body cosmetics at each visit. By appointment only.

Sunparks – Thermae
Sunparks De Haan; Wenduinesteenweg 150; 8420 De Haan; tel: 050 42 95 96; www.sunparks.be; Wed, Sat 11am–2pm (with swimsuit), Tue–Thu, Sat 2–8pm (nude), Sun 2–7pm (nude); coast tram (stop Sun Parks); map p.138 B4

The Sunparks holiday centre near the coast has a 'Thermae' bath complex that is open to the public as well as guests: it has a pool (indoor and outdoor), saunas, Turkish bath, and provides facials and body massages, as well as overnight accommodation deals.

p.138 C3
Pretty but tiny private sauna centre attached to a bathroom store for a maximum of four people, and really intended for two, so must be reserved in advance. It has a Turkish steam bath, sauna, infra-red sauna and a Jacuzzi. Just 4km (2.5 miles) from Bruges centre, it is easily accessible by bus from the city. Special arrangements

include a breakfast and champagne package. Tea, coffee, a plate of cakes and fresh fruit are provided free of charge.

Puur Spa
Torhoutsesteenweg 503; 8200 Sint-Michiels; tel: 050 67 44 44; www.puur-spa.be; Wed–Mon 8am–10pm; bus: 25 to Sint-Michiels Vogelzang stop, then 750m/yds walk; map p.138 C3

Below: Hotel Dukes' Palace spa and salt wall.

103

Parks and Gardens

Asmall city surrounded by lush farmland, Bruges' parks and gardens tend to be small and perfectly formed. The largest green spaces within the town have always been church property, the gardens of convents and abbeys: the largest is still behind the walls of the seminary of the former Abbey of the Dunes on Potterierei. To glimpse nature in the city, you need simply glance down a lush canal, sit on a café terrace in a tree-lined square or step into in a secluded almshouse garden.

Outdoor Spaces

Gezellemuseum and garden
Rolweg 64; tel: 050 44 87 43; www.brugge.be/musea; Tue–Sun 9.30am–12.30pm, 1.30–5pm; bus: 6, 16; map p.133 D1

The museum dedicated to the great Flemish poet and priest (1830–99) in the house that was his birthplace is backed by a pleasant garden, with shady benches and a number of exotic trees and plants.
SEE ALSO MUSEUMS AND GALLERIES, P.90

Graaf Visartpark
Karel de Stoutelaan; free; bus: 9; map p.132 A1

Situated just outside the city limits in the west, this park takes its name from Count Amedée Visart de Bocarmé (1835–1924), Bruges burgomaster for 50 years from 1876–1924 and a keen advocate of municipal green spaces. It was he who set about transforming the old fortified ramparts into a green boulevard around the city. The park was used as a driving practice ground in the 1960s and there is still a circuit where children can learn the

rudiments of the road, as well as a playground and tall trees.

Hof Sebrechts Park
Entrances on Beenhouwersstraat and Oude Zak; free; bus: 9, 41, 42; map p.134 B4

A tranquil oasis hidden behind houses, the Hof Sebrechts (Sebrechts House) park has had a chequered history. It, too, owes its existence to the French demolition of monasteries and convents: this was the vegetable garden of the Sisters of St Elisabeth's Convent, which stood nearby from the 15th century. City archivist Louis Gilliodts-Van Severen and his daughter bought the garden and adjoining 18th-century house in 1885, adding the monumental gate at the Oude Zak entrance in 1907. Surgeon Joseph Sebrechts, who worked at Sint-Janshospitaal, bought the domain in 1928, and hired a landscape architect to create the garden. After he died, the property fell into government hands. Plans to build on it were never realised, and it eventually became a car park. The city finally reopened the garden in

1982. There are benches, a children's play area and sandpit. In summer, the park hosts a sculpture exhibition.

Koning Albertpark
Koning Albertlaan; free; bus: 1; map p.134 B2

A broad strip of green that runs from the station to the 't Zand along the route of the former train line, from when the station was located on the 't Zand square. The garden was developed in the wake of World War II, providing much-needed employment to local men. Today it is a landscaped green cut-through; and not too disturbed by the ring road to which it runs parallel.

> The poplar-shaded courtyard of the Begijnhof de Wijngaarde *(see also Beguinages, p.28)* is one of the most serene and memorable locations in the city, especially in spring when daffodils carpet the lawn. The begijnhof takes its name – Wijngaard – from the vineyard that used to occupy this area, where grapes were grown for making vinegar. Visitors are asked to respect the rule of silence.

Left: a perfectly formed flock of geese on the canal ring park.

with the king at the wheel of their car. The residents of Bruges still call the park 'Botanieken Hof', after its original designation. The park is used for outdoor film screenings during the three-week Klinkers (cobblestones) festival in summer.

Minnewater Park
Minnewater, free; bus: 1; map p.134 C1

The Minnewater park is dominated by its tree-fringed 'Lake of Love' and the Kasteel Minnewater, a château-style restaurant with a scenic

Koningin Astridpark
Minderbroederstraat; free; bus: 1, 11; map p.135 D3

Koningin Astridpark (Queen Astrid Park) is one of Bruges' largest parks. It has a pond, wrought-iron bandstand (1859), children's playground; even a church, Heilige-Magdalenekerk (Blessed Mary Magdalene Church), built 1851–3, at the southern end of the park.

Like other green spaces in the city, the park occupies the site of a former monastery; a Franciscan abbey in this case. The land was purchased by the city around 1850 and converted into a botanical garden, becoming a big attraction with Sunday strollers. In 1935 it was given its current name, after the death in 1935 of the popular Queen Astrid, wife of King Leopold III, who died in a road accident in Switzerland

Bruges has a long history of maintaining its green spaces: a letter from Gervatius, Bishop of Reims, dated before 1067 (the year he died) praises the meadows, orchards and vineyards of Bruges, and the fertility of the soil. In the 12th–13th centuries, the city had several Boomgaard (Orchard) streets. The English word 'garden' is derived from the Dutch word for orchard, 'gaard'.

Below: the colourful bandstand in Koningin Astridpark.

105

Several *godshuizen* (almshouses) in Bruges have attractive, green, inner courtyards. Members of the public may enter when the gate is open; visitors are asked to enjoy the space in silence. Take a look at the 17th-century Godshuizen St Jozef and De Meulenaere on Nieuwe Gentweg, which are built around a courtyard garden with a tiny chapel and water pump *(see also Palaces and Houses, p.101).*

Above: tranquil Minnewater Park.

waterside terrace (closed at time of writing). The small garden behind is ideal for a picnic away from the crowds.

The origin of the lake's common name – the 'Lake of Love' – is the source of much debate. French novelist and poet Victor Hugo visited Bruges in 1837 and allegedly christened it the Lac d'Amour. It is said he was inspired by the word *minne*, medieval Dutch for 'love'. But local legend has it that the *minne* was in fact a watery ghost: that of Saxon maiden Minna, who fled the home of her father rather than marry the suitor of his choice. When her lover returned from fighting the Romans, he found her dead of cold and hunger by a stream in the woods. He built a dyke, buried her in the ground, then released the water to create a lake over her resting place. Whatever its origin, the romantic label has stuck and the park is a magnet for dreamy couples. In summer, the park is the venue of the free world music festival Feest in't Park, and the weekend-long Cactus Festival (entrance charge), a rock music event *(see p.92).* SEE ALSO CANALS AND BRIDGES, P.41

Ring Canal Park
A long, narrow, green belt around all but the northern

perimeter of the city follows the line of the old city ramparts, alongside the ring canal. The remaining four fortified gates of the walls punctuate the route, which can be undertaken on foot or by bicycle. A busy road also traces the ring canal, so it is not the most peaceful place, but it is ideal for a substantial ride, walk or run. The lawns around the windmills in the north-east are popular with sunbathers on fine days.

The park was created over many years, starting in 1876 on the initiative of mayor Count Amedée Visart de Bocarmé *(see p.104).*

Its north-west limit is the Ezelpoort (Donkey Gate). In the south-west, between Smedenpoort and the station, a small brick house in the trees is the Oud Waterhuis (Old Water House), an 18th-century pumping station where a horse-actioned pump was used to extract drinking water, which was then distributed to the various districts. Its origins date back to the 14th century. The gunpowder store of the Poertoren is on the southern tip, beside the Minnewater.

In the south-east of the park, the recently-added Conzett Brug footbridge

106

Above: the redbrick lockhouse in Minnewater Park.

The merchants and nobles of medieval Bruges loved their gardens, and made sure that painters included their well-tended plots in artworks they commissioned. *The Legend of St Lucy* triptych (1480) in Sint-Jakobskerk shows an orchard and garden in detail; and the otherwise shocking Gerard David painting in the Groeningemuseum, of the judge being skinned alive, shows a peaceful shady garden in the background *(see also Churches p.48; Museums and Galleries, p.85).*

across the Coupure means walkers no longer have to make a long detour to reach the opposite bank.

Beyond Bruges
Beisbroek
Zeeweg, Sint-Andries; www.beisbroek.be; park: daily, dawn to dusk; nature centre: Apr–Nov Mon–Fri 2–5pm, Sun 2–6pm; planetarium shows (occasionally in English): Wed and Sun 3pm and 4.30pm, Fri 8.30pm; park and nature

centre free; bus: 52, 53; map p.138 C3
One of two big country estates which stand side by side in the woods just a short distance south-west of Bruges. Beisbroek covers 80 hectares (200 acres), has trees, heathland, footpaths, picnic areas, a deer compound, a cafeteria, a castle that serves as an interactive nature centre, a planetarium and an observatory.

Below: neo-Gothic castle in Tudor City Park dating from 1904–6.

Tudor City Park
Zeeweg, Sint-Andries; tel: 050 32 90 11; daily dawn–dusk; beehives and botanical garden May–Oct Mon–Fri 2–5pm, Sun 2–6pm; bus: 5; map p.138 C3
Next to Beisbroek, the Tudor City Park covers 40 hectares (100 acres). There is a physic garden, beehives and Tudor-style castle, which is now an upscale restaurant, and reception and conference centre available for hire.

Restaurants

Bruges has a wealth of eateries – from simple cafés to Michelin-starred restaurants – and many excellent addresses within easy walking distance of the Markt and Burg. The city has a tradition of fine feasting and banqueting, and its 21st-century inhabitants uphold this tradition in style. This section recommends a wide choice of restaurants in all price ranges, and includes several addresses for the villages and towns outside Bruges, covered in the Areas chapter of this book. For an introduction to Flemish cuisine, Belgian beers and a description of typical dishes of the region, see 'Food and Drink'.

Markt and Burg

BELGIAN
Breydel – De Coninc
Breidelsstraat 24; tel: 050 33 97 46; www.restaurant-breydel.be; €€; Thu–Tue noon–2.30pm, 6–9.30pm; bus: 1; map p.134 C4
This long-established family-run seafood specialist between the Markt and Burg is the place to eat mussels in Bruges (when in season; expect quite a large portion), as well as lobster and eels. The few street-view tables make it possible to while away an afternoon watching the tourists in horse-drawn carriages while indulging in Belgians' preferred pastime: gastronomic indulgence.
Erasmus
Wollestraat 35-39; tel: 050 33 57 81; www.hotelbh.be; €€; Tue–Sun noon–3pm, Tue-Sat

Prices for an average three-course meal with wine:
€ = under €25
€€ = €25–50
€€€ = €50–75
€€€€ = over €75

Note that Bruges' restaurants are busy year-round and not just in peak tourist seasons. We advise that you book a restaurant for your evening meal in advance, otherwise you might struggle to find a table on the night.

6–10pm; bus: 1, 11; map p.134 C4
The modern-styled restaurant in the Bourgoensch Hof Hotel is a tippler's dream, with 16 draught beers (the list changes monthly) plus many others in bottles, selected to accompany the food: for example, crown of lamb with parsley and mustard, served with potato and bacon gratin made with Bush blond beer. With less outlandish menus than classy beer-cuisine joint Den Dyver (see p.110), it is also a fair bit cheaper. The menu changes monthly.
Kwizien Divien
Hallestraat 4; tel: 050 33 80 27; www.kwiziendivien.be; €€; daily noon–2.30pm, 6–10pm; bus: 1; map p.134 C4
Rather tucked away down a

side street beside the Hallen, the restaurant offers a Belgian menu featuring Flemish specialties, as well as French dishes. Fish, meat and vegetarian dishes – all based on local ingredients. There are tables in the sun-trap courtyard to the rear, where the only noise interruptions will be the clanging bells from the Belfry next door.
Lucifernum
Twijnstraat 6–8; tel: 0476 35 06 51; www.lucifernum.be; Sun 8pm–11pm; bus: 1; map p.135 C4
Unique venue open just Sunday evening for drinks and dinner. In the private house of showman Willy Retsin, his Peruvian wife prepares paella. Gypsy musicians play occasionally amongst the hundreds of strange paintings and sculptures that deck out this former Masonic lodge.
Tom Pouce
Burg 17; tel: 050 33 03 36; www.restaurant-tompouce.be; €€; daily 9am–11pm; bus: 1; map p.135 C4
This large but not imper-

Left: Bruges restaurants offer plenty of red meat and game.

South

BELGIAN
Bistro & Bar One
Arsenaalstraat 55; tel: 050 33 80 88; www.one-minnewater. be; €€; Tue 6.30–9pm, Wed–Sun noon–9pm; bus: 1; map p.134 C2
Snug and romantic small bistro alongside the canal close to Minnewater Park, with low beams and a large old brick fireplace. Duck down and tuck in to Belgian food like exquisite Flemish stew or homemade meatballs. A wide selection of beers accompanied by savoury snacks.
Christophe
Garenmarkt 34; tel: 050 34 48 92; www.christophe-brugge.be; €€–€€€; Thu–Mon 6pm–1am; bus: 1, 11; map p.135 D3
Definitely worth leaving the beaten track (but not by too far) for an excellent dining

Smoking has been banned in restaurants in Belgium since January 2007. Bars and cafés, however, do not have to respect this rule. Those that serve food must normally have a non-smoking area for this.

ing vines and bunches of grapes – but you are not here for the setting. The menu makes some concessions to Belgian tastes, but the pizza and pasta dishes are what you come for and are reasonably priced.

sonal restaurant enjoys an unrivalled position on the Burg. Although fish and Flemish cuisine dominate the menu, the quality of the food is definitely secondary to that of the location. Order a waffle or pancake, sit on the heated outdoor terrace and watch the world go by.

ITALIAN
Riva del Sole
Wollestraat 22; tel: 050 34 33 30; www.rivadelsole.be; €€; Thu–Mon noon–2.30pm, 6–10.30pm; bus: 1, 11; map p.134 C4
Follow the Italian students from the College of Europe to the place they say does the best pizza in town, and this is where they will take you. The interior decor fulfils all the trattoria clichés – fake climb-

Below: Erasmus is located in the Bourgoensch Hof Hotel.

109

Above: a standard tourist menu will feature most local favour-ites, though quality will vary from place to place.

experience at this unpreten-tious 'evening and night bis-tro'. The chef has won fans far and wide for his excellent way with no-nonsense staples, available till late into the night.

Den Dyver
Dijver 5; tel: 050 33 60 69; www.dyver.be; €€€; Tue–Sat noon–2.30pm, 6–10pm; bus: 1; map p.134 C3
Be prepared for an adventure in taste at this family-run house renowned for inventive beer cuisine that contrasts with the more typical Flem-ish beer-recipes such as *carbonnade flamande*. All dishes – like duck breast with guinea fowl and mint mousse in a Chimay sauce with caramelised figs, and peach and chicory stew – come accompanied by selected Belgian brews; desserts are prepared with local genever. Not cheap, but unique.

De Gastro
Braambergstraat 6; tel: 050 34 15 24; www.degastro.be; €–€€; Fri–Wed 11am–3pm, 6–10pm; bus: 6, 16; map p.135 C4
This stylish address has concocted a menu to please all comers, from snacks to Belgian classics and fusion-inspired dishes, while pan-cakes and waffles are served all afternoon. Prices are lower than the decor and smart presentation suggest.

Hertog Jan
Loppemsestraat 52, Loppem–Zedelgem; tel: 050 67 34 46; www.hertog-jan.com; €€€€; Tue–Sat noon–1.30pm, 7–9pm; no bus; map p.138 C3
This fabulous restaurant, a couple of kilometres south-west of Bruges' old town, has in merely seven years risen to become Belgium's third three-star Michelin restau-rant. Chef Gert De Mangeleer

and sommelier Joachim Boudens epitomise the new generation of Flemish cuisine, with highly creative dishes deserving of being exhibited in one of Bruges' many art galleries, such as the attention to aesthetic detail. Yet many of the ingredients used come from the owners' nearby farm, while the welcome and service are warm and atten-tive. There is a choice of set menu and à la carte.

't Huidevettershuis
Huidenvettersplein 10–11; tel: 050 33 95 06; www.huide vettershuis.be; €€; Mon–Fri noon–2pm, 6–10pm, Sat–Sun noon–10pm; bus: 1; map p.135 C4
An elegant canal-side eatery (with an entrance on a hand-some little square) specialis-ing in Flemish cuisine. The building, which was formerly the Tanners' Guildhouse, dates from 1630.

Marieke van Brugghe
Mariastraat 17; tel: 050 34 33 66; www.mvb.be; €€; Tue–Sat 11am–9pm, Sun 11am–5pm; bus: 1; map p.134 C3
Even though it is slap in the middle of tourist-ville, in the shadow of the Onze-Lieve-Vrouwekerk, locals still cherish this restaurant-brasserie-tearoom, which dishes up traditional Flemish fare: rabbit stew, beef cooked in beer and a great fish soup. The terrace for people-watching is an added bonus, but service can be a little frosty. (Do not confuse with the much less loveable place next door: they look like one big establishment.)

Prices for an average three-course meal with wine:
€ = under €25
€€ = €25–50
€€€ = €50–75
€€€€ = over €75

Belgium has three Michelin three-starred restaurants: the Hof van Cleve in Kruishotem, not far from Ghent, De Karmeliet in Bruges *(see p.119)* and Hertog Jan in the outskirts of Bruges *(see p. 110)*.

Above: 't Pandreitje's chef takes time out from his busy kitchen.

Maximiliaan Van Oostenrijk
Wijngaardplein 17; tel: 050 33 47 23; www.maximiliaanvan-oostenrijk.be; €€; daily 10am–10pm; 15 Mar–15 Nov closed Wed; bus: 1; map p.134 C2
Despite having as touristy a location as you can find in Bruges, adjacent to the Begijnhof and the Minnewater, Maximiliaan's achieves the creditable feat of not being entirely overpowered, but then it does have a lot of tables. Specialities include the traditional local stew, *waterzooï*, grilled meats and seafood.

't Pandreitje
Pandreitje 6; tel: 050 33 11 90; www.pandreitje.be; €€€€; Mon, Tue, Fri, Sat noon–1.30pm, 7–9pm; bus: 1, 6; map p.135 C3
Elegant and refined Franco-Belgian cuisine is served in spacious comfort in this Renaissance-era patrician house near the Rozenhoedkaai. Chef Guy Van Neste runs the kitchen and wine cellar, while his English-born wife welcomes guests. The seafood is excellent.

Salade Folle
Walplein 13–14; tel: 0474 36 25 33; www.saladefolle.com: €; Tue–Sat noon–6pm; bus: 1; map p.134 C2
This bright, contemporary café and tearoom serves good soups, salads, quiches and pasta in generous portions (the pasta dishes are rather average but the rest is good). Rustic blond wood tables are divided over two floors with a mezzanine. Good for vegetarians and lone diners.

De Visscherie
Vismarkt 8; tel: 050 33 02 12; www.visscherie.be; €€€€; Wed–Mon noon–2pm, 7–10pm, closed most of Jan; bus: 1; map p.135 C4
The subtle flavours of the sea are cooked to absolute perfection in this top-notch fish and seafood restaurant, situated right on the fish market (Vismarkt). A formal establishment where the mâitre d' will attend to your every whim, this is ideal for a special occasion with all the frills. A few meat dishes are also available.

Below: restaurant Maximiliaan Van Oostenrijk succeeds in providing quality Belgian food in a tourist-friendly setting.

111

Above: unsurprisingly, Salade Folle specialises in salads.

De Wijngaert
Wijngaardstraat 15; tel: 050 33 69 18; www.wijngaert.com: €; daily 11am–2.30pm, 6–10pm; closed Wed–Thu in winter; bus: 1; map p.134 C2
No-frills, friendly service assured at this grill restaurant, bar and tearoom along the well-worn tourist groove between the Beguinage and Onze-Lieve-Vrouwekerk. Well-prepared mussels, ribs and a lot more besides, but especially worth a stop for the house-speciality: sangría, made with red or white wine.

't Zwaantje
Gentpoortvest 70; tel: 0473 71 25 80; www.hetzwaantje.be; €€€; Mon, Tue, Fri, Sun noon–1.15pm, 6.30–8.30pm, Sat 7–8.30pm; bus: 1; map p.135 C1

Prices for an average three-course meal with wine:
€ = under €25
€€ = €25–50
€€€ = €50–75
€€€€ = over €75

If you have come to Bruges to indulge in romantic fantasies, this venue could be the icing on the cake, with its Tiffany-style lamps, mirrors, and candlelight. A local treasure that tourists have never really discovered, run by a welcoming family down near the Bargehuis off Katelijnestraat. Belgian-French cuisine is lovingly presented and served. The chef's chocolate desserts have won multiple awards, too.

FRENCH
Couvert
Eekhoutstraat 17; tel: 050 33 37 87; www.couvert-brugge. be; €€–€€€; Thu–Mon noon–2pm, 6–10pm; bus: 1, 11; map p.134 C3
Loving attention to French-influenced cuisine, service and presentation have earned this slightly back-street address a faithful following. The fixed price menu is inventive and seasonal – gratin of scallops and asparagus; baked guinea fowl with stuffed mushrooms and creamy parsley sauce – while the à la carte is brief but diverse. Romantic setting with white-dressed tables and brick-exposed walls.

Den Gouden Harynck
Groeninge 25; tel: 050 33 76 37; www.goudenharynck.be; €€€€; Tue–Fri noon–1.30pm, 7–8.30pm, Sat 7–8.30pm; bus: 1; map p.134 C3
Formal haven of top-notch modern French gastronomy in a 17th-century former fishmonger's behind Groeningemuseum. Chef Philippe Serruys stamps his flair on sensuous creations such as smoked lobster with fig and date chutney, Muscovite potato and Sevruga caviar. Eating here is a seriously luxurious experience. One Michelin star.

Duc de Bourgogne
Huidenvettersplein 12; tel: 050 33 20 38; www.ducdebourgogne.be; €€€; Tue 7–9.30pm, Wed–Sun noon–2.30pm, 7–9.30pm; bus: 1; map p.135 C4
A classic dining experience, with French-style dishes in beautiful surroundings and a canal view. Sup like a lord on lobster and roast meat in rich sauce among the artworks and tapestries. Good-value, all-inclusive menus, especially for lunch.

Malesherbes
Stoofstraat 3-5; tel: 050 33 69 24: €; Wed–Sun noon–1.45pm, 7–9pm; bus: 1; map p.134 C2
The all-female team is a winning combination in this simply decorated French deli and dining room in the so-called narrowest street in Bruges. With famously attentive service and a good atmosphere, it serves quality French produce, quiches and regional specialities. The deli is open from 10am.

The restaurants on the Markt are firmly aimed at the passing tourist trade and none are worthy of particular recommendation. Their terraces are fine for a drink and a view, but avoid dining here if you want to get good quality food for a reasonable price.

INDIAN
Indian Tandoori
Oude Gentweg 11; tel: 050 34 58 26; www.indiantandoori.be: €–€€; Wed–Mon noon–2.30pm, 6–11pm; bus 1; map p.134 C2
Although right in the heart of the tourist zone, this modest but excellent Indian restaurant is just off the main drag and so often overlooked. Seek it out for subtly spiced, authentic dishes from the sub-continent, made with the freshest ingredients and served with understated grace.

VEGETARIAN
De Bron
Katelijnestraat 82; tel: 050 33 45 26; www.eethuisdebron.be: €; Mon–Fri 11.45am–2pm; bus: 1; map p.134 C2
Locals pack in to this spot-less lunch-only restaurant with an atrium out back which opens in fine weather. You join a table wherever there is a seat and eat the day's soup or its one dish: a mixed platter that might include a gratin, a grain, and baked, steamed and raw vegetables (just choose small, medium or large; vegan option on request). The locals use it rather like an unofficial canteen and get talking to whoever they sit with. You have to ring the bell to get in, but once in the staff are very friendly. Take-out service of the day's menu is also available.

FUSION
De Stoepa
Oostmeers 124; tel: 050 33 04 54; www.stoepa.be: €; Tue–Sun from 11am; bus: 1; map p.134 B1
Sociable hangout near the station popular for its informal atmosphere and cuisine with an Oriental twist. Vegetarian-friendly and as good for a drink and a nibble as a proper tuck-in. The walled terrace-garden is a fantastic sun trap on fine days.

West

BELGIAN
Aneth
Marie van Bourgondiëlaan 1; tel: 050 31 11 89; www.aneth.be; €€€€; Tue–Sat 11.30am–9.30pm, Sun 11.30am–6pm; bus: 9; map p.132 A1
Local foodies who like their fish adore Aneth and book ahead to celebrate special occasions. The roomy detached house beside the Graaf Visartpark outside the ring road is well off the tourist circuit and worth the trip for top-class preparations of the day's catch, fresh from the coast and presented in style.

Cafedraal
Zilverstraat 38; tel: 050 34 08 45; www.cafedraal.be; €€€; Mon–Sat noon–3pm, 6–11pm; bus: 1; map p.134 B3
Impressive collection of 15th-century buildings given a contemporary makeover for fashionable dining (seafood is its speciality) on two floors and on its large back garden-terrace. Colin Farrell's character caused a scene here in *In Bruges*. Open for drinks only from 3–6pm.

Below: family-run 't Zwaantje is a local favourite.

113

Chagall

Sint-Amandsstraat 40; tel: 050 33 61 12; www.restaurant chagall.be; €€; Fri–Tue noon–10pm; bus: 1; map p.134 B4
Whether you are out for a few drinks or for a heart-warming pot of mussels in cream sauce, you may have to fight for a table on this popular bistro's terrace, which is perfect for people-watching and afternoon sun on the pedestrianised Sint-Amandsstraat. Classical music plays in the cosy, newly refurbished interior, which has an open hearth, wooden beams and stained-glass windows.

Grand Café De Passage

Dweersstraat 26; tel: 050 34 02 32; www.passagebruges.com: €; bar 5pm–midnight and later, restaurant Sun–Thu 5–10pm, Fri–Sat noon–11pm; bus: 1; map p.134 B3
Absolutely the best cheap eat in town; long brown café in Belle-Epoque style packed with tables. Locals love it and there is a youth hostel upstairs, so an atmosphere is guaranteed every night. Good for ribs and grilled food, served with either jacket potatoes or chips.

De Hobbit

Kemelstraat 8; tel: 050 33 55 20; www.hobbitgrill.be; €€; daily from 6pm; bus: 1; map p.134 B3
Popular and reasonably-priced ribs and grilled food restaurant – 'Middle Earth cuisine', they claim – across the street from renowned beer joint 't Brugs Beertje (see p.33). The decor is dark

Prices for an average three-course meal with wine:
€ = under €25
€€ = €25–50
€€€ = €50–75
€€€€ = over €75

Right: Cafedraal sells modern seafood in a revitalised 15th-century setting.

and rustic, with low ceilings and antique kitchen implements.

De Koetse

Oude Burg 31; tel: 050 33 76 80; www.dekoetse-brugge. be; €€; Fri–Wed noon–2.30pm, 6–10pm; bus: 1; map p.134 C3
This inviting restaurant has a rustic Flemish interior with a blazing fire in winter. It serves robust Flemish cooking, including North Sea fish dishes, spare ribs and excellent *frites*.

De Mangerie

Oude Burg 20; tel: 050 33 93 36; www.mangerie.com; €€€; Tue–Sat noon–1.30pm, 7–9pm; bus: 1; map p.134 C3
The young couple who run this restaurant have gained a reputation for their scrummy dishes and painstaking presentation – and a short menu featuring a starter and main course from each of four styles: 'refreshed classic', 'funky new style', Mediterranean and vegetarian; dishes are along the lines of filet of venison with juniper berries and Jerusalem artichoke sauce; and pike perch with aubergine caviar, tomatoes and chorizo oil.

Patrick Devos

Zilverstraat 41; tel: 050 33 55 66; www.patrickdevos. be; €€€€; Mon, Tue, Thu, Fri noon–1.30pm, 7–9pm, Wed noon–1.30pm, Sat 7–9pm; bus: 1; map p.134 B3
Star chef and wine-taster Devos gives his name to this chic-as-they-come temple to gastronomy in the historic 'Zilveren Pauw' (Silver Peacock) house, formerly the second residence of the abbot of Ghent cathedral. The 13th-century gabled frontage contrasts with the

stunning art nouveau interior, the result of a late 19th-century makeover that gives the impression of dining in a private club. The menu draws on fresh regional produce, complemented by suitably top-class wines.

't Putje
't Zand 31; tel: 050 33 28 47; www.hotelputje.be; €€; daily 8.30am–11pm; bus: 1; map p.134 B3
Facing the Concertgebouw, the crisp tablecloths and smart wicker armchairs set this large, popular hotel brasserie apart from the nearby run-of-the-mill pavement cafés on the 't Zand. Reasonably priced and good French and Belgian classics are served round the clock.

De Stove
Kleine Sint-Amandsstraat 4; tel: 050 33 78 35; www.restaurantdestove.be; €€€; Mon, Tue, Fri, Sat dinner from 7 pm, Sun lunch from noon, dinner from 7pm, closed two weeks in Jan; bus: 1; map p.134 B4
Homely and intimate De Stove specialises in Flemish

cuisine with the emphasis on salad, fish and steaks. Mouthwatering scallops on black pasta with tomato tapenade, and sea bream with couscous, stuffed aubergine and basil oil are just some of the pleasingly original menu items in this unfussy, intimate 20-seater, set in an old gabled house. At the lower end of this price bracket.

FRENCH
Guillaume
Korte Lane 20; tel: 050 34 46 05; www.guillaume2000.be; €€€; Wed–Fri noon–2pm, 7–10pm, Sat 7–10pm, Sun noon–2pm, 7–9pm; bus: 9; map p.134 A4
Bijou, whitewashed cottage on a terraced street off the tourist circuit near the t' Zand. Houses a popular, high-quality bistro run by owner-chef Wim Vansteelant. The menu includes a small but tasty selection of starters and main courses with a distinct Franco-Belgian flavour, such as mackerel stuffed with Liège potatoes and mustard ham.

In addition to all the restaurants listed here, many bars and cafés in Belgium serve a short menu of satisfying fare for empty bellies: principally soup, spaghetti Bolognese, omelettes and toasted sandwiches.

INDIAN
Bhavani
Simon Stevinplein 5; tel: 050 33 90 25; www.bhavani.be; €€; Thu–Tue noon–2.30pm, 6–10pm; bus: 1; map p.134 B3
Good-quality, authentic Indian cuisine – including delicious vegetarian dishes – served in stylish surroundings. Madras and tandoori dishes are specialities. The set lunch on weekdays is good value.

SPANISH
Bodega Lorena's
Loppemstraat 13; tel: 050 34 88 17; €€; Tue–Fri noon–2.30pm, 6–10pm, Sat until 11pm, Sun until 9pm; bus: 1; map p.134 B3
Spanish restaurant (not a bar) on a tiny alley off Simon Ste-

Below: De Koetse serves hearty Flemish specialties.

vinplein, which does authentic Iberian cuisine – a large selection of tapas, plus paella – in a dining room unchanged since the 1970s.

VEGETARIAN
Hashtag Food
Oude Burg 30; tel: 050 70 76 70; www.hashtagfood.be; €€; Mon, Thu–Sat noon–4pm, 5–9pm, Sun noon–4pm; bus: 1; map p.134 C3
Varied homemade vegetarian options including pasta, quiches, salads and bruschettas but also a wide selection of gourmet burgers for meat lovers.

VIETNAMESE
Buddhasia
Sint-Salvatorskerkhof 14; tel: 050 34 16 91; www.buddhasia-brugge.be; €€; Mon–Thu noon–5.30pm; bus: 1; map p.134 B3
Vietnamese cuisine with European touch. Go for the great traditional Vietnamese fondue, pho, steak Vietnam style or Peking duck. Good choice of options for vegetarians.

If you fancy immersing yourself in medieval Bruges, or have a family to entertain, try **Brugge Anno 1468** (Vlamingstraat 86; tel: 050 34 75 72; www.celebrations-entertainment.be; Apr–Oct Fri–Sat evenings, Nov–Mar Sat evenings only; bus: 3, 13; map p.132 C1.) A theme dinner venue in a former church, you can sup in Burgundian style while jesters, minstrels, dancers, falconers and fire-eaters recreate the 1468 wedding feast of Charles the Bold and Margaret of York. Various price packages available. Reduced for under-15s (free for under-6s). Advise two days ahead if vegetarian food required.

Above: fondue and other Belgian classics are served at Pietje Pek.

North

BELGIAN
Brasserie Forestière
Academiestraat 11; tel: 050 34 20 02; www.brasserie forestiere.be: €; Mon, Tue, Thu 11.30am–6pm, Fri–Sat 11.30am–2.30pm, 6–10pm; bus: 4, 14; map p.132 C1
Reasonably priced, popular and laid-back diner in an elegant town house with marble fireplaces and scrubbed pine tables. Light meals – pasta, quiche, salads, desserts – are served by friendly staff. Caters for vegetarians.
Brasserie Souffleur
Vlamingstraat 58; tel: 050 34 82 92; www.souffleur.be; €€; Fri–Tue 11.30am–11pm; bus: 1; map p.134 C4
This brisk and smart brasserie, across the road from the Stadsschouwburg (city theatre), is good for snacks and salads. It has a warming open hearth in winter and a sunny terrace streetside in summer. Excellent mussels and chips; afternoon tea served 2–6pm.
Curiosa
Vlamingstraat 22; tel: 050 34 23 34; www.curiosa-brugge.com; €€; Tue, Wed, Fri 11.30am–3pm, 6–11pm, Sat 11.30am–midnight, Sun 11.30am–10pm; bus: 1; map p.134 C4
Cellar tavern with a vaulted

ceiling and brick walls. Surprisingly tourist-free despite its proximity to the Markt, it serves a broad range of Belgian classics, including salads, steaks and seafood specialities. Spacious enough for larger groups.
't Oud Handbogenhof
Baliestraat 6; tel: 050 33 19 45; €€; Mon, Tue, Fri, Sat 6–9.30pm, Sun noon–1.30pm, 6–9.30pm; bus: 4, 14; map p.133 C2
Wonderful 'olde worlde' place in peaceful Sint-Gillis neighbourhood peopled by characters from Brueghelian paintings. Flagstones, wooden beams, gigantic fireplace, heavy oak furniture, and a hearty no-nonsense approach to solid Belgian cuisine – from steak, fish or mussels to snacks like omelettes and toasted sandwiches. The garden to the rear is shady in fine weather. Not a lot of tourists open the heavy door to step inside, and they are missing out.
Au Petit Grand
Philipstockstraat 18; tel: 050 34 86 71; www.aupetitgrand.be; €€; Tue–Wed 6–10pm, Thu–Sun noon–2pm, 6–10pm; bus: 1; map p.134 C4
Fuel up after a day's hard sightseeing on T-bone steak or rack of lamb at this pretty and popular address for

grilled fish and meat specialities. It is not enormous and
the locals like it here, so reservation is advised.

Pietje Pek
Sint-Jakobsstraat 13; tel: 050
34 78 74; www.pietjepek.com;
€€; Thu–Tue from 5.30pm; bus:
1; map p.134 B4
Behind its art nouveau
facade, this traditional (and
unashamedly tourist-focused)
restaurant serves up satisfying portions of its speciality
cheese and meat fondues,
as well as a limited menu of
hearty Belgian classics.

Zeno
Vlamingstraat 53; tel: 050 68
09 93; www.restaurantzeno.
be; €€; Tue–Fri noon–1.30pm,
7–8.45pm, Sat 7–8.45pm; bus:
3, 13; map p.132 C1
Run by a couple of young
perfectionists, this new
venture has a monthly menu
composed of eight courses
from which you can select

Prices for an average three-
course meal with wine:
€ = under €25
€€ = €25–50
€€€ = €50–75
€€€€ = over €75

---

four to seven, or else a faster
lunch option. The presentation is ravishing, and the
Franco-Belgian cuisine
excellent; but if you loathe
nouvelle cuisine this place is
not for you.

EUROPEAN
De Florentijnen
Academiestraat 1; tel: 050 67
75 33; www.deflorentijnen.be;
€€€; Tue–Sat noon–2.30pm,
6.30–10.30pm; bus: 3, 4, 13,
14; map p.132 C1
Stylish eaterie set in a modern retake of a medieval
interior. It has a lively buzz
and dishes up superb Italian-
French food, with painstaking

---

attention to presentation.
Credit cards accepted for
sums over €100 only.

FRENCH
Bistro Bruut
Meestraat 9; tel: 050 69 55 09;
www.bistrobruut.be; €€€; Mon–
Fri noon–2.30pm, 7–9.30pm;
bus: 1; map p.135 C4
Small and cosy bistro-style
restaurant overlooking the
most romantic stretch of
canal in Bruges, set in a
beautiful 16th-century building. Cousins Bruno and
Bas Timperman took over
the popular Chez Olivier
restaurant and opened their
own Bistro Bruut focusing on
local, seasonal ingredients
and serving innovative and
delicious French fare.

In Den Wittenkop
Sint-Jakobsstraat 14; tel:
050 33 20 59; www.inden
wittenkop.be; €€; Mon, Tue, Thu
6–10pm, Fri–Sat noon–2pm,
6–10pm; bus: 1; map p.134 B4
Mellow café-bistro lined with
retro enamel advertising
panels and run by a stylish
and friendly couple. Although
it describes its cuisine as
French, the menu includes
Belgian standards such as
waterzooï – made with lan-
goustines rather than white
fish or chicken. Lush terrace
to the rear.

FUSION
Tom's Diner
West Gistelhof 23; tel: 050 33
33 82; www.tomsdiner.be; €€;
Mon–Fri 11.30am–1.30pm,
4.30–9pm, Sun 4.30–9pm; bus:
3, 13; map p.132 C2
Convivial gem highly popular
with locals in an unprepos-
sessing neighbourhood,
with a candlelit setting
and exposed brick walls,
so nothing like a diner in
the commonly understood
sense. Blends Belgian
dishes with international

Below: mussels and chips served with the obligatory beer at
pristine Brasserie Souffleur

117

influences to successful effect.

ITALIAN
Trium Trattoria
Academiestraat 23; tel: 050 33 30 60; www.trattoriatrium.be: €; Tue–Sun 9am–9pm; bus: 4, 14; map p.132 C1

Authentic Italian deli, take-out and eatery in the old merchants' quarter where their compatriots once came to trade; this is the real thing, with home-made pasta and all the best produce from Italy. The deli counter and shop side sells wines, pasta, cheeses and hams.

VEGETARIAN
Lotus
Wapenmakersstraat 5; tel: 050 33 10 78; www.lotus-brugge. blogspot.com: €; Mon–Fri 11.45am–2pm; bus: 1; map p.135 C4

Popular and long-established 'natural' restaurant that serves lunches only. Very good value for the carefully prepared dishes using hormone-free meat in the daily dish of either lamb moussaka or lamb stew, plus vegetarian options.

East

BELGIAN
Bistro De Schaar
Hooistraat 2; tel: 050 33 59 79; www.bistrodeschaar.be; €€; Fri–Tue noon–2pm, 6–9pm; bus: 6, 16; map p.135 E4

This rustic bistro, with a pavement terrace beside the Coupure yacht harbour, provides an entirely different experience to city-centre restaurants that are generally full of tourists. A popular and friendly neighbourhood eatery, with an open grill-fire, it serves fish and meat dishes. Locals reserve tables so it is wise to do the same.

Bistro Refter
Molenmeers 2; tel: 050 44 49 00; www.bistrorefter.com; €€–€€€; Tue–Sat noon–2pm, 6–10pm; bus: 6, 16; map p.135 D4

The brainchild of Geert Van Hecke (chef of De Karmeliet, see opposite), Bistro Refter brings his culinary magic within the reach of mere mortals, and spares them the pomp and ceremony of the main restaurant – 'refter' means refectory. Dishes are variations on the bistro standards: asparagus served every which way; snails, fish soup, scallops and so on; the wine list is good and seating comfortable if not spacious. Reserve well in advance: everyone wants a piece of the superstar chef at a fraction of the usual price.

Ganzespel
Ganzenstraat 37; tel: 050 33 12 33; www.ganzespel.be: €; Fri–Sun 6.30–10pm; bus: 6, 16; map p.135 D4

Small ancient house on a residential street with a bed and breakfast upstairs and

homely feel downstairs, very reasonably priced daily menu comprises soup, salad, main course and beer, a choice of which will be explained by welcoming owner Nicky. Recommended for those on a tight budget.

In 't Nieuw Museum
Hooistraat 42; tel: 050 33 12 80; €€; Mon, Tue, Fri, Sat noon–2pm, 6–10pm, Sun noon–2pm; bus: 6, 16; map p.135 E4

A simple front room in a humble terraced house, decorated like an old brown café festooned with dried hops and with a roaring open fire. It serves home-cooked Belgian favourites including eels in green sauce, grilled prawns and mussels (in season), a variety of grilled meats, and simple oven-baked dishes such as lasagne, for no-frills dining in a warm-heart. Good beer selection and changing beer of the month.

De Karmeliet
Langestraat 19; tel: 050 33 82 59; www.dekarmeliet.be;

Below: an impressive array of cheeses are available at Trium Trattoria's deli counter.

€€€€; Wed–Sat noon–3pm, 4.30–11pm, Tue 4.30–11pm, closed 3 weeks Jan, 3 weeks July and 10 days Sept; bus: 6, 16; map p.135 D4
Step off uninspiring Langestraat through the great double doors and enter a world of jaw-dropping culinary creations in grand surroundings. A legend beyond Belgium's borders, De Karmeliet occupies a gastronomic class of its own, thanks to the genius of indefatigable owner-chef Geert Van Hecke. At the time of writing, one of just three three-star Michelin restaurants in Belgium.

De Nisse
Hooistraat 12; tel: 050 34 86 51; www.denisse-brugge.be; €€; Wed–Sat from 6pm, Sun noon–3pm and from 6pm; bus: 6, 16; map p.135 E4
Homely fondu specialist that also has a varied beer selection. Good hearty soups, garlicky prawns and seasonal specialities. Although slightly out of the way and doing little to publicise itself, it has established a faithful following.

FRENCH
Rock Fort
Langestraat 15; tel: 050 33 41 13; www.rock-fort.be; €€€; Mon–Fri noon–2.30pm, 6.30–11pm; bus: 6, 16; map p.135 D4
Diminutive fashionable bistro with a simple formula: good food – French with fusion influences – generous portions and stylish decor. Seating may be on bar stools so specify if this is not acceptable.

Sans Cravate
Langestraat 159; tel: 050 67 83 10; www.sanscravate.be; €€€; Tue–Fri noon–2pm, 7–9pm, Sat 7–9pm; bus: 6, 16; map p.135 D4

Above: Koto's sushi is freshly prepared and delicious.

The self-styled 'cooking theatre', due to the open kitchen in the middle of the room, does original and super-stylish food in a decor to match. The characterful owner of this Michelin-starred restaurant divides opinion between those who love him and those who hate him, but his culinary pedigree is unquestionable and the food – spit roasts a speciality – is guaranteed to win over all your senses.

JAPANESE
Koto
Potterierei 15; tel: 050 44 31 31; www.hoteldemedici.com; €€€; Tue–Sun 7–10pm, Sun noon–2pm; bus: 4, 14; map p.133 D2
Japanese food in stylish surroundings, in the Hotel Medici. Meat is tender and savoury, vegetables have just the right degree of crunchiness, sushi and sashimi sea-

Prices for an average three-course meal with wine:
€ = under €25
€€ = €25–50
€€€ = €50–75
€€€€ = over €75

food is fresh and bright, and the sake is warm. Teppan yaki grilled meat and fish are the speciality.

Damme

BELGIAN
De Damse Poort
Kerkstraat 29; tel: 050 35 32 75; www.damsepoort.be; €€; Fri–Tue noon–2.30pm, 6–9.30pm; map p.139 C3
A smart old farmhouse with an elegant dining room plus a large back garden for fine weather, serving Flemish staples with a seafood bent – eels, oysters, shrimps and sole – and teas between meals (3–5pm).

Tante Marie
Kerkstraat 38; tel: 050 35 45 03; www.tante-marie.be; €; daily 10am–6pm, Sat–Sun and holidays also 8–11am; map p.139 C3
Delightful tearoom and lunch restaurant serving light meals. Try the three-ingredients fish dish to sample the specialities of the region: tomato stuffed with shrimps, shrimp croquette, etc. The dining room is decorated in country-style

119

Above: Hof ter Doest's seasonal menu includes fresh game in autumn.

with lots of natural wood and there is a terrace for fine weather. Absolutely wicked pastries and cakes, and a fixed-price lunch menu with champagne on weekdays.

Lissewege

BELGIAN/FRENCH
Hoeve de Rozeblomme
Stationsweg 45b, Lissewege-Dudzele; tel: 050 32 35 97; www.derozeblomme.be; €€€; Fri–Wed 11am–11pm; bus: 42 to Dudzele then walk; map p.139 C4
Restaurant and tearoom with a nice sunny terrace. Extensive seafood menu including tasty salmon, cod, eel, lobster and shrimps dishes. Separate menu for children.
Hof ter Doest
Ter Doeststraat 4; tel: 050 54 40 82; www.terdoest.be; €€;

Prices for an average three-course meal with wine:
€ = under €25
€€ = €25–50
€€€ = €50–75
€€€€ = over €75

daily noon–3pm, 6–9pm; café: daily 9am–midnight and later, Sept–June closed on Tue evenings; train to Lissewege then walk; map p.139 C4
In a sprawling farm that rose from the ruins of the former Ter Doest Cistercian Abbey, this large, family-friendly restaurant with a vast terrace combines the hallowed qualities and fresh produce of its predecessors in an elegant country setting. Sample North Sea specialities – eels, shrimps, oysters and lobster – or a wide selection of game dishes in autumn.

Ghent

BELGIAN
Brasserie HA'
Kouter 29; tel: 09 265 91 81; www.brasserieha.be; €€–€€€; Mon–Sat noon–2.30pm, 6–10pm, Sun 9am–noon; tram: 1 (stop: Korte Meer); map p.136 C3
Elegant yet cool, the Handelsbeurs Theatre's café-restaurant serves refined but not too high-brow

French and Belgian cuisine – light and breezy for lunch, candle-lit romantic for dinner – to foodies and theatregoers alike. A fantastical multi-coloured modern chandelier graces the main dining room, and in the summer you can enjoy your meal seated on the lovely outside terrace overlooking the Ketelvaart canal.
Restaurant Valentijn
Rodekoningstraat 1; tel: 09 225 04 29; www.restaurant valentijn.be; €€€€; Mon–Wed, Fri–Sat from 6.30pm, Sun from noon; tram: 1, 4 (stop: Sint-Veerleplein); map p.136 C4
This small, but lovely restaurant in the hip Patershol district serves refined, wonderfully presented food. There are inventive set menus on offer and a limited choice of à la carte Belgian dishes. Good, attentive service.

EUROPEAN
Le Grand Bleu
Snepkaai 15; tel: 09 220 50 25; www.legrandbleu.be; €€€; Wed–Sun noon–4.30pm,

7pm–midnight; bus: 34; map p.136 C4

Set in a small Provençal-style house with a lovely terrace by the Leie, west of Sint-Pietersstation, this seafood specialist presents Mediterranean-influenced fish dishes and a wide range of lobster variations. A few succulent meat dishes are also on offer.

VEGETARIAN
Eethuis Avalon
Geldmunt 32; tel: 09 224 37 24; www.restaurantavalon.be: €; Tue–Sat 11.30am–2.30pm, closed first half of Nov; tram: 1 (stop: Gravensteen); map p.136 B4

Across the street from the Gravensteen, Avalon is a far cheerier medieval reference. Among its informal organic-vegetarian concoctions, home-made soup served with home-baked bread, followed by a slice of savoury quiche seems like lordly fare. The antique-tiled main room is a protected monument; there is also a charming small garden terrace for eating al fresco in the summer months.
De Warempel
Zandberg 8; tel: 09 224 30 62; www.warempel.be: €–€€; daily 11.45am–2pm, Fri 6–9pm, except public holidays; bus: 55; map p.137 C3

The menu at this informal lunch restaurant and local favourite comprises a one-dish mixed platter, with optional soup starter and dessert. The custom, if you haven't booked in advance, is to join a table with other diners.

For seafood fresh off the boat, head to Ostend's Visserskaai where stalls and restaurants deal directly with the fishing fleet.

De Haan

BELGIAN
Casanova
Zeedijk 15; tel: 059 23 45 55; www.casanova-dehaan.com; €€; Fri–Wed noon–2.15pm, 6–9.30pm; coast tram (stop: De Haan aan Zee); map p.138 B4

Good location on the promenade of De Haan with lovely sea views. The restaurant specialises in seafood: go for a turbot, sole fillets or mussels and you will not be disappointed.

Ipres (Ypres)
Old Tom
8 Grote Markt; tel: 057 20 15 41; www.oldtom.be: €–€€; Thu–Tue noon–2.30pm, 6–9pm, bar 7.30am–11pm; bus: 84 from Ieper station; map p.138 B1

A classic address on the Grote Markt, this hotel-bistro is favoured by Ypres locals as well as guests staying in its hotel rooms upstairs.

Tasty Belgian classics like shrimp croquettes, mussels and eels are served in professional and friendly style, although service can be slow when the terrace gets busy on sunny days.

Ostend

BELGIAN
Beluga
Kemmelbergstraat 33; tel: 059 51 15 88; www.beluga oostende.be; €€; Fri–Wed noon–3pm, 6–10pm; bus: 5 from Ostend station; map p.138 B3

Stylish bar-restaurant on the Ostend promenade that specialises in seafood with a French-Belgian theme, and serves anything from simple onion soup to Belgian caviar. Warm, welcoming and a bit more special inside than most other seafront addresses, although the food is still a fair price.

Below: the coast is the place to go for the freshest seafood.

Shopping

Bruges has a reputation for twee boutiques selling chocolate and lace, and there is no shortage of these, but there are also plenty of stylish shops in this small town. Belgians are not, generally, won over by the 'pile 'em high, sell 'em cheap' type of retail experience; they like to shop at leisure in pleasant surroundings with attentive service. As a result, the small, specialist boutique and family-run retailer continues to thrive here. Note that shops for chocolate, beer, books, CDs and beauty products are covered, respectively, under 'Food and Drink', 'Literature and Theatre', 'Music and Dance', and 'Pampering'.

The Shopping Map

Lace and chocolate shops (see p.125 and p.59) and other stores catering to tourists are concentrated on the well-worn groove between the Burg, Markt and Begijnhof, along **Breidelstraat**, **Wollestraat** and **Katelijnestraat**.

The main shopping area is located west of the Markt. The familiar chains, including Belgian department store, Inno, are found along **Steenstraat** and **Zuidzandstraat**, which runs from the Markt to 't Zand. The more fashionable boutiques are located in the parallel streets of **Geldmuntstraat** and **Noordzandstraat**, and in the **Zilverpand** shopping precinct, situated between Noordzandstraat and Zuidzandstraat. **Vlamingstraat**, to the north of the Markt, also has some good stores.

Department Stores

Galeria Inno

Steenstraat 11–13; tel: 050 33 06 03; www.inno.be; Mon–Fri 9.30am–6pm, Sat 9.30am–6.30pm; bus: 1; map p.134 C4

The Bruges branch of Belgium's premier department store, good for fashion, perfumery and accessories.

Design and Interiors

De Ark van Zarren

Zuidzandstraat 19; tel: 050 33 77 28; www.arkvanzarren.be; Mon–Fri 10am–6pm, Sat 9.30am–6.30pm, Sun school holidays and Easter–Aug 3.30–6.30pm, Dec Sun all day; bus: 1; map p.134 B3

Charming homeware store packed with romantic linens and accessories. The owners run a similarly stylish guesthouse near Diksmuide, towards Ypres.

Au Bonheur des Dames

Hoogstraat 38; tel: 050 33 63 63; www.desdames.be; Tue–Sat 10.30am–6pm; bus: 1; map p.135 D4

Beautiful store whose owner Sophie Verlinde has a talent for displaying floral fabrics, beads, glassware, picture frames and other items.

Callebert

Wollestraat 25; tel: 050 33 50 61; www.callebert.be; Mon 2–6pm, Tue–Sat 10am–noon, 2–6pm, Sun 3–6pm; bus: 1;

map p.134 C4

Sleek interiors shop selling a striking selection of glassware, cutlery and furniture by some of Europe's best designers. There is even a kids' section for style-conscious parents. On the first floor is the Artonivo design centre and gallery (Mon–Sat 2–6pm; free), which hosts frequent exhibitions of local designer craft items.

Dille & Kamille

Simon Stevinplein 17–18; tel: 050 34 11 80; www.dille-

Below: Dille & Kamille on Stevinplein for homeware.

Left: local designers Delvaux create luxurious leather goods.

Thu–Sat 10am–6pm; bus: 1; map p.134 B4

A striking boutique with clothes by top Flemish fashion designers, as well as hip international brands like Acne and Rick Owens. Womenswear by Dries Van Noten, Ann Demeulemeester, AF Vandevorst and Bruno Pieters, jewellery by Antwerp's own Wouters and Hendrix, and a small menswear section with items by Van Noten, among others.

Villa Maria

Gistelsesteenweg 18–28; tel: 050 31 07 44; www.villamaria. be; Mon 1–6.30pm, Tue–Sat 10am–6.30pm, Sun 10.30am–1pm; bus: 5, 15; map p. 138 C3

Villa Mary is the largest and most luxurious fashion shop in Bruges selling men's and women's apparel from both national and international clothing brands for over 40 years now.

Rue Blanche

Simon Stevinplein 16; tel: 050 34 79 38; www.rueblanche. com; daily 10am–6pm; bus: 1; map p.134 B3

This Belgian womenswear brand launched in Brussels producing knitwear in the late 1980s, but has expanded to a complete collection of tailored dresses and separates, whose unstructured, feminine style evoke French bohemian chic.

Jewellery and Accessories

Brugs Diamanthuis

Cordoeaniersstraat 5 (off Philipstockstraat); tel: 050 34 41 60; www.diamondhouse. net; Mon–Sat 10am–6pm, sometimes also Sun; bus: 1; map p.134 C4

If you are looking for a bargain, the magic words to look for on shop windows are *Solden* (Sales) and *Totale Uitverkoop* (Everything Must Go). Visitors from non-EU countries may be able to claim back value-added tax (BTW) on purchases in some shops; look for a sticker on the window or door. It is worth asking, particularly if you buy expensive items.

---

kamille.be; Mon–Sat 9.30am–6.30pm, Sun 11am–6.30pm; bus: 1; map p.134 B3

Bruges branch of the Dutch homeware store that has won a faithful following for its country-style kitchen utensils, table linen, wooden toys and gifts, soaps, teas, dried flowers and plants. Reasonably priced and good for gifts.

G & M Pollentier – Maréchal

Sint-Salvatorskerkhof 8; tel: 050 33 18 04; www.pollentier-marechal.be; Tue–Fri 2–6pm, Sat 10am–noon, 2–6pm and by appointment; bus: 1; map p.134 B3

Tucked behind Sint-Salvatorskathedraal, this antique print and map shop owned by Geert Pollentier also does framing. It may be the only place in Bruges to sell the 1562 Marcus Gerards map of Bruges (see the original in the Stadhuis, *p.81*). Prints date from the 18th–20th century, and include, on occasion, the work of Felicien Rops, a decadent *fin-de-siècle* artist from Namur. If the shop looks shut, the owner may be upstairs working on a framing job, so try later or ring the bell.

Fashion

It will not take you long to notice that the Flemings like to keep up appearances, both at home – see the neat-as-a-pin houses, with their window boxes and café curtains? – as well as in person: well-groomed and well-dressed, they are rightly proud of the recent generation of Belgian fashion designers who have achieved world renown.

L'Héroine

Noordzandstraat 32; tel: 050 33 56 57; www.lheroine.be; Mon–Wed 10am–1pm, 2–6pm,

123

Above: De Striep Club on Katelijnestraat has a good selection of Tintin albums.

In a beautiful building dating from 1518, this shop sells a sparkling array of fine diamond jewellery designed and produced by local craftspeople. The proprietors – a Danish-Turkish couple who met through the diamond trade and moved to Bruges over 20 years ago – also run the Diamantmuseum on Katelijnestraat *(see p.85)*.

Delvaux
Breidelstraat 2; tel: 050 49 01 31; www.delvaux.be; Mon–Sat 10am–6pm; bus: 1; map p.134 C4
Brussels family firm Delvaux has been working leather since 1829. Today, young designers keep the tradition alive in luxurious bags, gloves, scarves and leather jewellery.

Optique Hoet
Vlamingstraat 19; tel: 050 33 50 02; www.hoet.be; Mon–Fri 9am–6.30pm, Sat 9am–6pm and by appointment; bus: 1; map p.134 C4
Bruges family firm of opticians and eyewear designers. The Hoet label frames are limited edition and made of horn, stainless steel, titanium or gold. There are more wacky frames under the Theo brand.

Markets

Antiques and Flea Market
Dijver, with an extension at the Vismarkt; 15 Mar–15 Nov Sat–Sun 10am–6pm; bus: 1; map p.134 C3
In addition to being a source of bargains and fine antiques, the market stalls' scenic setting beside the tree-shaded canal makes this also a treat for the eyes.

Fish Market, Vismarkt
Tue–Sat mornings; bus: 6, 16; map p.135 C4
A limited number of fishmongers' stalls set up most mornings in the elegant 1820s colonnaded market.

For a small country, Belgium's fashion design roster is impressive; most trained at Antwerp's renowned Fine Arts Academy or Brussels' La Cambre school. Belgium's Fashion darlings include **Dries Van Noten, Ann Demeulemeester, Diane von Furstenberg, Martin Margiela** (formerly head designer at Hermes), **Raf Simons** (creative director at Jil Sander), **Olivier Theyskens** (ex-artistic director of Nina Ricci and formerly of Rochas).

Worth taking a look to identify the numerous species of fish, supplied that morning fresh from Zeebrugge and Ostend. The market area is occupied by wooden toy and craft stalls at other times.

Markt
Wed 8am–1.30pm; bus: 1; map p.134 C4
General market set in the square built for the purpose many centuries ago.

't Zand and Beursplein
Sat 8am–1.30pm; bus: 1; map p.134 A3
General market selling food and other goods.

Souvenirs

Lace was once the principal product made in Bruges and is certainly the premier souvenir today. While most lace on sale is machine-made, usually in the Far East, genuine hand-made lace can still be found, and some shops deal only in the hand-made product (while most sell a mix of the two). You can frequently watch ladies making lace items in the shops and the Lace Centre runs courses to train aspiring lace-makers. Hand-made lace is expen-

One of the best things about shopping in Belgium is that most shops offer a complimentary gift-wrapping service. Even at the busiest times of year, sales assistants will take their time to complete a beautiful presentation for one customer, finished with ribbons and bows: infuriating if you are in the queue and in a hurry, but if you are not it can make the experience a real pleasure. Remember to say that your purchase is for a gift when you are buying it.

Below: shop in the Belgian fashion stores, stock up on souvenirs or browse the markets.

sive: a large wedding veil or tablecloth costs upwards of €400.

Other Belgian products to look for, though most of them are not specific to Bruges, include modern **tapestries**, **diamonds**, **ceramics**, **crystal** (especially the hand-blown products of the Val-Saint-Lambert workshop in Liège), **jewellery** from respected modern designers based mostly in Antwerp and Brussels, and, if you can find them, **pewter** from Huy and hand-beaten **copper** or **bronze**, Dinanderie, from Dinant in the Meuse Valley.

LACE SHOPS

Several shops claim to be the only one selling hand-made lace, but this is not the case. Here is our selection:

't Apostelientje
Balstraat 11; tel: 050 33 78 60; www.apostelientje.be; Tue 1–5pm, Wed–Sat 9.30am–12.15pm, 1.15–5pm, Sun 9.30am–1pm; bus: 6, 16; map p.133 D1
A small boutique and craftshop close to the Kantcentrum (Lace Centre, see p.89), its owners insist on the real thing; all hand made by local women. You can look at specimens of old lace as well as stock up on supplies to try your hand at the craft yourself.

Claeys Antique
Katelijnestraat 54; tel: 050 33 98 19; www.claeysantique.com; Mon–Sat 9am–6pm; bus: 1; map p.134 C2
Specialists in antique lace since 1980, also selling antique jewellery. Antwerp-born owner Diane Claeys was born into a family of lacemakers and grew passionate about the craft, authoring several books on the subject. She has forged strong ties with Japan, where

she frequently lectures and runs classes in lace-making. She also holds residential courses lasting 1–3 days in her Bruges house.

Kantuweeltje
Philipstockstraat 11; tel: 050 33 42 25; daily 10am–6pm; bus: 1; map p.134 C4
A hand-made lace and tapestry specialist since 1895, where you can also watch lace being made by hand.

Unusual Gifts

Museum shop
Dijver 16; Tue–Sun 10am–6pm; bus: 1; map p.134 C4
Located in a former stable building in the courtyard opposite the Arentshuis, the city-run museum shop has an inspired selection of art books, jewellery, watches, games, postcards, posters and children's art books. One example is a satchel decorated with a Bosch triptych.

De Striep Club
Katelijnestraat 42; tel: 050 33 71 12; www.striepclub.be; Mon 1.30–7pm, Tue–Sat 10am–12.30pm and 1.30–7pm, first Sun of each month 2–6pm; bus: 1; map p.134 C2
Comic strips are Belgium's biggest literary export and De Striep Club is the best address in Bruges for comics, though most Belgian bookstores boast a healthy selection of Tintin books and other local comic stars.

De Witte Pelikaan
Vlamingstraat 23; tel: 050 34 82 84; www.dewittepelikaan.be; Feb–June Mon, Tue, Fri and Sat 10am–5.30pm, July–Aug Mon–Sat 10am–6pm, Sept–Dec daily 10am–6pm; bus 1; map p.134 C4
It is Santa Claus (or Sinter klaas) time all year round in this specialist Christmas shop, which sells tasteful tree decorations, garlands, teddies and accessories.

125

Transport

Close proximity to channel ports and an excellent national rail network put Bruges within easy reach of neighbouring countries and the Belgian capital, Brussels, which has extensive international transport links. This chapter outlines the main ways of reaching the city, as well as how to get around once there. Navigating the compact centre should be done on foot or by bike; although little of Bruges is officially car-free, driving is strongly discouraged: there are few parking spaces and most streets are one-way only. If you do arrive by car, this section gives details of where to park it.

Getting There

AIR

Most international airlines fly into Brussels Airport at Zaventem, just outside Brussels. Beneath the airport is a railway station, with direct trains to Brussels and Ghent. The journey to Bruges involves one change at Brussels North and takes 1 hr 30 mins. Brussels Airport (tel: 0900 700 00 [Belgium], +32 2 753 7753 [elsewhere]; www.brusselsairport.be).

Taken together, British Airways, easyJet and Brussels Airlines operate virtually an hourly day service between Brussels and London – less frequently from other cities around Britain. Aer Lingus flies between Dublin and Brussels. There are direct daily flights from many cities in North America and Canada, among them New York, Washington, Chicago, Atlanta and Toronto.

Ryanair flies from Edinburgh, Manchester and Dublin to Brussels Charleroi, from where charter coaches ferry passengers to and from Brussels in around 1 hr (Voyages Lelan, tel: 071 35 33 15; www.voyages-lelan.be; or buy a ticket on the bus). There is also a shuttle bus service from Brussels Charleroi to Brugge Railway Station. The journey takes about 2 hr (Flibco, tel: from Belgium 070 211 210; www.flibco.com)

Nearby Ostend airport, www.ost.aero, is used principally by cargo traffic or charter flights to Mediterranean resorts.

CAR

Bruges is located on the €40 motorway linking London with Istanbul. Drivers from Britain can travel through the Channel Tunnel on the Eurotunnel from Folkestone to Calais, a drive-on, drive-off train service that takes 35 mins, or about 1 hr from motorway to motorway. You can just turn up and buy a ticket, but it is worth booking ahead at busy times of the year to avoid a wait. Payment is made at toll booths, which accept cash, cheques or credit cards. The price applies to the car, regardless of the number of passengers or car size. Eurotunnel, (tel:

Above: Bruges is well connected by rail to the rest of Belgium.

Left: most people arrive in Bruges by train.

travel on Belgian railways to Bruges (within 24 hrs of the time stamped on the Eurostar ticket). There are reduced fares for children aged 4–11; those aged 3 and under travel free but are not guaranteed a seat. (For timetables and reservations, see www. eurostar.com or tel: 03432 186 186; from outside UK, tel: +44 1233 617 575. Note that there is a £5 charge for booking by phone.)

Fast intercity trains (IC) from Brussels to Bruges are modern and comfortable, with toilets but no refreshments. They are often crowded at weekends and in the summer. The main station lies just outside the old city. It takes about 10 mins to walk into town; the central shuttle bus from the station to the Markt is No. 1.

SEA
Cross-Channel ferries from the UK serve French and Belgian sea-ports within easy reach of Bruges by car.

Below: parking in the centre of town is a nightmare.

Aviation is 10 times more damaging to the climate than other forms of transport. To neutralise their emissions, many people choose to 'carbon-offset', an effort to balance the CO2 emissions of their journey through investing in a product that saves or stores an equivalent amount of carbon dioxide. Several organisations exist to calculate the CO2 cost of your journey, collect your donation and invest in renewable energy projects in developing countries. Two good organisations are Atmosfair (www.atmosfair.de) and Pure (www.puretrust.org.uk). But remember: offsetting does not reduce emissions or prevent climate change.

08443 353 535 [UK], www. eurotunnel.com). The service runs 24 hrs a day, all year, with up to five departures an hour, depending on the season and time of day.

From Calais, allow 1 hr 20 mins to drive to Bruges. From the €40, follow signs to Brugge Centrum for the centre of town.

COACH
A cheap way to travel to Bruges is by coach. National Express Eurolines runs one service daily from London (Victoria Coach Station) to Bruges, en route to Amsterdam. The journey takes about 5.5 hrs. There are discounts for young people and senior citizens, and the ticket includes the crossing via Eurotunnel. (For more information and to book Eurolines; tel: 08717 81 81 77 [UK; 24/7]; www.eurolines. co.uk; from Belgium tel: 02 274 13 50.)

RAIL
Bruges lies on the main railway line connecting Brussels with Ghent and the Belgian coast. Direct trains from Brussels to Bruges take just under 1 hr. For train times, see the Belgian railway SNCB/NMBS website (www.belgianrail.be).

You can travel from London (St Pancras) or Kent (Ebbsfleet or Ashford) to Brussels by Eurostar in under 2 hrs. The service runs up to 10 times a day, and your ticket will include free onward

127

P&O Ferries and DFDS Seaways serve the busy Dover-Calais route, each operating over 20 ferries daily; crossings take 90 mins. (P&O, tel: 0800 1300 030, www.poferries.com; DFDS Seaways, tel: 0871 5747 235, http://ferry.dfdsseaways.com) Calais is 120km (75 miles) from Bruges and the journey by car takes around 1 hr 20 mins.

Ferries from Dover to Dunkirk are operated by DFDS Seaways, which runs about 11 crossings each way daily, taking 2 hrs. (Contact or book on tel: 0871 5747 235; http://ferry.dfdsseaways.com) Dunkirk is closer to Bruges – 76km (47 miles) – and the drive takes just under 1 hr.

P&O Ferries also runs a nightly service from Hull to Zeebrugge (every other night in Jan), which takes around 12 hrs. Zeebrugge is 17km (10 miles) from Bruges.

Getting Around

ORIENTATION

Bruges is a compact town with all the main sights, hotels and restaurants located within the line of medieval ramparts (demarcated today by the ring canal). When looking for an address, it is helpful to know that a *reie* is a canal, a *plaats* or *plein* is a square and a *straat* is a street. If you are navigating without a map, the easiest way to get to the centre is to look for the octagonal

Two Bruges-based companies organise tours to Ieper (Ypres) and the World War I battlefields: Quasimodo: (not to be confused with bike tour company QuasiMundo; *see box, right*; Kapellestraat 87, 8020 Oostkamp; tel: 050 37 04 70; www.quasimodo. be) and Flanders Fields Battlefield Daytours (tel from Belgium: 0800 99 133; www.visitbruges.org).

top of the belfry. Elsewhere in town, church spires provide useful landmarks.

BUSES

Most places in Bruges are easily reached on foot, although you may want to take a bus from the station to the town centre. The city and its suburbs are served by a network of small buses operated by Flemish public transport company De Lijn. The 1 route runs from the station to the 't Zand, the Markt and back; almost all other buses also serve this route. A single ticket bought on the bus costs €3 from the driver (€1.40 with a Lijn Card and €1.95 for an SMS ticket) and is valid for 1 hr including any change of bus within the Bruges zone. Cheaper options include a day pass (€7 or €5 in advance), a three-day pass (€12 or €10 in advance) and five-day pass (€18 or €15 in advance) and a seven-day pass, which can be used for unlimited travel on buses and trams throughout West Flanders (€20); these passes are available at the ticket booth. Tickets have to be inserted in the orange scanner near the doors every time you board a bus.

De Lijn buses serve pretty much every town and village in Flanders and are very reliable. To plan trips out of

Below: one of the best ways to see Bruges is by bicycle; for details on renting a bike, *see right*.

Above: a row of Citroen 2CVs in Bruges for a rally.

town, the 'routeplanner' function at the company's website is very useful, but does require a rudimentary grasp of Dutch: www.delijn.be.

CAR
Parking within Bruges centre is almost impossible and navigation is difficult because of the network of one-way streets. Most tourists are advised by their hotels to leave their vehicles at the large car park next to the station (Stationsplein) in the south-west corner of the city, which has space for 1,500 cars (cheapest, and includes free bus ride into town), or in one of four other underground car parks in the old town. Some hotels have limited parking, but charges are usually high. For the station car park, claim a free public transport ticket for each person in the car by presenting your car park ticket at the office of De Lijn, the bus company operator, located outside the railway station, and telling them how many people are travelling in the car.

CYCLING
It is clear as soon as you arrive that Bruges is a city of cyclists. Although everywhere is within walking distance, a

bike allows you to cover a lot of distance in a short time, for a ride around the ramparts, to take in the outlying districts, or for a trip out of town. The most popular trip is along the tree-lined Daamsevaart canal to the charming little town of Damme, which is not well-served by buses. Take the minor road on the north side of the canal to avoid the traffic, which takes the road along the southern bank.

Several shops hire bikes by the hour, day or week. The most convenient option for those coming on a day ticket by train (and without luggage) is to rent a bike directly at the station, as you can get a combined train and bike rental ticket. The following places provide bicycle hire.
B-Bike
't Zand 34 (Concertgebouw); tel: 0479 97 12 80; www.b-bike.be; map p. 134 B3
Blue-bike
Railway Station; tel: 050 39 68 26; www.blue-bike.be; map p.134 B1
Eric Popelier
Mariastraat 26; tel: 050 34 32 62; www.fietsenpopelier.be; map p.134 C3
QuasiMundo
Nieuwe Gentweg 5; tel: 050 33 07 75; www.quasimundo.com; map p.134 C2

't Koffieboontje
Hallenstraat 4; tel: 050 33 80 27; www.hotel-koffieboontje. be; map p.134 C4
Bauhaus Bike Rental
Langestraat 145; tel: 050 34 10 93; www.bauhaus.be; map p.133 E1
Snuffel Backpacker Hostel
Ezelstraat 47-49; tel: 050 33 31 33; www.snuffel.be; map p.132 B1

WALKING
The compact scale of Bruges and the quasi absence of cars make it an ideal city for strolling around. It takes approximately 20 mins to walk from the railway station to the main square. The tourist office has mapped out several walks within the city. The walks are described in English on the website https://bezoekers.brugge. be/onfoot

Companies that organise guided bike tours in and around Bruges include: **QuasiMundo Bike Tours**, Nieuwe Gentweg 5; tel: 050 33 07 75; www. quasimundo.com; **Pink Bear Bicycle Company**; tel: 050 61 66 86, www.pinkbear. freeservers.com; **The Green Bike Tour**; tel: 050 61 26 67.

129

Atlas

The following streetplan of Bruges and Ghent makes it easy to find the attractions listed in our A–Z section. A selective index to streets and sights will help you find other locations throughout the city.

Map Legend

	Pedestrian area	✈	Airport / airfield
	Notable building	🚗	Car ferry
	Park	🚌	Bus station
	Hotel	ℹ	Tourist information
	Urban area	✚	Hospital
	Non urban area	🎡	Windmill
✝ ✝	Cemetery	🗼	Lighthouse
	Railway	⛪	Cathedral / church
)·····(	Tunnel	✡	Synagogue
	Canal	👤	Statue / monument
- - -	Ferry route	✉	Post Office

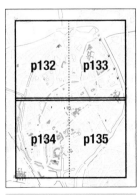

p132	p133
p134	p135

Ghent	p136 - 137
Flanders	p138 - 139

Bruges

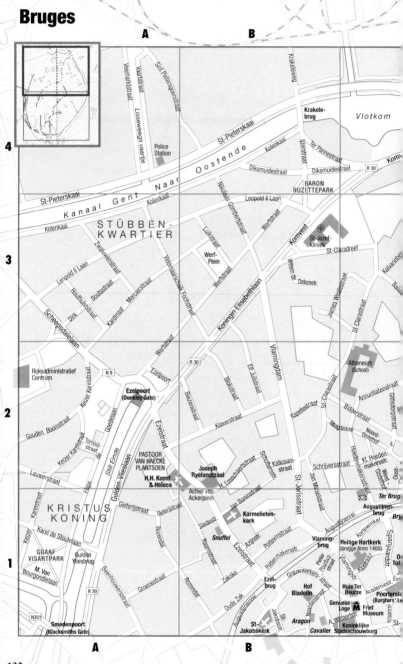

Bruges

D

E

N376

Fort Lapin

Walweinstraat

Warandebrug

Handelskom

R 30

Buiten de Dampoort

N374

Noorweegse Kaai

Kanaal van Brugge naar Sluis

Damsevaart Zuid

St-Bodelierdreef

De Tuintestraat

100 200 m

0 100 200 yds

4

Brandweer (Fire Station)

FORT-LAPIN

Dampoort

St-Leonardus-brug

Zuidervaartje

Sportcentrum (Sports Centre)

Komvest

Wulpenstraat

'S Gravenstraat

Kalvarienbergst.

Stokersstraat

Langerei

Potterierei

Haarhakkerstraat

Koeleweimolen (Cool Meadow Windmill)

Onze-Lieve-Vrouw ter Potterie (Our Lady of the Pottery)

Potterie-museum

Dijver

Duinstraat

Peterselienstraat

Leestenburg

Edestraat

Korte Sportstraat

Sportstraat

Paradijsstraat

Buiten Kruisvest

Dampoortstraat

Kanaal Gent Naar

3

Julius en Maurits Sabbestraat

Duinen-brug

Bisschoppelijk Seminarie

Ter Duinen

Groot Seminarie Duinenabdij (Abbey of the Dunes)

Duinen-abdijstr.

Peterselienstraat

Nieuwe Papegaaimolen

Naar

Koolstijk

Doghelaan

Kanaal van Maanderstraat

ne Nieuwstraat

Oliebaan

Oliebaan

Hemelrijk

Kazerne (Barracks)

Oostende

2

T-GILLIS

1. Lange Raamstraat
2. Sarepta
3. Sterstraat
4. Korte Raamstraat

Gotje

Snaggaardstraat

Snaggaardstraat

Schuttersgilde Sint-Sebastiaan (St Sebastian Archers Guild)

St-Janshuismolen (St John's House Mill)

R 30

Dampoortstraat

Buiten Kruisvest

Snaggaard-brug

Elisabeth Zorghestraat

Kruisstraat

Ropenstraat

Speelmansstraat

Engels Klooster (English Convent)

Carmersstraat

Rolweg

Guido Gezelle Museum

Hugo Verrieststraat

Bonne Chiéremolen

t-kerk

St-Gillis-koorstraat

Collaert Mansionstraat

2.

Kadaster (Land Registry)

Langerei

Potterierei

Rijkepijnders-straat

Ropenstraat

Korte Ropen-straat

Rolweg

Stedelijk Museum voor Volkskunde (Folklore Museum)

Albrecht Rodenbach-straat

Stijn Streuvelsstraat

GUIDO GEZELLE WARANDE

Schuttersgilde Sint-Joris (St George's Archers' Guild)

jen-Handstraat

enbrug

Adornes

Carmersstraat

Korte Rijke-pijnderstraat

Kantcentrum (Lace Centre)

GEZELLE

Kruisvest

illiskerkstr.

houden-Handrei

Carmers-brug

Blekersstraat

Strostraat

Jeruzalemstraat

Balstraat

Jeruzalemkerk (Adornesdomein Jerusalem Church)

Peperstraat

KWARTIER

Kruispoort-brug

hof

Genthof

Scholin-werkers-straat

Strooi-brug

St-Anna-straat

Yenkatastraat

Kant Werkstersplein

Sint-Streuvelsstraat

Langestraat

Kruispoort

1

nsdag-

Spiegelrei

Koning-Straat

Koningstraat

St-Anna-plein

Kant

Rodestraat

ST-ANNA

Vuldersreitje

Bauhaus

Kazernevest

in's Relais Huis terdam

Konings-brug

Verversdijk

St-Annakerk

Sint-Amand-straat

Korte Joost de Damhouderstraat

Timmermansstr.

Vlamingstraat

uis de Croon-hoco Story

Korte Ridders straat

Europa College

Sint-Anaker-straat

St-Anna brug

Verbrand Nieuwland

Police Station

Nieuw Gerechtshof (New Courts of Justice)

annstraat

St-Walburgakerk

Molenmeers

Minnebo-plein

Koopmansstraat

Essebom-straat

M A R K T   B U R G

D

E

133

Bruges

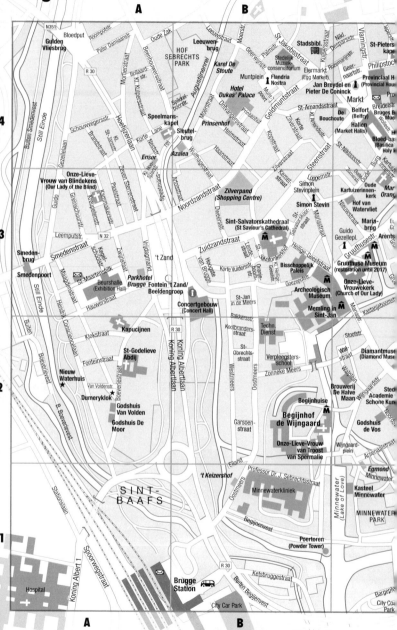

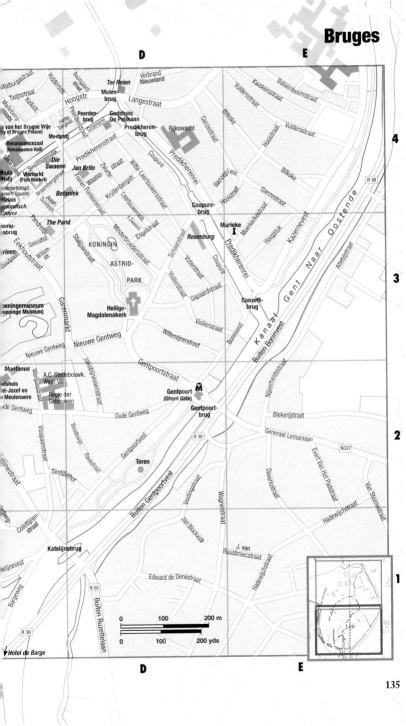

Bruges

135

Ghent

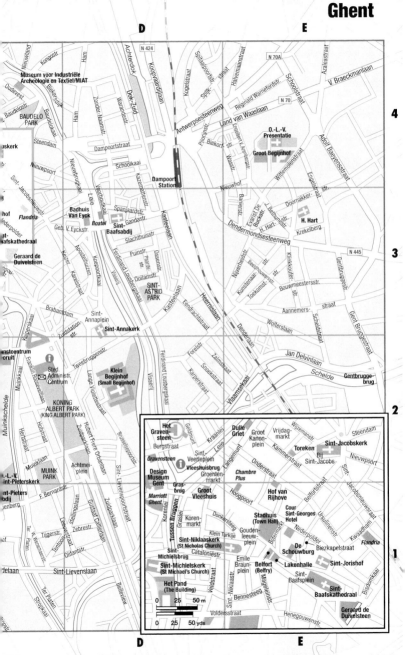

Ghent

137

Flanders

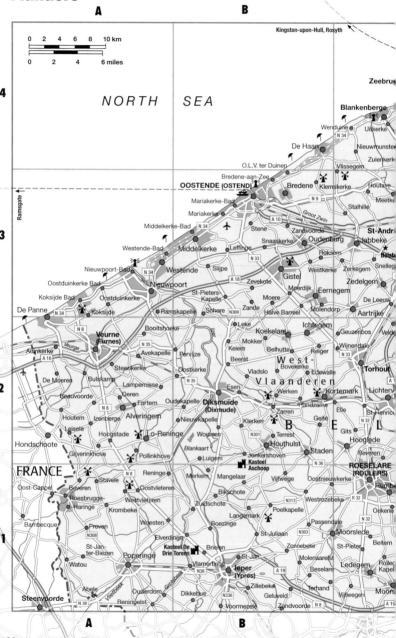

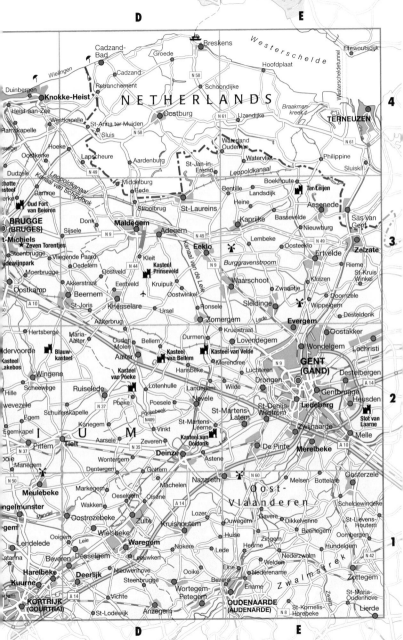

139

Selective Index for Atlas Section

St-Salvatorskerkhof 134 B3
Steenhouwersdijk 135 C4
Steenstraat 134 B4
Timmermansstraat 133 D1
Verversdijk 133 D1
Vlamingdam 132 B2
Vlamingstraat 134 C4
Vrijdagmarkt 134 A3
Vuldersstraat 135 E4
Werfstraat 132 B3
Westmeers 134 B2
Wijngaardstraat 134 C2
Zonneke Meers 134 B2
Zuidzandstraat 134 B3

Ghent

PLACES OF INTEREST
Archeologisc
    Augustijnenklooster
    Sint-Stefanus 136 B4
Badhuis Van Eyck 137 D3
Bargiebrug 136 A4
Begijnhof Dries 136 B4
Belfort (Belfry) 137 E1
Bijlokemuseum 136 B2
Boekentoren (Book Tower)
    136 C2
Botenhuis 136 A2
Congrescentrum/ICC 136
    B1
Contri-Butiebrug 136 A4
Cour Sint-Georges Hotel
    137 E1
De Opera 136 C3
De Schouwburg 137 E1
Design Museum Gent 137
    D2
Donkere Poort (Dark Gate)
    136 B4
Dulle Griet 137 E2
Ekkergembrug 136 A3
Europabrug 136 A2
Gentbruggebrug 137 E2
Geraard de Duivelsteen
    137 E1
Gerechtshof 136 B3
Gravensteen 137 D2
Groot Begijnhof 137 E4
Groot Vleeshuis 137 D1
H. Hart 137 E3
Het Pand (The Building)
    137 D1
Hof van Rijhove 137 E1
Hof van Sint-Antonius
    136 B4
Huis van Alijn 136 C4
Klein Begijnhof 137 D2
Klooster der Dominicanen
    136 B3
Klooster van de
    Ongeschoeide

Karmelieten 136 B4
Koning Albert 1-brug 136
    B2
Koninklijk Museum voor
    Schone Kunsten 136 C1
Kunstcentrum Vooruit 137
    C2
Lakenhalle 137 E1
Leiebrug 136 B2
Leopoldskazerne 136 C1
Museum voor Industriële
    Archeologie en Textiel/
    MIAT 137 C4
Onze-Lieve-Vrouw
    Presentatie 137 E4
Onze-Lieve-Vrouw Sint-
    Pieterskerk 137 C2
Rabot 136 B4
Roze Marijnbrug 136 B3
Sint-Annakerk 137 D3
Sint-Baafsabdij 137 D3
Sint-Baafskathedraal 137
    E1
Sint-Elisabethbegijnhof/Oud
    Begijnhof 136 B4
Sint-Jacobskerk 137 E2
Sint-Jorishof 137 E1
Sint-Martinus 136 A3
Sint-Michielskerk 137 D1
Sint-Niklaaskerk 137 E1
Sint-Paulus 136 B1
Sint-Pieters Abdij 137 C1
Stadhuis 137 E1
Stedelijk Museum voor
    Actuele Kunst/ SMAK
    136 C1
Toreken 137 E2
Velodroom 't Kuipke 136 C1

STREETS
Begijnengracht 136 B4
Belfortstraat 137 E1
Belleview 137 D1
Biezkapelstraat 137 E1
Bijlokekaai 136 B3
Botermarkt 137 E1
Burgstraat 137 D2
Coupure Links 136 B3
Coupure Rechts 136 B3
Dok-Zuid 137 D4
Donkersteeg 137 D1
Emile Braunplein 137 E1
Ende Were 136 A3
Ferdinand Lousbergskaai
    137 D3
Geldmunt 137 D2
Gordunakaai 136 A2
Gouden- leeuwplein 137 E1
Graslei 137 D1
Groentenmarkt 137 D2
Groot Kanonplein 137 E2

Hoogpoort 137 E1
Hoogstraat 136 B3
Kammerstraat 137 E2
Kasteelaan 137 D3
Keizer Karelstraat 137 D3
Ketelvest 136 C3
Klein Turkije 137 D1
Koning Albertlaan 136 B1
Koning Leopold II-Laan 136
    B1
Korenlei 137 D1
Korenmarkt 137 D1
Kortrijksepoortstraat 136
    C2
Kortrijksesteenweg 136 B1
Kouter 136 C3
Langemunt 137 E2
Mageleinstraat 137 E1
Martelaarslaan 136 B3
Nederpolder 137 E1
Neermeerskaai 136 A2
Nieuwewandeling 136 A3
Onderstraat 137 E2
Ooievaarstraat 136 A4
Opgeeistenlaan 136 B4
Oude Houtlei 136 B3
Papegaaistraat 136 B3
Phoenixstraat 136 A4
Sint-Antoniuskaai 136 B4
Sint-Baafsplein 137 E1
Sint-Pieters-plein 136 C2
Stropkaai 137 C1
Ter Platen 137 C1
Theresianenstraat 136 B3
Veldstraat 137 D1
Vrijdagmarkt 137 E2
Zuidparklaan 137 D1

Flanders

TOWNS OR SETTLEMENTS
Aalter 139 D2
Aartrijke 138 C3
Adegem 139 D3
Alveringem 138 A2
Ardooie 139 C2
Beernem 139 D3
Blankenberge 138 C4
Bredene 138 B3
Bredene-aan-Zee 138 B3
Brugges 139 C3
De Haan 138 B4
De Panne 138 A3
Deerlijk 139 D1
Deinze 139 D2
Desselgem 139 D1
Diksmuide 138 B2
Duinbergen 139 C4
Eeklo 139 D3
Eernegem 138 B3
Evergem 139 E3
Gent 139 C4

Gistel 138 B3
Harelbeke 139 C1
Hooglede 138 C2
Houthulst 138 B2
Ichtegem 138 B2
Ieper Ypres 138 B1
Ingelmunster 139 C1
Izegem 139 C1
Jabbeke 138 C3
Knesselare 139 D3
Knokke-Heist 139 C4
Koekelare 138 B2
Koksijde Bad 138 A3
Kortemark 138 B2
Kortrijk 139 C1
Kruishoutem 139 C1
Kuurne 139 C1
Lederberg 139 E2
Ledegem 138 C1
Lichtervelde 138 C2
Lo-Reninge 138 A2
Maldegem 139 D3
Mariakerke 138 B3
Mariakerke-Bad 138 B3
Merelbeke 139 E2
Meulebeke 139 C1
Middelkerke 138 B3
Moorsele 138 C1
Moorslede 138 C1
Nazareth 139 D1
Nevele 139 D2
Nieuwpoort 138 A3
Nieuwpoort-Bad 138 A3
Oostduinkerke Bad 138 A3
Oostende 138 B3
Oostkamp 139 C3
Oostrozebeke 139 D1
Oostvleteren 138 A1
Oudenburg 138 B3
Pittem 139 C2
Poperinge 138 A1
Roeselare 138 C1
Ruddervoorde 139 C2
Ruiselede 139 D2
Rumbeke 138 C1
St-Andries 138 C3
St-Michiels 139 C3
Staden 138 B2
Tielt 139 D2
Torhout Thourout 138 C2
Veurne Furnes 138 A2
Waregem 139 D1
Westende 138 A2
Wielsbeke 139 D1
Wingene 139 C2
Zedelgem 138 C3
Zeebrugge 138 C4
Zelzate 139 E3
Zomergem 139 D3
Zulte 139 D1
Zwevezele 139 C2

141

Index

Insight Smart Guide: Bruges
Edited by: Rachel Lawrence
Author: Katharine Mill
Updater: Magdalena Helsztynska
Update Production: AM Services
Maps: Carte
Head of Production: Rebeka Davies
Picture Editor: Tom Smyth
Cover pictures by: AWL Images (main)
Getty Images (bottom)

Fourth Edition 2016
© 2016 Apa Digital (CH) AG and
Apa Publications (UK) Ltd
Printed in China by CTPS
Distributed in the UK by:
UK: Dorling Kindersley Ltd, A Penguin
Group company, 80 Strand, London,
WC2R 0RL; sales@uk.dk.com
Distributed in the United States by:
Ingram Publisher Services,
1 Ingram Boulevard, PO Box 3006,
La Vergne, TN 37086-1986;
ips@ingramcontent.com
Distributed in Australia and
New Zealand by:
Woodslane, 10 Apollo St, Warriewood,
NSW 2102, Australia;
info@woodslane.com.au
Worldwide distribution enquiries:
Apa Publications (Singapore) Pte,
7030 Ang Mo Kio Avenue 5,
08-65 Northstar @ AMK, Singapore
569880; apasin@singnet.com.sg

Contacting the Editors
Every effort has been made to provide
accurate information in this publication,
but changes are inevitable. The
publisher cannot be responsible for any
resulting loss, inconvenience or injury.
We would appreciate it if readers would
call our attention to any errors or
outdated information. We also welcome
your suggestions; please contact us at:
hello@insightguides.com
www.insightguides.com

Photography by: Photography by:
Adornes 70tl, 70tr, 70br; Age
Fotostock/Superstock 100; B-In 94-
95tc; Chris Coe/Apa 81b; Jan Darthet
81t; Jerry Dennis/APA 4t, 5tl, 5c, 5b,
9t, 10, 13t, 15b, 26b, 27b, 29b, 35t,
38b, 39b, 40, 41, 47b, 50, 51, 59, 72-
73tc, 79b, 80t, 84bl, 105b, 107t, 125c,
132-133; Daniël de Kievith 16, 21t,
21b; De Reyghere 76b; De Tuilerieen
66t, 66b; Die Swaene 64b; Glyn Genin/
APA back cover t & b, 2-3tc, 2b, 3b,
5tr, 5cl, 5cr, 6, 7t, 7b, 8, 9b, 24b, 28b,
30b, 31b, 32, 33t, 33b, 34t, 36b, 37,

43b, 45bl, 45br, 46-47tc, 48, 49, 52b,
45-55tc, 55b, 56-57tc, 57b, 58, 68,
73b, 78b, 80b, 84br, 90b, 104-105tc,
110, 114t, 114c, 114b, 116, 117, 120,
122-125tc, 122b, 124, 125t, 125b,
126b, 127b, 128bl, 128br, 129; Getty
Images 28-29, 42-43, 62t, 62cr, 62b,
63tr, 63bl, 63br, 75b, 78-79, 82-83,
86b, 89b, 96-97, 96b, 101; Global
View 25b; Jean Godecharle 99b; Tony
Halliday/APA 13b, 14, 15t, 17b, 20, 44,
106, 107b; Hotel Jan Brito 67; iStock
22/23, 60b, 61bl, 119, 126-127tc,
130/131; Britta Jaschinski/APA 34bl,
34br, 35b, 36t, 95b, 118; Bob Krist/
Corbis 30-31tc; Joris Luyten 56b;
Maximiliaan Van Oostenrijk 111b; Mary
Evans Picture Library, 74b; A Nowitz/
APA 108-109tc, 121; The Pand 65b;
The Print Collector/Alamy 88; Public
domain 61tr, 62cl, 85; Roger-Viollet/
Topfoto 63tl, 74-75tc; Ronald Grant
Archive 77t; Scala, Florence 84t;
Shutterstock 18; Sunparks de Haan
102-103tc; Stadsfotografen, Stad
Brugge 76t; The Swan Hotel Collection
103bl&br; Toerisme Brugge/cel
fotografie Stad Brugge 83b, 86t, 87,
89t, 91b; Toerisme Brugge 98-99tc,
111t, 112, 113l, 113t, 115; Toerisme
Brugge/Daniel de Klevith 90-91tc, 92-
93tc; Toerisme Damme 17t; Walburg
69; Gregory Wrona/APA 4b, 11, 19,
24-25tc, 52-53tc, 71

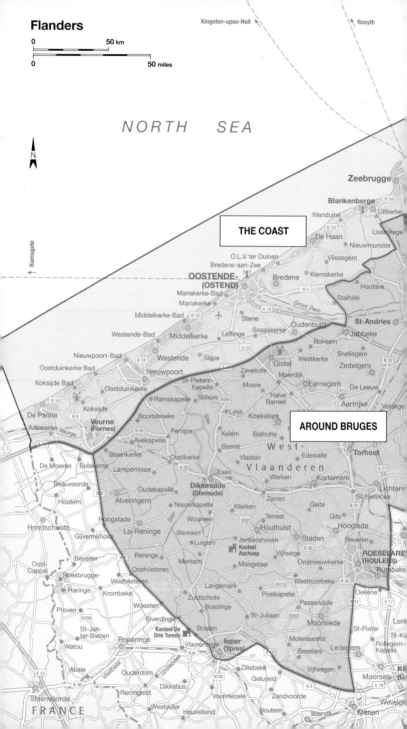

Flanders